A *RiverVerse* Novel. First Edition: May 7th 2014
ISBN-13: 978-0692023907 / ISBN-10: 0692023909
Copyright © 2014 by Tom Reagan

On The Cover:
Photograph by Alexander Smirnof
Used by paid license.

Contact the author:
https://www.facebook.com/tjamesreagan
tjamesreagan@gmail.com
http://tjamesreagan.com
@tjamesreagan

Also Available by T/James Reagan:
lovetrust
beach house burning
Leeds House
Famous For Nothing
Southland Tales: The Complete Saga

"It's harder to MAKE glass than BREAK glass.. Forward progress is difficult.. Backwards is as simple as ONE mistake." ~ Ice T

FOR:

I&A

I'm sorry.

EMPIRE WASTE

a novel by
T/JAMES REAGAN

EMPIRE WASTE

TABLE OF CONTENTS

EMPIRE WASTE

THE COLLECTION

"There are some nice pieces, but it doesn't come together. I can't deny the occasional brilliant moment, but it's not an experience," Karen tells me.

I nod as though I'm considering this warning, but Karen's too late opinion is useless.

After working tirelessly for months, I've finally finished the Spring/Summer collection for the recently relaunched "Andrew Lorrie" luxury fashion line.

I am Andrew Lorrie.

Given these facts, if this line is deemed to be a massive failure, I'm aware of who will be blamed.

"This is my vision," I say, hoping it sounds definitive.

"Then we should've also designed eyewear as an accessory... at least for you," Karen tells me in her awful monotone voice.

Karen, who is at least 41, with a painfully last decade hairdo, is a woman I'd prefer not to dress in my Spring/Summer collection, so I merely respond, "If you're telling me the singular vision I've established for this line doesn't work, then it's time for me to work on my double vision. Get me a tequila."

I don't want a drink, but I want to remind Karen that she's my assistant and not this line's stylist. She should be assisting me, not confirming all my worst fears.

"Scratch the tequila," I say, amending my order, "Get me a water instead." There's a pause, then I say, "No, not a water, get me a Vitamin Water." This correction is necessary because I know that we don't have any Vitamin Waters in the fridge, so Karen, being my assistant, will have to walk to the Duane Reade to buy me the drink. I don't hand her any money so she'll have to pay for it, then get a receipt and request a two dollar reimbursement through a formal process. This is how I've decided to deal with Karen's feedback. I want her to feel as desperate as I do.

I know that Karen is doing her job, assisting me, by presenting a potentially valid critique of my collection, but right now what would really assist me is someone saying, "Andrew, you aren't fucked," or at least, "Andrew, you might not be fucked?"

Where was Karen's *assistance* when I was sketching?

Where was Karen's *assistance* when I was choosing fabric?

Karen's too late opinion is nothing more than an attack on me.

"What do you think of the girls we have walking for us?" I ask, because we have an incredible casting director in Gregor Hampden, and I know it will lift my spirits to hear about the talent we've assembled.

"I think that most of the girls are walking for trade so I'm afraid they'll be disappointed," Karen tells me.

After being reminded that a lot of semi-inspiring fresh faces aren't getting cash for walking tomorrow, I begin to re-prioritize. "Don't worry about the Vitamin Water. What can you get me to fix this collection?" I ask, hoping to come away with some pieces the girls will accept with a smile.

"To fix this, you're going to need a pair of scissors," Karen says.

"To use on myself or..."

Karen slaps my arm, then explains, "If we were on TV, we'd take a pair of scissors to these clothes after one of the models accidentally ripped a piece and her clumsy edit inspired you. I can get Ferranina in here. Do you remember her during that fitting Lux was sick for? Ferranina is like a walking hurricane. A hurricane who's *really* bad at English."

"I'd prefer to wait until tomorrow before these clothes are torn apart," I decide.

"Suit yourself. You should have sided with the TV answer though. Always side with the TV."

Wondering how permanent my thrashing will be, I ask, "We agreed that we would only live stream the collection right? If they miss it, then we'll post a link to the gallery on *style.com*, but the video should be one-and-done."

"We'll have the live stream up on the site and it won't cycle back to the beginning once it's over," Karen confirms.

"Good," I say, relieved.

"However, it's inevitable that someone will record the live stream and upload it to YouTube. Since you fired the intern that makes the copyright claims, it'll stay up there until long after you or I die."

"Why did I fire the intern?" I ask, without recollection of this moment.

"You described him as a 'shitty employee, even by spoiled trust fund kid standards,' then he threatened to tell his dad, then you said that your line was probably fucked anyway and his dad already knows it, then he compared you to your brother, then you threw a computer monitor at him," Karen recaps, affectionless.

"LCD or one of those old style monitors?" I ask.

"LCD. I don't think it even broke. I think we still use it. I think we were looking at runway tests of Lux on it earlier today."

"I don't remember this," I say.

"I had gotten you a lot of tequila that afternoon," Karen states plainly.

I begin to feel lost in the high-ceilinged downtown penthouse loft that the Chinese investors are paying for. The space was supposed to make me feel at home creatively. It's totally open, surrounded by white walls, and floored with Brazilian teak hardwood that's now riveted with imperfections caused by the sharp heels of the shoes I've designed. My muse, Lux, has walked in every piece, every pair of shoes, and her mark has been made on this space. The Chinese investors won't be getting their security deposit back.

My collection clings tightly on 35 rented gray department store mannequins that have been lined up in rows like stick armed soldiers ready to march into a battle that they're both outnumbered and unprepared for.

Not willing to leave things as they are, I demand, "Call Lux."

"Come on, Andrew. It's midnight. Let the girl have a life. She pretty much lives here at this point."

"I need Lux here," I say, and this bothers Karen, but I don't care because Karen is bothering me.

Lux is my muse. Her jet black hair. Her razor-straight bangs. Her long, wide Asian eyes. Her perfect proportions- towering at a lean 5'10". I'm only interested in *her* opinion.

Tomorrow, the front row will be filled with the people who matter to me, and the critics will stand.

Lux won't be in the front row, and she won't be on the runway. She will, however, be here with me tonight, working on the line.

"Call Lux," I demand again, this time with an edge, and my assistant takes out her phone.

THE POINT OF NO RETURN

I sit in a square arm black leather chair in the center of the loft, my collection surrounding me. I sip from a bottle of Fiji water, wishing it was a tequila, but feeling in control because it isn't.

Lifting up my phone, I look at my face in the reflection of the glass. I turn my head slightly to the right, hiding a crooked nose by working my angles- a technique I've learned from the girls I've photographed. I notice new lines. On either side of my mouth, I find two ripples that get more severe when I smile, so I never smile. My eyes are still a piercing blue and the purple blood pooled below them clashes alarmingly with my pale complexion. Fine cracks at the far corners of my eyes continue straying, running to my hair in the way raindrops streak across the body of a speeding car. My hair flops down and covers the cracks. Thank God for my long, full hair. Thank God for L'Oreal brown/black hair dye and Elnett hairspray. My teeth are stained from a thousand cups of coffee and too many "social" cigarettes, then bleached with the Crest Whitestrips I wear while streaming TV shows I secretly watched throughout my teenage years- time capsules of a more innocent era/ Smooth faces- old actors, fresh/ The speed of it all stripped away/ A forgotten patience we once had, then lost/ A time when I didn't need extremes to feel excited. An experience that now can only exist through nostalgia.

I hear the door to the loft open with a clank, as the metal crossbar is pressed down then released. After a moment, the door slams shut, then the loft is filled with the click-click-click of heels on the hardwood.

"Unless you're designing pillows and duvets, I don't want to be here," Lux's tired, husky voice echoes to me. I don't turn around. I continue to face the collection. Beyond the mannequins is a static view of a brick building across the street. All of the bricks fit together so perfectly that Karen must find the building to be quite an *experience*.

A hand cups the right shoulder of the custom made sky blue dress shirt I'm wearing. I've never actually released a menswear line, but when I was dabbling in very androgynous suits, I made myself a new wardrobe to get the feel for the tailoring.

I look down at Lux's unpainted nails, yellow from the different coats that I've applied, then stripped, throughout this past week. Lux doesn't have to be ready for tomorrow because she won't be walking the show. The next color that finds its way onto Lux's tips will not be selected by me. This makes me a tiny bit jealous. Lux is the girl I want to dress, yet she'll never wear another piece from this collection ever again. I filmed her walking back and forth in the loft, in each piece, so I could see my designs in motion. Since I have all these videos on my laptop, Lux doesn't need to walk this show because it's already been done. Most importantly, if I was to cast Lux, the industry would immediately take note of her, then they'd take her away from me.

Since Lux's continuation as a working model is assured by my success. I called her here so she can assure me that I will be successful.

"Do you like the clothes?" I ask, still facing the collection.

"Yes. For the millionth time," Lux says, staying behind me, knowing which part of her must be modeled at the moment.

"Karen doesn't think our work comes together. She doesn't think it's an experience. She told me this during my final walk through," I recap, so that Lux can provide the sympathy I demand.

"Karen's expertise is in getting you vodka tonics," Lux reminds me. Since Lux is *my* model, who I'm constantly calling back to the loft, she knows everyone behind the scenes, yet she's a stranger to the girls who will be backstage tomorrow.

"Karen didn't get me any vodka tonics tonight," I say, and Lux pats my shoulder as a small way to acknowledge that I'm attempting to fix this instead of just throwing another computer monitor.

"So, Karen didn't get you a drink, then she told you that you're a massive fuck up who's doomed?" Lux either points out or attempts to clarify.

"Sure did," I say, accepting this criticism again.

"I don't think you're a fuck up," Lux assures me.

"But you *do* think I'm doomed," I respond slowly, looking at my collection that, apparently, doesn't come together.

Lux, seemingly reviewing something other than the garments around us, says, "I think if you do what you have planned, then yes, you're doomed. I also think Karen is being a little shit about this very good collection so that you'll pull back on your... plan."

"This plan is me doing what I've always done," I maintain.

"What you've always done is dramatically doom yourself," Lux reminds me.

"They invited me back so I'm going to go through with it."

"They invited you back because Karen has been issuing statements about how much you've changed."

"And I haven't," I sigh, trying to find Lux's reflection in the wall of windows at the edge of the loft, but there's always a mannequin in the way.

"And you haven't," Lux confirms. After a sigh of her own, she tells me, "I kind of love you for being Andrew Lorrie, always, without fail, but I also don't know how I'm going to pay rent if this collapses for us. If this fails..."

Suddenly, screws are tightened in places I was unaware they were needed. Our future seems to be held together with invisible bolts that are constantly loosening, requiring close attention.

"I can help you with your rent," I say.

I need Lux behind me for this to work. For me to create again, I need Lux right where she is.

"You've already helped me, Andrew. I haven't started paying off the first debt."

"It's not a debt. You aren't indebted to me. That's the difference between designers and agents. You owe me nothing beyond your presence. It's not just about your body being this Andrew Lorrie golden ratio. It's you. You're doing more than just standing behind me. You're, I don't know, holding me up."

Lux cups my chin with her hand, then tells me, "Tomorrow... make sure you do it your way, because your vision amazing."

THE BAR

Lux slips her fingers between mine, and it's exactly what I need.

We leave the loft, then walk the street without a specific destination.

Eventually, we cab to an East Village bar that Lux likes.

The music is too loud.

We leave the bar.

We find another bar.

Lux hides in the bathroom while I order us drinks.

Lux is 27, passing as 22, holding on to the false hope that someone will believe that she's not old enough to legally drink. She's Asian, so it sort of works, for now. Lux has no more than ten more years left before it all falls apart, and the collapse will be tragic. When it happens, I will avert my eyes and lie to her. It will absolutely change things between us.

Before we entered the bar, Lux provided her boilerplate demands- "I don't want people to see the bartender checking my ID/"Let me hide in the bathroom, while you order/"I want something with tonic. And alcohol. I think you can intuit which ingredient is more essential/"Text me when it's safe to come out."

My beer, and Lux's gin and tonic, sit coaster-less on a perfectly square faux wooden table.

I angle my legs toward where Lux will sit because I've already read all the bumper stickers on the foosball table in front of me- a black sticker advertising a vegan website/ A white sticker with red lettering that displays the ominous message "YOU DON'T HAVE TO BE HERE"/ A pink sticker that reads "social!heavy."

Past the table is a dark red wall, and on the wall are shitty paintings, no doubt painted by the son of the guy who owns this dive.

"Thirsty?" I text, and before I can look up from my phone, Lux slips out of the bathroom, then sits down next to me.

We exist outside of our comfort zone of the loft for the first time in a long time.

Lux drinks her drink, I get her another, then she drinks that too.

Once she has a buzz, Lux hands me her phone and shows me pictures of people that she's mentioned before, but I've never met.

She tells me stories- some I've heard, some are new. The stories I've already heard become more frequent as I keep replacing Lux's glass.

When I make my fourth or fifth trip back to the bar, I flirt with the bartender. She dances a slow groove to the chillwave song that plays over speakers that I can't locate. I tell her I'm going to steal her moves. I tell her I'm going to use them in the back room. She laughs. She flirts back, and for a moment, I feel 22.

I bring Lux what will most likely be her last drink of the night. This accelerates her agenda, and she immediately launches into a last-ditch effort to get me to do the right thing. Just as she asks me not to go through with my plan for tomorrow, a black girl comes rushing toward us in a drunken panic. She thuds down next to Lux, and tells us that she's on a date with a guy she had been exchanging messages with. She met him on a sketchy free dating site. We ask her where her date is, and she tells us that he's Russian- he's in America though- he's outside smoking a cigarette. The black girl says that she rushed over because she decided to pretend to have to puke. Lux and I express that we're skeptical if mere vomit is enough to deter a Russian. I ask the black girl why she doesn't like her date. The black girl says that when she mentioned she was meeting up with her friends at the bar, the Russian asked what race her friends are. The black girl felt, and continues to feel, this question was out of line.

Lux freezes up and leans into me lightly. This action, I assume, is supposed to indicate that Lux wants me to be quiet. It truly doesn't matter. The black girl is as drunk as Lux.

When the black girl's two friends show up, they triumphantly confirm that the Cold War with the Russian has come to an end; he's gone home for the night. One of the black girl's friends is white and the other is Asian.

We turn away from the girls, and I accept Lux's phone. She shows me more pictures of people we've discussed, then she reminds me why they're significant. Everyone seems tangled in a web of remote interconnectedness.

"You know a lot of people," is all I can think to say.

People who can steal her away.

"The internet is bizarre, man," Lux summarizes, and this makes me hand her phone back.

In a way that's completely unsettling, she admits, "I relate to that drunk girl. I'm on all these weird sites."

"What does that mean?" I ask, my body shifting so that my left leg is curled under my ass, and I stare straight at Lux's perfect profile.

"I don't know," she says.

"Is everything okay?" I ask.

Lux nods, but says nothing. Her eyes glaze, then they fix on the foosball table.

No one says anything for a long period of time.

Lux points out a boy smoking an electronic cigarette and we mock him.

I pay the tab, and Lux smokes a Pall Mall outside.

We walk for a while, even though we need to get a taxi.

Lux tells me some sad things about her family that I'm not sure how to react to, so I just give an empathetic exhale, then say, "Wow, I'm sorry."

THE STRANGERS

I drift backstage inside the air-conditionless warehouse the Chinese investors reluctantly rented out for the show. After a quick survey of the area, I'm pleased with how the girls look- all of them, except Galina Mirov. Galina looks strung out, and probably is, if I'm to believe the libelous text messages I got from a booker (not Galina's) who was bitter that the girl *she* sent over wasn't cast. Gregor informed me that the rejected model looked like an anthropomorphic human/mouse hybrid and not in the charming Mickey Mouse way. When the booker got wind of Gregor's assessment, she resorted to telling me why the rest of my models were defective in hopes that her girl would seem like she fit in with the theme.

Galina sits, posture slumped, staring at her phone, which appears to be turned off, and I realize the booker is probably right. I briefly consider giving Galina a bag of heroin so she'll kick off, but Karen is always cagey about buying drugs for the models. She says that it's debasing to fill out an expense waiver for the drugs she fronts the money on.

While moving slowly backstage, I try to appear like an experienced craftsman double checking his calculations before his vessel pushes off for a choppy, thrilling, tiring, inspiring journey. What I'm really doing is looking for the models that I'm friends with, but the models I'm friends with now host TV shows, and head up charities, and run lifestyle websites, and raise their kids full time- all the while doing Splenda sweet spreads in magazines that show up on the end caps of every Wal-Mart checkout line in America.

These new girls around me are an army of Amazons that Gregor searched (and sometimes begged) for. Gregor and I worked well together while assembling this group. We had an understanding. We wanted new blood. We wanted fresh faces. Right now, I just want someone I can count on to perform.

In a flash-forward, I see all of these overgrown children putting my designs on backward, tripping in my shoes, stomping on my trains, then inarticulately describing my work with quotes like, "This collection is really fun, really thrilling, really now, but also vintagey."

I will take an eye out with a four-inch heel if I hear the made-up word, "vintagey" uttered regarding my designs.

When I notice the hovering cameras, I back into a corner, out of frame, and watch as a poorly dressed interviewer for one of those YouTube fashion channels bounces from model to model, getting statements from the girls. She seems to have varying degrees of success, largely depending on where the model is from. Gregor and I plucked these girls from all over the world. Well, not Africa, but the rest of the world was on the table. Well, not Haiti either, but I think their airport was under six feet of water or something anyway. The interviewer keeps asking the girls, "If you could vacation anywhere, where would it be?" and, "What locale does Andrew's style remind you of?" As this continues, it seems like she's trying to help these girls imagine a place more peaceful and habitable than backstage at the first Andrew Lorrie collection in 8 years.

THE RUNWAY

I watch the dressed models get placed in an orderly line, and I'm suddenly reminded of how good it feels to release my work into the world under my own name. I peek out at the impatient crowd, and I see that my front row seat has been taken. Everything is going as planned.

A blur in my periphery- almost certainly Karen- is squeezing between two models that are at least a full head taller than her. Before the blur comes into focus, I move quickly to a side exit that dumps out to the left of the audience.

I have to move fast because Karen is doing her best to keep me from making a huge mistake, and I can't allow her to succeed.

Nodding twice to acknowledge the smattering of confused applause I receive when the crowd recognizes me, I make my way to the front row. The audience is expecting a man on his best behavior. A pre-show quote that was widely circulated- "This collection will be happier and more contemporary, because *I* am happier. *I* am more contemporary. I promise you this,"- had assured the industry that they'd be meeting a new man. The reality is, I never actually said those words, and they're completely untrue- the statement was Karen's creation. She seems to have a gift for finding the right words, as long as she's not directing those words at me, and this is why I keep her on my arm like a wife or daughter.

Walking parallel to the runway, I make it to the halfway point of the front row, then I stop.

I look to my right and I see Harlan Pulchra.

Harlan is an ethnically ambiguous fashion editor. To be more precise, Harlan is an *online* fashion editor for a site that doesn't create new content, it merely "reports" on the industry. Some old lady who's "fashion royalty" sits to Harlan's left, and to his right is a straight boy who I know for a fact fucked a 40-year-old man to get a supporting role on a CW show about twink magicians. I begin to wonder what the boy might have done to get this front row seat, but whatever it was, I'm confident he earned his place, so I allow him to remain seated. The buyers can sit close and ask me questions about my collection. Hell, the buyers can do whatever they want. The CW stars can sit close. I'd love to dress these young celebrities since half of them are playing undead characters that seamlessly fit in my aesthetic. I refuse to extend any courtesy to Harlan because his lack of mercy made my return nearly impossible.

Eight years ago, Harlan's "breakout moment" was a hatchet job of an essay for *FashionCut* that went viral. The piece was about me- about how awful I am, about how- I'm directly quoting here- "*Andrew Lorrie should never be allowed to design or show another collection ever again. The only time Mr. Lorrie should be allowed near a sewing machine is so he can make soccer balls for two dollars an hour to support himself, as he hides out in Honduras, far away from the normal and good people in the fashion industry.*"

"I need to have a word with you," I say to Harlan. He catches my stare, then his eyes dart to where my finger is pointing. I can see that he thinks he's going backstage. I allow him to think this because it will make him all the more embarrassed and hurt when he finds out that he's very wrong.

The boxy, maybe-Mexican, Harlan gets up and follows me. The crowd watches us, and I make sure to walk with a casual speed so they can see exactly what I'm doing.

When we reach the door that leads backstage, we don't enter it.

I turn and we walk along the edge of the crowd.

"Andrew, where, uh..." Harlan begins to ask.

He seems to realize that, yes, he *is* receiving special treatment because of his article, and no, this treatment is not an ass-kiss or a fruit basket to show that I view everything is "water under the bridge."

We walk up to two very tall girls, whom I don't recognize, but I pay attention to. Both girls give me a fashion bitch-stare, and I become simultaneously excited and worried by their presence. *These* are the type of girls I want to buy pieces from my collection, not the Karen-looking women who can afford my prices. I glance at the first girl- black, impossibly clear skin, her shiny hair pulled tight in a ponytail- then to the other- Puerto Rican, puffy lips, saucer eyes, vaguely reminiscent of another model from another decade that used to walk for me. This second girl is either someone Gregor cast, or is the best part of my past coming back to haunt me, and I'm less than scared about either possibility.

"Girls, meet Harlan Pulchra. He'll be watching the show with you," I say, making the introduction.

"Is this a joke, Andrew?" Harlan asks.

"No. You were in my seat," I say simply.

"You're going to sit and watch your own show from the front row? How much attention do you need?" Harlan asks disdainfully.

"I could ask you the same question. Is there a problem with your seat? Well... I guess it's not really a seat, it's more just a space," I say, pleasure dripping down me in sparkling waves.

"You're going to make me stand for this entire collection?" Harlan asks, not accepting his place.

"No, I'm going to *let* you stand," I say, then the girls make an, "OoOo," noise that pleases me greatly.

"You do know that I'm the editor of *FashionCut*?" Harlan states, trying to throw his weight around.

"Correct," I confirm. The nearby crowd focuses on this discussion, making their own notes, beginning their own stories for their own websites.

"You do know I most certainly will write about this," Harlan tells me, and I say, "Good. *FashionCut* didn't waste their money sending you here."

With more seats to rearrange, I walk past the security guard who I personally instructed, and paid, to have any critic thrown out if they moved from where I relocated them to.

I return to the front row- to no applause this time- just a confused silence.

I feel the buzzing excitement of doing things my way, right before presenting the collection I designed, my way.

When I sit down, they'll cut the lights and a Sky Ferreira song will start, then Cori Poorman will open the show.

Flush with revenge, I become content by merely moving Harlan, instead of making all the critics migrate to the back of the crowd, as I had originally planned. I'm about to take my seat, when the old woman who's the editor of an irrelevant magazine and is praised as "fashion royalty," leans over and hisses at me, "Did Harlan just get invited backstage? He only writes for a website, you know. My readership-"

"-how rude of me," I interrupt, but she keeps going, "After all those awful things he wrote about that last Andrew Lorrie collection, now you're brown-nosing him for it? You can't sway us by buying our silence."

"You're right. I need to acknowledge that you're unbiased and will write about my collection's merit, regardless of my actions," I say, faux warmth filling my voice.

"Exactly," she responds.

"Come with me," I request, holding out my hand. The fashion royalty grabs her purse that costs more than a crown, then grasps onto my wrist and hoists herself out of the chair.

Like a man walking his mother between the pews at church, I move slowly down the aisle with this old bat.

Like a man sick of his mother's bitching, when we turn the corner and head toward Harlan, I ignore the woman's string of complaints.

Like a man desperate to pawn his problems off on someone else, I leave the old woman with some strangers. This is a gesture I refused to do with my own mother, but I'm more than happy to do it to this lady.

Need and fear collide when the woman's complaining syncs up with Harlan's threats, and out of instinct, I lock arms with the familiar looking Puerto Rican girl, then begin my return to the front row. This how I've fashioned my life- beautiful women are constantly rescuing me from myself.

It would look bad to have an open seat in the front row; it will make me look great having this girl next to me.

The buyers keep their seats. The celebrities keep their seats. The rest of the critics and editors look down at their phones so they don't catch my laser stare.

This stare has become my inadvertent trademark. Most models fear this expression, and only Lux knows what it really means. She understands it's how I search the world- on guard, ever aware, never looking away.

Bound to me by our locked arms, the eerily familiar model quietly asks, "What the fuck are you doing?" It's a question posed with excitement, not judgment.

"Are you supposed to be backstage right now?" I ask her outright.

"No," the girl responds, while the weight of a faltered dream colors those two simple letters, turning them into a sentence. She must have stolen someone's invite to get in here. She must think that she's about to be shown out.

"You're very beautiful," I say to her, as we make our way back to the front row. The girl is tall and olive, with naturally puffed lips. Under heavy eyebrows are long, lean, deep eyes. Above her eyebrows stretches a crease-less massive forehead. Her ears stick out a little too much, but this somehow only adds to her appeal. Her hair isn't dyed- it's not burnt to shit from heat. I notice that she might be as tall as Lux, and I'm tempted to bring her backstage so she can walk for me today. This is an Andrew Lorrie girl, and I want her either next to me, or on my runway.

"Your seat," I say, presenting the girl with what once was Harlan's chair.

Everyone is looking. No one seems entertained. Some seem curious. Some just look like they have to pee. Others seem worried I'll come for them next.

"I can't," the girl tells me. This hesitation seems like another warning, and I'm tired of well-meaning women trying to stop my self-destruction, so I inform her, "I insist." I use my blue-eyed stare to convince her there are no other options.

"I'm Madeleine," she says, sitting down.

"I'm Andrew Lorrie," I admit, finally taking a seat.

"I know. I love your work," she tells me.

The lights click off and the girl's Lux-like vote of confidence arrives perfectly-timed at the beginning of the show.

"Do you even care anymore?" a critic behind me asks.

"Too much," I respond.

THE RETURN

Sky Ferreira's "American Dream" pumps out of the giant speakers that bookend the matte black set. The background looks like the monolith in 2001...

if those monkeys had succeeded in knocking it down and the fall caused a uniform crack through the middle of the slab. Cori Poorman, a silent movie-actress-in-another-era, is the first model down the runway.

"American Dream" is playing simply because the Chinese investors felt that having a song with "American" in the title would help us. "The American Dream" was provided to me as a theme, despite the chilling fact that the American dream is dead. As is the status quo now, my American dream was delivered thanks to the Chinese.

The makeup I picked for the show is traditional Andrew Lorrie. It's facial bruising meets the perfectly smooth porcelain complexion of a bisque doll. This is a look I've always loved and Karen has always hated. She continually asks me where the romance is, and I faithfully maintain that the makeup is brimming with romantic notions. Karen usually counters with, "I only see the Andrew Lorrie version of romance, which, frankly, is pretty scary."

When we were doing the makeup tests, Cori- no doubt prompted by Karen- asked me, "Isn't this a little... severe?"

Moving behind her, I asked, "Did you have a china doll as a girl?"

She nodded, then giggled, as a powder-coated makeup brush tickled her cheek.

"And how'd you feel about your doll?" I asked.

"I loved her," Cori said, smiling, not that far removed from being a little girl. "And she scared me a little. And she comforted me," she added, like she was thinking back on a time that must have been both shockingly far in the rear view mirror and also still somewhat present. With this context, she accepted my vision, and she asked no additional questions.

When our mutual understanding was solidified, Cori wordlessly announced herself as my opener. I tapped into something she had hidden, while she tapped into something waiting to burst out. It was an undeniable chemical reaction.

The other girls were found through castings, through favors (this explains the 5'7" Chinese girl in the tenth look), and some were fresh faces that captivated my team for one reason or another.

The music thumps out, sonically bleaching everything, and I watch as the models parade down the runway in a near-neutral way that mixes focused street walking with the cadence of a determined, well-oiled robot. These girls look like they're possessed. It's impossible to tell if they're happy or not, and this is good because they're probably miserable. Their shoes are tall. Their heels are pointy. Everyone in the front row can see the divots being pierced in the runway.

These little holes are being stamped with machine-like regularity, leaving a mark, further complicating things for the next girl.

The fabrics I used for this collection are webbed, "...almost like a Spider-Man outfit," I told the Chinese investors. They were pleased that I chose an American superhero. I assured them that Spidey was the most American hero besides Captain America and Superman. We universally agreed that Superman is more menswear or swimwear, and girls can't really pull off the underwear over-the-pants look, while guys can because it makes their dick look bigger. This lie allowed me to eliminate the color red from the collection completely, and I focused on reptilian browns and greens. They made me use blue, but I was okay with that. Blue fit. Red didn't.

I wanted everything to look like scales. I wanted these clothes to look like they could be shed, just as a snake sloughs off its skin. I was inspired by a memory I had from elementary school when a boy named Ian brought in his pet snake and told us about how it would wiggle out of its skin every so often. This was very exciting to a group of children not yet comfortable in their own skin. It felt promising, until Gretchen asked, "What did his old skin look like?" And Ian responded, "Exactly how it looks now."

This moment stuck with me and now mirrors my own transformation. My work is not a caterpillar turned butterfly; it's a snake becoming the same snake- only older, newer, a little better, but mostly the same.

The idea of shedding skin led to this collection being about layers. It's visible in the vest that's open, except for the second-to-last button, worn under a coat cinched with a belt. Blue satin clings under the vest, then lace slides down into a loose asymmetrical skirt that, despite how it looks, the model can't wiggle out of. A voyeur may believe that the garment could simply fall away, and the audience of this show is exclusively comprised of voyeurs. By wrapping lace in careful angles, I've complicated things. Everyone is waiting for it to all fall apart, but I've engineered my work so that this is an impossibility.

The clothes pass by me and I hope that they look as good from the back wall of the warehouse as they do up close.

"American Dream," ends, but the show does not. After a single second of pin-drop silence, Sky's "Lost In My Bedroom" begins as the collection builds. The one runway veteran we were able to afford- the one person getting paid real money- Maryna Mauden, is closing the show in a piece that I view as the culmination of all my efforts.

Each look that passes by feels like a New Year's countdown to the final dress. My young models surprise me with their poise and power. These 17-year-old girls parade up and down the runway in clothes that will be sold to women who won't reach the heights scaled by their younger predecessors. Piece after piece, a collection born out of pain becomes healed by the possibilities provided by the girls that I chose to help me.

I hold my breath as my final girl, Maryna, arrives as a force so strong that the hot warehouse seems to time travel to a romantic Victorian moment that never existed in all of history, until now.

She cannot be followed. Nothing can come after Maryna.

She ends the show as Sky wails away, *"It's just what I imagined."*

The buyers need one last look- one reminder of my greatness- so I allow for the conventional "Halloween parade" style final march. All of the girls return to the runway, and in an orderly fashion, they show off all of the looks in rapid-fire succession.

I don't stand up for applause, I don't hop on the runway and give a wave. Instead, I walk in tandem with Maryna, as she forms the tail of the parade and makes her way backstage.

Once behind the curtains, Maryna and I find each other again. I watch as her purple lips bend into a smile, a mimicry of my pleasure with this moment.

"We are American dream," Maryna tells me, in her thick Russian accent.

THE COLLECTION

Things go from beautiful to ugly, but it makes my collection look that much more breathtaking when pressed so closely to the press.

Security lets anyone with a green invitation into the makeshift press room. The asshole fashion journalists and bloggers crowd around me and it's clear they're unhappy with my actions.

Things have gone exactly as I've planned, so far. My girls just did an incredible job with my fully-realized collection, now it's time for me to become Frankenstein's monster facing the pitchforks.

Karen appears amongst the vermin, and says to them, "Andrew thanks you for your support, but he won't-"

"-waste too much of anyone's time here, I know this isn't your last show of the day, and I dislike doing this, so start firing questions," I interrupt her, unwilling to have someone cover for me when I'm capable of speaking for myself.

The journalists force Karen back, discarding her because she just makes everyone's life more difficult.

I know that the first question- and most of the follow-up questions- will have nothing to do with the clothes that I just showed. I'm prepared for this, but I keep my rant locked away until I'm provoked. Maybe the musical chairs that kicked off the show will be enough for a mean-spirited headline, and we've gotten the ugliness out of the way before the clothes even walked.

"What statement are you making by putting nobodies in the front row, while making well-respected editors stand?" an overweight woman aggressively asks me, while holding her phone out to video my response.

"One could interpret that as a statement that I regard editors as less than nobodies," I say, scratching my crooked nose.

"They made you. We made you," an old gay guy with a pomp tells me.

"No. They didn't. You didn't. You destroyed me eight years ago," I remind them. I don't yell this. My cool is so icy that the warehouse becomes a bearable temperature.

"And still no change," the old guy responds, shaking his head.

"This is a brand new collection. Change," I say, holding out my arms. "I just showed a collection, you are aware of that, right? Are there any questions related to what you just saw?"

"How do you respond to the people who say that you're racist when you cast, and that this show is missing P.O.C.?" a white girl asks me.

I raise an eyebrow, then mumble, "Who's Poc? Who is she signed with? I don't think she was at our castings…"

"It stands for 'people of color,'" the white girl snarls.

"Oh, well, who's calling me racist? Show me some quotes," I request.

"The fashion community is saying that you're racist because of your casting and your history," the bitter white girl says.

"The fashion community," I repeat, then ask, "So the fashion community just wants to discuss the difficult issues, right?"

There's a silence, then the bitter white girl says, "We want to talk about a glaring omission of black and Latina models on your runway. It has to be addressed."

"Because that's what the fashion industry does, correct?" I ask, training my glare on the white girl. She avoids eye contact because she's used to people immediately walking away from her when she starts talking. I move my gaze across the crowd of raised phones, and I try to hold back a tirade that's been building for eight years. I hate every person in this room, and I ask them, "The fashion community addresses the serious issues, right? As I now understand it, the most serious issue the fashion industry is currently facing is… am I a racist? So, am I?" My question hangs there, but I keep talking before the mob can answer with certainty that I am. "That's the most important issue in fashion, correct? The 'industry' has spoken, so let's discuss my 'racism,' and we can put the other issues to the side. There *are* other issues, you are aware of that, right? I think we can all agree there aren't just a couple of problems with the industry," I say. No one attempts to agree or disagree. I stare these disingenuous pigs down, then I unleash the anger that I wanted to stay buried, "Let's not worry about fashion's other trouble points. Let's not acknowledge that puberty doesn't begin and end at 14. Let's not acknowledge that women have hips. Let's not acknowledge that most of these girls are underage. Let's not acknowledge that some of these girls are literally killing themselves to be out there on that runway. Let's not acknowledge that we're robbing childhoods, and providing no adult guidance. Let's not acknowledge that we're pulling girls out of school to work in an industry that only wants them for four seasons. Let's not acknowledge that there are photographers verbally and sexually assaulting girls. Let's not acknowledge that some girls are being trafficked in foreign markets. Let's not acknowledge that there are agencies putting girls in debt for a job that they were promised would help their impoverished parents get *out* of debt. Let's not acknowledge how in arrears so many of these companies and magazines are when it comes to paying for work that has already been completed. Let's not acknowledge that we're teaching these girls- and the girls who obsess over these girls- that you have to look one particular way, and if you don't, well... Let's not acknowledge that a girl can have a bad season because she's 16 fucking years old and her body is changing more than it ever will for the rest of her life. This is regardless of stress or eating habits. You'll never say that a girl had an 'off-season' because she's experiencing normal physical changes that come with maturity. That silence speaks volumes, while you speak in volumes and volumes of SEO-baiting online articles about the fact that there isn't enough of a type of model that *you* like. It's shitty. You're sustaining a predatory industry, while also making it a cannibalistic industry. You're collapsing the empire from the inside, just for a little attention. You all list yourself as 'editors' and 'writers' on your little social network profiles, then you attack words that I said so long ago because none of you understand words. You understand cuts, and fabrics, and faces, but not words. It's not my responsibility to teach you, but I won't stand by and be the villain of this industry. So. Yeah. My models for this collection were white- not all of them, but a lot of them were. I hope that 'the industry' can find it in their selective hearts to forgive me. Or... I'll remain the villain and you can move on to addressing the laundry list of problems that I just recited. Whatever works for your article."

THE IMPERIAL HALL

The limo is being driven by a young white guy who's not the recent immigrant, in-his-own-world, hands-free cell phone talker that I usually get in this city. He's friendly. He probably lives in Brooklyn. He's probably having his rent paid by his father, but he needs to hold down a day job to manufacture the illusion he's doing his best "in a tough, unforgiving city." He probably has a band. His jaw isn't strong enough for him to be a wannabe model, but then again, that hasn't stopped boys before. The driver informs me- "Busy week/"It didn't go as bad as you think it did. I mean, yeah, I was parked around the block when the show happened, and I have no idea what happened inside, but.../"It could have been worse. It's not like the angry mob burned down the building. They didn't even try. I would've seen it/"Shouldn't you have champagne right now/"Do you want me to stop and get you some champagne/"Was I supposed to bring champagne/"Forgetting the champagne won't impact my tip, will it?"

I fake a phone call, mainly to get the driver to stop talking, and also to get my mind off the fact that I really could go for some champagne.

The driver plugs his phone into the AUX and plays a song with a droney, hollow, not-quite-hip-hop beat. A voice ripples, "*I caught you in a time, we planned broken designs,*" and I put my head between my legs.

Stuck in traffic, no sign of progress, I listen to voicemails that went ignored for the past week- "Hey, it's Dan. I'm not sure if you saw my text, but, yeah, we're going to Heathers at like 11 tomorrow if you want to come with/"Can you stop answering my e-mails with 'use your judgment?' This is your collection, but we're practically making design choices here. Call Eunmoo and get your ass out to Milan for the last two pieces/"Yes, Andrew. This is Eunmoo. My daughter come by studio. Please help her. I know she short. Can you fix dress on her/"Okay. The last two pieces are shipped. You didn't make this easy. The least you could do is pick up your fucking phone/"Do not come to this meeting with Eunmoo's daughter. Don't do it, Andrew. Your old statements are still circulating because of that fucking YouTube clip being posted all over *TFS*, and you're going to make everyone uncomfortable if you show up. And don't worry, I won't tell Lux that Eunmoo's daughter is going to be our Asian face for the show."

I listen to the messages a second time to make sure that the voicemail about meeting Dan at Heathers wasn't from last night. Heathers was the first bar that

I took Lux to, and if I showed up, ignored Dan, then walked out, I'll never hear the end of it. I slide through my phone. No confused texts. No additional voicemails. Given Dan's overbearing personality, I feel confident that he wasn't at Heathers when I was.

Dan Carrington is tangentially involved in this line- floating in and out of various castings- never really accomplishing anything noticeable. Gregor had worked with him before, and Dan is hard to shake after he gets that introduction he fights tooth and nail for. He's one of those people that orbits relevance, then name drops others to inflate his stature. He has no purpose, yet I see him at too many parties for him to be completely irrelevant. Since I'm unable to derive his point, I put up with him. I can't afford to burn bridges because I'm such a natural pyro that if I start doing it intentionally, I'll end up completely isolated.

When the driver announces we've arrived at The Imperial Hall, I grab my camera off the seat next to me, then over-tip the kid so he won't sell *The New York Post* a fake story about me. He seems to question the tip and begins to make change. "Keep it," I say, using the money as a penance because the Chinese investors are covering the bill for the car and this makes me feel guilty for what I've done.

I step out onto the sidewalk, then make my way toward The Imperial Hall, a basement club that was introduced to me by a transsexual internet phenom turned sort-of pop star, turned social investment golden guy... girl... whatever. Two years ago, my management suggested that I should design her tour outfits, and after flying out from LA to New York to interview for the gig, I had a sit-down meeting with her. She immediately informed me, "It's going to be hard to hide the cocks with some of these cuts, we're going to have to tuck," then she grabbed my hand, and we made our way to The Imperial Hall. As soon as I arrived here, I knew I had found a place that offered everything I demand from a Friday night.

I walk inside The Imperial Hall, this time without a transsexual, which is probably a negative because the fashion bloggers would pull back on their attack a little if I had an unsnarkable date. They'd say that my arrival with this golden boy-girl somewhat "dulled Lorrie's harsh words that were spat earlier in the night," and that I "temporarily pacified the turmoil with a moment of masculine softness."

The heat of the crowd in the windowless basement rushes toward me, as do the models, and I immediately feel welcome. I'm offered congratulations and club drugs- I decline both.

I immediately take off my suit jacket and place it on one of the leather sofas that line the wall. I know I'll never see the jacket again and I'm okay with that. The clothes are no longer important tonight.

Matthew's band is already playing. The crowd is already slamming into each other- dancing/ Kissing/ Moshing/ Together/ Separately.

I turn my Fujifilm Finepix S1000 camera on, then I back up to the end of the rectangular basement. My first snap is of the entire scene. Uneven stones- some over a foot and a half long- have been mortared together to form the walls. The archways are vaulted. The ceiling is a lumpy gray stucco.

My camera flashes and the strobe briefly syncs with the drumbeat of Matthew's energetic indie rock. Models and their boyfriends bounce to the music. Shaggy-haired boys strangle green beer bottles. Sweaty girls with slicked back hair check their text messages. Models with champagne flutes and wine glasses arch wide goofy smiles for my camera. They're off the clock, but still working as models for Andrew Lorrie. They're buzzing from the alcohol and fulfilled from the music they bop to. A band-boy, who's definitely *not* a male model, glides with his Fender, as Matthew continues to croon out his lyrics. I don't pay attention to the words. Matthew's problems are insignificant. Matthew could fuck anyone at this party, besides me. Matthew is in the moment. Matthew could've walked for my womenswear line; he's that appealing.

I'm struck by a surge in the crowd and my lens is redirected.

The drummer of Matthew's band falls into focus. He's watching the crowd as the mayhem hits a fever pitch, but he never misses a beat. It's like that scene in *I Love Lucy* where Lucy is working an assembly line, and she keeps going faster and faster as the pace of the conveyor belt speeds up. Eventually, Lucy fucks things up, as was required of her character. Matthew's drummer keeps going faster, and he doesn't fuck things up, as is required of his character.

I scan the scene through my viewfinder. I don't photograph anywhere near the perimeter sofas because they're probably lined with the critics who are desperate to take a load off their feet after standing for the entirety of my ill-advised press conference. A girl in a baseball cap with an alien on it pulls a model in an ill-fitting 80's dress across the mess of the mosh. Elbows and arms crash in waves around the girls. A boy wearing eyeliner hoists a black model onto his shoulders, and the black model runs his hands along the wet gray ceiling. A messy-haired model tries to heal a gash on an injured boy's head merely by holding out her hands to project energy. A long, lean girl is hoisted up by the dense crowd, but without a stage to surf to, she's just passed around. Everyone clutches their beers carefully so if they get kicked by the girl, they won't have to go back to the over-packed bar. A bizarre looking girl wearing a mesh top, who's a model merely because of who her mother is, licks Matthew as he sings. For a moment Matthew loses his lyrics and laughs into the mic. The falter is temporary, and the song resumes as the girl in the mesh top dances back into the mess of bodies. His eyes fixed, Matthew sings to a girl at the edge of the party- possibly his girlfriend- certainly a girl I don't know- certainly a girl disappointed in Matthew's conduct (or at least in his setlist). The models at the party pick their boys, or leave to call their boys. Or girls. Everyone couples up. I snap the unlikely duos. I brought all these people together; the start of something. The boy who was supposed to be healed by the model's raised hand aura suddenly passes out. The model shrugs, then merely declares, "It worked." Tall girls who didn't walk for me stand in rows and smile for my camera. No one is camera shy. Everyone is sweating. More hugging and more mayhem. More kissing and more thrashing. More hands and more heavy breathing. Glances are exchanged. Numbers are exchanged. The daughter of the famous model, being somewhat undesirable, is regularly exchanged. No one smokes cigarettes. Someone lights (turns on?) an e-cigarette. It reminds me of the bar last night. I look for Lux. I find her. I point at the boy with the plug-in cigarette.

Beyond the boy, I see something far more interesting.

THE GIRL

I hand my camera to Lux. She's standing with the girl, Madeleine, from the front row. Madeleine looks like she belongs here. I'm happy that she came, even after she heard my speech. Most of the models showed up for this after-party. Some didn't. The buyers moved on to the next show. The Chinese are absent. At least a couple of critics are probably waiting to tell me off. Most of the critics are probably home writing scathing posts about how terrible I am.

I'm comfortable leaving my camera in Lux's care. Before I saw her, I momentarily considered giving it to Galina, which would have been a huge mistake. If I did that, the only way I'd get the photographs from tonight would be if Galina's pawn shop of choice sold the camera to a girl with a blog.

I immediately make my way to the girl who stole my attention. She stares at nothing particular, yet scowls with a directed displeasure.

I approach the girl because she's wearing one of my designs.

She's wearing one of my designs from the show this afternoon.

She's wearing one of my designs from this show this afternoon, and it's not the design she walked in.

She's wearing one of my designs from the show this afternoon, and it's not the design she walked in, *but it should have been.*

The girl looks like she doesn't want to be here. While she seems shy, annoyed, and above it all, she also exudes an aura that matches my vision for the piece. It's almost as though I was designing for this girl, despite having never met her. The only comparable feeling to this moment is dreaming of a person before they appear in your life.

The piece this girl is wearing is made of a special cobalt blue velvet that has a tendency to look like curtains when the material is loose, so I painstakingly crafted the entire garment to be tight, cutting it precisely so it wouldn't gather. A skinny black belt cinches the model's slim waist to keep everything flush to her long, slender body. A sheer but sturdy black leopard lace is carefully sewn into the velvet, wrapping around the piece. The neckline is V cut, to create the illusion of cleavage, but anyone with boobs would fall out of the dress. This girl has no boobs, but the dress hides this, unless she's viewed from her profile. It's the model's long arms that prevent the dress from being a perfect fit. The black lace sleeves end immediately at her elbows, instead of past her elbows as they did on Lux. The piece touches the floor, as I had intended, but in a place like The Imperial Hall, where everyone is crushed together, this holds this girl back. Based on the model's present expression, the dress isn't the only thing holding this girl back.

I remember discussing this model with Gregor, but I certainly wasn't this taken by her during casting.

The model has a massive waterfall of brown hair that frames her pale face, but that's only the beginning of her intriguing look- it's the thick, sharp eyebrows/ It's the tight eyelids over brown eyes/ It's the slightly wide, but small, nose/ It's the biggest, reddest lips that mostly stay pressed together in a near grimace/ It's those gapped front teeth that occasionally make an appearance when the party clicks into some special combination of events that unlocks this girl's scowl/ It's the hint of another ethnicity/ It's her features, which are exaggerated in the way that never wins a girl the prom queen crown, but does win the quiet envy of the prom queen.

"Nice dress," I say to the model, admiring my work, admiring her.

"I'm so happy with it. When your assistant mentioned a chance for trade, I knew exactly what I would choose," the model says in a small voice. She has a domestic accent, and I'm thrilled to find that her shyness isn't because she's unfamiliar with the language- it's because she doesn't know any of the other models.

The girl's voice is perfect, but her words make me recoil. If Karen offered the girls trade immediately after the show, it means that she believes none of this collection will go into production, and the Chinese investors would prefer to have a smaller bill than a bigger collection. It's cutting losses. It's not standard procedure. It's throwing everything overboard so the ship doesn't sink as fast. It's revenge for my actions today.

I tell the girl, "You really don't have to take trade. I mean, I can get you some cash. This is your first show, right?"

Gregor had informed me that a lot of the girls we found were fresh off the boat/plane/train/their parent's minivan, and this girl is no exception.

"Yeah. My first," she confirms, biting her blood red lip.

"What's your name?" I request.

"Isabella," she says.

"Isabella what?" I ask.

"I think I'm just going to keep it at Isabella. There's already an Isabeli, but not many Isabellas," she tells me.

This girl is correct; she exists above the other models tonight.

There are not many Isabellas.

I nod at her statement and purr, "Isabella in blue velvet."

She smiles at this, understanding the Rossellini fueled joke, but she doesn't overreact to the reference. A movie frame pops into my head- Dennis Hopper, armed with a gun, cradling a blue velvet robe in his arm. I will become that evil old man if this piece is ever taken back from Isabella. There's no way that would happen. This piece is hers now. I'd sooner turn the gun on myself than take back the blue velvet.

When I first saw Lynch's *Blue Velvet*, it was unique, haunting, thrilling, and I immediately wanted to show everyone else what I had "discovered." I feel precisely the same way about seeing Isabella in my blue velvet dress. I want everyone to notice us tonight, and tomorrow, and the next day, and so many days after that, for a long time, in a vast number of basement bars and backstage areas. A future begins to assemble, and I make a promise- "I'll get you paid, in addition to the piece, but-" I add gently, Matthew's music almost drowning me out, "-normally, you don't leave with trade immediately after the show."

"Oh. Sorry. Karen said..." Isabella responds, embarrassed, trailing off.

"Seeing you in that look fixes things," I tell her, acknowledging this out loud. Tonight, with youthful waves crashing in a static massage, the tension in my shoulders dissipates, and I view my return as an unquestionable success.

"What needed fixing?" Isabella asks me, and the music is too loud and she's too quiet, but my eyes never leave her lips, so I'm able to respond.

"You didn't hear the tirade I went on after the show?" I ask, and now it's my turn to be embarrassed.

"Yeah, I did. But that's you. And you aren't fixed," Isabella says.

"No. I'm not fixed," I say, and my eyebrows raise for some reason, then I go into a small panic. "That wasn't a come on," I quickly add.

"Oh. Ew," Isabella says simply, then moves past it, "I noticed you didn't mention established designers plagiarizing up-and-coming designers when you were listing problems in the industry," and this proves that she thinks there are problems too.

My answer to this is simple, "I design based on my own pain, not my Google search history. I suppose that the experiences I can't get past might be similar to the pain someone else is exorcising, but nothing I've ever created has ever been a choice. It was essential for me to create that piece you're in."

When Isabella doesn't respond to this, I ask, "Who's your agency? I want to know where to send the check to."

"Just let me keep this piece. I like it. Any money I make would go directly to paying my agency rent, then it would be gone. This dress will last until I'm too old and gross to wear it," Isabella tells me, looking down at the slice of my pain wrapped around her.

"Exactly. You can use the money to stay in a model apartment as an investment. Don't you want to live in New York? Isn't that the dream of, uh, everyone in this room?"

"I have money from graduation. My agency will upfront the rent."

"Are you sure you want to stay in New York?" I ask, trying to figure out if *I* want to stay in New York.

Isabella nods an unassured confirmation.

"Where are you from?" I ask, because I'm unable to pin the associated geography of her slight accent.

"California," she says, then smiles an apology.

"Me too," I say, but she already knew this, so I ask, "Are you in school back in California?"

She provides another unsure nod, then says, "I've taken a couple of classes at a community college."

"But you're choosing this as a career now, right?" I ask, leading her.

She winks her left eye closed for a second, thinking over her answer, then decides, "I'm going to give it a shot."

I look at the beautiful girl in my perfect design, and I feel very confident in my talents. I want another shot at dressing this model.

"Good. I'll need you again," I say, then I turn and see another very different too-perfect girl walk into the party.

Suddenly, the night changes, again.

This late arriving girl possesses an instantly recognizable facial symmetry so profound that when people criticize her, the best they can come up with is to say, "Yeah her face is great, but her hands seem sorta weird." High cheekbones meet cat eyes, and puffed lips hover over a pointed (but not pointy) chin. Her jet black Liz Taylor hair is gracefully flopped to the left side of her face, almost covering one of her eyes- those arresting eyes that make interviewers ask, "Is your father Asian?" They know her mother isn't Asian because there are 50-foot billboards of her mother's smiling non-Asian face looming over every freeway in America. The fashionably late girl is so uniquely gorgeous, people have a hard time believing that multiple ethnicities didn't collaborate on the creation of this perfect specimen. I know for a fact that they didn't, and this makes me leave without my jacket, my camera, or a goodbye.

THE FALLOUT

For some reason, I read the reviews. Most of the aggressive attacks on me don't mention the clothes. All of them mention my post-show interview. None of them address the issues I brought up. All of them call for my removal from, at minimum, the fashion industry, and at most, the planet earth.

After the video of my "meltdown" spreads across the fashion blogs, I close off. I read everything, I listen to everything, I respond to nothing.

The calls from the panicked Chinese investors go unreturned.

A "promo blitz" is canceled.

A "not the cover story, but listed in bold text on the cover" feature is "postponed."

An "I told you so" e-mail from Karen (all 19 paragraphs) is eyeballed then moved right into the trash.

With this Andrew Lorrie collection, I was supposed to finally receive what most people would consider to be the "fruits of my labor." It was my chance to make more money, get more power, and to redeem myself. My contract provides me with a salary for the line, as well as a percentage of the profits. I don't check my bank account. I don't receive any sales projections for the line.

To look at my savings could potentially provide confirmation that I've failed and nothing was gained.

More time passes. Enough time for the reportage of my show to reach the print magazines. One popular fashion magazine, available at the few remaining newsstands in New York, features not one, but three articles about my show- none of them positive. Some of the articles are authored by people I regarded, up until recently, as friends. These articles, after I read every word, are torn out of the magazine, balled up, set on fire, then crushed by the heel of my beat up black Dr. Martens. The ash on the carpet is tracked around the room, leaving a ghostly carbon char that the maids spend a considerable amount time attempting to remove.

What finally gets me out of my drink and brood cycle is Lux's husky voice yelling over the phone, "You can't do this to me!"

I had neglected to consider how Lux would be affected by my actions. It was implied that my creative team would proceed on to the next opportunity without me. Karen, Gregor, Mandy, and all of the fresh faces would move on. It would be fine, for everyone, except Lux. Most people in this industry run from one show to another. Not Lux. For Lux, I'm the only show in town. Her call is the jolt that snaps me out of my self-pity celebration. It's the call that gets me out of bed and into the shower. It's the call that gets me into a clean black V-neck T-shirt and an army green knit soft cotton cardigan. It's the call that makes make realize, yes, people *can* be hurt by "only words."

I skip dinner, and return with Lux to the bar we went to the night before my show. I hope that it will remind her of the cozy, too hot, just the right amount of intoxication filled night we spent together in the back room.

Lux's hair is pulled back in a ponytail, except for her razor-straight bangs. She's wearing a thin gray tank top and what appears to be, based on strap count, two different bras. Black tights are matched with DvF ankle boots.

My hands shake as I find out just how far things can swing off course in a short amount of time.

Lux and I make each other happy; I want to remind her of that.

I want to remind her of my humanity.

This time, Lux doesn't hide in the bathroom. She orders a drink and they don't ID her. She seems okay with this. I try to figure out why she accepts the bypassing of a mandated formality, then I realize it's because it means she'll get her drink faster. Our prior night in this bar now seems to be a memory that's fading into the distance. The games and the cute humor Lux and I once enjoyed together are now absent.

When we get back to the square table and sit down under the unflattering lighting, I see that Lux has bags under her eyes. It's possible she didn't hide in the bathroom because she's already spent a significant portion of her day closed off in a tiled cell, acting younger than she truly is.

Lux ordered a vodka tonic this time. It's close to the drink she had before.

I ordered the same PBR, but I didn't flirt with the bartender, and she didn't seem to remember me.

None of the amusing interruptions occur- there's no black girl, no Russians, no douche with an electronic cigarette. Just us. All of the excitement is gone. The bar that was so hot the other night, is now somehow cold.

Lux stares at the foosball table as though she's reading the stickers, but she's already seen their clipped messages and there's nothing new stuck there- nothing to demand this much attention. Lux needed my presence earlier, but now she seems to loathe it.

"Why?" Lux asks me, and there are too many questions requiring an answer for me to know how to respond.

I assemble a general explanation that applies to so many different issues, "I thought I was going to open people's eyes to-"

"-speaking of that, you could have fixed this by doing the logical thing."

"Which was?" I ask.

"This sounds stupid," Lux says, "This sounds selfish, but it makes sense. If you had used me in the show, then-"

"-nothing would have changed," I immediately promise her, "Next time, you'll walk. This line wasn't right because-"

"-an Asian girl doesn't fit with your 'American Dream?'" Lux asks, not looking at me.

I have to laugh, and I remind her, "My 'American Dream' was mandated by Asians. I had-"

"-I know. You had an Asian. A fucking five foot seven inch Asian walked for you," Lux says with disdain. She must have watched the live stream because she never uses the invite I send to her. Despite this, she cared, and she watched. She's always cared, more than Karen, almost as much as me.

"Can I also just say that seating shit felt very deliberate," Lux tacks on.

"It wasn't. It meant nothing. Madeleine- the girl- she was just standing by the wall, and-"

"-and you sat her in the front row to fuck with me."

"I didn't. You're blowing this out of proportion," I say, embracing the seating topic because it truly was born out of innocence. "It's not like she was my date or something, it's not like she's my new muse. I don't need a new muse." I want to end this by saying, "I still have you," but that assurance escapes me.

"Ah, so this is me blowing things out of proportion? I bet that's going to be your excuse a lot when people call you out for what you did after that show."

"I bet people will be blowing a lot of stuff out of proportion, so, yes, I'll defend myself," I say.

"Maybe your proportions are off," Lux suggests, channeling Karen.

"I base them on you," I say, then I shoot Lux a smile. She didn't expect this hybrid of a compliment and a joke. I catch her giggle before she snubs it out.

After almost forgiving me, I see Lux shut down completely. She's not going to let me out of this one.

Lux doesn't have another drink. This time, she stands up, then walks away.

"We're not done," I yell to her, as she passes the bathroom she used to hide in.

Lux doesn't return to clarify if I meant tonight or if I meant in the industry.

THE SECOND OPINION

I text Lux that I'm sorry.

Two 151 & Cokes later, I receive a response, "The collection is done."

I'm approaching the point of drunkenness, but I can still hear sober me begging, *Not another massacre/Don't wreck something else/Not again/Just go back to your hotel room/Don't complicate an already very fucked situation/You're going to complicate things further, aren't you?*

I pay my tab, and I half-hope that I will find Lux outside chain-smoking Pall Malls, waiting for me to emerge.

Out on the sidewalk, I look both ways, but Lux is gone.

I take out my phone, then pause, because I have nowhere to go, and no one to text. I swipe over to my contacts, and I search for another voice of reason. Anyone who has texted me, "Are you okay?" in the aftermath of the show is disregarded. I stop scrolling when I see the name of a person that I wanted to hear from, but haven't. The next contact in the row is a name that I recognize from shows past, and I burn for a blanket of nostalgia.

Mandy, my makeup lead, is the person I *need* to meet with tonight. She didn't text me because she knows how I deal with failure, and it's not by socializing- it's not by moving on- it's by closing myself off/ it's by studying everything that's been said/ it's by second-guessing/ it's by convincing myself that I'm right and everyone else is wrong.

Mandy is white, 29, and pretty in the way that when she arrives at this bar, men will look at me with envy. She's programmed in my phone as "Amanda," so the name under her is "Anastasia."

Anastasia walked for me four straight shows early on in my career. She has a Russian name, but she's Ecuadorian. Now that she's "aged out" of the industry, she's become an actress and activist. She articulately argues the same points that I screamed about to the fashion press after my show. Having Anastasia next to me will be a good way to figure out just how wrong my actions were.

I text both girls.

Mandy responds back with a bright text, confirming that she's still in New York, and she'd love to meet up. I'm well aware that I don't need to apologize to her. Mandy was booked for multiple shows every day of NYFW so my implosion didn't affect her professionally. She left after her team finished the looks for my show, then she started different looks, at a different venue, for a different designer.

Anastasia responds back to my invite with, "Yeah, I think that would be good," and I become both scared and appreciative

We agree on meeting at a small French restaurant that always has open seats at the bar.

I begin walking and the quicker I move, the soberer I feel. I don't hail a cab because I need time for the alcohol to vacate my pores. Sobering up is the only way I'll be able to articulately explain my questionable post-show actions.

I find the restaurant without doubling back or checking my phone. There's still a bit of summer left in the air, so the large doors are propped open, allowing for a warm cross-breeze that encourages drinking. I haven't been here in years, but as soon as I walk inside, I feel like this is the perfect place to meet with my girls again. The entire length of the L-shaped bar is empty, except for a lone woman in her late 30's who has her brown hair pulled back in a silky ponytail at the vertex of her skull. She's wearing a tan silk blouse tucked into an olive pencil skirt. What captures my attention beyond the fashion notes is the fact that she's nursing a glass of white wine while reading a book.

I feel that my ability to read people allows me to intuit how to dress them, but when I see a woman reading at the bar, I'm lost as to who she is. Does she have the book because she doesn't have anyone to go to the bar with, but she wants to be in a social setting? She could get a better bottle of wine- a full bottle of wine, cheaper- if she just read her book at home. The lighting is dim and the sun has set, so the woman has to push the book near one of the candles flickering in a jar on the bar. Reading- a task that most people do on a glowing screen now becomes even more difficult when it involves a well-worn book in a poorly lit French restaurant. The woman has to be meeting someone. Is she killing time until her date arrives/ Is this an online relationship finally jumping into the real world, and the woman is cramming to read all those books she listed on her dating profile/ Is she a student, changing her path later in life, and could she have advice for me?

I decide to talk to the woman with the novel- to confront my confusion- to profile her being.

Taking a seat next to her, I ask, "What are you reading?" then I point at the book, as if this clarifying action is somehow necessary.

"*The Fountainhead*," she says.

I know that this choice has political implications, but I'm not sure what those implications are.

"Have you read it?" she asks me, and I immediately realize this woman is Dutch. I'm good at recognizing accents. I've made a lot of small talk with a lot of beautiful Dutch women. For a moment, I think back to the girl, Isabella, that I met at The Imperial Hall, and I question why her accent threw me after living in LA for so long, then I question where Isabella is now.

Before I'm exposed for having no knowledge of Ayn Rand, I sidestep the Dutch woman's question and mention I started reading *Infinite Jest*, just because it's the longest book I own. This is a lie. It *is* the longest book I own, but I'm not reading it. I bought it on my Kindle because it was two dollars. I had briefly hesitated before I clicked "Buy," and I tried to think of who this money would go to. A man with no children, who is dead, was getting my two dollars. What type of abyss did that cash enter? Did his widow get the money? I can't imagine that's an easy check to cash. I also can't share any of these thoughts with the Dutch woman- not this early into our budding friendship- so I say, "The novel is great. Already loving it."

She nods at this, and tells me, "I'll add it to my list."

I feel confident that, yes, this woman did want someone to speak with her, and, yes, I will be the person who attempts to make her night out not feel like a waste. Without letting an awkward silence materialize, I consistently keep a rich topic of conversation at the forefront of our interaction.

In New York, girls too often flee the bar after a single glass of wine, only to go home to their too small apartment and feel totally alone. I don't want the Dutch woman to perform this ritual, and I don't want to resort to texting Lux again, so I seek a temporary connection to keep everything hopeful.

I casually mention that I just showed at NYFW, then she casually mentions she's a historian who was "kidnapped" by New York seven years ago. I resist the urge to admit to her that the only reason I'm interested in history is because I want to steal from it.

Mandy arrives, and the Dutch woman senses that the one thing that bonded us for this short moment was our mutual loneliness. To put a close to our interaction, she finishes her wine, then makes me type the name of my clothing line into her ancient Blackberry. I briefly consider making a joke, "You really are into history," as I raise the phone, but that's not how I want to end our small moment. When she googles me in the cab on the way home, she'll learn I'm a dickhead. No sense in making the announcement now.

Mandy greets me with a big hug- a funeral procession embrace. It's a grasp so tight and so close that it's almost as though she's searching for confirmation that my heart is still beating after everything that's happened.

Mandy is wearing a black drop neck knit sweater with a black tank top underneath. She also has on flats and dark wash jeans- a uniform of a girl always on the go, in and out of New York and LA.

We sit down at the bar, in front of a flickering candle in a jar, and Mandy either doesn't notice I'm drunk or she's just used to seeing me like this. I order myself a Stella, and Mandy gets a glass of red wine. The Dutch woman with the book leaves. I don't know what I accomplished with her, and that makes me want another woman with another book to appear so I can try once again to crack this elusive breed. I want to apply what I learned tonight so I can confirm the universality of my observations. A collection of tall Dutch girls walking down a runway with purses that look like thick novels I've lied about reading begins to flash fast in my mind, but I don't have the chance to realize this inspiration, unless someone else's name is on the purse.

Mandy lets me exist in my moment, and she doesn't immediately bring up the obvious topic, unlike Lux who demanded answers before we even sipped our drinks. Mandy tells me about her other shows. It's all eye makeup with her. That's what makes conversation with Mandy so rich. No matter what, she'll pay attention to my eyes, and so much of how I emote comes from my stare. Sure, she'll think of ways to make me look better- how to eliminate those dark circles, how to even everything out, but I know it's because she loves me, not because she can't stand the way I look. I see a beautiful woman and I want to dress her; Mandy sees a beautiful person inside and she wants to fix their outside to match. Everything she tells me indicates this.

I get an update on her twin sister, who went to mortuary school, but was turned away from an externship because it was feared that her tattoos would make people feel "uncomfortable" about her working on their dead loved one-like there was going to be some dark ritual involved with Grandpa Dan's corpse. Mandy spruces up the story with a happy ending by noting that her sister is becoming a herbalist. Makeup on the tattoos. Makeup on the mistakes. There's the mention of the last time we saw her sister- when she was dating a guy in a band that was playing Warped Tour, and we stayed at their apartment, eating cold pad Thai on the floor after a long night at a diner-themed bar in Philly. It was a time when Mandy was out of college, out of love and trying to find her place. Now Mandy is dating a guy with a good job, and she has her own place with him, while her sister is lost. Twins, but they keep jostling for who's older. In the end, Mandy is infinitely young, but she's stable now.

Our eye contact is broken when Mandy's phone vibrates on the bar. "I have to flag down Ana," she tells me, then drifts out to the street, leaving her phone with me- an assurance that she will return, that she's not abandoning me.

I search the restaurant for women reading books, but only find mismatched couples frowning at each other.

When Mandy returns with Anastasia, I feel everyone in the restaurant focus on the edge of the bar. I see the envy I predicted, and I bask in it. If people knew who I am, they wouldn't envy me.

I hug Anastasia. She's wearing a white cotton strapless eyelet dress with a sweetheart neckline and a shaped bust. She arrives looking exactly how I remember her- almost too busty for fashion, almost too muscular for fashion, almost too annoyed at me to show up here, but interesting enough of a person that none of it detracts from her glow.

Just as Mandy did, Anastasia begins "catching up" with me. She lists all the things she's doing outside of the industry. Her conversation topics are so far from fashion that I realize Anastasia wasn't lost earlier; Mandy left me for a moment so she could provide a preemptive warning on where the conversation had gone, where I am mentally, and where we will collectively have to go when the time is right.

As one of the accomplishments that she's been collecting off the runway, Anastasia mentions, "I was on *Law & Order*."

"The one with Ice T?" Mandy asks.

Anastasia nods, and in the dim candlelight, I notice her freckled nose. I think about the white pancake makeup I put on this beautiful olive girl and for a moment I become one of my own critics. To move past this, I continue the softball conversation, asking, "Did you meet Ice T?"

"No," Anastasia says, shaking her head, "He's usually only in one scene where someone needs to comment on how unacceptable rape is, even to a street-weary reformed gangsta."

"It's good to have checks and balances," I say.

"So, I was a prostitute," Anastasia continues her story casually. When my face manipulates into a mask of concern, she adds, "On the show. I was a prostitute *on the show*. And I don't work method," then she fast forwards to the point of her story, "They gave me an outfit and when I put it on, half my ass was hanging out. I figured I'd be sitting in court for the entire scene so I wasn't worried, but the director kept having me get up so he could give me notes, almost like he had some sort of agreement with the crew."

"What was it like on set?" Mandy asks, and I want to stop the conversation because losing Mandy to TV would be a waste of her high fashion makeup talents. Living in California, Mandy is bound to get into TV or movies, but I'll do everything in my power to advise her against it. Fashion has a tendency to push talent away for trivial or imagined reasons, and this is why I aggressively hold onto anyone who was born for this industry.

"Like I said, being on set was a lot of standing around," Anastasia tells us, robbing the moment of any glamour. "My lawyer was a total pervert. It almost seemed like he auditioned to be my John, and when he was given another role, he simply chose to stay in character for the part he originally read for."

"Did you win your case?" I ask.

"I don't remember. I think the ruling found me 'gross, but innocent,'" Anastasia says, and the whole hooker moment begins to feel inconsequential, which is how I demand it should end.

"Did you live?" Mandy asks.

"Yes. I lived," Anastasia laughs. "I was in court."

"You were a hooker on *SVU*- that does seem like death on a platter," I say.

"I died in the mafia movie I was in," Anastasia offers, as though this would satisfy us in some way.

Carefully, I ask, "Were you..."

"No," she says, sensing my accusation, "I wasn't a hooker in that movie. I was a mom. I had..." she leans over to me and whispers, "...black kids. I asked the director, like, 'How did this happen? You know I'm not black right?'"

"What was his response?" I ask, trying to see how another professional fields a question like that.

"He said that I got the role because I'm not SAG and I'll work for daily minimum and pizza. Same for the kids."

"Was the movie any good?" I ask.

"After I died, I became detached," Anastasia remarks.

"What happened to your black kids?" Mandy asks with concern.

"I don't know, but they're going to have some questions, that's for sure," Anastasia responds, but it doesn't answer the question, and I feel a shift begin to happen. This discussion is too close to *the* discussion. There's a rumble on the bar and I feel the drinks shake. The Vietnamese bartender, who hopefully knows more French than English, senses my wordless anxiety and she brings me another draft of Stella. Mandy asks the bartender if there's a spare outlet she can use to charge her phone. The bartender takes out a power strip from behind the bar and tells us that after the hurricane last year, this restaurant was one of the few places in the city that had power so they would charge patrons' phones while they drank. "Good tips when texting is involved," the bartender tells us.

"So, after I left the show..." Mandy says, getting down to it, but I feel depleted like her phone's battery.

"Yeah, Andrew. What *was* that about?" Anastasia asks.

Both women immediately become devoted to having this conversation. They seem to be searching for the reason why I am the way I am, still.

"I think... I wanted revenge," I tell them, and it doesn't feel good to admit that to these women, but I'm infinitely glad that they're patiently listening to me. I willed this moment into existence so to flee from it now would make me look foolish, again.

Mandy, in her warm way, laughs, like she's not following, then says, "You got your revenge." She shakes her head like she can't believe my response, then explains, "The line was your revenge. It was you, and it was now, and it was exciting. You showed them what they were missing all these years. You proved that your brother isn't a better designer than you are."

When Mandy says this to me, it makes complete sense. Before the show, I was sure that my revenge would come when I "fixed" the industry. I wanted to prove to every person in the room how hypocritical they have become.

"And, as an advocate for models, you had some amazing points-" Anastasia adds, "-but the thing is, Andrew, we make those points separate from the collections because this is an industry, and you have to respect the machine because-"

"-I don't have to respect the machine. I *don't* have to respect the machine. The machine is broken. We have to apply the fix where machine exists," I say, too loud, as I defend what I previously said too loudly.

Anastasia puts her hand on my tensed arm and says, "You're one man. I'm one woman. I *know* I can't do everything as a single woman in the industry so I find other advocates to provide support, to spread out the heat, to show people that this is a group of ex-models, or retired designers, or current designers- like you, who demand change. The difference between a crazy person ranting to himself, and an expert making a passionate point, is that one of them is in a dialog and one of them is a madman cornering apathetic onlookers. You turned into the guy on the subway, holding up a heavy book, demanding that people repent, while the audience is just trying to get to the office so they can do their job."

I stare at the candle on the bar, then at Mandy's glowing phone next to it. "You're right. You're both right," I admit, under my breath, and I desperately want to blow out the candle because Mandy keeps trying to look me in the eyes, and I can't return the gesture.

"What do I do?" I ask.

There's a pause peppered with the sounds of the city, then Mandy answers my question, "You need to stick to designing for other people. I don't think Andrew Lorrie for Andrew Lorrie brings out the best in Andrew Lorrie. That may sound like a broken solution, but... you're kind of a broken man."

The broken man sits between two women who have it together, completely. I'm not forced to apologize, I'm merely asked to make sure this doesn't happen again, for my own good. They encourage me to continue doing the things I do well, then hand off the things I don't do well to someone who *does* do them well.

Mandy has embraced fashion. Anastasia has left it.

Mandy still looks beautiful. Anastasia is the best-dressed girl in the restaurant.

I become aware that you never truly leave the industry. You never abandon that feeling of being the best version of yourself that fashion offers.

The clothes will always be there, and right now, that's a rare virtue.

THE PRINCIPAL'S OFFICE

I walk into the loft, and I find that items are already being removed. Evidence of my existence is being cleaned up.

I watch a man in a navy blue jumpsuit carry away the computer monitor I threw, and I say to him, "Be careful with that."

Karen sits in the square leather chair in the center of the rapidly emptying space. She's in *my* chair. This is a chair that I'll have to leave behind because it was already here when I arrived. It's someone else's chair. It's anyone else's chair, besides Karen's.

I walk across the loft and nod to the Latino men who are carting out the mannequins. I'll have to argue to get my army of plaster girls back, a familiar discussion.

"I just saw your e-mail. Sorry about the delay," I say, stepping in front Karen, my right hand in the pocket of my tight black dress pants, my left hand rubbing my neck, just under the collar of my custom made sky blue dress shirt.

Karen stares at my bent elbow, then her eyes move up slightly to the even bricks outside the window. After considering something, she looks back at me and copies the glare that I give someone when I'm about to lose control. She stands up and tells me, "I'm going to remind you of this fact, one last time."

This will not be brief, so I brush by her, then sit down in the chair.

Karen looms over me, antagonizing me with her dreadful pantsuit. This one is cream colored.

"You're a good designer. You put together a very creative collection for your return," Karen tells me in her monotone voice that now seems baked with fatigue. I know that I excel at making beautiful dresses so this preface doesn't soften the blow for what she's about to tell me. "But the world isn't against you, Andrew. We aren't lining up to 'catch you' in some big scandal."

"I don't think that," I say, staring over her shoulder, to a naked mannequin being picked up by a fat man, then carried away.

"Then why do you look to undermine me at every point, when all I'm trying to do is save you?" Karen asks.

I put my elbows on the edge of the chair, then my fingers press on my widow's peak, and I explain, "It was my obligation to speak up because I finally had the power to change things. There's this silent trauma going on and-"

"-it's not silent," Karen interrupts me, "You just have to understand that fashion can be an escape. I think you already know that. I think that's why you make Mandy do the girls' makeup so extreme. The thing is, you have to let other people escape with you, Andrew."

"I follow my instincts," I say, as a way of accepting blame, while also making it seem as though I had no control over the situation. I want Karen to believe that there was only one possible path for me to take after the collection showed.

In response, Karen provides a recommendation, "Let the industry at least get out of the general vicinity of your work before you unleash your hate. They aren't mad at you specifically, they're angry at the casting tastes in fashion.

You're just an example they can challenge because you don't have that many minorities on your runway and you're a dumb-ass when you argue."

"You don't understand. I've had to deal with articles that-"

"-people will always write articles, Andrew. Have you ever been on the internet?" Karen asks me, knowing that I've been pouring over every perspective of this event, even if the opinion is coming from a sheltered teenage girl who knows nothing of the world. "You need to change, and only then is there a chance that the industry might take notice of your points. People aren't looking at you as being racist, they're looking at the system, then you put yourself in the middle of it and, yeah, they start looking at you. I'm tired of it. I'm tired of you asking for my help, then fleeing when I try to give it. I'm very tired, And-"

"-so what's next?" I interrupt. This begins to feel like a breakup that's happening as my stuff is already being moved out of the common space we once shared. The timeline continues moving so fast that the events are getting jumbled. I need to slow things down. I need the promise of a future.

"Next, you listen to me," Karen says, her voice almost gaining inflection. "Next, you beg. Next, you apologize. Next, you say you're wrong. Next, you blame your meds. Hell, blame anything and anyone you can and hope that something sticks."

"Who's going to believe that's genuine?" I ask. "Shouldn't we wait until things, I don't know, die down? I just showed a collection. I'll stick around in the city a bit instead of going back home. When the bloggers move on to someone else, I'll make a statement about how deeply sorry I am, then I'll tell them that I'm going to verbal rehab or something."

"We already have a meeting set up for tomorrow," Karen tells me, not taking a break. "You aren't leaving the city, not yet."

This is Karen's career at stake. I can see her loyalty battling her better judgment. Right now, her loyalty is winning and this makes me want to return the favor.

"Okay, you're right, I do owe the Chinese an apology," I say, standing up.

Karen shakes her head, "Oh, no. Be perfectly clear on this point, the Chinese investors want *nothing* to do with you. There is no meeting with them. Ever again."

"Then who's the meeting with?" I ask.

"A prominent designer is interested in having you revamp his stale ready-to-wear line," Karen tells me, and Mandy's advice repeats like a ghost-whisper in my ear.

"I don't do ready-to-wear. Too boring," I say, flipping my hand dismissively, knocking away the echo.

"Fine. I'm going to this meeting tomorrow with or without you," Karen says.

"You'd leave?" I ask.

"Absolutely. So you have two choices, come with me, or say goodbye."

THE BAILOUT

"No. Fuck you! No!" I yell back at Karen, as I head down West 36th toward 7th Ave.

"We had an agreement," Karen says, her heels clacking behind me.

"This is a fucking set up and you're sick for it," I growl.

Morning commuters stare at me, trying to figure out if I'm on a cell phone call gone wrong or if I'm just a crazy person. I'm fleeing the sound of Karen's heels, searching for a subway line or a taxi so I can escape back to the Hilton and resume soaking in regret.

"This is you running away from me when I'm trying to help you. After all the shit I mentioned yesterday, here you are today doing exactly what you promised you wouldn't," Karen points out.

Once again, a person in my life who's trying to save me from me is in an argument with me because I'm convinced what's about to happen isn't "me."

I make a decision that I know is stupid, and I turn around.

I walk back to Karen.

I walk back to the office building on West 36th.

I walk into Michael Lorrie's international headquarters for the first time ever.

Karen failed to mention that the meeting she brokered happened to be with my brother. I'm aware that this meeting exists as a way for Michael to finally get me up to the 8th floor so I can see just how much more successful he is than I am.

I've never felt that there was a rivalry between myself and Michael, but I'm not sure Michael shares this perspective. We design in totally different ways, and we have different sensibilities. We've always been talented, in the same industry, but there's been no overlap between what he does and what I do, until, possibly, now.

On the off chance this opportunity is real, Michael probably wants me to design his line because it will make a good story for those asshole journalists.

It will be a unification decades in the making.

Michael and I rose to fame together, both paying our own way to study at MAFTA- the McCarthy Academy For The Arts. We worked separately, never comparing notes, never sharing the wannabe models we would use for our separate fittings. Michael is one year older than me, so the final project from my first year coincided with Michael's second-year project, and both collections ended up showing on the same day. Michael and I received widespread acclaim for our work, and we individually generated the type of buzz that our peers neither garnered nor warranted. Two weeks after our collections showed, I was told that there were private collectors lining up to look at my work. Four weeks after our collections walked, Michael and I saw checks for our looks. Three months later, we saw our looks on celebrities. Our "little projects" spread rapidly.

I didn't know how to deal with a rise that was too fast and too easy. Michael, however, seemed more well-equipped to handle the sudden interest. It was almost as though he expected this reaction to his collection, and the only way he would've been lost is if he premiered his work to casual compliments and quiet admiration. There's an alternate reality somewhere out in the universe where Michael's collection didn't take off, and I'm sure that in that reality my brother and I are kinder to each other than we are in the reality I'm about to face.

Michael will not be understanding of what I did. He will not comprehend why it was necessary.

They were always easier on him. Maybe because he was easier on them.

We were referred to, first by the *New York Times*, then later, by every other journalist on the planet, as "Fashion's Oasis." This nickname was not established because our collections were unexpected beauty in the middle of a disorienting desert of fashion, we earned it because, like the members of the once-popular Brit-rock band of the same name, we were two highly gifted brothers who simply did not get along.

People attempted to figure out how heterosexual brothers, raised under the same the roof in Upstate New York, could both become fashion's wunderkind. Journalists wondered how our collections could be so vastly different when our points of reference and DNA are so similar.

My shows and collections gained notoriety for being theatrical- a direct contrast to my personality.

Michael's shows have always been reserved, refined, and careful- a perfect reflection of his personality, or at least the personality he presents to the public.

This caused a rift. The industry expected me to act with the same flamboyant energy that my collection was bedrocked with. Interviewers usually described me as a, "surprisingly subdued Andrew Lorrie," and noted, "*While known for his wild collections, one-half of 'Fashion's Oasis' comes off, as- dare I say it- a little boring,*" and then there was the much reprinted, "*...obviously drunk, seemingly unable to care why I was sitting at his table, Andrew unloaded mean spirited and expletive-filled rants directed toward all within shouting proximity. Unfortunately, I was bound by my assignment to remain close him so I received much of the abuse doled out that rainy afternoon.*"

Michael and I have always viewed fashion's role in our lives in two completely different ways. I encountered fashion when it stormed into my life and took over, changing me completely into the man I've remained to this day. For me, fashion was an awakening/ an infinite buzz/ an addiction/ a requirement for being. One day, a switch was flipped inside of me, and I began to notice everything as colors, textures, materials, and choices.

In contrast, Michael has always controlled fashion, inviting it into his life as a curiosity. I firmly believe that, if Michael discovers that he possesses another talent that yields the possibility of making even more money than what the fashion industry is willing to throw at him, he'll never sketch another skirt in his entire life.

This is the aspect of Michael's personality that could be fueling today's meeting. He's a good businessman, and it's possible he sees the benefit of having extra time to ensure his lines yield a constant flow of big checks and headline acclaim. It's realistic to consider that Michael is willing to forgo the labor of putting together a ready-to-wear collection so he can instead focus on building an empire.

Fashion is about knowing what you want, sketching it so others realize what you want, sending them off to create what you want, then modifying the details, until you're holding exactly what you wanted in the first place. The final piece won't look the same as the sketch, but it should *feel* the same.

With all of this as a backdrop, I decide to take the meeting because I want to continue designing beautiful clothes for God's finest creations.

"Thank you," Karen says to me, as we wait for the elevator.

I wave off this pleasantry, then I remove my custom made, vented backed, notched collar, black blazer. The design feature I'm most proud of in the blazer is the ribbed pinstripe I worked painstakingly to create. Thin ribs in the material give a look of stripes, but the entire blazer is solid black. Designing this piece was a dreadful experiment to go through. After I received the final product from my team, I pretty much let the idea go because I, the consumer, got what I wanted, and I didn't want to repeat the process for a women's cut. I could tell Michael about this, but he wouldn't give a shit. I'm not interviewing for a job, I'm about to do some heavy lifting and the blazer will only get in the way.

The steel doors open, and Karen walks inside the elevator, watching me the entire time, making sure that I follow her. I do.

I'm unable to hit the "8" button because it looks like a rotated infinity sign, and I begin to feel like my soul is on sale.

Karen's unpainted finger jabs the 8, then the doors close.

A red number counts higher, while I create a countdown in my head.

When the doors open, we're immediately greeted by a black girl in her late 20's- cute, well dressed, bad legs. "Hi, I'm Jessica. I'll take you over to Mr. Lorrie's office... Mr. Lorrie," she introduces herself, stumbling over the bizarre situation we've found ourselves in. Jessica appears to be Michael's secretary. I can't be sure if he's fucking her or not because no one knows if Michael fucks anyone or if he just stares in the mirror and jerks off to his own reflection.

"Call me Andrew," I request, distancing myself from Jessica's employer. She nods agreeably at this, almost relieved that I'm not as awful as the reputation my name evokes.

The busy segregation of Michael's workspace is completely different from the barrierless loft I crafted my last collection in. The layout on the 8th floor is distinctly corporate- set up in a way that professionals would find familiar and trustworthy. Cubicles create a labyrinth, slicing up a space that is better suited left wide open. The "back office" employees sit in a stereotype of a workplace, but I notice the offices that line the perimeter sport stained hardwood floors, hardwood walls, and acoustic ceiling tiles- all of this exhibiting a luxury and attention to design otherwise absent in the center of the space. Since the cubicle monkeys have no windows, they're forced to look at giant ad campaigns for a brand that they realistically can't afford on their salaries. There's activity buzzing all around us, but none of the tasks can be directly correlated with putting a line on the runway or in stores. It's MacBooks, and frowning people at each other's desks, and young women on their phones looking at Facebook. This is the business end. This is what I've aggressively avoided. I don't even know what my accountant's name is- I just trust he or she is there, and I trust that he or she is doing what I'm paying him or her to do. The Chinese had handled all of this business garbage for me. Now, maybe the people in this office will take over that burden.

It's my hope that Michael realizes his passions- money, status, and control- can become his sole focus if he allows me to freely pursue my passions- design, fittings, and runway.

Maybe, this alliance can work- Michael shaking hands and laughing at stupid jokes, while I make sure there are 30 or 40 well-dressed models parading down the runway with the predictability of an anxious calendar.

The one obstacle- besides my relationship with Michael- is the fact that either I have to design in Michael's style, or he has to trust me to create in my own way, while keeping his hands off of what I'm doing.

This inspires questions that follow me, as I follow Jessica.

Do I tone down the makeup to match something that you might see on the face of a girl dancing at any club in this city?

Do I shorten my shows and zigzag my runways so the front row goes on forever, and people can brag about their experience at M.Lorrie F/W to everyone who will listen?

Do I re-brand this stagnant ready-to-wear line to reignite interest and anticipation?

Does Michael hand me over his high fashion line in addition to RTW, then just circle back and take all the credit?

After reading all of those articles attacking me, I no longer desire the front page acclaim. My name mirroring the name on the tags now feels toxic to me. An absence of my name means I don't have to worry about being called a racist after my final look shows. Gregor was never accused of racism, despite casting my last show- the same show that "confirmed" I was a racist. The blame was placed on the guy whose name was embossed on the invitation. As a result, I now intensely crave comfort, freedom, and protection. Only after my three needs have been met can I pursue change in the industry.

Jessica stops at the door to a corner office, then knocks twice, and she receives an annoyed, "Enter," as a response.

The door opens, revealing Michael at his desk. This is the first time I've seen my brother in three years. When our mother- the last monument keeping us coming back for Christmas- passed away, there was simply no reason to go back home, and no home to go back to.

Michael is wearing a pure white dress shirt- unbuttoned to the third button, and a black vest- also unbuttoned. He hasn't shaved in maybe three or four days, but it's a calculated stubble. I presume that Michael still doesn't own razors and continues to over-tip an elderly barber to take a straight razor to him every couple of days. Michael has always been attracted to the idea of being a man in the big city, living his life in a way that most have abandoned in favor of modern convenience. The shoe shining/ the *Wall Street Journal* copies from the newsstand/ the barber- all of it has been part of Michael's routine since he left upstate. I'm impressed that he has the same amount of hair he's been holding onto for the past decade. He started balding in his mid-20's, then somehow stopped balding further. Now he looks like he has the world's largest widow's peak. I train my eyes on the tuft of flat hair in the center of his head in hopes of making him self-conscious.

Michael stands up to greet us, but he stays behind his desk to establish authority. "Welcome," he says, and no one shakes hands or hugs.

Michael gestures to the open chair on the other side of his desk. Michael's chair- cream colored, supportive headrest, plush armrests- dwarfs the chair I'm offered- small, thin, also cream colored, short backed, no armrests. His office is wood paneled in two different styles. The floor's wood paneling is made up of long, interlocking boards of chocolate birch. The wall consists of textured fusion wood panels that are all an inch thick and a foot long. The wood appears to be a mix of wheat oak and red oak. I suspect this wall is comprised of very thick stained shims or possibly manufactured laminate because the stretch of uninterrupted pattern is far too uniform in its jaggedness. Behind Michael is a view of the city, and to his left is a giant black and white photograph of himself, sitting in an office that obviously isn't his office because we're standing in his office and it looks nothing like the one in the picture. I turn, and see that directly across from Michael's desk is a flat screen that silently plays a runway show. I instantly recognize my collection strutting toward me, and I have to look away. Michael catches this and he smiles. I'm not surprised that he sought out a copy of the live stream.

I sit down in the smaller chair, and for the first time, I notice that there's another man in the office. The man- most likely Michael's accountant- doesn't stand up or offer his chair to Karen. He's asserting himself as a part of this discussion, yet his wardrobe attempts to also confirm he's an "everyman New Yorker" and not "the man." A well-worn navy blue Yankees cap is supposed to provide a casual ease that's offset by the very businessy matte black Oliver Peoples Denison glasses he wears underneath the brim. I presume the glasses are meant to indicate that the man is prepared to review documents. Frown lines parenthesizing a smirk tell me this man is over 30, but a lack of gray at his temples tells me he's not 40, or maybe he just has the same secret I do. The cranberry turtleneck under the black blazer shows that this man is used to the frigid temperatures that Michael works in. I'm aware of this chill as well, but I know I'll break into a sweat as we begin to argue, so I keep my blazer on my arm.

Karen remains standing because she's not offered a chair. She doesn't complain about this, and after a beat of silence, Michael warmly asks, "Jessica. Could you take Karen around and introduce her to the team?" The way he requests this doesn't feel like a brushoff- it feels like he's bestowing an honor- because Michael possesses an extremely calming voice. Every word that leaves his mouth is a posh assurance, and it's lush with condescension mixed with wisdom. If I was to find myself in a life or death situation, I'd want Michael there because he could talk me out of going off the deep end, or if death was certain, I'd want to make damn sure he's coming with me so he doesn't exploit my "tragic passing." The all black collection/ the teary post-runway speech/ the supreme freedom of not being restricted by the baggage of the past- Michael's plan for dealing with my passing is ridiculously predictable.

Jessica leads Karen out of the office, closing the door as she leaves, sealing me inside of a room that feels like a coffin.

Michael leans back in his chair, looking past me to my collection that's running on the TV. He's purposely placed this show behind me, a gesture that, in a way, I mimic. Quickly, I convince myself that it doesn't matter what Michael thinks of my most recent designs. When I saw Isabella in blue velvet at The Imperial Hall, I was captivated by one of my designs, and this gives me confidence.

"So, how are things?" Michael asks, but I know he doesn't want an answer.

"Who's this guy?" I ask, motioning to my right.

"We need to set things up before he's introduced. Patience, Andy," Michael tells me, as though I'm a child.

"Set things up, then," I say, because Michael loves monologuing, and I know that he's prepared something for today.

"Karen told me about the situation with the Chinese pulling your funding. Your line is essentially dead and you're in a corner," Michael gleefully recaps.

"Did you call Karen, or did she call you?" I ask, my hands already beginning to clench into purple fists.

"I called her. Karen wouldn't contact me. She wouldn't do that to you," Michael says, not because he's defending Karen, but because it has to be clear that all of this is a plan that he's hatched himself.

"Don't worry, I'm not going go broke and sell off our last name to Target or something. You can relax," I say.

"I can't relax, Andy, because, by an unfortunate series of events, our brands have a very similar name."

"That series of events is brotherhood," I remind him.

"Be that as it may, I need to know that you're employed, so I'm willing to offer you a job," Michael says.

I stare past my brother, out into the world, and try to completely shut off my brain, but before I'm able to, Mandy's advice replays in my head. I'm being offered the exact solution she proposed, and if I turn down this opportunity, I'll be turning my back on everyone I love just so I don't have to work with someone I should love, but don't.

"What's the job?" I ask, forcing the question out of my lungs.

"I want you to design my ready-to-wear line," Michael says, then immediately adds, "I know you're a little more high fashion than that, but think about this as an experiment- a challenge. Think of it as a change." Michael punctuates this with a smile because he knows he's just struck my Achilles heel.

I nod at this, and since I can't refuse the job, I decide to lay out some test demands to see what it will be like working for Michael. "I won't even consider designing for you unless Karen can come along with me," I say.

"Well, there are some things you have to understand," Michael responds, clasping his hands together, calmly speaking to me as though he's a doctor discussing a diagnosis. "The position you'll be taking... it doesn't justify an assistant. It justifies an intern. You can... audition them. I know that you have very specific preferences. Consider it making up for the high co-pays in your health insurance plan."

"If I can't bring Karen, then we don't have anything to talk about," I say, standing up so I can go retrieve my assistant.

"Andy. Relax. Sit down. I know how important Karen is to you, and the company is really booming right now. I'm not sure if you've seen the financials, but I can have Jessica e-mail you a copy. Michael Lorrie has a multitude of open positions that your friend seems to be qualified for."

"I need her assistance," I say, my hands gripping the back of the small chair.

"I'll make sure that she's close by, but you won't own her. I will," Michael says.

I lean on the chair, processing this, then my mind seeks a distraction, and I rediscover the Yankees fan.

"You have an assistant who does nothing," I say, pointing at the man in the baseball cap. "Get rid of this guy and give me Karen."

"James isn't my assistant," Michael says with a small laugh, like the idea was foolish.

"Oh, is this the introduction? Have we reached that portion of the program?" I ask.

The Yankees hat wearing asshole glances at Michael, then stands up and extends a hand. In a throaty voice, he tells me his name, "James Pickens."

"Andrew Lorrie," I say, shaking his hand, and in my periphery, I see that the mere mention of my full name causes Michael to wince.

"If this guy isn't your assistant, is he at least on your team?" I ask.

"Now? Yes. He is," Michael confirms.

"Boom," James says, sitting back down.

"He just reacted to that by saying 'Boom.' Who *is* this guy?" I ask, taking a seat, because this asshole is a bigger asshole than I initially anticipated when I saw the Yankees hat, and I need to know how he's going to undermine me.

"He's a photographer," Michael says, and this means nothing.

I'm a photographer. Michael's a photographer. Everyone is a photographer. Feeling threatened by a photographer is like feeling threatened by a high school student- the only thing to be envious of is their proximity to hot young girls.

"Would I know your work?" I ask the "photographer," playing along.

"Absolutely," James responds.

"Who have you shot?" I ask.

"Everyone," he tells me.

"Names," I request.

The baseball-capped idiot takes out his cell phone and snaps a picture.

"Recognize this rascal?" James asks me, turning the phone so I can review the screen.

I stare at a blurred picture of myself, and even through the motion streak, you can tell I'm angry.

"Are you kidding me, Michael?" I ask, turning away from James.

"He's going to shoot the campaign for the new Michael Lorrie ready-to-wear collection which will walk under the name 'M.Lorrie.' I'm sure you know that already- it's highly a recognizable name," Michael says, then smiles, again.

"This is the guy you're trusting your new campaign with? Where the fuck did you find this clown?"

"He comes recommended," Michael says, and James nods, recommending himself.

"By?" I ask.

"By social!heavy's producer," Michael says, and I feel myself blanch.

"I think you're familiar with social!heavy, am I correct? You're connected to that group of girls in a rather interesting way, aren't you, Andy?" Michael asks.

"Man, small world," James says.

"Why is it a small world?" I ask slowly.

"I don't know, why is the sky blue?" James responds, then makes a goofy face at Michael.

"Tell him your story," Michael prods James.

"Martin Turner," James says, letting the name hang between us, trying to bond over our tangentially related social!heavy connection. "He sort of... discovered me. There was a pretty big buzz around me because of my part in the social!heavy mythology. You probably read the piece on *OxygenWaster*."

It's at this moment that I realize James Pickens is a re-branded Jimmy Pixx. The "photographer" Michael has hired is a celebrity paparazzi. I say nothing. My hands shake. That photograph on James' phone isn't the first time he's snapped my picture.

"I like social!heavy's new single..." Michael says, then he asks a question he knows the answer to, "What was the original lineup for that band, Andy?"

I mock him with bitter aggression, "You're shooting your new campaign with a paparazzi. Fuck, and I thought my company was mismanaged. I mean, come on."

"He has a... skill set that I find... necessary for this new collection," Michael says cryptically.

"And who's your face?" I ask, desperately trying to change the subject, since the current subject is being presented as a pointed threat.

"Irina is the face of the ready-to-wear line," Michael announces.

"Isn't she 30 by now? She's been working for at least 15 years," I say.

Michael swivels an LCD monitor that's sitting between us, and suddenly I'm staring at Irina. The bright blonde hair/ the pointed chin/ the cat eyes/ the dark eyebrows/ the spattering of freckles/ the poreless skin, the thin upper lip/ the thick lower lip/ the forever long legs- all of it is new, and now, and classic, and iconic.

I don't recognize the editorial on the screen, but it's one of the hundreds of stunning stories that Irina has been a part of.

"Yeah, I'm aware of what she looks like," I comment listlessly.

"That's a test shot. From last week. Shot with a cell phone camera," James clarifies.

"Last week? That was shot last week?" I ask.

"Yeah, and that's just the start of what I'm going to show you," James says to me.

"You and James will have a great time working together," Michael assures me. "I think you might have more than just some acquaintances in common."

I say nothing, and I realize that I'm trapped.

THE MISSING GIRL

Sitting at a table that's pressed tightly against the brick wall at Lazzara's, I give Karen a complete recap of the events that transpired in Michael's office.

After digesting the offer and taking Michael's personality into account, Karen asks, "So how'd you two leave it?" The question is posed with a detached preparedness, because Karen knows that this is where the reliable disappointment of Andrew Lorrie will set in.

"We have another meeting on Thursday," I say, acknowledging that I'm going to accept this job, but my inflection makes it clear that I'm not happy about it.

"Andrew," Karen says, then her voice almost pitches up, "Are you going along with the plan?"

Her wording, "The plan," reminds me of who the photographer is, and why Michael brought him on board. To protect the people I love, I confirm, "Yes, I'm going along with the plan."

This brings an ease to Karen that had been absent from her demeanor for months. When the check comes, Karen buys me dinner, knowing the charge on her card can't be expensed, but she seems confident that she'll have a job again soon enough, so she's willing to treat me.

I ask her to join me on Thursday, and she instantly agrees.

"I'll take this out of your hands/"I'll do whatever it takes for this to work/"I'll stop trying to micromanage your life/"I'll protect you from Michael," Karen promises me.

I say a quick goodbye, then make my way to 7th Ave, alone.

When I pass by West 36th, I don't turn toward the direction of my hotel- I keep walking down 7th. I text Lux to see if I can get my camera back because I want to download the pictures from my after-party. I'm hopeful that Isabella's image is somewhere in the background of one of the pictures because I'm growing increasingly aware that she'll be a key to this new collection.

When I don't get a response from Lux, with equal parts reluctance and desperation, I text Dan Carrington because he has the type of sticky connections that gain him access to the phone numbers and names of fresh faces. Dan is in the background of so many candid model pictures that girls presume his importance when they meet him. My text to him reads, "New model- Isabella- walked for us. Who's she signed with?"

Reaching out to Dan may cost me a night this week, but the fact that my name can do nothing for him in this city now might save me from this mandated responsibility. I have no other choice than to cast a wide net to find Isabella. My work computer has been seized by the Chinese, and all the records of our castings are on Gregor's computer, but Gregor isn't answering the texts I send him- a gesture that's supposed to tell me to cast the next show by myself; he's not willing to line up my victims anymore.

If I have a picture of Isabella, then I can track down her agency. A quick e-mail of the shot to a couple of contacts will yield a lead.

Walking past a massive screen advertising a Kanye West concert that isn't happening for months, I'm reminded of the TV in Michael's office that played the live stream of my show. For once, things seem to go my way, as I realize that Isabella walked for me, so I can find her on the stream. This gets me to turn around. I don't cab back to my hotel room, instead, I choose to walk because I'm currently unemployed. I remember that the Chinese are paying my hotel bill, and I'm not sure if they've already stopped payment on my room. They definitely should've already stopped payment on the minibar (if they're smart) (which they are) (but they're also trusting) (so maybe I can get drunk tonight).

My phone is clutched tightly in my right hand, and when a text vibrates my fist, I stop walking completely. The message, from Dan Carrington, reads, "@the Liberty. It's a Blend party 4 girls not in Milan. Come."

"Which four girls?" I mumble to myself, then I realize the party is "for" girls not in Milan.

Blend, one of the better agencies in the city, is constantly grabbing new girls from various overstuffed mother agencies, and this party is so close that I can't think of an excuse of why I shouldn't stop by and ask around about Isabella.

I make my way to The Liberty, practicing the excuses I'll use to escape Dan, but before I have to employ one of them, I spot an oasis in the form of Isabella, in blue velvet, smoking a cigarette, outside the bar.

I dash across the street, then try to act casual on the approach.

Isabella is standing alone, and she doesn't attempt to speak with two male models who walk out of the bar and light cigarettes.

I lock eyes with Isabella and I feel my gaze becoming too intense, but she looks past me, in the same way I looked past Michael in his office.

She finally gives up her charade when I'm 15 sidewalk squares away, so I point at her feet, then raise my finger up to her neck. She nods at what I'm pointing out, and I give her a thumbs up.

Her thick, blood red lips permit a smile, then, with the same confidence she walked with on that runway, she makes her way toward me.

"You don't have to do that," I yell over the noise of the traffic, pointing at her purposeful approach.

"It's just how I walk," she says to me.

"No, I mean the red badge of courage," I respond.

We stand, close, the city requiring us to get closer, to raise our voices.

"Huh?" Isabella finally says, not sure how to respond.

"The clothes. You don't have to keep wearing this blue scarlet letter," I say.

Isabella's face instantly goes slack and she becomes a ball of nerves. Looking away from me again, she stammers out, "I know. I knew it. I'm sorry. I don't know... how things work-"

"-relax. I'm projecting," I say. I want to touch Isabella's arm, but then I remember the lace doesn't fit her arms right, and this makes me want to take her back to my hotel room, undress her, then fix her lace while she watches TV in a bathrobe. The dress looked normal on Lux's arms, and on Galina's arms, but on Isabella, the imperfection was revealed. I designed this dress incorrectly and it took Isabella's inspired beauty to show me my error.

"Know what? I tried to project today too," Isabella reveals.

"What did you try to project?" I ask, genuinely interested in her, still.

"What you said to me at the party."

"You really have been paying attention," I marvel.

Isabella puts her cigarette out on an off-white column, then she looks at the black mark she made. "I had to. That was my first show, like, ever," she says.

"You didn't do any other work before my show?" I ask, in disbelief that her walk could be so focused and searing without hundreds of practice runs.

"Not on the runway. I did local modeling, and I was scouted... but not by an agent. It was some cokehead photographer."

"This sounds bad. This sound like some sort of human trafficking..."

"No, it's legit. I think. I don't know. He set me up with my mother agency, then your assistant liked me," Isabella says, retracing her steps to the runway.

"I liked you too," I say, trying to make her feel better about this unsteady career choice.

"You weren't at the casting. Some guy named Gregor was," Isabella tells me.

"I, uh, work... worked... closely with Gregor, you know," I respond, the complications of the situation becoming obvious.

Isabella nods at this.

"Why are you still wearing a piece, that, in all likelihood, will lower your stock?" I have to ask.

"Because my stock is worth nothing. Because this piece is worth something. Because I feel like *someone* with it on," Isabella says, and it's an unexpected moment where she actually lets me in.

"Do you want another piece from the collection?" I ask, dying to dress her in everything I've ever designed.

"I can't afford it, I don't have a job," Isabella admits with a shoulder sliding sulk.

"You're a model," I remind her.

She has to shake her head in disagreement. Deny the classification, fight the reality. If she was to accept the fact I presented her with, it would set something in motion, and it would create a responsibility.

"I'll get you another piece. It'll be yours. And not trade," I promise her.

"I can't take it," she tells me.

"Can't take this conversation with me?" I ask, only because I'm confident that's not what she was referring to.

"Your designs," she says.

"I think you already did take one of my designs. I have proof."

The model smiles, revealing the gap between her front teeth.

I review her completely, again, because it allows for the release of endorphins without anyone getting hurt or brain cells being destroyed. Isabella is the single success to emerge out of an otherwise total failure.

"I've saved all the pictures of your collection on my phone," Isabella tells me.

"You didn't," I say, a little bit of my own insecurity battling to equal hers.

"I have, look," she responds, then takes out her phone from a purse I didn't give her- a purse that's not designer. I begin to fear what this bag does to my piece, but then I remember the piece is from a "disaster" of a collection. This model managed to sell me on a garment that never will go into production because it's not good enough.

Isabella holds out her phone to me, but I don't take it. I ask, "Could you show me how to navigate between pictures, I have a different model." It's the truth- I have a better model- but the reason that I say this is because I don't want to swipe past the final picture of my collection and end up looking at one of Michael's designs from his much more successful and well-received collection. At least I can be sure that Isabella doesn't have any M.Lorrie ready-to-wear saved on her phone.

We begin to scroll through the pictures and, sure enough, she's downloaded HQ shots of every look from the collection. All of the files are meticulously named- the model's name next to the "Andrew Lorrie Spring/Summer" distinction. I have to start talking to keep from tearing up. "So you're a Blend girl?" I ask, peering into the bar to see if I recognize any of the bookers.

Isabella nods.

"Why are you still in New York? The show's over and the models have moved on. What did I do to your career..." I start to say, then I sputter out a laugh.

Not accepting my self-pity, she responds, "Stop it, drama queen."

"You're right, but I'm sorry that you have this unintended baggage from being involved in what I did," I say, because it's a reality.

"Funny you'd say baggage. That kinda explains my 'uniform.' I only brought a backpack's worth of clothes here so when my agent was like, 'You need to network at this party,' I started getting ready, but all of my clothes make me look like I'm cosplaying Wednesday Addams so I wore my 'model uniform' to salvage some hope I'd be taken seriously."

"The Addams Family look is very 'Valentino' right now," I note supportively.

"I like looks that are more 'Andrew Lorrie.' This dress is the only thing that makes me look like a model. The first time I put it on, I actually felt like I wasn't playing dress-up," she says, but her eyes are back on the screen of the phone. She nervously flips through pictures, too fast for any of them to be reviewed.

"I can't imagine anyone else walking in that piece. On or off the runway," I tell Isabella, and it's the truth.

"That might be one of the problems with your line," she says, then her smile reappears as she appreciates her own joke.

"Ouch," I say, taking mock offense.

"It's not so bad being one of your problems," Isabella tells me.

THE CALLBACK

Without a single sketch attempted, my next collection is already well underway. A new model has saved me from myself, and I feel ready to create again.

Before I sent Isabella back into The Liberty, she programmed her number into my phone, then I sent a text to her reading, "This message is redeemable for one free Andrew Lorrie piece."

Isabella has become *the* essential inspiration for the M.Lorrie RTW collection I'm going to design.

I've decided to send Dan a bottle of very good wine as a thank you for the tip about the party. Hopefully, the gift will pay my debt, and I won't have to meet him at a bar later this week.

Since Karen still hasn't arrived for our Thursday morning meeting, and there's no way I'm going into Michael Lorrie HQ alone, I take out my cell, momentarily entertaining the idea of sending a, "It was good to see you," text to Isabella. I notice that she didn't include her last name when she added her number in my phone. She stayed true to her branding, and her distance.

I didn't ask where she's staying in the city, but I find myself beginning to worry about her living situation.

I text Gregor, "Where are the Blend model apartments? I'm working on some castings," and I add a displeased-looking emoticon to indicate I'm not doing this for fun or pleasure.

"I'm sorry, there was something about a lost autistic kid in the subway and the trains were all messed up," Karen says, finally appearing beside me. I glance at her, and I'm relieved to see she's wearing a brown polyester pencil skirt and white blouse instead of her usual uniform. "Is this the right move?" I ask her.

Karen fixes the flipped collar on my sky blue dress shirt, then tells me, "This is our *only* move." No eye contact. No smile. No attempts to calm me down. Karen doesn't misdirect me like she tried to the night before my self-destruction. We face each other for a moment, neither of us confident, both of us knowing we have no other option but to make this work.

We walk into a funeral that demands our attendance because the body will never be revived and the family would hold it against us forever if we didn't show up.

A silent entrance into the building is complemented by a silent ride up in the elevator.

Jessica greets us on the 8th floor, and a wordless walk to the corner office gives me time to mentally prepare for Michael and his buffoon paparazzi.

We enter Michael's office, and I notice that an additional chair, off-motif, has been dragged into the office so Karen can sit between James and myself.

Karen and I quickly sit down and an awkward silence hangs. I look back to make sure my collection isn't still running on a loop on the TV. It isn't. A news report showing the Seaside Boardwalk on fire plays on mute. I don't rule out that Michael had something to do with the fire.

I turn, to watch with mild amusement as Karen and James run through a quick introduction- both of them wearing a mask of professionalism that they think Michael respects and demands.

Michael and I don't even attempt to make small talk. The meeting hangs silent, stuck at a moment where normal brothers would tease each other or share a fond memory that had recently resurfaced. We're two designers obsessed with nostalgia, yet we never talk about the past; we never reminisce. I wonder if this is due to the fact that neither of us ever expended the effort to keep the good moments alive because we were too busy coping with our own demons. Maybe it's a control thing. Right now, in real-time, Michael decides what happens. He's the boss. This is how he's set things up. I've entered into this world because it's the only place I'm welcome anymore.

"Here's what's going to happen with my ready-to-wear line," Michael announces. He doesn't field opinions, he doesn't interview us for the job, he merely assumes that we've accepted the open positions, and now he wants to show off. "M.Lorrie is under-performing," Michael admits.

That name. The first thing I'll do with the ready-to-wear line is rename it. My last name brought me here, but it's a roadblock in my relationship with Michael. It's possible that if we remove the "Lorrie" name from the RTW collection, it will also remove one of the many problems I have with my brother. I'll think of a new name, then I'll convince Michael it was his idea. Simple.

"I want to inject some high fashion elements into the runway collection, then I'll tone them down for production," Michael says.

This is nothing new. I've followed a similar process on the pop star and celebrity lines that I ghost designed. Customers love black clothes, but runway photographers don't.

"You'll design the collection, within my aesthetic," Michael says to me.

"What will the approval process be?" I ask.

"You'll get together with Karen, you'll sketch out the line, I'll approve the sketches, then off we go."

"So I still get an assistant?" I ask, forcing Michael to confirm that Karen is on the payroll.

"No. We discussed this. You get an intern," Michael responds, frustrated that I'm not following.

I point to my right, "But Karen-"

"-Karen is the stylist for the line," Michael says. "The accessories sector is booming. She's my point person to get a complete line of accessories ready this season."

I blink excessively as I process this, and I cannot look at Karen.

"Understood," I finally say, my mouth dry.

There wasn't enough money for an assistant, so I have a stylist.

"I have a fantastic team assembled. You're not going to be a lone man. You'll have more than enough assistance. I have a dedicated ready-to-wear crew waiting to make your vision to happen. You'll show them the direction to go in, then you'll keep refining what they bring you until we've found something special," Michael says. Just when it begins to feel as though he putting faith in my talents, Michael practically steps on his own words to add, "James will work closely with you so that he gets the feeling of the collection, then he'll implement a large scale campaign. I've been toying a lot with his role, and I've decided that, due to his connections and his great eye, he'll also cast the runway show."

I make a noise of displeasure and disagreement, but Michael lifts a hand toward me and continues regaling us with his plan, "James is still our photographer, don't worry. In the same way that you'll design and cast, James will photograph and cast. It's a lot of responsibility for you both, but I trust that you'll get excitement drummed up for what we're doing."

"I work with Gregor Hampden to cast," I say.

Michael laughs at this, possibly because it strays from his plan, or possibly because Gregor would rather send the models to death camps than down a runway in my designs.

"No casting director from here to Japan will work with you," Michael informs me. "I work with James. You work for me. Therefore, you work with James. You've really left me no other option."

I don't look at James because I already know he's sporting a dumb grin.

"James was actually the one that suggested we use Irina," Michael tells me brightly.

"Yeah, I saw the picture, but you never answered my question. How old is Irina? Why are you using her again? Don't you feel like you're repeating yourself?" I ask, revisiting the subject that was brushed off with a photo that *must* have been heavily photoshopped.

"So you *were* paying attention to my work," Michael says, pleased that I remembered the times that Irina has walked for him in the past. "What happened to that quote, 'I'm not even familiar with what he's designing and selling, so if you see any similarities between our pieces, it's a genetic coincidence,' that you'd prattle off when I was mentioned in your interviews?"

"The Irina campaign was huge. I couldn't avoid it," I defend myself.

"You certainly couldn't," Michael says proudly.

"So you're circling back?" I ask, knowing that this will bother him.

"I'm not circling back. I'm moving forward."

"Then you need fresh blood," I respond, my motives hidden.

Isabella in blue velvet made me feel like a new designer. I don't want a supermodel wearing what I design this season. A runway-tested girl like Galina did nothing for me when she walked in the exact same piece that Isabella has captivated me with. It was Isabella and Cori that inspired me as I watched my last show. Maryna was incredible, but she closed the show, and I know it would bring Michael great pleasure to use her merely as runway filler. This would be a statement that even the best of Andrew Lorrie only registers as "acceptable" Michael Lorrie.

"While you're right- I do need fresh blood- Irina is my choice, and James will photograph her."

"I know someone," I blurt out.

"Some new blood?" Michael asks.

"Yes... yes," I say, making sure I'm careful with how I represent this, "She walked for me. You're going to have to get over that fact, but it was her first show. You'll instantly agree when you see her aga-"

"-haven't caught your full show yet," Michael dismisses me, and I call him out on this lie immediately, "It was running on the flat screen behind me during our last meeting."

"I could only watch so much before... well..." Michael trails off.

"I want you to bring her in for a go-see," I say, then look to James, who opens his eyes wide like he wasn't listening and had been caught.

Michael clears his throat, then says, "I thought I made myself clear-"

"-listen you brought me-"

"-don't interrupt your boss," Michael snarls at me.

I pause for a moment, and when it's clear I have the floor, I say, "You brought me here because I can help you. It's in both of our greater interests to put the best possible line on the best possible girls. You have to trust me on this."

"Wait, what's the go-see girl's name?" James asks.

"Isabella," I respond.

"Isabella what?" Michael asks.

I blink rapidly.

Michael nods at this.

"Will you consider her?" I ask.

"She's already walked for us," Karen says.

"Once," I growl.

"Heads didn't turn," James says.

"Maybe that's my fault," I respond.

"Maybe," Karen repeats, without any inflection to color the statement. It's neither an accusation nor an acknowledgment, yet it's also both.

"How long have you been in New York, Andy?" Michael asks, changing the subject.

"Most of my life," I respond. "There was the LA detour..."

"Oh," Michael says. He sounds surprised, "I thought you lived in Connecticut."

"I've never even been to Connecticut," I say.

"Couldn't tell that by looking at you," Michael responds.

"Is that supposed to hurt my feelings?" I ask.

"Not that part of our conversation, no," Michael says, then he arrives at the reason why he asked the question in the first place. "I've set aside hotel rooms for you and-"

"-that won't be necessary. I have a place to stay," I respond. I don't need my home life tied to Michael Lorrie as well. Michael is trying to make sure that every aspect of my existence is under his control. I'll live on the street before that happens, and at about 5 PM tonight, that might happen. This morning, despite my best attempts to walk with purpose across the lobby of the Hilton without being noticed, the Latina desk girl spotted me and informed me that I'll be checking out tonight if I can't provide a valid credit card for billing.

"How do you have a place here?" Michael asks, "After Mom... well... didn't you decide to stay in LA?"

"It's always been my plan to stay in New York after fashion week," I lie.

"Oh. I see. Things have been going as planned lately?" Michael asks.

"I know why I'm here, and I know the job that needs to be done," I say, getting up.

"Andrew Lorrie. That's why you're here," Michael says, not standing.

"Deep. I'm here because I'm me. I get it," I say.

"No. Your clothing line," he responds.

"I don't need your gloating little-"

"-and I don't need your attitude. We have a meeting tomorrow that you will be attending. Do not make me regret this because I don't do well with regrets."

"Is that a threat, Michael?"

"It's whatever you chose to interpret it as."

"I'm interpreting it as a threat."

"Then it sounds like I can confirm your attendance tomorrow."

THE CALL FOR HELP

Sitting next to Karen in the back of the car that Michael is paying for, I break into a cold sweat over the fact that I mentioned Isabella. I now believe that Michael will find her, then he'll do everything he can to take her away from me. I had mentioned Karen during the first meeting and she was brought on, so I figured that maybe the same thing could happen for Isabella.

Karen remains silent for most of the ride, and when I cancel our dinner plans out of fear the silence will continue throughout the afternoon, she asks, "Do you need to stay with me?" She's been on the receiving end of so many of my lies that she's always aware when I'm not telling the truth.

My natural response is to ask Karen to research all the affordable apartments within 10 blocks of Michael's office, but Karen is no longer my assistant, and she hasn't reminded me of that fact yet, so I ask her, as a peer, "For apartments... should I, um- I don't know- make an ad on Craigslist?"

Karen says that a man of my age shouldn't have roommates, and Craigslist will land me a roommate/ Karen says that I don't have the money to get the type of apartment a man of my age should have in New York/ Karen says that I have to be "cautious and practical" if this new arrangement is going to work/ Karen says that I have to call Cassie.

"Absolutely not," I respond, contemplating telling the driver to stop so I can get out of the car and walk away from this conversation.

"She still has the house and not only is it only a half hour outside the city, but it's also fully furnished and unoccupied."

"How do you know that? We don't know that," I say, hoping for an excuse.

Karen takes her phone out of her purse, then brings up pictures of Cassie in LA. The pictures were posted yesterday.

"What's your excuse, Mr. Lorrie?" Karen asks. I know that she chose "Mr. Lorrie" to remind me that she has no ulterior motives with her actions because, if I fuck things up, she doesn't have to clean up the exploded body parts that I leave in my wake. If I ruin things, Karen will continue to work on my brother's line, as I'm tossed away like an LCD monitor.

I take out my phone and select Cassie's number. I trust Karen's judgment because my other options are to either put up my own credit card to continue staying at the Hilton or I can accept Michael's offer. I'm too cheap to do the first and two smart to do the second.

Karen stares at me, as I bring the phone to my ear.

The call is about to predictably ring out, then Cassie's voice crackles over the line, "Andrew…"

"Cassie…" I say, popping open the door of the car as it remains parked a red light. I give Karen a quick wave, then I begin making my way toward the Hilton. I'm already gasping three steps in, not from fatigue, but from nerves.

"Listen," Cassie says, and I hold my strained breath. The situation is totally in her control. "I'm sorry, Andrew. I really was going to call. I know how much was riding on that collection, but I couldn't be at the show. I had… other engagements."

This apology feels like a trap, specifically because I made no request for Cassie to attend my show. Of course, it would have helped to have her there, but the thought never occurred to me to invite her. I convince myself that I'm being played, because if this sympathy is coming from a sincere place, it means that my collection was bad enough to inspire my perennially bitter ex-girlfriend to put aside my egregious betrayals in our failed tryst so she can tend to the even deeper gashes that I inflicted on myself.

"We could have used you," I say, and what I mean is, "I could have used you."

"I wouldn't have saved you," Cassie says. When I balk, she adds, "You don't want me on the runway right now. I look like I should be modeling snowsuits. When I see my ass in the mirror I feel like someone should be playing the violin next to me. It's tragic."

I laugh at this exaggeration because Cassie looked fantastic in the pictures that Karen showed me.

I hear in her building giggle that Cassie is pleased by my unwillingness to believe her. I can picture that smile, the real smile, the sincere smile- not the smile everyone sees on those billboards.

I move down the street, feeling pathetic and needy, shame washing over me. If Cassie was treating me worse during this call, I would feel better about my collection. The niceness she's employing again makes me think of a funeral.

Before my recent failures can be recapped in vivid detail, I lower myself to a point that I didn't want to venture to. "I have to ask you something," I say, and immediately Cassie responds, "I knew this was going too well. I knew we would end up in this place." She sighs, not tired, just frustrated that she still has to deal with me again.

"Speaking of places…" I say, trying to brighten up my tone.

"I can't control Sienna," Cassie tells me. "I didn't know she was going to be at your after-party. I would have told her it's a bad idea, but she currently isn't taking my calls because of the last time I gave her advice."

"The house in South Orange," I blurt out. I steady my voice and begin treating this call like I would any other business transaction. I explain, "I want to rent the house from you."

Cassie is silent, most likely running through my motives in her head. "I'll have to check to see if we have a tenant," she finally says.

"You don't. Yet. I want to be the tenant."

"How do you know if I have a tenant or not?" she asks.

Lying, I say, "Karen went online and-"

"-oh. Karen. *That* is happening again."

"No. No. Karen is assisting me with-"

"-I'm aware with what Karen assists you with," Cassie says, and I anticipate her hanging up at any moment.

"That's not happening."

"What is this, Andrew? Now you're willing to go back there? When I'm in LA? The house you devoted your entire life to escaping is now your dream home? Will she be staying there too?"

"Who?" I ask quietly.

"The fact that I have to clarify that makes it worse."

"I'll pay you," I beg. Suddenly, the solution I didn't like is the *only* solution I will accept.

"Whatever, Andrew. The keys are under the mat. Or in the mailbox. Or maybe that last tenant kept them in a fake rock in the landscaping. I don't know. The keys are there. Just don't sleep in my bed," Cassie tells me. "Listen. I have to go. Enjoy your Jersey vacation. I'll make sure I keep paying the bills. I know how much it sucks to be completely in the dark while living in that house."

And, with that, we end the conversation the way it started, dwelling on my failures.

THE BUMBLING SIDEKICK

I text Lux that I have good news, and she doesn't respond because the text sounds like a lie.

When the phone finally vibrates, I look down at the screen and find an unknown number demanding that I, "Meet with James."

"Who is this?" I text back.

"Michael," the mystery number responds, then another text arrives, providing an address to a restaurant only blocks from my hotel.

I have to be checked out by 5 PM- a half hour from now- so I'll have to show up to the restaurant with my luggage. If Michael didn't plan this, he lucked into a situation that will expose me as a liar.

I'm relieved that the card still works for my room at The Hilton, and with a clock ticking, I pack everything into my red hard-case Briggs & Riley suitcase in a matter of minutes.

I've custom made my entire wardrobe so that it fits in this suitcase, along with my laptop, and everything I need for my face and hair. I go to great lengths to make it as easy as possible to escape, because that's what my personality demands.

I roll out my baggage, and let the door lock behind me.

As I'm walking on West 42nd Street between 7th and 8th, a throaty voice says to me, "Crazy how different this place is now."

I glance to my right, and find James keeping pace with me, awaiting my response. I quickly realize that the meeting has already begun. I keep walking, even though the only reason I'm headed in this direction is because I have to meet with the person next to me.

"It used to be prostitution, drugs- a mess here," James says.

"And now?" I ask.

"Disney," he responds, glancing up at a billboard for a *Thor* sequel no one asked for.

"I thought you said it was different," I joke.

James looks at me, wondering what I meant.

"Kids with fucked up childhoods having meltdowns later in life," I clarify.

I can see James that doesn't don't know if I'm talking about the drug addicts, the prostitutes, or the Disney girls. Understanding that it doesn't matter, he lets out a rapid-fire laugh, then grabs the sleeve of my leather Saint Laurent jacket and pulls me into some fuck awful tourist restaurant that's just outside the Regal Theater whose digital billboard commands, "UPSIZE YOUR MOVIE. SEE IT IN RPX."

I drift behind James, as we navigate a Tex-Mex place that contains no Mexicans besides a busboy who cleans empty Coronas off the small circular tables that are surrounded by stools upholstered to look like Native American drums. James traverses this place like he's a regular. He has a confidence that- combined with his stupid hat- makes him look like he belongs here. If I force

James to do all the things Karen used to do, this attribute could be extremely beneficial.

James leads me past a bar lined with bottles of tequila and low-quality import beers that we freely let into America, while the guys who brewed the stuff were shot at with rubber bean bags when they tried to follow their product.

We seat ourselves in a booth, away from the human slugs and mouth breathers around us. James distances us from the mayhem of the tourists for privacy, and I'm almost curious about what he has to tell me. Michael didn't send us to this circle of hell and it becomes clear that James has information to give me before I walk into whatever my brother has set up.

I look across the table and endeavor to display my displeasure about being here. James adjusts the brim of his Yankees hat, and this simple gesture causes me to look at the six other assholes in the restaurant who are also wearing Yankees hats.

James is a tourist. He probably refers to New York as, "The greatest city in the world," despite the fact that the places he frequents in Manhattan can be found in literally every other city in the entire world.

"Man, daddy issues, huh," James remarks, the comment slipping out of the side of his mouth.

"What?" I ask, my face becoming a scowl.

James looks at me in disbelief, then says, "Outside, on the street, we were getting somewhere."

"Right, Michael texted me an address-"

"-no, you and I. We were connecting," James says, sincerely.

"About... Dads?" I ask, not connecting.

"You mentioned that whole Disney thing, and you're well aware that I used to chase those girls with my camera. We were making a breakthrough. We were acknowledging our common ground," James informs me.

I revisit the interaction.

James used to be a paparazzi. I have a small amount of notoriety.

James found me on the street, and when he started talking to me, I talked back.

As a paparazzi, James must have viewed this as a deep connection.

"Gotcha," I say, giving in to James' alternate universe. "No. No daddy issues here," I assure him.

"Right," James balks.

"My father was good. He was responsible. He had rules, not many, but they were important to follow."

"And have you followed them?" James asks, pleased that his conversation starter somehow worked.

"I haven't followed his rules as carefully as Michael has," I admit.

"So Michael is the favorite son?" James asks, obviously on Michael's team.

Luckily, a waitress nears our table, and James whistles, puts up a peace sign, then points to a Corona sign. She nods to acknowledge the order.

After this meeting, I have to take the train to South Orange, so I become focused on avoiding Michael *and* getting drunk enough that NJ Transit will seem tolerable.

"I can't be sure who the favorite Lorrie son was," I say, continuing the conversation because I'm hoping James will pick up the tab. He probably already has a Michael Lorrie corporate card.

"So you're both constantly fighting for that clarity?" James asks.

"No. Nothing to fight for. Our father, no matter how many collections we showed, no matter what we accomplished, always smiled, then said, 'Good going.' No one has ever started a war for 'good going.' Our dad didn't really care about what we were involved in. He never viewed fashion as a career. He never viewed our work as art."

"How'd that make you feel?" James asks, propping his chin in the palm of his right hand.

"Like I knew my dad really well, and I was prepared for his response. I was never surprised. I was never disappointed."

"Ugh. How functional," James says, and our beers arrive. This puts me at ease, and I smile, then say, "Right?"

James takes a swig of his beer, then fixes his cap again. "So you must have Norman Bates Oedipal Macbeth Mommy issues," he assumes, seeking what caused the rift between myself and Michael.

"Not really. Our mother was a great woman. Church lady. Literally."

"Ah, Catholic guilt?" he says, pushing for the source of the strain.

I run my hand across my cheek and feel an uncharacteristic stubble. Stubble is Michael's thing. I'm always clean shaven, otherwise, I begin to look like him, but with a better hairline. "Sure, there's some guilt going on. I have some of that. I'm not sure about Michael though. He would go to mass on Christmas, but other than that... not sure."

"What the fuck? How are you guys so damn broken, yet also so successful?" James asks. The paparazzi burns to understand my history with Michael so he'll know where the fault lines are.

"Because we've never had an obstacle to overcome. Because we have the Lorrie ego."

James takes a sip of his beer, then looks over at his contemporaries. He removes his hat and puts it on the table. James has a full head of inch-long black hair. He looks younger without the hat.

The drinking, the silence, the personality change- it's clear that James has daddy issues, and he was hoping that I have them too. He must have thought that, in the same way those daddy issues could've pushed me apart from Michael, they would become a bond between two men in one of the ugliest chain restaurants on the east coast. I begin to pity James, so I ask him, "How about *your* dad?"

"What about him?"

"Good relationship?" I ask, then I hold my breath because I'm afraid of what type of genie I might be rubbing out of the lamp.

"Martin Turner has this really great story about how he got into photography and it mirrors how I felt about my old man when he was around," James tells me, and I have to hope this isn't a tangent. "Problem is, Martin found out how to use his pain. And I'm..." there's a pause, then making an ax with his hand, James hacks at the table, and says, "Martin was with me, every day, taking the same exact pictures I was taking, but he had this story, and this talent, and he connected with people instead of chasing them. Now he only takes a picture if he wants to. No one tells Martin Turner what to photograph," James says. He puts his hat back on, then takes off his glasses.

"So, you have issues with Martin Turner's daddy issues?" I ask.

I know the story that Martin tells, about how his sisters inspired him to get into photography. Martin's father would regularly insult his own daughters, so Martin devoted himself to showing sensitive women their true beauty- starting with those his lived with, then branching out. Martin Turner not only brought a measure of humanity to the industry, but he also accomplished something that I neglected to do. I am in debt to Martin Turner.

"OxygenWaster said that I tried to pull a 'Martin Turner' with that story about how I got a ticket for social!heavy's first show, but that wasn't me making up some bullshit. That moment changed my life. That moment is why I'm sitting here. Sure, the job at CTV didn't work out, but I have some nice editorial work, and I've scouted some great talent," James tells me, competing with a man who isn't at this table, applying for a job he already has.

James is inextricably linked to social!heavy, and because of this bond, he'll also be linked to me. This world of recognizable names has made everyone a slave to associations, and despite my lack of wealth, I'm part of this web so I remain tangled.

Surprisingly, James does end up connecting with me today.

I pay for our beers, then we leave the restaurant.

Back out on West 42nd, James looks at my luggage, then says, "I'll walk with you to Penn Station."

The meeting is called off, and I should be relieved, but I begin to fear that James views this as some sort of a date, and to avoid an embarrassing situation, I say, "You know I'm not..."

"Happy with this arrangement? Yeah, I know. I guess I just need your help because..." James gets close to me, then he says, "I can't fuck this up, and you can't fuck this up, so let's listen to Michael and, uh, walk each other to the train, like friends."

James is an ass, but he doesn't tell me what to do, beyond the "don't fuck up" advice that is universally provided to me by every single person in my life, so I walk with him to Penn Station. There's too much in the way for me to be friends with James, but I decide I won't attack him, because I'm tired of delivering self-righteous verbal diatribes. I swallow the anger I have toward James, and I don't confront him about the destructive photographs he sold of me with my friend.

THE ABANDONED HOUSE

As soon as I step off the train, I take in South Orange at night, and I think, *Ah, this place. I know this place.*

The train clatters away, descending further into New Jersey, and I do the same. I struggle to get my hard-case down the train station's unforgiving stairs, and avoid reviewing the brick facade to my right, because it reminds me of the view at the loft I once had, then lost.

I make my way past the bakery/ past the Starbucks/ past the diner/ then across the street. A bus roars by, and for a moment, the whooshing noise mixes with the chattering wheels of my hard-case, drilling me with the type of headache that tends to arrive at the end of a non-committal night of casual drinking.

I don't receive any texts or calls during my walk, because the only person who wants to speak to me is a guy who used to go by the moniker of "Jimmy Pixx," and this new reality makes me want to climb into bed and never get out.

I'm reminded of Cassie's one demand, *Don't sleep in my bed.*

I begin to wonder who's sleeping in my bed in LA right now, then I cease caring because I've left that life behind. I will endure in this colder East Coast climate, until I figure everything out- only then can I return home.

I never thought I'd end up back in South Orange. Not like this. Not alone.

It takes me 20 minutes to walk to the house on Scotland Road.

I take a deep breath, then round the overgrown bushes that line the front of the house.

The dual-level monument to my *first* try at happiness with a model remains untouched, static, empty. The stone first floor still stands solid and unblemished. Two white Doric columns reach up on either side of the front door and support my favorite feature of the house- the long, thin porch that can be reached from my old bedroom. I decide that this is where I will sketch my collection. It's where the neighbors will see me, and offer unassured waves. It's also where I'll yell down to the cops when they show up to question me about who I am and why I felt it was okay to enter Cassandra Wolfe's home while she was out of town. They won't have the context to know that I belong here. No one in the neighborhood will have that context because the last time I was supposed to be here, I wasn't.

I approach the house, then hoist my luggage up the five steps to the front door. Under a brown mat with barb-like quills, I find a lone golden key.

Before I put the key in the lock, I leave my luggage, then I walk around to the side of the house, to a line of trees. I use my cell phone as a light so I can collect branches dry enough and big enough that they'll stay burning for a while in the fireplace.

Tonight, I'll have a fire and some drinks. I'll pick up where I left off.

I didn't steal anything from the Hilton's minibar, but I'm confident that- because this is Cassie's house- there will be numerous drink options available.

Returning to the front door, I balance the kindling atop my hard-case, then I key inside my past.

I listen for an alarm, but I'm met with silence. I shut the door, then flick on the light, ready to confront my once-home.

I find myself in a living room I helped decorate. It looks the same- paintings by artists who OD'd/ antique furniture/ hardwood floors/ empty space. It's not the look of the room that becomes important, it's the scent that grabs me and confirms to my brain that, yes, I am home.

I pick up the kindling, then make my way to the far right corner of the room, to the rolling wooden door that usually refuses to stay on its track, but when I pull on it, the door slides easily, revealing the book-lined study. This will be my office when the weather kicks me off the balcony.

Old intentions resurface. The books I never read. A piano I never learned how to play. Now, I have time. Ready-to-wear isn't as complicated as what I'm used to putting on the runway so I'll have a new freedom to circle back on my old life.

I throw the kindling in the fireplace, then search the bookshelf for the copy of *Ulysses*. When I locate the green book, I pull it out, carefully. Lifting the cover, I find the rusty can of lighter fluid. The text of this copy of *Ulysses* had been sliced out so that the lighter fluid could be concealed. I did this because I once told Cassie I was a Boy Scout, and she got such a kick out of it that I never had the heart to tell her it was just a joke. Since I was the "Boy Scout" of the house, it was my job to start the fire when it got cold. I would collect the kindling from the side of the house, then sneak in the library while Cassie was making her drink, and I'd use the lighter fluid. *Ulysses* became the hiding spot for the fluid because our copy had an unlabeled green spine and this meant that when Cassie was browsing for a novel to pack in her carry-on as a time waster that would occupy the remaining hours after her MacBook battery died on an intercontinental flight, she wouldn't accidentally take a can of lighter fluid on the plane. I didn't want to deal with the tabloids reporting on my girlfriend attempting to "Zoolander" an airliner. I secretly wish I was unable to find the novel, because it would've made Cassie laugh to discover this trick. Maybe the laugh would be short-lived. Maybe she *did* find it, and she kept *Ulysses* in the library as a reminder of all the nights by the fire that were predicated on half-truths and secret plans.

I grab a book of matches, then ignite some loose pages of a *Vogue* that I find next to the fireplace. I toss the beautiful editorials onto the fluid covered kindling, then stare at the growing fire. When I met up with Mandy, I was bothered by the flame of the candle on the bar, and now here I am turning the living room into my bar and stoking the fire.

With the first task of the night completed, I begin my search for alcohol.

I find that the roll top desk next to the piano where I used to keep the booze for guests now only contains bills. Unopened bills. I move away from the desk, making my way to the stairs. I flip on the lights in every room I enter, slowly revealing a house I never forgot. I decide to tour the home fully, instead of piecemealing it. I have no desire to drag out the rediscovery process, fearing what I'll find every time I enter a room.

I climb the stairs, and on the second floor, I make my way to the spare bedroom. All the shades are drawn so the room is completely dark, but when I flick the light on, the same space is bright and bursting with life. Pictures of Sienna/ pictures of Cassie/ pictures of models I've met and consider friends are all affixed to the wall in an unbroken border. Good memories form a perimeter around the guest bedroom. I realize that the shades must stay closed so the photographs don't age. The fragility of memories creates tombs. I flick the light off, then head to the master bedroom.

I stand in the door frame of *our* bedroom. A slice of yellow light from the streetlamp cuts through the room and I find myself drawn to the angular spotlight.

A question arrives in my mind, as I search the dark- *When Cassie said that I couldn't sleep in her bed, was she referring to the bed we once shared or the bed in the room lined with photos?*

Burning to know if Cassie lingers in this room like she does in the guest room, I walk back to the light switch and flick it on.

I'm immediately rocked by a wave of nostalgia. Everything gives me pleasure to revisit, and my eyes remain thirsty for this aged spirit. Seeing that so much of this room has remained unchanged makes me feel like Cassie could walk through the door at any moment, but I know that there are reasons beyond geography that make that fantasy impossible. I have to focus on the subtle differences to remind myself that everything has changed. There's a new comforter on the bed, but the cherry wood frame remains pressed up against the dark green wall to my left. The door to the balcony is draped with the same soft white doily curtain that I would always see Cassie peeking through when she woke up late and wanted to find me. The smiles that Cassie and I exchanged between that door are probably burnt onto the glass- there was that much heat between us. Directly in front of me is the long oak dresser that Cassie bought for me to keep my clothes in. The fact that my entire life easily fits in a suitcase is because this dresser was the only space in the house where I was allowed to store my clothes. It was a safeguard that Cassie employed to keep my designing in check. She saw how, when I had finished sketching out my work pieces, I would sketch out possibilities for myself. I've never had a menswear line because I'm the only guy that I'm interested in dressing. I'm my own Lux in that way. Cassie could recognize that, often, I wasn't in need of inspiration, I was in need of restraint. She was always convinced that Karen and I had an affair, but when I would sneak out of the house at night, it was about my passion for creating *just one more piece*, not getting a piece. Karen was the only one who understood the thrill of being paid to do the best thing in the world. This dresser was a way for Cassie to keep me from spending every free moment I had creating. She figured that, when my collection was completed, I'd have to focus on the model in my bed. Sometimes, that didn't happen, and kept designing, for me. She let me retain whatever pieces I wanted, but she kept me from turning her house into Andrew Lorrie HQ II. In hindsight, if this restraint wasn't placed on me, my trajectory may have been different. Would I have branched out in menswear professionally? Would I have delegated the designing to someone else, then just collected the praise? None of that second reality has the romance of fashion so this alternate timeline makes me feel no regret or resentment toward sticking with womenswear exclusively.

When I leave the bedroom, I don't continue down the hallway to the final door because I can't confront what it conceals. No matter what is behind that door, it will hurt me.

I make the decision that I'll stay in the master bedroom tonight. I allow myself to do this because there's no sign that it's Cassie's room anymore. In the re-done guest room, Cassie is *everywhere*. I want to stay in the guest room, but I want to obey Cassie's rules more.

Returning downstairs, I find a bottle of beer in the fridge. Prying off a Heineken cap, I walk back into the library, then scan the lines of books I had intentions of reading once upon a time. Eventually, I select *Portrait of The Artist as a Young Man*. When I was a young man, I spent a couple of hours with Joyce. I destroyed his work so I could hide a secret. I've chosen to give his words a try as an apology to James' ghost.

I started my night by having a beer with James, and that's how I'll end my night as well.

The pages turn, and the bottle empties.

When the fire dies out, I place a bookmark in the weathered novel, and I feel as though Joyce's spirit has accepted my recompense.

Getting ready for bed, I hoist my suitcase up the wooden stairs, then roll it into the master bedroom.

I reach for a drawer in my dresser, but I realize that when I open this drawer, I'll find Cassie's husband's clothes. I only have this one dresser to store my entire wardrobe and it's probably filled with another man's shirts and pants, designed by another designer. I don't have a menswear collection, but Michael does, and because of this, the drawers stay closed. The space in this house that Cassie granted me has been revoked. She didn't tell me this when she gave me the house for the fall/winter. This sends me to bed. I pull back the new comforter, slide under the new sheets, and I feel myself squirming to the side of the bed I used to sleep on.

Not drunk, alone, I long for someone to join me in this empty house. This longing is immediately slashed through and negated when I hear the floorboards in the hall pound with frantic footsteps. I beg God to make the sounds go away. I peer around the room to see if I can find a weapon. It's pitch dark except for the light from the window that provides a triangular yellow spotlight on the floor.

As the noise in the hall gets louder, and closer, I remain perfectly still. No one knows I'm in this house besides Cassie, and she's in LA. The possibility of a silent alarm triggers in my mind, but I would've seen the lights from a patrol car if it pulled in the driveway.

This unknown noise has my full attention, then a chill overcomes me, when two people appear in the slice of light in the center of the room.

I stare at a boy and a girl.

The Boy is long haired, skinny, tired-looking, but happy-looking.

The Girl is flat chested, feline, and dangerous looking.

The Girl is only wearing a towel. The Boy is wet with what appears to be sweat, instead of the shower water that's rolling down The Girl's tan body. Both of them are framed in the intrusion of the light.

The Girl laughs, yet protests, as The Boy approaches her.

My eyes are fixed on The Boy and The Girl. I say nothing, afraid of alerting them to my presence.

There's a split second of a standoff, then The Girl looks to the right and sees a cup of tea on the long dresser.

The Girl picks up the tea, then The Boy speaks, and my hair stands on end. He says, "You wouldn't." The Girl raises an eyebrow. Neither The Girl nor The Boy move. Then, they both move, swiftly. The Boy grabs the towel and pulls it off The Girl, and since The Girl's left arm is no longer pinned to her body, she splashes the tea onto The Boy. The screams and the laughter mix to the point that I don't know who's laughing, and who's shrieking, and who's outraged, and who's having the best night of their life.

The Boy and The Girl fall back into the shadows and disappear. The room is silent again. Part of me hopes that I see The Boy and The Girl again. Another part of me wants to warn them that these moments will replay forever inside the house on Scotland Road, so make them great and don't worry about the future... worry about each other.

THE TRAIN STATION

I sit down on an empty bench, and I rub my hand down the dark green painted iron armrest. The long wooden slats between the iron must have been freshly sanded and stained because the public plaguing graffiti that litters New Jersey is missing here.

Across the tracks, the boldface message "THE DAWN OF A NEW EMPIRE" floats above an ugly green sky in a foreboding looking ad. The murky background surrounds an alien, hive-like structure. Bright lights bounce off an otherworldly arched glass ceiling. Purple supports run between the panes of glass like veins, giving the structure a sinister pulse. At the bottom of the ad, in boldface, reads, "EMPIRE CITY CASINO."

I look behind me and find a sign displaying sketches of six faceless, sexless people. Instead of being white or black, the people are shades of gray. A green banner runs across the center of the ad and in white script is scrawled, "You are not alone," then, under that, is the question, "Feeling desperate, depressed or suicidal?" A number is provided to call. It's clear this sign is for white people, since they are the ones who jump in front of trains, and the gray shades may have been used to indicate a dark cloud depression, instead of racial ambiguity.

Next to the anti-suicide sign, is a sign explicitly prohibiting smoking at all stations and platforms. The placement of the signs seems purposeful. If your life is falling apart, and you really need a cigarette, but you're told by a sign you can't have that cigarette, you'll probably need a suicide hotline to consult. A smoker's a smoker when the chips are down.

Back across the tracks is a real estate advertisement featuring three smiling, non-threatening white people with their "casual" nicknames in quotes.

Further to the left on the platform wall, is a red ad that demands, in boldface yellow font "GET BACK TO HAPPY" then proclaims that "New Jersey is open for the summer" as six panes of actors pretending to be a family smile while they ride a roller coaster, and smile while they enjoy a dinner, and smile while they're at the beach, and smile while they ride a merry-go-round. In the final pane, the actors are replaced by an image of an orange-pink sunset behind a giant, dark, phallic lighthouse bursting up through the center of the soft sky with thick brush sitting at the base of the structure. I think this last image is intended to indicate that your wife might let you fuck her if you take her to New Jersey.

Uniformly, each ad promises a better world than the one that brought us all to the train station today.

Beyond the other side of the tracks, mere feet away, is a movie theater.

Everything in front of me is calling me to escape. Every message tells me that I'm not where I should be.

The train's horn can be heard in the distance.

I watch as the commuters group together near the edge of the track.

THE MEETING

I'm staring past Michael, placing my focus on a cloudless September day. Karen isn't here. I don't ask why she isn't at this meeting, since she's the stylist for the line and no longer my assistant. If she was still my assistant, she'd have to be here. She isn't, so she isn't.

James is here. He's still wearing his Yankees hat, still wearing his glasses. I notice that he's also wearing mascara.

Michael looks at me, reviewing my shirt- a self-designed piece featuring a blue vertical stripe print, a basic collar, and a patch chest pocket- and I think he's trying to figure out if the shirt is from his menswear collection. This makes me happy that I never went into the fuck boring world of menswear. Copies of copies. No adventure. No room for the artist.

"Just so you have the perimeters, you'll focus on the womenswear collection. Menswear will be the focus for my team, due to your inexperience and the fact that it shows earlier," Michael tells me, almost as though the shirt I'm wearing revealed my inexperience. "James will learn about casting, and you can learn about menswear- for the future. I'm confident that both of your skills will transfer over," Michael says, breaking out of the trance my shirt put him in.

"I have no passion for menswear," I say.

Michael shakes his head indicating that I'm incorrect.

No one says anything.

Michael picks up a black cell phone off his desk, then tosses it to me.

I turn the phone on and see that the Verizon logo is set as the background.

"This isn't mine," I say, about to hand it back.

"That phone must remain charged at all times," Michael says, reaching over the desk, dropping the charger in front of me.

"No thanks. I already have a phone," I say, taking out my personal cell, showing it to him.

"Now you have a business phone. You didn't have me programmed into your old phone," Michael says.

"You can reach me on my personal. It has really good battery life," I assure him.

"I want a phone devoted to your Michael Lorrie responsibilities. In fact, I want a phone where my PR girl can immediately get through to you when you begin spouting off your hateful, racist opinions to anyone who will listen. Think of that as the 'putting out fires' phone," Michael says.

"There won't be any fires to put out," I mumble, through my teeth.

"Says the man leaving gasoline footprints everywhere he goes."

"Good imagery," James compliments Michael.

"Thank you," Michael says, eating the pleasantry.

I take the charger and slide it into my pocket.

"Aren't you going to get James' phone number?" Michael asks.

James looks at me, waiting to be treated as an equal.

I stare at Michael, while I hand over my glorified tracking device to James. "Program in whatever you want, Sparky," I say.

"Enter your name as 'My Partner' in Andrew's phone. It will remind him of my vision each time you call," Michael instructs James.

I'm positive that James will carry out this silly order.

"Don't hesitate to call Andrew," Michael says, "He can be useful, despite what you might hear from the Italians, and the Chinese, and the fashion press- "

"-what's my phone number?" I interrupt Michael.

James calls his phone from mine, then tells me the number, and I write it down on a post-it that I grab off Michael's desk. I accept my new phone back, and I don't look at what name- James/ Jimmy Pixx/ My Partner- has chosen as his electronic identity.

"Could I-" I start to pose a question, but I immediately stop when I imagine the climbing debt I'm accruing with my brother.

"Could you, what?" Michael asks me, open, accepting.

"Could I have some business cards?"

I ask this not because I want documentation that I'm an official Michael Lorrie employee- even though I haven't signed any contract of any sort- but instead, because I want to throw around the fact that I already have a new job, while those spiteful fashion editors are sitting at their shitty old jobs, writing new snarky articles because their libelous piece on me is no longer relevant thanks to my speedy recovery. More importantly, I want business cards to present at Isabella's agency so they don't fear that I'm trafficking their clients to some underground show where I'll be dressing everyone in S&M inspired garments that I made on a sewing machine in a studio apartment in Bushwick.

"Why do you need cards? It's so... 80's," Michael comments. I eye the business cards sitting in an iron stand on his desk, then say, "People are going to be reluctant about what they're signing up for here. My line and your line are both 'Lorrie' lines and that will confuse the models."

"It's true, I've already confused several models," James says.

"Yes, models *are* easily confused, aren't they?" Michael responds sincerely. "I really wish you used a different name. I *was* born a year earlier after all," he mentions.

"We started using that name commercially on the same day," I remind him.

"That's what my lawyers tell me as well," Michael says, as a legal battle I didn't know existed is exposed.

"Michael, I'm your brother, why the fuck are you fact checking our conversations with your attorney?" I ask.

"Don't worry, it doesn't leave their office. Attorney-client privilege," Michael says, as though this should calm me.

"I'm not worried about you leaking the information, I'm worried that you think that's okay," I tell him.

"Our name is valuable," he responds. "The Lorrie name- based on what *we* built, separately- has value. I'm not going to have your intern make me a pie chart on which one of us did more with the name, because it doesn't matter, but let me put it to you like I put it to my lawyers- if you're Google, you really, really need to own goggle.com. Do you know why?"

"People make mistakes," I respond.

"Exactly. And most of them are too dumb to notice they've made a mistake," Michael says. "A girl could easily buy an Andrew Lorrie piece when she had been saving up for a superior Michael Lorrie piece."

"You're absolutely right," I say, and Michael leans back in his chair a bit, because he wasn't able to successfully hurt my feelings the way he wanted to.

"One- we need to get me business cards," I count on a finger, then I hold out a second finger, and say, "Two- we need to re-brand M.Lorrie because it's only a letter away from being my collection."

"You want to rename M.Lorrie?" Michael asks me, almost waiting for the punch line.

"Sounds like you do too. Sounds like this name thing is an issue," I say.

"What do you think we should rename the ready-to-wear brand?" Michael asks.

I provide no suggestions, because if I do, this renaming won't happen.

I look to James, and he immediately surrenders, holding his hands in the air.

"We need to re-brand M.Lorrie," Michael says, as though he just plucked the thought out of thin air. He writes none of this down, but it will be revisited. I'm relatively sure that he's making recordings of everything that happens in his office, channeling some sort of Nixonian paranoia.

I fix my hair, and continue, "Beyond the name, what else are you willing to change about this label?"

"It needs to ride the line between now and the future," Michael says. "Previously, we seemed to be stuck in *the past*," he admits, and this accurate statement is possible only because Michael had nothing to do with the line.

"Do you have a mood board?" I ask.

"Not my job," Michael says, keeping his distance, fortifying the perimeter.

On the surface, it appears that I'm being given the privilege to design this line as I see fit.

Of the two Oasis brothers, Michael is regarded- without question- as the dependable genius- the Noel. I'm the irrational, exciting one- the Liam. Michael is now trying to look like the exciting dependable genius. I think I can get him to that place, and I don't give a shit if he has that title because it's a distinction I've never sought to achieve.

"How involved will Irina be?" I ask, and this innocuous question seems to anger Michael, but I'm not sure why.

"Irina will be very involved," Michael snaps. "Both of you could be replaced long before Irina," he tells us. Michael does this as a defensive move. Irina is at an age where she could be viewed as disposable in the industry, yet Michael has locked her in as an exclusive. At first, I didn't understand why he would do this when he's looking for a 'future-now' collection, but then I remembered that Lux is 27 and I'm constantly demanding her presence.

Irina is Michael's Lux, and as long as I can have my Lux, I will gladly put up with his.

"Ever since Irina took that season off for... traveling or whatever, she seems to have worked out her Brazilian anger issues, which is extremely positive," James says, then feels the need to add, "I'll do anything she asks of me. It will be a true collaboration."

Michael is calmed by the acceptance he receives, and I become envious of the opportunities he can provide to his muse.

I can't wait, and begin texting on my personal phone in the middle of the meeting. I want to celebrate tonight with Lux. I miss her.

THE STITCHES

Lux agrees to meet me, and a hopefulness that had been absent from my life returns.

In an effort to wrap up this never-ending meeting, I agree to accept a Michael Lorrie executive board member's 20-year-old daughter as my intern, in exchange for keeping Lux on as my fitting model.

"Is she cute?" is James' only question about the intern.

"I don't know," Michael says, "I've never met her."

"What if she's fat?" James asks, suddenly worried for the line.

Michael genuinely considers the point, then says, "Jessica will verify, but the girl is 20, how fat could she possibly be? It's hard to get fat in only 20 years. It takes dedication, your body is literally working against that goal when you're young. It's science."

I stand up, then I demand that Michael shakes on the agreement that, as long as this board member's daughter is under 140 pounds, Lux will stay employed by M.Lorrie. He happily extends a hand, and this is the first time I've touched my brother in years.

It's essential that Lux has a job, so I don't lose her to another designer. If she premieres on someone else's runway, she'll be *his* girl. She'll land *his* campaign. The money she'll make on that campaign is far more than what she could make this season with me. I decide that, if she walks for someone else, I'll leak her real age. I'll make sure everyone knows she's 27. I'll write this fact in the sky over Milan if that's what it takes. I cannot lose Lux.

As Jessica walks me to the elevator, I tell her that she looks pretty, because she does. She smiles at me, then asks, "Are you sure you're a Lorrie?"

The elevator opens and it becomes my escape pod.

Outside, the street is bursting with energy, and I flee underground for relief. This city has become a place I don't recognize and cannot keep up with.

On the subway, I check my phone at least ten times while in transit, afraid that Lux will cancel on me.

My cell doesn't vibrate once during my ride, and I arrive early at the semi-nice restaurant whose name I always forget, so Lux lovingly refers to it as "the place where I threw up in my purse that one time." Luckily, that event has only occurred in three places in the city- the other options being Webster Hall and a UES apartment owned by an heiress who might be dead now. I originally found this restaurant merely because of the proximity to Lux's apartment and the Yelp review that declared it "a great place to apologize to an angry woman."

This is not the first time I've invited Lux to this restaurant with that review in the back of my mind.

Peering past the old men that dine around me, I finally see my muse, as she arrives, unhurried.

She's wearing an open-knit, circle neck, long sleeve, mod striped black and white sweater and a leather skirt. On the crown of her head is a black Annie Hall hat.

"We're back in business," I say, standing up, then pulling out Lux's chair.

"North Korean investors?" she asks, then turns her cheek to me, so I can kiss it, and I do.

"Worse," I say, rounding the table, heading toward my chair.

"No!" she gasps, instantly knowing what happened, while having none of the details.

"Yeah," I say, searching her face. I find fear. I find sympathy. I find the feeling of *Ah, I remember this man. I've been here before. I know this feeling.*

"I'll be designing M.Lorrie," I announce.

"Shit. I did not... wow... this is... Andrew? You're... taking other people's advice?" Lux stumbles over our new reality, then picks up the drink menu to recreate our old reality.

"How do you know that I didn't come up with this plan?" I ask.

"Because you're psycho about your brother," Lux says, putting the drink menu down, then craning her neck to look for the waitress.

"I'm going to be less psycho," I promise demurely.

"Does this..." Lux starts to say, then shakes her head, removing the thought, like her brain was an Etch A Sketch.

"Of course," I say, filling in her question with the answer.

"Really?" she asks, then smiles.

"I can't do it without you," I say.

"I think you could do it without anyone," Lux tells me, aware that my drive cannot be redirected and passengers are optional.

"It almost came down to that," I respond coldly; "I'm fixing things," I add warmly.

Lux nods at this, then she's saved by the waitress. She orders a drink named after a zip code, or it might be the combo to a safe or- who knows- it might even be a series of numbers that kids send in a text when they're willing to blow each other in an even trade of satisfaction.

I order a Heineken, then the waitress takes my drink menu.

"Are you okay with your..." I ask, stopping short of the subject because I'm afraid Lux will walk away.

The fringe of Lux's high fashion bangs moves up and down as she nods, hopefully aware that I'm referring to her always tumultuous money situation. My question regarding the well-being of an unsteady model temporarily makes me flash on Isabella, but I don't indulge in this mental tangent, because I haven't heard from her since she took my number. I think about how many numbers exist in my personal phone merely because they were a means to end a conversation I had no interest in continuing. I make a note to text Dan Carrington to see if he's seen a girl in blue velvet at any industry parties.

"So, who's fresh? Besides you, who should I be looking at for this collection?" I ask. I need Lux to mention how impressed she was by Isabella that night in The Imperial Hall. "And do you have my camera?" I tack on, desperate for my photographs.

Lux puts a finger up, then reaches down into a purse that I didn't even notice. This oversight is possible evidence that the accessories responsibility is better suited for Karen.

Lux places my old Fujifilm Finepix s1000 on the table.

"Matthew took a picture of his balls with it," Lux informs me.

"Thank you," I say, taking the camera, then I add, "Thank Matthew as well."

"No. It would ruin it for him," Lux says disinterestedly, "He doesn't photograph his balls for the accolades."

Before I fully process what I'm doing, the camera is powered on, and I take a picture of Lux. I capture her image before the look on her face turns to an annoyed snarl.

"You're next to Matthew's balls now," I say.

"A girl model cliché," she says, giggling.

The waitress brings us our drinks, and I'm happy that the conversation has made it this far.

"So. Give me girls. Who do I re-use?" I ask. Since James is casting the show, I'm just going to pick the people I want, then I'll tell James to shut the fuck up and accept the perfect line of girls I've assembled. "Galina is on drugs right?" I search, desperate for model gossip because discussing models whose lives are falling apart always makes Lux feel alive.

"Yeah," Lux responds casually, barely alive. "Galina is on Paxil- or something that's like a speedier Thorazine."

"Oh, is it good?" I ask.

"If you like eating chalk," Lux says, then takes a sip of her drink.

I try to keep the mood light, so I say, "I'm not against it if it will make me stop crying during those 15 second YouTube ads."

Lux smiles, and says, "The one about the baby dog."

I nod, then clarify, "I meant is Galina on illegal drugs?"

Lux takes a deep breath, "She was bitching that her prescription for Enzotrend expired and the doctor wouldn't give her more, so she made her mom go to the doctor and pretend like she was performing OCD rituals just to get the script."

"Enzotrend is a clothing line, isn't it?" I ask, confused.

"Maybe. Actually- that could be it- she didn't book Enzotrend, so she started getting Candrol from her mom to deal."

"Candrol is a restaurant in LA, isn't it?" I ask.

"Maybe. It's possible Galina didn't book Enzotrend, so she started regularly eating at Candrol, and she's using the coke that her OCD mom buys her to make sure she doesn't get too fat to book Paris."

"Is Galina doing any drug that an inner city person would do?" I ask, providing a specification that now seems necessary.

"Galina lives in a city," Lux says, opening her eyes, wide.

"Fine. Whatever. She can walk the show. This is impossible," I say, no longer able to navigate these models. The new girls make Cassie look well-adjusted.

"You seem stressed, Andrew," Lux casually mentions, "Are you just booking Galina because she has the prescriptions you need?"

The waitress returns, and we order.

"Sort of genius, just make sure she has her own stash or she'll never show up to walk for you," Lux adds, returning to Galina like there was no break in the conversation. "Remember the taxi incident?"

"What's the taxi incident?" I have to ask.

"Where did she even get that piano wire?" Lux asks, like I know what she's referring to. I stare at the bubbles in my beer, until I remember that Galina almost killed a cabbie for "being crude." The exact details of what he did that was crude proved to be vague at best. All of the charges were ultimately dropped because Galina is so pretty that- yeah- the taxi driver probably did do something crude... but could you blame him?

Setting the record straight, I say, "It wasn't piano wire, it a guitar string. When Galina's dad was visiting, she took him to see Bryan Metro who was performing some charity gig for his grand-kids school. Backstage, Bryan gave Galina a guitar string that she put in her purse to please her dad, but she doesn't give a fuck about old people so she caught a cab immediately after."

"Oh. I relate," Lux says, not looking at me, "The taxi story seems more understandable now. It's like The Godfather with cuter girls and more drugs."

"I think the part you're referencing happened in The Godfather Part II," I say, then add, "At least it wasn't in The Godfather Part III."

"Hey, Sofia Coppola was in The Godfather Part III," Lux responds.

"Good point. At least The Godfather Part III was better than Somewhere."

Lux looks at me from the tips of her fridge and says, "Somewhere was The Godfather of Stephen Dorff movies."

"If we don't count Britney's 'Everytime' video as a movie," I note.

"That's not a movie- that's an experience- that's transcendent," Lux says.

Feeling a bizarre confidence because of how well my apology has gone, I allow myself to ask, "Do you know that new girl, Isabella?"

"No. Who's that?" Lux asks.

"Someone," I say. I couldn't respond, "No one," because Lux would instantly know I'm lying.

A rhythmic vibration freezes time for a moment, and I consider it might be Isabella calling. Lux looks down at her purse, then takes out her phone. My personal phone sits on the table- steady, silent.

After reading the glowing screen, Lux looks panicked, then she tells me, "I have to go console my roommate."

"What happened?" I ask, starting to stand up.

Lux holds out her palm to keep me from joining her, then she fills me in, "Her boyfriend broke up with her, and she's a psychotic bitch now."

"She wasn't before?" I ask, remembering Lux's stories.

"No. Before she was just a bitch. But she's the most dependable bitch in New York so I owe it to her to be there. *Being there* is sort of what she does. It's not what I do, but I know how important it is so, today, it's going to be what I do."

"She's never at the apartment when I visit," I point out.

"It's a different type of being there, Andrew," Lux says, then the model transforms into a girl and walks away from me.

"Lux," I yell across the restaurant. Everyone looks at me, besides the girl walking away.

"Andrew, I have to," she responds, over her shoulder.

Lux was there for me the night before my last collection. Being there *is* what she does. I want to tell her that, but she's already gone.

THE AGENCY

I wake up when my personal phone makes a blip of a noise, indicating I have a text.

After sitting on the edge of the bed for four minutes, I walk over to the dresser and pick up the phone.

The text reads, "Isabella lives in one of the BK Blend apts."

I thank Gregor in a gushing text, complete with smiling emoticons and an open-ended, "I owe you."

I iron a French cuff, spread-collar brick/cranberry hued long sleeve shirt of my own design, then a pair of black pants that I sewed myself on my portable sewing machine that I left in LA. I'm about to get dressed, but I leave the shirt and pants on the ironing board.

I reach back into the suitcase, then I take out a black V-neck T-shirt and a pair of Vigoss women's jeans with the tag ripped off. The Gucci loafers I had set out are traded for my black Doc Martens. I'm not going to a business meeting, I'm taking a trip into the city so I can help a friend. I make sure I'm dressed appropriately for the task at hand.

Downstairs, I maneuver through the kitchen and find absolutely no food.

I look around to make a supermodel joke to someone, but I find no one. Not even The Boy.

I go back upstairs, to the room lined with pictures- Cassie's room- and I look through her closet for a travel bag that I can use to store the business cards, my work phone, and its charger.

The options I'm presented with are vast in number, but limited in practicality. I find a rectangular black quilted Chanel bag with no outside logo besides a small gold boldface CHANEL near the zipper. The strap is leather so I don't have to worry about the look of a chain giving away the fact that I'm wearing my ex-girlfriend's accessories around New York. I fill the bag with my few personal items, then toss in some *Vogues* to make it look like I have lots of important business documents that I need to carry with me at all times.

I throw on my leather Saint Laurent jacket and begin my walk to the train station.

On the walk, I brainstorm ways to get a meeting at Blend so I can lay claim to Isabella before she's booked solid. The cards become essential because even Lux was hesitant to believe in this new deal.

I call Jessica from the pre-programmed "business phone" Michael gave me, and when she picks up, I stammer out, "Hi, uh, Jessica. It's Andrew. Lorrie. Michael's brother."

"Yeah, I saw on the screen," Jessica says, but not in a bitchy way- just in a way that confirms she's confident about my identity. It feels good to know that she wanted my number, and she programmed it into her desk phone.

"Listen," I say, careful not to give this girl an order, because I'm not good at this type of stuff. Karen is good at this type of stuff, but Karen is not responsible for this stuff anymore, so I continue, "Yesterday, I spoke with Michael, and he mentioned getting me -"

"-business cards?" Jessica asks, reading my mind.

"Yeah, he didn't write it down so..."

"He never writes anything down. He must have some sort of genius mind to remember everything," Jessica marvels, and she's either covering for her boss' skeevy surveillance tactics, or she's a fucking idiot. "I have your cards on my desk," Jessica informs me.

"Oh. Already?" I ask. The business card thing was going to be my excuse. I was supposed to be told that the cards will arrive in eight-to-ten business days. I was supposed to have a week filled with hand-wringing procrastination before becoming equipped to march up to the Blend office and beg them for their incredible new find. Now that I have the cards available to me, I don't want them.

"My ex is in printing so I got them done super-fast," Jessica says.

"You still print with your ex?" I ask, admiring this.

"Sure, I think part of the reason that we broke up was because we never had any money, so- I don't know- I guess I like to give him some business when I can," Jessica explains, and I begin to wonder if Michael offered me this job for a similar reason.

"I think that's sweet," I say, because I don't want to suggest that Jessica is manipulating her ex-boyfriend by reminding him that he has to resort to accepting acts of professional charity.

"Thanks, Andy," Jessica says.

"Andrew," I correct her, and it ruins the casualness of the call, so I add, "My dad was Andy. I like Andrew. I wouldn't want my dad associated with my, uh, behavior."

"Ah, hookers," Jessica says.

"No. I would never-"

"-joking, Andrew. Your cards will be here. See you in a bit," Jessica says, then ends the call.

I realize that I'm the boss' brother. I've somehow assumed the role of the insane, never-play-by-the-rules guy who got his job because of nepotism; this all feels very New Jersey via New York. In a workplace where Jessica has to confirm the structure of everything, she seems to appreciate that there's a younger brother too apathetic to get on her case about anything beyond what name he likes to be called.

On the train, I google the location of the Blend offices so, in a role reversal, I can go-see them.

Address in hand, I pop out in front of MSG, then I taxi down to Watts Street, without getting my business cards. After my googling unearthed rumors of Blend wrapping up their girls in a couture version of indentured servitude, I understand that I'll have to control the flow of information. I don't want Blend to be able to easily contact me... yet. If they're mismanaging Isabella- just as they have with new faces in the past- I *will* move Isabella to Elite. Elite takes care of their New York girls. They study their girls, then cater to the specific model's personality, strengths, crossover potential, and versatility. Isabella was sent to Blend by her mother agency in LA, then they placed her in an overcrowded fuck awful model apartment in Brooklyn until they figure out what they're going to do with her.

Isabella needs to like New York, and she's not going to like it living with six other girls that are more conventionally attractive and outgoing than she is.

If Isabella hates New York, she'll leave, and if Isabella leaves, she'll resume community college. After that, with a little catch-up, she'll be deep into the school year, working toward a life that doesn't include modeling. She'll haunt my design table, and I'll feel that every future collection is incomplete if she becomes a ghost.

I hop out of the taxi when I see a long, black awning bearing the name "BLEND" in bold type. More than just an attention-getter, more than just the symbolism for the slender monochrome-clothed models inside the building, the awning is practical because it keeps the girls shielded from the elements as they leave the agency, then step- beautiful face first- out onto the ugly streets.

I make my way up to the sixth floor, to the Blend offices, and when I enter the all-white space, I notice a man in a Yankees cap.

James is already at Blend.

For some reason, my first instinct is to hide, then I realize that James is the amateur casting director for our show, and I'm the designer. We're partners, like my business phone tells me. James is making introductions, and this could be a perfect segue for me. I can look like I'm late for a meeting, instead of showing up unannounced like a creep. I'm the Liam of fashion's Oasis; why would I show up for a meeting on time?

There are two women- one agent and one model- standing with James. The model is blonde, blue-eyed, fair-skinned, and speckled in beauty marks. She's wearing a lightweight black jumper that- thanks to the positioning of her tall frame- I can see has a slit back. The exposed skin and the dotting of birthmarks feels oddly intimate, and I keep this in mind for the future.

"I'm really worried about the North Pole," is the first clear thing I can hear from the model. I don't know her name, but I recognize her from a *Numero* editorial, and she might have been discovered by *Teen Vogue* or one of those modeling competitions that used to run on TV.

"The North Pole? I'm also worried," James says, his eyes bugging out as though he doesn't believe the odds he found someone who shares his passion. "That whole Santa thing is bizarre. We shouldn't be teaching children that fat old men with white beards will give them presents for being agreeable. Because-ya know- that's exactly what happens in real life. Those candy canes are-"

"-no. Here's what I'm talking about. Look at this," the model says, showing James something on her phone, "This is the North Pole."

"Beautiful," James marvels.

"-that used to be all glaciers and now it's water," the model says.

"And what beautiful water it is," James responds, not understanding what's going on.

The other woman- the agent- watches all of this unfold while wearing a calm smile.

James looks up from the picture, notices me, then says, "Get a look at this, Andy."

"Andrew," I say, then sport a tight-lipped smile.

I walk over, then review the image on the phone- an artfully drab landscape of very blue water surrounded by white snow. My photographer's eye makes me suspect that this is a computer generated desktop background.

Thinking he's helping his cause, James begins telling me, "The North Pole might be a new destination location. Look at this beauty. We might be able to shoot a great campaign there, as long as their airport isn't in the middle of n-wait, what are you doing here, Andy?"

"Tragic about the North pole. If only we could keep it as cold as James' heart," I say to the model, and she smiles at me, finally getting the reaction she originally wanted. The agent next to the model smiles as well, because she seems to view me as a human being with the ability to articulate independent thoughts, unlike James.

I begin my introduction, without a business card, "My name is Andrew-"

"-you don't have to introduce yourself. I'm Anne. I'm Arianna's agent," the woman says, then gestures to the environmentalist/model at her side.

"Arianna, you were beautiful in *Numero*," I say, and the model blushes.

"Anne, can we pop into your office for a moment? James and I are working on the early stages of a line, and you could be of assistance to us," I explain, trying to sound docile.

"We're partners," James says, aligning himself with me because I'm doing better with Arianna.

"It's come to our attention that Blend signed a girl who will be very important for our spring line," I purr.

"Who?" James asks, then I shoot him a dagger of a glance.

Anne takes me by the elbow of my leather jacket, and says, "Let's chat."

James looks torn between staying with the model and following Anne.

"Don't leave without me," I instruct him, verbally pushing him out of the business conversation. James winks at me, and I find it unnerving.

I enter Anne's office, then close the door behind me. The windowless space is covered in old style Polaroids of beautiful girls and framed pictures of what I presume to be Anne's dog.

I take a seat, setting my bag on the floor, then I lean slightly over the messy desk, and I say, "I *need* Isabella."

Anne looks at me with a blank expression.

"She walked for my last collection," I clarify.

Anne nods at this, "Right. So you're... working on... your new line?" she asks carefully.

I lower my voice to a whisper, then say, "I have some information that I'm going to need you to keep under your hat. Frankly, I want a working relationship with you, so that's the only reason why you're the one who gets this info."

This excites Anne, and judging from the fact we must be about the same age, I realize that, despite the fact other agents would probably fear giving their models to me, Anne- one- doesn't know who Isabella is, two- wants my exclusive information, and three- might want to sleep with me.

"I'm designing M.Lorrie ready-to-wear now," I whisper.

A smile slides across Anne's face, and she says, "Andrew, congratulations. I never thought- wow. Very exciting."

"Thank you. It certainly *is* exciting. I think it could also be exciting for some of your girls," I say. I circle the Isabella issue so I don't come off desperate, and I mention, "Arianna has a great look." I can hint at my interest in the speckled model, despite the fact that she might be totally wrong for the line, because James will likely creep out Arianna, to the point that she'll never agree to show up to a Michael Lorrie casting.

"What do you need from Blend?" Anne asks.

"I'm going to be one hundred percent honest with you," I say, but this is a lie, "We already have a face for the collection, but there's a smaller role that Michael wants to utilize in order to develop an exciting new fresh face, and I think Isabella is perfect for the opportunity."

Anne cranes her neck back a bit, studying me, then she turns to her laptop and starts hammering keys. She squints at the screen, raises an eyebrow, then she says, "You have her for your Spring collection."

"I'd like to shake on that," I say.

Anne reaches across her messy desk and our hands lock.

"You are going to be a very happy woman this spring, compliments of the Lorrie brothers," I promise, standing up.

Anne nods at this, then makes a request, "Andrew. Take care of her. The girl seems lost."

I pause for a moment, and I take her words to heart. "I think I'm a little lost too," I say, my stare fixed on the chair I just got out of.

"You must be," Anne responds, "You have no idea how many times I tried to get you into my office when you were working on those vanity lines."

"You're weren't supposed to know I was involved," I whisper in a flirty mock-secrecy.

"I know an Andrew Lorrie design when I see it," she purrs.

I grab my bag, thank Anne for her time, then I walk out of her office to collect my dead weight. I force myself to accept that James somehow put into motion a series of events that ended with me getting Isabella for this collection.

Today, James and I worked as partners.

I find James, model-less, holding a pile of tear sheets, observing the comings and goings around him.

"Vamanos, James. We have a meeting," I say.

"Did he text you?" James asks, visibly hurt that Michael might have left him out of the loop.

"Nope. I'm scheduling the meeting," I respond, feeling good, needing my business cards, bouncing in a groove, until James informs me, "Arianna couldn't stop talking about your Chanel purse."

I ignore the comment, and I leave Blend with a renewed drive.

On the elevator ride down to the street, James says, "Michael put me up at this beautiful hotel. *Beautiful hotel*," he emphasizes.

"I have a house I'm staying in," I say.

"Oh, I know. Cassandra Wolfe's place, right? Quaint."

"Who told you that?" I ask.

The elevator doors open.

James quickly walks out, so I have to catch up to him. My Docs hammer the awning-covered sidewalk, my Chanel purse bops at my hip, and when James senses I'm close, he tells me, "Relax, dude. I saw you take the Dover train, and I knew you had a love-nest out there with Cassandra about two decades ago."

"Where'd you get that information from?" I ask.

James steps out into the street and immediately hails a cab in a serendipitous way. This ex-pap might be a douche, but he has an aura about him that greases wheels and makes things happen. He's slowly becoming as much of an asset as he is a liability.

We get into the taxi, and James leans forward, then says "Michael Lorrie. The office, not the retail store. West 36th."

Our trip underway, he turns to me, and explains, "I'm not stalking you, I merely felt a little curious last night, and *OxygenWaster* let me keep my password to their system, so, of course, I had to read your file."

"You read my file?" I repeat, mentally negating the momentary friendship I allowed myself to have with James.

"Yeah, dude. I did it to help our working relationship. I didn't want to read the file, but you don't have a Facebook page," he says. "Well, you have a small fan page, mostly populated with awful racists, but no personal page."

"How'd you know about the house?" I ask.

"We have a list of all our P.O.I.'s previous addresses," he admits casually.

"P.O.I?" I ask.

"Person Of Interest," James says, explaining proudly, like it's an industry term. "It was going to be Targets Of Interest, but that was deemed 'too predatory.'"

"And you still have access to this database?" I ask.

James pulls his cap down a bit, then says, "Sure, I do. I mean, I shouldn't be accessing it, but I'm kind of a computer whiz. If you hack enough cell phones for pictures of famous peoples' buttholes, you can pick up tech skills pretty fast."

THE INTERN

Jessica hands me a box of business cards as I step out of the elevator onto the 8th floor.

James, trailing behind me, asks where his cards are, and he's met with the appropriate amount of silence.

While walking back to Michael's office, I slide off the top of the skinny box, then I select one of the crisp white cards. A massive MICHAEL LORRIE is stamped in raised lettering, taking up almost the entire surface space of the card, while my name, in tiny font, is printed at the bottom. A phone number I don't recognize is listed on the bottom of the card.

"Thank you," I say to Jessica, and she moves close to me, then whispers, "I think your business cards made me miss my poor business-card-making ex."

I consider this for a moment, then say, "If you still feel that way tomorrow, let me know, and I'll mention to Michael that his name could be bigger on the card, then you'll be able to call your ex with an excuse to chat."

Jessica giggles at this, then wishes me luck as I open the door to Michael's office without knocking.

Glancing up from an iPad, Michael says, "Nice Chanel purse."

"Thanks," I respond coldly.

"I have one too," says a girl- not a model- who's sitting on a chair from a cubicle that's been relocated to the far corner of the office. I take note of her distance from Michael, and I envy her seat.

"Very nice," I say, as the girl lifts a similar looking Chanel purse.

"Twins," James adds, smiling at everyone as he enters the office.

I sit down, and drop my bag. The girl puts down her purse as well, then she walks over to me and extends her hand, greeting me with, "Hi, I'm your intern, Jessica."

"Perfect," I celebrate, popping up from my chair, "You're skinny! Ever since this whole internship thing was mentioned, all I could think about was how my life would be ruined if you were fat." My eyes are frantic with joy, as the contract for my fitting model is solidified.

"You're not really shattering any stereotypes of the fashion industry, are you?" Jessica responds, retreating back to her distanced chair.

"Huh?" I ask, looking to James for help, a desperate act.

"Body shaming," Jessica says.

"Body shaming?" I ask, then add, "And what are you talking about? I'm straight. I'm a straight designer. I am definitely shattering stereotypes."

The intern stares at me. She's about five feet tall/ not fat/ tan/ huge eyes- the usual. She wears black framed glasses that are nearly a copy of James'. I'm sure she'll get along fine here. She has my purse, James' glasses, and Michael's name on her checks.

I try to start over because this girl isn't just *the* intern, she's *my* intern. "That was a joke. I joke around," I warn, as though I'm priming her for long days of sexual harassment.

"Using your majority-status sexuality as a joke isn't funny to me," the intern says.

"Fuck. You have a fashion blog, don't you?" I say, flopping back down in my chair, my joy fleeting fast, as it usually does.

"I have over 4,000 followers," the intern says, putting her nose in the air.

"Okay," I say, accepting this merely because it'll get Lux on the payroll.

I review the intern's outfit. She's wearing red pumps whose designer I can't identify, a black pencil skirt whose designer I can't identify, and a white polyester peplum top with cap sleeves and a darted bust- designer also unknown. "Did you say your name is Jessica?" I ask, just now processing this.

She puts her messy black hair behind her ears, then nods by pushing out her chin twice.

"Michael, you don't rename all your employees 'Jessica' when they start, do you?" I ask.

Michael smiles, then asks me, "I don't call *you* 'Jessica,' do I?" He pauses, looks down, then adds, "Well, now that you're carrying that purse..."

"Can I get you anything?" Intern Jessica asks, hopping into the conversation, protecting me from this harassment.

I pause. I don't want this intern to dislike me, so I try to get things back on track by asking, "Could I have a coffee, black, please?"

"Sure," she says, then leaves the office.

Despite the contentious introduction, Intern Jessica strikes me as a younger, better-dressed Karen.

"I'm having a get-together at my apartment tonight," Michael announces.

"Very nice," I respond.

"Will you be bringing someone?" he asks.

"Pardon?" I cough out, fidgeting, sweating.

"To the party. I'm going to make an announcement to some close friends about you joining the team. Will you be arriving with a guest?" Michael asks.

Isabella. I want to bring Isabella to this party. I want to protect her from Michael, but I also want her to join me tonight because her presence would continuously remind me of why I'm going down this thorny path. Isabella is proof that the world isn't as terrible as Michael and his friends would force me to believe.

"No. I'm going alone," I say, and this statement confirms my isolation and solitary existence.

"Shame," Michael responds, not in the *That's a shame* way, but instead in the *You should feel shame for what your life has become- it's shameful* way.

"I'll be there, dude," James says, but Michael ignores him, and stares at me directly. "Even if you don't bring her tonight, you are aware that we're going to have to leverage your renewed thing with Cassandra," Michael says.

"What thing with Cassie?" I ask.

"Well, now that you're back living with her..." Michael trails off.

"I don't remember telling you where I'm living. I don't remember that being your business," I say.

James hops in again, "Cassandra is actually in LA right now. She's filming a jewelry ad," he says.

"And how do you know that?" I ask.

"She's a P.O.I. of mine. Remember?"

I find comfort in the information James is providing, because it means that Cassie is currently out of Michael's manipulative reach. I'm assuming that James told Michael about my living arrangements, and Michael inferred that I must be back with Cassie if I'm staying at her house. If he researched this further, he'd know about the commercial, and this topic of conversation would've been tabled for a later date.

Intern Jessica reappears and provides me with my much-needed coffee. I glance quickly at Michael to see if he'll give me an indication of if it's proper to tip the interns. Michael's blank expression reveals nothing, and my intern returns, tip-less, to her distant chair.

To make it clear I'm in the house alone, I tell Michael, "You'll have to make the Cassie thing happen. I'm paying her rent to stay at the house. Nothing bizarre or forgiving about it. She'd never skip the jewelry commercial gig to show up for a little get-together, so maybe you should just reschedule..."

"A tiger is involved in the shoot," James says, then raises his eyebrows like this carries some sort of implication.

"Yes, Michael. A tiger is involved," I say, sarcastically. I hear Intern Jessica stifle a giggle, and this tiny show of support makes me change my answer. "Actually, put me down for a plus-one for tonight," I announce.

"Certainly," Michael says, "Just let Jessica know who you'll be taking, when you find her."

"Jessica," I say, standing up, turning toward the chair in the corner, "You're going to a party tonight."

Jessica's eyes light up, but then they lose their light when they dart to Michael.

"We'd love to have you," Michael says, then adds, "Now that we've confirmed you're not fat."

James laughs good-naturedly at this, but I don't because I know this isn't a callback to our earlier conversation, but instead a threat to Jessica that if she expects to be seen outside of the office, she has to keep up her appearance.

Welcome to Michael Lorrie.

THE FASHION PEOPLE

I don't allow myself to notice any of the details in Michael's apartment because he's invited me here to show me a tale of two Lorries. Michael thinks he's living in the best of times, and it's clear he views my life as the worst of times.

In the apartment, I float, distanced from it all.

I need alcohol and a beautiful woman.

I let Intern Jessica join the social circle in the center of Michael's living room because I don't want to be around her once she starts drinking.

On the way to the party, the single topic of conversation was about how Intern Jessica doesn't know how to properly educate her friends that reverse racism doesn't exist. My suggestion, "Stop oppressing them and it will be easier," was immediately disregarded with a snarl.

"Do you want a tour of the place?" Michael asks me.

"From here to the bar," I say.

"I don't think alcohol is exactly what you need to make a good first impression," Michael responds.

"Tour's canceled. Gotcha," I say.

I begin to look for James, and this search is an indication of how bad this party is.

"Hey, isn't the face of our collection supposed to be here?" I ask Michael.

"No. I never said she'd be here. I never said that. I never said Irina would be here," Michael repeatedly responds to my single question.

I only brought Irina up so I could see his reaction, and now that I have the reaction, I presume that Irina turned down the invitation. She said no to this party and there was nothing Michael could do about it. This makes me smile. I begin to look forward to working with Irina. She has the power to do the shitty things I can only fantasize about.

I try to hang on the edge of the well-dressed group of partygoers, looking involved, yet never becoming encouraging of the pointless exchange of words that's happening with no clear signs of connection. I'm frozen in a state of disbelief that this is what now passes for communication.

Someone says that they called their girlfriend today.

Someone asks if it ended in a fight.

A second person asks if it ended in a fight after a, "Pshh," noise is made.

Someone says, "Damn."

Someone says, "Figgies."

Someone says, "Don't say that."

Someone says, "Don't say, 'Don't say that.'"

Someone asks, "How do you know I shouldn't be saying that she shouldn't be saying that?"

Someone says, "We need tacos."

Someone says, "Yesss," enthusiastically.

Someone asks, "Tacos?"

Someone says, "Tacos."

Someone says, "Pink tacos."

Someone says, "Nooo."

Someone asks, "No to tacos, or no to being crude?"

Someone responds, "Both?"

Someone asks, "Was that a 'Can I have both?'"

Someone says, "In my mouth."

Someone says, "Tac-ho's," with that specific emphasis.

Someone says, "I like it spicy."

Someone says, "I like mild."

Someone says, "Figgies."

Someone says, "I just realized you're abbreviating 'figures.'"

Someone laughs disparagingly at this.

Someone asks, "No tac-hos?"

Someone says, "You can't cheat on a diet."

Someone says, "Diets aren't like boyfriends."

Someone says, "Stop. Not the time."

Someone says, "I've heard that before."

Someone says, "The oven is on fire."

Someone says, "I think you mean the stove."

As no one rushes into the kitchen to put out the fire, my phone vibrates, and I honestly believe it's a text from Satan asking if I'm enjoying his stage play.

I look down at the screen and see that it's an incoming call. I swipe the call to answer it, and I hear a familiar voice ask, "Hey, can you talk?"

My pause is involuntary and too long, "Of course," I say. "Of course," I repeat, drifting away from the nobodies masquerading as human beings.

"My agent told me to call you... and... uh, I could use... someone."

"I'm coming over. Text me an address," I say, then I end the call.

I make my way to James, who I now realize is with the model, Arianna, from the Blend office. Knowing that James already has a focus for the night, I ask, "Do you think you could make sure Intern Jessica gets in a cab tonight?" then I hand him a fifty.

"Sure, dude," James says, then looks to Arianna to flaunt that he was given responsibility, like a real person.

I turn to walk out of Michael's apartment, but I'm stopped by a hand on my shoulder. "Where are you going?" my boss asks.

"To help a friend," I say.

"But you can't stay to help your brother?"

"I have every intention of helping my brother," I respond, then add, "Tomorrow."

THE MODEL APARTMENT

The apartment in Brooklyn is as filthy and dark as I expected it to be.

"Come on," Isabella says, then I follow her through the model den, pausing for a moment when I recognize the guy on the sofa because he's in the ad for my cologne. Not *my* cologne- that opportunity was never presented to me, and if it was, I wouldn't know where to begin. He's in the ad for the cologne I wear.

Isabella and I move through the noisy space, each model-resident seemingly working on some sort of droney musical side project. I'm shocked by the number of abandoned food containers everywhere, and when I look closer, I see that most of them still contain food. The apartment doesn't smell bad, but it doesn't smell good either. The air has a weight to it that makes me aware it's there.

Even in basketball shorts and a gray t-shirt, Isabella looks like a model, but she looks like a model, apart.

When we reach her room, she says, "Sorry you have to stand, but..." and she doesn't need to finish her statement because the places that I could sit are covered in clothes. For a girl that only brought a backpack worth of possessions to the city, I begin to wonder how she could create such a mess, then I see another mattress on the floor, under more clothes, and I realize that Isabella doesn't have her own room.

When the door to the room is closed, the air gets even heavier.

"I hate it here," Isabella says, and my worst fear is realized.

"Have you gone to any castings?" I ask.

Isabella sits down on the cleaner of the two mattresses, then says, "Yes, but I come back to all of this, and I try to sleep, but there's always music playing, and I have to be a bitch and ask them to turn the music off, and they do, then I go back into my room, and, louder, they start recording a cover song of the song I made them turn off."

"We need to get you out of here," I say.

"That's the plan."

"But we need to keep you in New York. It's important that you stay in New York," I say, attempting to cover up the fact I'm begging.

"No," she responds.

I nod, then offer, "Alright, let's get you set up in Jersey. With me. I have a house."

"I'm not going to stay at your house," Isabella balks, like the idea is ridiculous.

"We'll figure this out," I say, putting my hands on my hips so I don't reach for my phone. I refuse to call Michael, even though his hotel room offer would solve this problem.

"My best friend here doesn't speak English," Isabella says, punctuating the Blend apartment experience. "She laughs a lot though."

"Come on. Pack your stuff," I say.

"You're letting me go home?" Isabella asks, looking up at me.

"No. I'm giving you a new one."

Isabella purses her lips, considering my offer.

I can't pack for Isabella because I don't know what she owns. Everything in this apartment seems at once communal *and* discarded.

"I want to go home, Andrew," Isabella says, "I appreciate you talking to my agent and all, but even she admitted that I arrived after fashion week castings so it's going to be a while before I book something else. I'm just sitting here, wasting time and money."

"I'm taking rent out of the equation. You'll stay at my house in New Jersey. You can have your own room-"

"-you're nice," Isabella says, "I'm not sure if this is some penance for what's happened with your collection, and I'm not sure why you've chosen me to be the person you help, but you have enough going on right now, you don't need *this* too. *This* isn't going to help. I'm going back to school."

I walk toward the door, but I stop myself before I make my exit.

"Do you want to be a model?" I ask the model.

I look back; Isabella shrugs.

"If you leave New York, you'll never come back to the same opportunity," I warn, informing her of a reality.

"I can come back for your show... if you still want me to."

"Sure, you can, but you're in your prime right now. There's a clock that's ticking," I tell her as a metronome clicking in the room next door backs up my statement. "You have all the time in the world for community college. Think about the people in your classes. I bet half of them are my age and that's because the option to attend classes will always be there. *This* option... unfortunately... unless you're Irina, has an expiration date. Don't end up like the discarded food all over this apartment," I warn.

Isabella stands up and grabs a backpack off the dirty carpet. "Meet me out front in 15," she says, then she goes to work packing her life back into the bookbag. She and I both seem to have a habit of cramming our entire existence into a single piece of luggage. We're two people who rely on a fully-furnished home to continue on. Somehow, we keep finding that home when we need it, but we're absolutely stubborn bastards before the move-in.

"I'll be out front," I say, then I leave the room.

As I walk back through the dark apartment, a black girl with a bouncy afro corners me in a stretch of cornerless hallway, and asks, "Where are you taking Isabella?"

"She needs to be alone for a bit," I say.

The black girl follows me, as I move by a dish-filled sink, and she reminds me, "If there's a problem, Isabella can shut her door here."

I point at the shirtless guy on the sofa who's wearing headphones and singing at full volume while playing an unplugged electric guitar. "She can't shut that out," I say.

"Who are you, sir?" the black girl asks, "Why is this your problem?"

I turn around and reach into my pocket, then pull out a business card.

The girl takes the card, then moves it so that it's under the light of the bare bulb hanging from the ceiling. "Shit. You're Michael Lorrie?" she asks.

"No. I'm Andrew Lorrie... my name is in that really tiny font on the bottom of the card," I admit.

The black girl squints, trying to read the microscopic type.

"Are you a model?" I ask the girl.

"I'm trying, sir," she says.

"Don't call me Michael and don't call me sir, and call me on that card if you're having trouble with the industry," I instruct her. "I want you to program my number in your phone."

She looks at the card again, then says, "You designed the dress that Isabella loves."

I nod and it feels damn good to confirm this fact.

THE ROOMMATE

The village of South Orange seems at odds with itself. The residents- New York commuters- are so bitter and hateful that they want to extinguish almost everything that sustains the village. They're fighting off Newark/ they're fighting off the university/ they're fighting off all of the reasons the village still exists. If the residents had it their way, a perimeter wall would be constructed and the only businesses inside it would be a dry cleaners and a Dunkin' Donuts. The residents here want everyone to go away and that's why Cassie and I chose the house on Scotland Road- it was the closest thing we could get to a castle with a moat and a reasonable New York commute.

"I know the only reason you demanded to carry my backpack was so you could steal the dress back," Isabella says, as she walks down the train station stairs in front of me.

I find myself finally able to run my hand along the brick wall at my side because Lux is speaking to me again. Everything isn't fixed with her, but I know that once I start to sketch, I can bring her back. Lux is still excited about fashion; she's just worn down by the world. The routine of fittings and daily collaboration will help her claw out of whatever shit she's currently going through. It's sad- Lux kept trying to pose as an 18-year-old, until she ended up feeling like a confused teen.

Since it's a warm night, and Isabella isn't wearing heels, I decide we'll walk to the house on Scotland Road.

The trip seems quicker tonight, most likely because I finally have someone to make it with.

My work phone vibrates, and I check the screen. "The Intern has been sent home safely in a cab," reads the text from "My Partner." I'm tempted to text back "And Arianna?" but I'm in no position to send such a message because I'm approaching my model ex-girlfriend's house, with a young model by my side.

"Nice going, Andrew. I like your house," Isabella says, as we round the bushes and head toward the front door.

"*This* is Cassandra Wolfe's house," I say.

"Wait. Are you joking?" Isabella asks, stopping before the staircase.

"Nope," I say, popping my lips, signing the house over to Cassie once again.

"Are you messing with me?" Isabella asks, as her long legs take the stairs two at a time, allowing her to reach the door before me.

"I wish I was," I say, climbing the stairs.

"Can I check out the inside?" she asks.

"That's the plan," I respond, sliding in front of her, then keying into the house.

"I can't wait to go through Cassandra Wolfe's stuff. This is going to be incredible for my blog," Isabella gushes, walking inside.

"Please stick to the fashion side of it," I request, flicking on the light.

"What's the other side?" Isabella asks.

"You'll find it almost inextricable from the fashion side, so don't post anything," I warn.

"Relax," Isabella says casually, "They won't even know I'm here. The content will just appear on the internet. That's how it happens."

"That's how *what* happens?" I ask, making my way to the staircase.

"Everything," Isabella responds, as we climb the stairs.

On the second floor, I have to make a decision regarding which room Isabella will get. Cassie said that *I* can't sleep in her bed, but she never said anything about Isabella.

I move to the door of Cassie's room, then flip on the light. Isabella looms over my shoulder, at least four inches taller than me.

"Holy shit, are these all Cassandra's pictures?" she asks, storming into the room, then pushing her long hair back so she gets an unobstructed look at every photograph.

"Yes, they are," I confirm, happy that she chose this room instantly.

"These are..." she starts to say, then trails off, getting lost in a photograph of a makeup-less Cassie combing her hair, her robe coming open, one of her breasts exposed.

"Make yourself at home. Bathroom is down the hall. Kitchen is downstairs, empty," I realize aloud. I'm an ill-equipped host and I have to avoid the consideration that maybe I haven't thought this plan through. "I'll get some groceries tomorrow," I promise, then amend my morning schedule.

Everything I'm saying is falling on deaf ears, as Isabella slowly moves around the room, studying each picture.

"Let me know if you need anything," I say.

Isabella turns to face me, and in a small voice, she says, "Thanks, Andrew."

I nod an acknowledgment, then walk out of the room, and close the door behind me.

When I enter my own room, I leave the door open.

I don't have to warn Isabella about The Boy and The Girl, because they'll never enter her room; the pictures assure this. The knowledge of what happens *after* would collapse the loop they appear to be stuck in. Nothing would be worth replaying if The Boy and The Girl were able to see what happens next. The pictures insulate Isabella from the looping imprint. If she does encounter The Boy and The Girl in this house, it would mean that I'd have to answer questions. I'd have to provide an end to the story that began here, and that would most likely lead to a second, very similar ending. I could claim that I've changed, but Isabella has watched me for so long, and she knew details of my life before I met her. She can intuit that I'm the same person I've always been.

Cassie's request that I stay away from her bed seems less offensive now. It's possible that she wanted me to see The Boy and The Girl because I had worked our failed relationship out in so many collections, but those pieces are now floating somewhere in the world- in closets and consignment shops- so, in a way, the pieces are missing. I now know why the oft-vacant house on Scotland Road was never sold; it would be like selling a home movie. The memories aren't just stuck to the walls- the memories are trapped inside the walls. Meanwhile, I'm just trying to keep Isabella in the house for a single night.

With everything coming together- business cards confirming that I'm employed, Lux confirming that she'll remain my muse, Isabella arriving in my temporary home- I realize that it's finally time to create.

I open my suitcase, then remove my sketch pad and the special pencils that I use to make sure my lines come out steady, even when my hands are shaking for a drink.

An hour into my preliminary sketches, I find myself churning out nothing but versions of Isabella's face. No designs flow after her neckline- that's where the drawings stop.

This is the problem with being a designer. A special face will come along and change the rules. My piece has to be *at least* as good as the face that struts along with it. The divine girls will *always* get cast, that's a given, so I know they'll be stepping onto that runway and I'll have to come up with something better than this easy perfection. It becomes a challenge to create with a skill that surpasses God's, all the while knowing that God does not lose. This is why there's a Michael Lorrie purse named after Chloe Warren. Our art, and the resulting products, are secondary to God's masterpieces.

I put the sketchbook away, then I slide into bed.

I stare at the open door, then I look to the yellow triangle of light on the floor. Neither the door frame nor the patch of light ends up breached.

Eventually, I close my eyes, but moments later, a creak of the floorboards jolts me instantly awake.

THE FACE

I buy waffles and bagels from the waffle place that used to be a bagel place, but apparently still sells bagels so they don't alienate their old customers. I quickly walk back to the house on Scotland Road because I'm afraid Isabella will die of hunger while I'm gone. Food was everywhere in her last apartment, yet Isabella is still underweight.

Before I leave for work, I don't write out any instructions or emergency numbers, because that would be dad-like. I leave a hundred dollar bill on the counter, because that's not something a dad does, it's something that a friend does when they invite you to live with them, then they realize they didn't think things through, at all. It's also a bribe to get her to stay.

I take the train to the city because James won't stop texting me that: "We've hit the jackpot. Irina invited us to her condo/"We're going to the home of one of the biggest models in the world/"Do we bring a gift/"I'm bringing red wine. Bring a baguette/"Do we need to get permission slips from the Jessicas for this, or are off-site meetings allowed?"

In front of the American Felt building on East 13th, James rushes over to me and informs me that I'm late- I know that- and that I have forgotten my baguette- I laugh.

James is panicking, telling me if I'm not prepared to be the baguette to his Merlot, then this is going to be a rocky collaboration.

The doorman lets us inside without questioning who we are, then we take the elevator up to Irina's floor.

James is worried that Irina will recognize him from the time he took pictures of her when she was shooting a highly under-wraps September issue cover.

"We need to be good guests. I've already ruined one of her Septembers, I can't afford to fuck up another," James tells me, and I gladly take the lead by knocking on the door.

James fixes the brim on his hat, while I fix my hair.

Surprisingly, Irina answers her own door. She's wearing a white lace top with horizontal stripes and a rounded neckline that doesn't show off her jutting collarbones, but does show off her tight stomach. A pair of 90's CK jeans grip Irina in a way that I'd like to. She looks 22 and magazine-perfect. This immediately endears me to her.

We exchange greetings that are cool, reserved, and professional.

As I walk into the condo, I admire the beautiful hardwoods, the high ceilings, and the blown-up versions of Irina's editorials as wallpaper.

I'm approached by a Jewish guy, probably around 25, wearing a navy blue NYPD hoodie and black shorts. He has a glowing energy to him. Empathetic eyes, a muss of curly hair, and a five o'clock shadow are the first features I notice beyond his clothes and aura. The man instantly starts talking to me like I've shown up to buy his gently used Honda. "Find the place okay? Not bad, huh? Thanks for keeping big bro at home. Great guy, but... evil. Just kidding." He pats me on the shoulder of my leather jacket, then continues, "But he definitely seems like the evil brother. I can say that because I'm dating the evil sister in a family."

I'm charmed by this man's rapid-fire delivery that peaks with perfect comic timing. He shakes my hand and gives that respectful frown that men give each other when they don't have a reason to hate each other, but also aren't thrilled that this introduction has to happen in their home.

The man then gives James an aggressive stare. No hand is extended.

James backs down and looks to Irina for help.

"This is Regis," Irina says, in her slight Brazilian accent that becomes less detectable every year.

"Is Regis your agent?" James asks.

"Nope," Irina says.

"Then why's he here for our meeting?" is James' next question.

Regis starts to respond, "Because I'm-"

"-Regis lives with me. He's my boyfriend," Irina says, making it clear that Regis will not have to qualify himself in his own home.

"Regis... interesting name. Do you have a nickname? How about Reeg?" James asks, instigating. James has been challenged, and instead of backing down and sticking to the plan he made me agree to, he's acting like a stubborn asshole. Suddenly, I believe that James and I might learn to get along because we have a mutual hatred of being "taught a lesson."

I'm forced into the role that James adopts in Michael's office, and I attempt to cool things down by saying, "We're not negotiating a man's nickname here."

"You don't like Reeg?" James asks me.

"Reeg is like what you call your Middle Eastern friend because you can't pronounce his real name," Irina says, and I realize that she's enjoying watching James fuck around with her boyfriend.

"I don't even have a Middle Eastern friend," Regis responds, almost confused.

"That's because you *are* the Middle Eastern friend, Reeg," Irina says, giggling, then she glides over and provides some consoling contact that heals her boyfriend instantly.

"I was born in Virginia," Regis says, sliding out of Irina's grasp, but smiling at this game because it won him affection from a woman that any man would die to be pressed against for a single moment.

"That's such a Reeg thing to say. Your accent is barely detectable," Irina continues, her own accent barely detectable.

I point to the bottle in James' hand, so that our hosts see he has a gift- a peace offering- a way to take the edge off.

"I brought red wine," James mentions, visibly satisfied that "Reeg" has been instituted, and Irina ran with his game.

Regis snatches the bottle out of James' hands because he won't allow the enemy to give his girlfriend wine. "I'll get some glasses," Regis says, then smiles at James for a lingering moment. When James was Jimmy, he didn't wear glasses. Regis clearly wanted Clark Kent to be aware that no one is believing his "disguise."

Irina looks at Regis, then at James. Purring, she asks, "Did you two used to fuck or something?"

"I'm going to get some glasses, then I'll refresh your memory about how we know this guy," Regis says.

James immediately looks down at the hardwoods, his hat hiding his shame.

Irina leads us over to a steel table that looks like something out of a morgue. The table, and its corresponding chairs, seem almost medical, but their pointed edges provide a stationary danger.

"If we fold up the leaf and push in all the chairs, the table turns into a monolith," Irina tells me, a hint that she might have seen the backdrop to my runway collection.

"How 2001," James says, sitting down at the table.

"Inappropriate," Irina says, pointing at James, "I might be Brazilian, but I wouldn't bring a piece of the towers into my condo in some ironic re-purposing."

"I mean like the movie," James says.

Irina gasps, "The one with Nicolas Cage or the one with Robert Pattinson where it zooms out and you're like 'Oh shit, his dad's office is in the towers?' Spoiler alert."

"The Kubrick movie," James responds, uncomfortable.

I quickly take a seat and interrupt the conversation. "I just want to put your fears at ease-" I start to say, and Irina points at me, "-you don't apologize for that. Don't," she demands.

I nod appreciatively at this. I already feel as though my connection and collaboration with Irina will be rich. She's not a dumb model, nor is she merely an apathetic hanger for my clothes. She'll be involved in the creation of this line in a way that I'm open to, because seeking the assistance and assurance of gifted women, like Lux or Karen, has done more for my career than any investor or fashion editor has.

Regis reenters the room with the wine already poured into four glasses. It took him some time because he had to find a tray- in this case- a fashion magazine. By its thickness and the date on the spine, I know why he chose this magazine as a tray.

Carefully, Regis lowers the balanced glasses onto the table. I reach past James, claiming my wine. I decide I'll start drinking, even though it's barely lunchtime.

Carefully, Regis lowers the balanced glasses onto the table. I reach past James, claiming my wine. I decide I'll start drinking, even though it's barely lunchtime. Before I take my first sip, I notice James glancing down, through the jungle of stems, to the September issue that Regis has used as a tray. James' eyes dart up, then watch as the calculating sommelier sits next to the cover girl.

Regis picks up a glass of wine, further revealing the cover. The iconic image is of Irina, wearing a sleeveless red satin V-neck gown, holding a gun to the head of a female model (ID unknown) who has a black bag tied around her head. The model wearing the bag is also wearing a schoolgirl outfit. The bold typeface across the bottom of the cover, "America's Gun Problem," wraps up the entire concept and still gives me chills, even now. When I first cracked open my copy of this hefty magazine, the article that accompanied the cover did nothing to move me. It was an unnecessary appendage; the article simply existed because a very good photographer and a very good model wanted to create an image that got people talking. This is another problem with the fashion industry- the people who have something to say should be able to speak through their medium, and that should be the final word. The entire haymaker punch happened on the cover of the magazine, while everything inside was just tough talk. How boring is the bark *after* the bite.

This cover was brought to the table as a reminder of what happened behind the scenes at this shoot. This picture of Irina- unquestionably one of the most powerful images she's ever been a part of- almost never made it to print. A paparazzi leak of the shoot, orchestrated by Jimmy Pixx, nearly caused the cover to be pulled. James' grainy photos were combined with the headline that Irina was "sexualizing and trivializing violence." Parents argued that this cover would create *Handgun Chic* in the way Kate Moss created *Heroin Chic*.

If I was a piece of shit pap, I would argue that the leak made the picture even more controversial and cemented the mag's status as the "must-own" fashion issue of the decade. If I was any other photographer besides James, I would argue that a truly iconic moment was partially unveiled, in low resolution, like someone took a picture of The Mona Lisa before da Vinci was finished with the portrait, then the grainy picture was printed on postcards that were sent to every gallery in the world.

On a professional level, it's nearly impossible to defend James' actions, and this- again- makes me feel a connection to him. We're two men who have committed a series of mistakes that not only defy logic, but also challenge the basic standards of human conduct.

Irina removes her glass from the magazine, and Regis says, "Cheers," merely because it puts the focus on James.

When James removes his wine glass, the controversial cover is fully revealed.

We all bring our drinks together with a soft clink.

I look to Irina through the gauntlet of glasses, and she's smiling. It's now clear to me that she's always been aware of James' identity. We were invited to Irina's condo as a test. I know that our actions today will dictate how she views us for the remainder of this collection.

"He fucked your cover," Regis says, casually.

"Reeg," James grits, despite the fact that the magazine is sitting on the table, and we've all taken note of it.

Irina asks, "Why did you do that, James?" and I immediately realize that she's mimicking my intense stare as she puts James in a trance that he doesn't dare break by angling his hat. This is her way of letting me know that she's also researched me; she didn't blindly fall into any of this. The next time I execute my stare, I'll be channeling what I learned from seeing Irina do it.

Studying Irina is always exciting because I don't need anything more than what she's presenting me with. Her expressions are fireworks- all of them beautiful to watch- none of them regularly spaced. I can't look away because I'm afraid of what I'll miss.

"It was my job to take those pictures," James says, then he clears his throat.

Irina's finger slams down onto the masked model, growling, "And this was my job."

James finally regains his motor skills and lowers the brim of his Yankees cap.

"Care to hazard a guess on whose job was more important on this day?" Irina asks.

James' brim is too low, so his hand scuttles across the steel table, searching for his wine glass.

"How much money did you get to almost ruin one of the greatest moments of my career?" Irina asks.

James slowly pushes his brim up with his pointer finger, then mumbles, "One thousand dollars."

"Regis is going to provide you with a bill for my fee. I hope Michael is paying you well, because what I get paid to be photographed is a lot more than what you got paid for my picture," Irina, the businesswoman, says.

"I just want you to know..." James raises his throaty voice, trying to prove something. "...I'm going to collaborate with you on this collection, and I'm going to shoot you like no one ever has before. I've photographed everyone, but *you* are my only focus," he promises Irina.

Irina laughs. She puts her hand over her mouth. She apologizes, then she laughs a little more.

"Does that reaction mean you don't have faith in me?" James asks.

Irina continues to smile and her expression's meaning is clear.

"Okay, but seriously, do you like my art?" James asks.

"It's not art to take a picture of someone as they accidentally flash their pussy," Regis responds.

"*Accidentally*," James repeats with a scoff.

"Ah, yes. Blame the girl," Irina says.

James looks to me for help, but I'm smiling at it all, entertained.

"I'm not blaming anyone because nothing bad happened," James says, then adds, "And you're wrong. My photography work for the blogs *is* art. Haven't you ever seen- I don't know- a painter, or an art... person. I mean, yeah all of them starved to death or whatever, but there are movies about painters, and in those movies, the painters will paint naked girls. For example, remember Jack?"

"Jack?" I ask.

"In Titanic. He was a painter or sketcher or something. Maybe he was... a... charcoaler?" James stumbles, his point becoming Titanicesque.

"Of course, Jack from Titanic. May he rest in peace," I respond.

"You wouldn't say Jack from Titanic's work isn't art. You would never question Jack from Titanic," James tells Irina. "And what I do is no different."

Regis begins his rebuttal, "The girl that Jack from Titanic was painting-"

"-Rose," James interrupts

"Right," Regis says, "Rose posed for that picture. Remember? She wanted Leo-"

"-Jack," James corrects.

"Right," Regis responds, shaking his head, "Rose wanted Jack to draw her like one of his French girls."

"Well, yeah, in that situation. I mean, they were trapped on the boat. Have you ever been on a cruise? Between the bad comedians and the excursions, it's... I digress. The point I'm making is that there's a chance maybe all of these great painters only briefly saw a nude girl, then they kept the image in their spank-bank and accessed it when it was time to paint."

"You're an adult male who just used the term spank-bank," Regis points out.

"I don't get what your problem is, Reeg. I used the term correctly."

"There is no correct way for an adult to say spank-bank," Irina offers.

"Sounds like a certain model's spank-bank has been foreclosing on some bone-loans," James says to Irina.

"You might be the dumbest person I've ever worked with," Irina says, a small amount of respect dotting the statement.

"You work with other models," James says.

"Precisely," Irina responds.

A sly smile gets passed around the table, until everyone wears it, besides James.

"We should have invited the sinister one," Regis says, looking at me, "This one is boring."

"I'm just observing," I say.

"Observing what?" Regis asks.

"Our dynamic," I respond.

"And how would you describe our dynamic?" Irina asks me.

"We're all so fucked up that this might actually work," I marvel.

THE DINNER

As soon as I step inside the house on Scotland Road, I'm struck by the smell of food.

I find Isabella hunching over the stove in the kitchen. She's wearing the same basketball shorts and gray T-shirt she had on at her old apartment. On the counter are assorted bags- most of them appear to contain boxes of tea and bottles of Diet Coke. I notice the open package of Asian noodles on the island, then I try to memorize everything Isabella bought herself, so I can buy the same items the next time I go grocery shopping. I'm confused about how, without a car, Cassie and I went shopping. Groceries seemed to just appear in the house. Maybe we had them delivered? I have to assume that Cassie went and got them when I was with Karen, hatching our grand plan to design clothes that would cause the world to change out of their cardigans.

"Usually, when you abduct a girl, you at least chain her to the bed or something," Isabella says, not turning to face me.

"Good point, did you pick up any chains at the grocery store?" I ask, sitting down at a small black table that's pressed against the wall to my left. I don't sit at the island counter because it reminds me of when my mother would cook for me, and I would sit at the counter and annoy her. I don't want to be Isabella's father, nor do I want her to be my mother.

I used to sit at this black table when Cassie would cook for me, but the event was so infrequent that the association is a fuzzy memory.

"No chains. I'm not going to abduct myself," Isabella says, turning off the burner.

"I think you did abduct yourself, in a way," I respond.

"I moved to the East Coast after one booking," Isabella acknowledges, then pouts. I'm not sure what this gesture is supposed to indicate. After sitting with Irina, whose face carefully instructed me as to how I should feel, Isabella's expressions require me to pay attention. In case her frown was to portray disappointment, I remind her, "The designer who booked you will be providing you with a career."

"The designer who booked me is dangerous when it comes to careers," Isabella says, lifting the pot from the stove, then pouring out the extra water into the sink.

"People forget that shit," I say, "The equation is all about time."

"Some people work not to forget," Isabella tells me, and I fear that The Boy and The Girl visited her last night when she left her room for a glass of water.

I close my eyes.

"Sometimes it might be easier to forget, but if you do that, you're setting yourself up for the same pain," Isabella reminds me.

I keep my eyes shut.

"And on the flip-side, not forgetting will keep alive the potential for a second chance. Without remembering why someone is amazing, you might just write them off. You might never speak to them again."

"You know how I am with nostalgia," I say.

"You're trying to manipulate the memory. That's something else. That's scarier," Isabella says.

I nod at this, and when I open my eyes I find that, instead of sitting at the island, Isabella chose to sit at the little table with me. She opens a package of chopsticks and stirs her noodles with them. I'm not sure where she got the chopsticks, and I get embarrassed that she might have assumed my general lack of preparedness extended to silverware.

I need to make sure that Isabella- now outside of New York- is given reasons to return to the city, to learn it, and to love it in a way that every teenage girl is capable of. "Is Blend... treating you how you want to be treated?" I ask.

"You know how we were talking about abducting girls?" Isabella responds, spinning her noodles. I nod. "Well, what's the opposite being abducted?" she asks me, then takes a bite of her dinner without breaking eye contact.

Lightly, I say, "Orphaned. The opposite of abducted is orphaned."

"They're going to orphan me," Isabella says, definitively.

"They can't," I respond, confident in my pact with Anne.

"Really? They can't abandon me? Am I in Milan right now, Andrew? Gee. Milan sure looks like the suburbs of New Jersey. They didn't mention that in the brochure."

"You're new. People need to digest your look bec-"

"-because I'm ugly," Isabella says, with a laugh devoid of joy.

"Bullshit," I respond.

"Then tell me, what's going on with me? I guess I have such 'unique features?' I guess I have such a 'striking face?' I guess I'm 'androgynous, yet alluring' to people? Everyone who meets me finds a way to say that when they look at me, they have no idea what the fuck is going on."

"You're intriguing," I say, explaining why people keep looking. It's a trait that not many girls have, but when they do possess it, it's impossible to describe and incredible to feel.

"You too can be an overgrown girl with no discernible hairstyle if you eat noodles every day and simply don't seek out others, at all, ever," Isabella says, selling what she considers herself to be.

"You don't get it," I say, then add, "You will. They will. Then you'll be in Milan."

"And where will you be?" Isabella asks.

"Hopefully backstage," I say, and with that, I wish Isabella a good night, then head upstairs.

In my room, I don't sketch, but I feel my inspirations colliding. I know that it will only be a matter of time before this collection pours out of me in 50 sketches.

I lay in bed and try to organize everything that's happened since I destroyed my career, again. Before I can get the influences situated and my body comfortable, I hear the heavy steps of too-big feet. Feet perfect for the size I design shoes in.

The footsteps are different, but not totally dissimilar to thumps The Girl's feet make.

The footsteps remind me of what I was put here to do- have girls walk for me.

Teetering on the edge of sleep, the moment feels unreliable. I pretend to be asleep because I don't want to scare my visitor away.

I don't know what the question was that brought her to the bedroom, in the same way I don't know what's convincing her to stay.

I feel her watching me. She's appeared, as she always does, like an otherworldly being. When I sneak a glance, I see that she has a bright light in her hand, a cell phone. She doesn't need my charger- we have different phones. She doesn't need medical attention because she isn't whimpering or panicked. What she needs seems to be what I need, and as I feel her settle onto the other side of the bed then burrow under the covers, I begin to fight sleep tooth and nail, but the comfort surpasses my effort and I drift off.

THE STUDENTS

We never fuck because she doesn't want to.

We never kiss because she doesn't want to.

We never touch because she doesn't want to.

We never go to bed together, but every morning I wake up with her next to me.

"Do you know that Cassandra has a topless bust of herself in the picture room?" Isabella asks me.

This statement makes me sit up.

The cold, early October air pushes the drapes into the room like they're reaching for the bed sheets.

I smile when I see Isabella's happily parted lips- still red, even without lipstick. It's clear Isabella has taken a perverse pleasure in her discovery.

"How's her bust look? Maybe we can move it in here," I say, my eyes squinting from the morning sun pouring into the room.

"Ew. Are you turned on by Cassandra's sculpture?" Isabella asks.

"I'm not sure. Think you can put in a good word for me?"

"You're weird. It's weird. I don't like it. I think it's staring at me," Isabella tells me, and I begin to wonder if she's just making an excuse for why she sneaks into my bed after I fall asleep.

"Well, are you doing anything bizarre in that room that the Cassie statue has to be worried about?" I ask, presenting a mock-accusation.

"No. Just changing."

"And?"

"That's it," Isabella says.

"Doesn't seem so bad. Cassie has seen tons of beautiful models change; I'm sure her sculpture is just as professional about it."

"She hasn't seen a girl changing in her house with her ex," Isabella says, then quickly corrects, "Those are two mutually exclusive events- the changing, then the... you know."

"I know," I say quietly.

Her house is how the house on Scotland Road remains. Isabella views me exactly how she views herself- a guest within these walls- someone just passing through. I tried to plant roots here once, and I'm not searching for a second chance now. The Girl and The Boy are that second chance, and I know how it will end for them.

I get up from the bed and walk over to the door that leads out to the balcony. I've been neglecting my favorite feature of the house, but today, I decide to step outside.

I squint up at the sun, then watch the clouds move like gridlocked New York City traffic.

Inside the room, I hear Isabella's bare feet thump in the direction of the hallway. She doesn't join me on the balcony.

It's morning, a time when we go about our responsibilities, separately.

I'm unable to motivate myself to sketch because I know what I'll sketch. I'm unable to motivate myself to go into the office because I don't want to be shackled with the rules that I know are coming, and this mentality allows me to easily rationalize my continued inaction.

There's no chair on the porch so I sit on the ground, and look out at the neighborhood. No one's outside, despite the nice weather, so I'm alone- a reality I once worked for, but now don't enjoy. I regret leaving the bed, but I know that my flight prevented an argument. Isabella's choice of words got to me, but calling her out on what she said would make me no better than the fashion bloggers who scrutinize every word or design, so I embrace the morning and take pride in the fact that I'm doing things the right way this time.

My body begins demanding coffee before any major task is attempted, so I stand up and I'm about to return back inside, when a white van pulls into the driveway. The vehicle doesn't turn around- instead, it parks. I watch the driver's side door until it opens and a heavily tattooed, well-built guy gets out of the vehicle. He checks his phone, looks at the house, then looks back down at the phone. I'm about to let the guy know that he has the wrong place, when, under me, I hear the front door open. Moments later, I watch Isabella approach the van. She tells the guy something, then they move to the side of the house, out of my sight line.

I immediately dart back inside and try to figure out how I'm going to confront this secret meeting.

My heart is racing as I make my way through the house.

When I burst out of the side door, Isabella looks at me, then her gap makes an appearance, framed by a nervous red smile.

"I'll pay for it, don't worry," Isabella says to me.

"Pay for what?" I ask with urgency.

"You- Cassandra- we- have no internet. It's not acceptable. I called this guy and convinced him to do a Sunday install. They never do Sundays. Don't send him away because we've already ruined his weekend so we might as well get internet," she says.

"Thanks for doing that," I respond, while quietly marveling at the step Isabella took, all by herself, to make a permanent connection in this home. I had meant to get the internet set up, but something was always happening- another task always demanded immediate attention. With two cell phones, I was able to limp along without hopping on my laptop. There was always a reason why I couldn't call the cable company and deal with that headache.

"I'll pay for it," Isabella repeats, almost like she's expecting a fight.

"You don't have to do that," I respond.

"I'm bribing this guy with the hundred dollars you gave me that first morning, so I should cover a couple of months, since you bankrolled the install," she says.

I marvel at a girl who got on the phone, then, off the books, got this very undedicated looking guy to take time out of his weekend to install our internet. I get a little annoyed with Isabella because she doesn't seem to have the same drive for her career that she has for WiFi. It would be much less effort for her to pursue modeling jobs, and the payoff for her hard work would be even better than high-speed internet.

The cable guy is staring at both of us, questioning what's happening here, and my eyes go wide.

"The hundred dollars was for groceries... I gave her money... for groceries," I say, desperate to explain this situation. For the first time, I feel dirty about Isabella staying in the house. It's the type of embarrassment I'd feel if someone looked at my search history. With this parallel drawn, I let the guy get to work. I choose to focus on the fact that this mystery guest will provide relief and internet to both myself and Isabella. This is a confirmation of her comfort here- it presents a possibility of permanence for the season.

Isabella and I spend our Sunday talking about all the stuff we're going to show each other once the cable guy has connected us to the world. I try to reinforce the success Isabella achieved when she took control of the situation, in hopes that she will continue to be proactive in her life. With Lux, I want her all to myself. With Isabella, I want the entire world to appreciate her like I do. I don't know why there's a fundamental difference in my treatment of these two remarkable girls, but to seek equality now would complicate things more than I already have.

After the cable guy leaves, a film festival begins, and we watch LL Cool J battle Michael Myers in *Halloween H20*, then follow it up with a miscast movie called *The Listeners*.

As dusk approaches, I find out a possible source of Isabella's laziness when it comes to pursuing work.

Cassie's giant LCD TV in the living room begins to play a rerun of *Tristan's Landing*, and Isabella lies across the sofa, her MacBook at her side, her long legs stretching across the red cushions.

"Do you know anyone who smokes?" Isabella asks me.

"This feels like a trap," and I say, "Everyone I know smokes. Literally everyone."

"No. I mean pot. I need pot. Sitting around the house is my thing, but I need my resources," Isabella tells me.

"Your resources being?"

"Internet. Pot. Noodles. A cup. A bowl," she lists.

"Well, South Orange *is* a college town," I point out.

"Okay. Let's go," Isabella responds, closing her MacBook.

"I'm not going with you onto a college campus so you can buy pot," I say.

"Come on! Lazy Sunday!" she cheers.

"Exactly, being lazy doesn't usually involve walking a quarter mile."

"A quarter mile walk is the lazy man's marathon," Isabella tells me. "It'll be good for you to get your marathon out of the way early in the month!"

"Yes. It's a marathon. I'll stay here and work, and you can go get the weed."

"I don't know where the college is," Isabella says, employing a strategic pout.

"Walk out the side door. Walk to the road. Make a right. Once you hit South Orange Ave, take a left onto South Orange Ave. Walk on South Orange Ave until someone offers you pot. On the off-chance you make it to the college before this offer is made, walk to the far gate until you'll see a little guard house. On the off chance the security guard is out of pot, go onto campus."

"That's like 60 directions, what if I have to walk home high? It'll be dark. We live in New Jersey," Isabella strings together hypothetical scenarios that I find difficulty in viewing as legitimate concerns.

When I realize that I'll end up spending my afternoon alone, with my door locked, watching portions of at least 20 different clips on XVIDEOS, I decide that maybe a walk is the healthier alternative. I get up and sigh, "Come on."

"We're going to go buy pot?" Isabella asks, excited.

"You are. I'm going for a walk," I say.

I throw on my leather Saint Laurent jacket and a pair of Ray-Bans even though the sun is setting. I leave the house, while Isabella- in black jeans and a non-designer jean jacket- hurries behind me.

I follow my own directions to the university, while Isabella tells me about the calls she's had with Anne- the sneaker job she turned down because it was "too sporty"/ The lookbook that she had no interest in because of the pervy photographer shooting it/ The Noxzema commercial she didn't audition for because she felt like it was "too far from fashion." I want Isabella to work, but I know that she's being smart. She's not an amateur in this industry, despite her amateur status. She's studied the careers of girls based on their *TFS* threads and *models.com* timelines. Isabella should establish herself in the fashion industry, *then* pursue the commercial stuff. Noxzema girl turned haute couture runway model is not a common story.

Having an easy discussion, while enjoying the mild fall weather, makes me admit that Isabella was right, this *is a* nice way to spend a lazy Sunday.

We walk together, but the closer we get to campus, the more I notice Isabella's youth. She could be a student; I could be a professor. Those who can't do, teach. Those who can't teach, either build an empire with a wall of hype and safe collections, or falter in an industry that doesn't really care if they can "do," when they chose to "do" it with a steady rotation of white models.

On campus, Isabella's crippling shyness makes it my responsibility to be the random old creepy guy asking children if they have drugs to sell. Unwilling to assume this role, I say, "I'll be at mass."

"Seriously?" Isabella asks, like I had just revealed I'm a consultant paid by her parents to get her onto the campus of a four-year college, and the final step of the plan was now complete.

"I'm going to go to mass. The 6 PM started four minutes ago," I say, eying the brownstone church to our left.

"You don't go to church," Isabella tells me.

"And where did you receive that information from? Wikipedia?" I ask slyly.

"I hope God strikes you down before you can walk in there," Isabella says, frustrated at herself- at her shyness- at my abandonment- at the faith I have in her to accomplish this task without me.

"So you believe in God? Would you like to join me?" I ask.

"If God carries out my lightning bolt wish, I'll go to church," Isabella tells me, shooting daggers at me with her eyes.

"We'll just have to see," I say, then I begin walking toward the chapel.

I enter the church, bless myself with holy water, then thank the Lord for keeping me lightning bolt free on my travels. My eyes run down the rows of pews filled nearly to capacity with students so happy to be in school with their friends that they'll accept any event that allows them to spend time together. The electric possibility of love seems to connect this campus in a way that wasn't present the last time I attended mass here, years ago. I see that not only has the facade of the chapel has been repointed and cleaned, but the inside has also been remodeled. I walk along the left edge of the church, close to the brown wooden pews. The mural under the sanctuary arch has been touched up, brighter. The ceilings have been repainted- gold leaf accents have been added on the wood trusses and they resemble arrows, alternating between pointing up and down. I don't review the possible meaning behind this choice. I allow none of what I see to feel like a message because I'm afraid of what I'm being told.

I find an open seat toward the front of the congregation, next to a middle-aged black woman. She's also alone and I feel relieved that I'm not sitting at the end of a row of perfect teens.

In the sanctuary, the Virgin Mary stands, arms open, as an assembly of angels play trumpets and burn incense around her. Isabella arrived on campus for weed, I arrived for incense.

Like the vastly different fashions the students now wear- like the new details of the church- the simple prayers I grew up reciting have also been revised. Entire phrases have been changed out and new language has been introduced. In the time I've been alive, even the basic prayers of the church have changed, and I haven't. Information divined from God is more malleable than I am. I'm hushed about everything because I don't know where the new additions will come in. Reciting the old words will expose me as a man who has run from his spiritual duty for a very long time. I have to mumble through the service, and I imagine Isabella, outside, mumbling in the same way, as she tries to find the words to a chant that the rest of the students are spitting out effortlessly. I wish she was here with me. She makes it easier to believe in Him, even when she doesn't believe.

I follow along exactly with what the black woman next to me is doing. I make sure that my glances are casual and warm instead of exuding the usual intensity I'm guilty of.

I fumble along until we reach the sermon regarding Luke 14. The parable of the wedding feast is discussed in a sing-songy manner by the priest.

I try not to draw any parallels to what I hear, but they're too clear.

"For everyone who exalts himself will be humbled, and he who humbles himself will be exalted," is how the parable ends, and I realize that these are not just words on a really old piece of paper.

After mass, I find Isabella sitting on a bench on the green, waiting for me to return.

"Did you get what you were looking for?" I ask her.

Isabella looks up from her phone, nods, then asks, "Did you?"

THE RULES

It's Monday morning, and I'm ready to go. I'm hopped up on a pumpkin spice latte that, unprovoked, Intern Jessica brought me. When I asked her how she knew exactly what I needed today, she told me, "Everyone likes pumpkin spice lattes."

The caffeine jolt carries Intern Jessica, myself, James, and Karen to the space that Michael is going to lease for us.

Sitting on 42nd street, the workspace begins as a hallway about as thick and long as a standard fashion runway. There are three perfectly square rooms to the left, and these separate rooms mean that the entire collection won't appear in front of me at all once.

When I was doing work for a couple of pop stars' lines, the space I was designing in was an old movie sound stage. Working in this giant, freeing box increased my affection for open spaces, despite the fact that a leak in the roof meant having to re-dye and blow dry a garment that took weeks to ready. When I arrived in New York, the space that the Chinese provided for me was perfection- a stretching, open, single level loft. It was a jungle of steel beams, with no walls except for the exterior, thus making it my favorite of all the locations I've worked in.

I turn to Intern Jessica, and explain, "I need an army of mannequins. I'll quit if I don't get my mannequins. I require them. This is non-negotiable."

"Fascinating," James murmurs, walking behind us, "Andrew Lorrie has a mannequin clause in his contract. How Jacksonesque."

"We can get a couple of mannequins, but most of the pieces should stay on hangers. We're going to review everything separately," Karen tells me.

"My last collection, you told me, wasn't an 'experience.' How are we going to figure out if what we're making is an 'experience' when we have to play a game of 'Clue' just to find specific pieces of the collection?" I ask.

"It was Miss Scarlett wearing the pepperpot-revolver-inspired piece in the sewing room," James says, pleased with how quickly he assembled this joke.

All three of us stop walking and look back at James.

"That was a 'Clue' joke," James clarifies, and we all nod.

Somehow not yet immune to moments like these, James flicks the brim of his Yankees cap, then pushes past us, attempting an escape in the wrong direction.

Karen, undeterred, follows James and explains in her monotone way, "What you boys have to understand is that there's a uniform proven structure that we'll need to follow now that we're working under someone else. Both of you had a lot of freedom at your old jobs."

I follow close behind Karen, and remind her, "All I've done these past few years is work under someone else."

"No. You haven't. You've done whatever you wanted to, then some airhead millionaire would make six notes on your collection after a seven-minute long meeting. You'd disregard the notes, she'd forget she made them, then the collection would hit the runway two months later," Karen says. Despite presenting a simplification of the situation, Karen is essentially correct in her recap.

"We always showed on time," I say, following the team into the room at the end of the hallway.

"Only after I would wrestle with half of Italy," Karen reminds me. "It made it to the runway after multiple last-second conference calls and next-day shipping costs that practically matched the retail price of the garments."

"Set your mannequins up in the hallway," James interrupts the argument.

Intern Jessica looks shocked. She writes this idea down.

I glance at James, and he attempts an uneasy smile, wondering if he just *Clue*'d himself again. "That's actually good," I say, making my way to the door. I review the long hallway. Once I'm satisfied, I reenter the room, calm, and when I stand next to James, his smile finally gains a relative stability.

"Okay. Go. Give me the rules," I prompt Karen.

She pauses a moment, knowing I'm going to ridicule whatever she tells me.

Karen is a person who always does her job, so despite already knowing how this ends, she goes through the requirements, "First, I'm going to need a mood board."

"Then, uh, make one," I say, itching my nose.

"You're going to be bound to the mood board," she tells me.

"No one is bound to the mood board. Come on Karen," I say, feeling like I stepped into a F.I.T. class.

"How are we going to get this collection to be cohesive if you won't do the things that'll make that happen?"

"Trust me?" I ask in a voice that comes out almost too cutesy.

"No. We need more than just your sketches this time. When you sketch, it comes from all over the place, and the sketches are so damn good that we end up going with them, but I need to reign you in. This is ready-to-wear," Karen reminds me.

I turn to Intern Jessica, and say, "I need you to send me a .zip file with all the designs from Michael's past RTW collections."

I turn to Karen, "That's not to say we're going to use the past pieces as the benchmark. I just need a sample of where we'll be coming from."

I turn back to Intern Jessica, "It's important you get the entire collection. Not the stuff from *style.com*. There's got to be more detailed pictures of those clothes."

I turn to Karen, "I'm going to pay attention to what's been done because, that way, at least I don't have to worry about getting my ass sued by some 'designer' from fucking Etsy that's convinced I stole her stuff. I'm going to incorporate items that Michael- or his design team- almost got right."

I turn to Intern Jessica, "Get the samples from the archive. I'll review them, then I'll design this collection in a way that channels M.Lorrie's spirit."

I turn to James, "Photograph this entire space, then request some petty cash so we can buy a sledgehammer."

"I can get you a sledgehammer," Intern Jessica says, like it's a pumpkin spice latte.

"Don't get him a sledgehammer," Karen warns Intern Jessica.

"It's gonna be a lot more work to take these walls down without one," I say.

THE TOUR

"Finished @ Blend. Meet me?" reads the text from Isabella that arrives as I'm watching James flip through his phone. He's looking for a picture that he took a couple of years back. This single photograph will be his inspiration for the future pictures he's going to take for M.Lorrie. I hate him for wasting my time, yet I can't help but suspect that once he heard I want to pull pieces from the M.Lorrie archive, he decided on pulling some of his own archived items. This feels like the flattery one might feel when they notice that they're being copied by their little brother, then I remember how all of this started and that idea is immediately buried- its existence, a cancer.

"Did you have anything else planned for today?" I ask Karen gently, while she shakes her head at poor baffled James.

"Jessica, Andrew will need the archive photos in the next three days," Karen says, then she tells me, "You're free to go."

I look to James, to see if he wants to leave too, but his focus on his phone is intense, and I assume he doesn't even notice I'm still here.

The moment I turn to escape, James asks, "Is your work phone on right now?"

"Yeah. Why?" I respond, keeping my distance.

"Show it to me," he demands, putting his own phone in his pocket.

I go from looking at James, to glaring at James.

He walks up to me and holds out his hand.

I take out my work phone, then give it to him, somewhat worried that he'll resume his google image search with it, and I'll be forced to stay.

James presses on the side of my phone, then Isabella's face appears on the lock screen- a picture I capped from the live stream because anytime I try to take shots of Isabella with the s1000, she shies away and lovingly tells me to, "Fuck off with that camera."

James looks at the picture, then up at me. "She one of our options?" he asks.

I take back my phone, and I say, "Not an option. A must."

James nods once at this, then lowers his head so his hat shields his eyes.

The conversation seems to be over, so I walk out of the building, to an unfamiliar part of 42nd street, and I text Isabella, "Where are u? I'll come get u."

I don't have a car available to me like my brother does, but I do have a desperate need to find Isabella, so one of the thousand yellow taxis that buzz around this city will become mine for the afternoon. I don't care about the cost, I want to take Isabella wherever will make her happy. I want her to fall in love-with the city.

"I'm under an awning," Isabella texts back, the response coming off as very "model."

"The awning in front of Blend?" I send to her.

"Yeah. That one," appears on my screen.

"I'll be there in 15," I text, then immediately hail a cab.

Once inside, I watch the cab's TV as it plays an episode of a talk show featuring Kelly Ripa and a football player interviewing a sleepy looking actress.

I realize that Isabella didn't make it past the Blend awning without texting me for help. It feels good to come to her rescue, but I also realize that I need to teach this girl the city. If she's going to get to her go-sees on time, she needs to at least have some idea of where to walk after the awning ends.

I lean forward in my seat, and ask the cabby, "If you could give advice to someone who's new to the city, what would you tell them?"

"Take cab often," the cabby says in broken English, and I can't fault him for his entrepreneurial spirit.

We pull up to the Blend building- the ride taking twice as long as it should have- but I still promise the cabby, "I'll give you a good tip," so that he'll continue to be our driver for the afternoon.

Isabella, in black heels, black jeans, and a black tank top, struts the length of the awning like it's a runway. Being a model is built into Isabella's DNA; even if she never had the opportunity to slip on designer clothes, I'm positive she'd still influence the way her peers dress. She's ahead of the curve. She already has the blue velvet dress and access to the closet of one of the world's biggest supermodels. Isabella went from having nothing to wear, to having everything only a hanger away.

The moment Isabella gets in the cab, she asks me, "So, what should I see?"

I'm not sure how she knew that I was anxious to teach her about the city, but I love that we don't flee back to the comfortable house on Scotland Road and instead choose to enjoy this perfect October afternoon.

"I generally take the models to Lincoln Center or Bryant Park," I say.

"Why haven't you taken me there, then?" Isabella asks, not offended, but instead curious, and a little insecure.

"Because Bryant Park feels European. I take the girls there because they're..."

"Exotic. European. And I'm a Cali girl," Isabella says, as though this is a tainted distinction. As though "Cali girl" is a low-grade beef patty.

The cabby waits, the meter runs.

"Which is your favorite?" Isabella asks, looking out the window, back up at the Blend building.

"My favorite what?"

"Building," she says.

"The Chrysler Building," I answer instantly.

The cabby interprets this as me giving him a destination. The car is put in drive.

"We're going to go in the Chrysler Building," Isabella informs me.

"Then what?" I ask.

"That's not how you should react when someone suggests you visit your favorite building," she responds.

This is an uncharacteristic curiosity from Isabella. She doesn't typically make decisions on a whim. She doesn't fly where the wind takes her. She might not even know that the Chrysler Building is in New York. This should bother me, but it doesn't- it makes me like her more. It makes me want to go to the Chrysler Building with her, so I can show her one of the best monuments this city has.

"You're absolutely right," I say, as a general statement.

"I know," Isabella responds, then wipes a hair out of her mouth. I'm seeing flashes of confidence in this shy girl and it spurs excitement and vitality in an old man.

"How far is the Chrys-" she starts to ask, then says, "-oh, wait. You're not so good with estimates."

"I, uh, might have undershot the traffic earlier," I say, keeping the blame on myself, because our lives hang in the balance of whatever this cabby has planned.

While we make our commute to my favorite building, Isabella watches the rest of the steel landscape, but she remains engaged with me, asking, "What were you doing when you weren't designing?"

"Rehab. Relationships. Partnerships," I list.

This pulls Isabella's eyes from the window. She stares at me, then asks, "Wait. Partnerships like..."

I squint at her, then I realize what she's hinting at, "What? Oh. No. More like, I've been... freelancing."

Immediately understanding what I've revealed, Isabella screeches, "Andrew! Who did you ghost for?"

"I can't tell you," I say. Now I'm the one looking out the window.

"Come on, Andrew! This is like finding out Truman Capote wrote To Kill a Mockingbird. This stuff is my life. History *is my life*. This is a secret history. Blogger mode, deactivated. Roommate mode, activated. Spill."

"I'm not worried about the blogger response. I'm worried about the roommate response," I say, then I start to bite my nails.

"I will burn down the Chrysler Building," Isabella threatens, and I feel her fiery gaze on me.

"Celebrity lines," I say, with shame, "When a celebrity would get a spot at some fuck awful off-the-grid fashion week, I would design the line, then the person who had the line's namesake would go on stage and rap beside a model, while commenting on the fact they, "Kill more niggas than both swimmin' and diabetes.""

"Can you not?" Isabella says, her demeanor changing.

"See? I knew it wouldn't go well," I respond without anger.

"I could do without your editorializing," she specifies.

"I could have done without the rapper's editorializing," I counter.

"I could do with some names," Isabella says, softening, becoming cute, exploiting me like she was a rapper.

THE BACKSTORY

The truth is, my "grand return" after "being away for so long" actually arrived at the end of a string of non-stop underpaid jobs designing as the "Creative Director" of various celebrity "run" lines. I always signed extensive contracts that demanded, above all else, that my participation in any given line remain totally under wraps at all times. The name and the face of the collection would receive the buzz of whatever I created.

Most of the celebrities I worked with were West Coast-based, so I was able to finally escape New York and its toxic scene. I found it far easier to keep a low profile in a place that was filled with people way more interesting than an aging fashion designer. I easily worked in secret because LA is not a fashion capital. Leaving New York freed me from a community of critics that deemed me so unfit to be near a needle that I probably couldn't even get a piercing without being attacked in writing on the internet. In LA, the discussion of cuts and construction always centers around flesh, not something that covers flesh.

I was bailed out by the entertainment industry when the fashion industry decided that I was "absolutely unacceptable." There was a new trend, which favored my skills. With the collapse of the music industry, record labels had to convert themselves into "talent factories." The blueprint was set by bigger acts, like U2 and Jay-Z, but it trickled down to the new artists simply because their fans could be easily exploited, even if they don't buy records anymore. The record companies became entertainment companies, then began to sign pop stars, socialites, hot sluts, and famous for nothing P.O.I.s to what they called 360 deals. These deals resulted in a company pimping the image of their client in every way possible. Sure, music was still a part of it, but the revenue from the Vevo views, the T-shirts, the notebooks, the concert tickets, and, finally, the fashion line were all a bigger part of it. I had to design at such a level that name models could be booked and top fashion editors would be forced to attend the show in a bid to seem "current." When we wouldn't do runway, my collections would verge into ready-to-wear territory. Most of the time, the runway show was part concert, so I would be able to work fully in the high fashion capacity I'm comfortable in. The actual line that was sold in stores was created by someone else, not me. A tug of war resulted on some projects when my style became too obvious and sunk the fantasy that some 16-year-old, lip syncing, pop-princess-in-the-making was creating beautiful clothing every moment she wasn't taking a half-nude selfie. I was asked to create more of the amazing pieces I had crafted in the past, while making it look like the celebrity client was intricately involved in the designs. Most of the time, I was able to achieve a balance by quietly convincing the namesake of the line that my ideas were their ideas. I would google the star who hired me, then I'd very loosely relate portions of my designs with things I saw in various pictures. "You were drinking water in Santa Monica once, and that inspired the wave-like texture of this piece," I would tell them, then they would say things like, "Yeah, as I was drinking that water, it, like, became part of me, and I knew that it would be used again for something other than, ya know, piss." I became a master at presenting the illusion of choice. That being said, there were some things I wouldn't budge on. I needed a big space to design, I needed my mannequins, I needed my team, and I needed my corpse brides. Mandy, an incredibly talented makeup artist, proved to be my equal when it came to these brides because, each time, she would switch the makeup enough that it was a totally different look, but I would always approve of what she did because she took the parts that I loved-the macabre/ the romance/ the history of it all- then she'd make it *now*, for that very moment. Purples would be traded for yellows. Tiny geisha lips would get Betty Booped. Mandy quietly carried out my bidding, and we all left feeling good. The company I worked with consistently kept me employed, as their temporary stars continued to have a "passion for fashion," then, mere weeks later, a "passion for domestic violence and DWI."

After I proved myself for a decade, the Chinese investors came calling. They were smart. They saw my work, they felt I did my time, and they allowed me to have my rebirth. By this point, I was exhausted. Coffee was downed to get me up in the morning. Heineken was a sleep aid. The bar nights and the coffee shop dates were my non-contractual social events. I filled myself with chemicals, merely to get through the damn day; my hands shaking- sticking anemic girls with pins during fittings. My models would march down the runway like purposeful, intense robots, and that's also how I navigated life. Eight hours of sleep was the norm until six years ago. Six hours of sleep was the norm for two years after that. Four years ago, I averaged four hours of sleep a night, except for when I'd sleep for 14 hour periods during my time off. I was catching meals in the form of Hidden Valley granola bars that could be slipped into suit pockets, pants pockets, and the flaps of design portfolios.

It was the half a pint of Chinese food that the model- fresh on a break with her girlfriend- brought to our fitting/ It was the slice of pizza I ate while walking between meetings/ It was the overpriced popcorn I crunched while catching a late show at the Arclight because I was so hopped up on coffee I couldn't sleep.

Everything was compounding, and I refused to stop, because I was afraid that if I got out of the rotation, someone who worked cheaper, with no baggage, would be designing the collection that would allow me to get all my emotions out safely.

The Chinese, unaware of any of this, swooped in and promised to let me use my own name on the line. No more hiding. It was supposed to be a relief. It was supposed to be a weight lifted, a mask removed, handcuffs sawed off. At the same time I was falling apart, I received the break that I had worked all those past collections for. To merely get through this experience of triumph and trouble, I created illusions to secure everything from collapsing. It was about the custom made and modified clothes that I created for myself, even as I dropped weight from my already frail frame. It was about the Tommy cologne that always ensured I smelled fresh. It was about the hairspray that kept me from looking disheveled, even after the windiest of commutes. If you look okay, smell okay, and aren't out committing hate crimes, people will think you're fine. You can even occasionally cry, and they'll still assume all is well, because, frankly, it had become commonplace. *FashionCut* listed "crying" in their "Trending" section with the comment, "Emotions are *in* this season."

The problem with consistently working hard is that someone will eventually take note of your dedicated work, then they'll provide you with that opportunity you always felt you were more than qualified for. By the time this happens- by the time your hard work has compounded year after year- you should be pursuing vacation, but no one can wait, no one can understand how you'd pass up your dream just to sit by a pool, so you immediately go to work, when it's the last thing you should be doing. Being offered the experience of a lifetime is a shot of adrenaline that will trick you. Your instincts will say, *slow down*, but you convince yourself that slowing down could mean death.

I know this because I watched, from afar, as Cassie went through this. She was away too long, always working 12 hour days, the stress aging her. She knew that she'd look even more run-down in the future if she kept this pace, and that would stifle her booming career. With every exhale of her cigarette, she would see the face of a younger Cassie in the smoke, then she'd watch it fade away. Later, Sienna went through this, and she ruined an opportunity she always craved. Even Irina- a superhuman woman by all accounts- took a year to just travel the US, *searching*. Irina arrived here from Brazil and achieved the American dream within a month, but she eventually cracked under the rigorous demands of fashion, and set out to discover if America offered anything *beyond* the American dream. She needed *more* if she was going to stay here. She searched across the country, and she must have found something to anchor her. Maybe she just found Regis, love, someone who "got it."

I'm jealous of Irina, because I've never allowed myself that vacation, and I look much older for it. I've never stepped away from the industry for a breath of fragrance-free air. Lux claims that I engage in self-sabotage, but if I do, it's certainly not intentional. Never once have I felt programmed with the feeling that, *I don't deserve success so I will ensure failure.* My self-sabotage was more self-neglect, being run ragged, then never mending myself. A stitch in time saves nine has a literal parallel in my industry, yet I still ignored the saying, probably because there were nine other voices all speaking to me at the same time, holding up other pieces that also required emergency stitching. My collapse was characterized by shunning social situations because I was simply too busy. Maybe that was an excuse. Maybe I was afraid that someone would detect that I was unraveling and they'd ask me to a take "some leave" while Karen stepped in and simplified everything. The pieces were always slices of my pain, and I was constantly afraid they would infect Karen if she tried to "fix" them.

The clients I found myself designing for had a blink-and-they're-gone shelf life. If I stepped away, I couldn't come back two seasons later and pick up where I left off. In two seasons, the line was always abandoned. The celebrity would predictably collapse under the same weight I was struggling to lift, so I'd always stay on. I have a need to be the one designing the line until the tombstone is carved. That completion is the most fulfilling feeling I've had pump through me. I could never be like Yves handing down my name to a worthy successor that people will tear apart. My work is the alpha and omega. I engage in the pinnacle of creation. This process gave me religion and brought me back to God. Now, every day, I work tirelessly to inch closer to Him.

THE BRUSH OFF

Isabella and I walk out of the Chrysler Building at the same time I complete the verbal wiki of my career- leaving out most of my failures, keeping in all the cautionary tales.

Isabella claims, "I knew all that," but her reaction to various key revelations hinted that she didn't.

"How do you know my secrets?" I ask, toying with her, "Did your fashion blogger friends tell you?"

"Hey! We're the most supportive and excitable demo you have!" she says, mock offended, as we dodge people who all seem to be carrying heavy bags or tiny dogs.

"You bloggers are very supportive, when I'm not offending you," I say, then add, "Which seems to be rarely."

"Listen, they'll be happy now. I'm your safety net. I'll call you a sick fuck when you misbehave, then you'll become better. I'm-"

"-you're you," I say, trying to explain that she changed my mind about fashion bloggers.

I've never met anyone as difficult and interesting, in equal measure, as Isabella.

"Exactly. Plus I'm half Mexican, so that wins you-"

"-wait. You're half Mexican?" I ask. The girl who knows everything about me tells me something I should already know.

"Yeah. Isn't that why I was cast?"

"No. You were cast because you fit with my vision."

"Well, the fashion bloggers will like this collection," she declares, moving past the compliment.

"Until one of your little queen bees picks up on my interview from the last collection and calls me out for being a racist, or a bigot, or an enemy of the misandry movement. I can't win. It's constant judgment from people with half-knowledge of virtually everything," I spit.

"Half-knowledge, huh? Bring a random collection up on your phone, and I'll tell you who designed it and what season it was," Isabella challenges me.

"I'm sure you will," I say.

"That doesn't sound like half knowledge to me."

"There are two types of fashion people influencing the industry now- the collectors and the craftsmen," I explain, dodging a group of Asian tourists that appear to be photographing Isabella like she's a skyscraper.

"Care to elaborate?" Isabella asks.

"Sure," I say, "I'll draw a parallel for you. Let's take the auto industry as an example. The collectors go on car websites to look at the latest concepts, they dealer-hop to test drive the new models, and they can name all the old classics. Same goes for the fashion world. The collectors increase the value of old models and increase the demand for new models. They're an important part of continued demand, but they could all disappear tomorrow and industry would roll on. The assets to the industry- the people who can't be replaced- are the craftsmen. You remove the craftsmen and you don't have an industry. These are the guys who are building the concepts that the collectors go crazy for. These are guys that might not know the name of every new craze rolling out, but when a classic needs to be rehabbed into something new and fresh, they're the only ones you'd trust to do it. They're the ones who get dirty."

"So, you're a craftsman and we're all just your disciples?" Isabella asks.

"I'm only half a craftsman," I state.

"You said there are only two types."

"I did. I'm a rare breed," I say, then smile.

Isabella's pace gets faster, her long legs challenge me to keep up, as I challenge her to do the same.

"Am I the first model you've brought to your favorite building?" Isabella asks, hopping topics, avoiding traffic. I'm not sure if this question arises from her desire to distance herself from the other models that I've taken on city tours in the past, or if it's to figure out if she'll be "just another girl" who went on "one of the many" trips to the Chrysler Building.

"I've only ever taken Lux," I tell her.

"You don't, like, have a secret wife named Lux, do you?" Isabella asks- a half joke.

"No. I have... a secret model named Lux."

"I'm not following," Isabella responds.

"You can meet her today," I say, excited that my two muses can finally connect. If this doesn't get me inspired to sketch the line, nothing will.

I reach into my pocket and take out my phone. I see it's my work phone so I slide it back in my pocket, then I find my personal cell.

"Why do you have, like, seven cell phones?" Isabella asks. "Were you holding out on me? Are you selling pot? Did you just want someone to walk you to church? I would have walked you to church... for pot."

"No, Michael gave me a phone so that he can reach me at all times," I say.

"Isn't this the same guy that you hadn't seen for three years before he offered you the gig?" Isabella asks, aware of everything fashion gossip related.

"Now, we're connected at the hip," I sigh.

After selecting Lux's name in my personal cell, I count the unanswered rings crackling over speakerphone.

Finally, after six rings, right before voicemail, Lux answers, "Hey."

"What are you doing?" I ask.

"I just got back to my place," she responds.

"Perfect. We'll pick you up," I say, then my personal cell beeps, warning me that the battery is dying. "Hold on. I'll give you my work phone number. Text me on that phone so I have you programmed in."

"You have a work phone?" Lux asks, finding this amusing.

"Yeah, it's for my new project," I say.

"Michael gave you a phone so you can feel like shit that he doesn't call you? Damn. Your family..." Lux says, taking a misplaced pleasure in this.

"Thanks for noticing," I say, then I immediately switch the topic of conversation, "My work phone number is-"

"-I don't want to go out. I'm not ready," Lux quickly tells me.

"You said you just got back to your place," I point out.

"Right, then I changed out of my model clothes," Lux responds.

"Okay, let's meet in 20. I have to freshen up too," I say, trying to compromise.

"You only call me when you're ready. I know you were at work today. I bet I can guess your outfit," Lux says, completely correct, as always.

"I've already sweated through it with all this walking around," I say, then I immediately look at Isabella and shake my head to indicate I didn't sweat through my clothes, and she shouldn't be grossed out by me. I've become aware that I may have an attraction to Isabella that isn't present with Lux.

"You don't get it. I can't go out, Andrew. I'm broke," Lux tells me- a sobering reentry into the conversation.

"No problem. My treat," I say warmly.

"What's your treat?" Lux asks coldly.

"Us. Hanging out. Together. I need this, Lux," I say. I sound desperate, but I let Isabella hear this because I know I'll be having the same conversation with her at some point in the near future.

"Do you need me at work tomorrow?" Lux sighs.

"I do. Well, actually, you have to meet with Michael, but I can walk you right up to his door. I won't be able to make the meeting because I have to go with James to Flurry, but we can catch up after, and you can tell me everything."

"Okay," Lux says, then there's a long silence.

"Okay, I'll see you tomorrow," I say.

"Bye," Lux responds.

I look to Isabella, and for the first time since I've met her, she's not enough.

THE QUIET MODEL

James and I walk out of our early morning meeting at Flurry after finding agents and bookers, but no models in their office. I casually reviewed some tears of the new Flurry girls that are beautiful women, but not Andrew Lorrie for M.Lorrie material. I make a decision that the Blend girls are more in tune with my vision, even though I haven't seen a Flurry girl in person since my last collection showed. I'm working off pure instinct, and my instincts are true, so there's no second-guessing.

We step into the elevator, and on cue, James notes, "Flurry went well. I'm going to meet up with one of their girls tonight."

Despite the fact that I don't believe him, I still find it necessary to say, "James. Don't."

"Oh really, Andrew?" James asks.

When the elevator doors open, we both try to walk out first. I push my way ahead, and James follows me, ranting, "Care to tell me where you're going now?"

"Not your business," I say, putting on my Ray-Bans.

"But what I'm doing tonight *is* your business?" James asks, straightening the brim of his hat.

"You volunteered that information," I say. "I'm not going to volunteer any information."

"I bet you're going to see a model tonight," James says. "And if you lie to me, I'll find out. It's part of what I do. I find out things that people want kept secret, then I show what I found to interested parties."

"You're right, James. I'm meeting a model tonight. Good detective work. You can close your case."

"Why is it okay for you-"

"-this is work-related," I say, never slowing. I don't look for a cab because I'd be trapped inside it with James.

"My meeting is more work-related than your meeting," James says, like it's a competition. I nod at this. In a devious voice, James purrs, "You'll get my first screener tonight."

"Can't wait," I say, not pursuing additional information.

"Is your work phone charged?" James asks.

"Yes. Stop asking me that."

"Let me see it," he demands.

To get James to go away, I stop walking, then take out the phone, showing him that it's charged because I only use it if my personal cell is dead.

"Cool. Good. Cool," James says, then asks, "Wanna split a cab?"

"I'm going to Brooklyn," I say- a lie. I need to meet Lux at the Michael Lorrie offices.

"Too poor for my blood," James says, backing away like I hoped he would.

I step out into the street and hail a cab.

Getting inside, I tell the cabbie to head to West 36th, then I relax back in the seat and begin texting Lux.

I assume that her interview with Michael is over, but I didn't receive the typical text that, "Michael isn't asexual, he definitely wants to butt-fuck himself," or, "Your brother is like you... if your body was being inhabited by an alien and his only frame of reference for human behavior was a 5-year-old GQ magazine he found at the train station." There's no text at all about how the meeting went, and this worries me.

Lux doesn't interview well. Her private school education enhanced her incredible intelligence, but left her socially crippled. A class of the same 50 kids, year after year, forced Lux into searching for a talent that would define her and make people think differently about the tall Asian girl who kept to herself. Her lack of confidence is a result of half pursued genuine talents that she never stuck with long enough to see them become a revelation. The drawing hobby/ the occasional violin performance/ the small and sparsely updated personal style blog- all of it shows infinite potential and zero follow through. Nothing is completed. Loose ends dangle everywhere. Drawings are finished, photographed, posted to the internet, then... it's a mystery what happens to them. There are no small gallery openings. Nothing ends up framed- or if it does- those frames are in the back of a closet, not on a wall. Another case of raw promise limited by second-guessing. Lux is always able to make the right call when it comes to my designs because the final say and the credit remain mine.

"RU in front of Michael's?" I text.

"No," Lux quickly texts back. I wait for additional information, and four minutes later, I receive a message that's only a hyperlink. I click on the link, and I'm presented with a map of her exact location. I read the address to the cabby, and he doesn't acknowledge me, but he clicks on his blinker and we swiftly change course.

Twenty minutes later, we arrive at a brownstone that matches what I see on the Street View. I take off my Ray-Bans, then look out the window, and I watch Lux. She's waiting on the stoop, studying something on her phone. Unable to help myself, I admire her outfit- she's wearing a dark, drop waist dress made out of what appears to be rayon. The pattern on the dress is of roses- purple and blue, scattered in the hundreds. The piece has a high neck, with three distinct gathers in the middle of the Lux's chest bone. It would have been formless if Lux didn't cinch it with a thin leather belt. The dress ends above her knee and she's wearing forest green Wang sandal boots. She looks great and Michael couldn't argue that point.

Lux notices me, and she puts her phone in her purse, then carefully steps down the stairs.

I slide over, as Lux gets inside the cab. Once she slams the door shut, she leans across the seat and gives me a loose hug, then tells the cabby her address.

"Did Michael make you meet him here?" I ask, peering out at the brownstone, feeling uneasy.

"No. Uh. That's my therapist's office," Lux says, the taxi pulling away, the brownstone in the rear view.

"Fuck. Great. You had to visit your therapist right after the meeting. So typical for Michael. He might as well just have a therapist move into the vacant 7th floor of his building so we don't have to waste swipes on our MetroCards getting to therapy," I growl hatefully.

"Chill," Lux says, opening her big eyes even wider, "The meeting was fine. Everything... is fine."

"So you'll still be fitting with me, right?" I ask.

Lux nods.

"You'll still do the muslin draping with me, right?" I ask.

Lux nods.

"So he hired you?" I ask, my eyes flickering with excitement.

"Yeah," Lux says, then she glances out the window.

"Exclusively, right? He got you as an exclusive... right?" I ask, sounding desperate, not caring.

Lux nods.

"You aren't working with anyone else, right? Nothing for the 'other Lorrie' line right?"

Lux nods.

"Promise?" I ask.

Lux nods.

I'm beaming. I want to text my brother and suggest we grab lunch. I want to thank him for believing in my team. I want to apologize to him for being so cagey and paranoid. I don't make this call, and I don't send a text because I'm afraid that, if I do, Michael will realize how truly happy Lux makes me, then he'll make sure she never works with me again. I say nothing. I preserve my pleasure. In a small gesture of thanks, I finally forward Michael and his legal team the signed contract that Intern Jessica had scanned for me. I didn't go to a lawyer to review the contract- I merely checked to make sure I wasn't giving up the rights to my last name, then signed the document.

Michael has accommodated both Karen and Lux, but I can't let him know how important Isabella is to me. Instead, I need James to convince Michael that Isabella is also worthy of joining what could be one of the best ready-to-wear collections of the decade. For this reason- and this reason only- I accept that my relationship with James must be one of mutual respect.

The cab stops in front of Lux's walk-up, and I pay the rancid smelling driver, then Lux and I both get out, wordlessly agreeing to have lunch in the apartment.

As we climb the stairs, Lux trails behind me and grumbles, with hesitation, "Michael said that the collection is RTW."

"Yeah," I respond, trying to sound bright and excited.

"Ready-to-wear is below your skill level," Lux says. I can't stop climbing the skinny stairwell or she'll sense that this situation isn't ideal for me creatively. She knows she's right, but I don't want her to know she's right, so I begin a speech, taking gasps of breath between each point, "The charm of ready-to-wear is that there are no fully beaded pieces, no feathers sewn in individually, it's very customer focused. It provides us with so much more time than we're used to having. Those large pieces we would obsess over are taken out of the equation. It's chess vs. checkers. Both are fun, but with one of them, you can sit down with just about anyone, and they'll totally understand what's going on, what's at stake, and how it all ends. With this collection, I'm going to make it checkers, but it's going to be drinking checkers where each mistake carries a penalty, and the bigger the loss, the more fucked up you are. I agree with you though, we do have to raise the stakes because, on paper, this task is too simple, and I'll have too much time to ruin everything."

After my excessive response, a simple question is asked, "But, like, how are we going to make a part-time job our entire focus?"

"I think I'm going to call a meeting tomorrow," I say aloud, realizing it's time.

"Tomorrow?" Lux asks, not taking out her keys, just standing in front of her door.

"Yeah, tomorrow," I say, figuring it out in my head, taking out my work phone so I can send another e-mail to Michael.

"Can it be in the morning?" Lux asks, and I look up from my phone, then say, "Sure. In the morning."

THE PLAN

In the far room of the workshop, I look at Lux, then I look at Mandy's image on the MacBook screen- the webcam giving her skin a purplish tinge that she would sometimes give my corpse brides. I look at Michael's Jessica, then I look at Intern Jessica. I look at the seamstresses, then I look at James. Finally, I look at Michael, then I begin to share my timeline, "By the 20th of October, my collection will be sketched. Michael has to approve the sketches, and if he requests additional sketches, that's exactly what he'll get. After the sketches are signed off on, here's where I'm different- I'll have very rough versions of the pieces sewn here. If you're trying to understand what 'rough' means, it doesn't mean sloppy, the fits will be perfect, but I'll be using muslin instead of the fabric Michael approves. October 21st, until Midnight on November 16th, we will work, as a team on these muslin pieces, five days a week. Once I have the pieces on Lux, and I like them, I'll put them on my mannequins alongside the sketches, then I'll walk Michael through the collection. When he approves what we've created, we'll finalize the fabrics, then send everything to the Italian team as an early Thanksgiving present from America. While the pieces are being sewn, we'll work on the shoes, and I'll collaborate with Karen as she creates the accessories. When the Italians are done, they'll send the finished pieces back, as our early Christmas present, then it's a scramble. Your late winter is going to be miserable. If you aren't able to work this way, then speak with HR. If you *are* willing to work this way, bring your suggestions to me and donate your time. This is ready-to-wear, but we're treating it like a full Michael Lorrie collection. I'm not trying to make an Andrew Lorrie collection, however, I am Andrew Lorrie, so we are going to do things Andrew Lorrie's way, with Michael Lorrie's leadership." I can't look at Michael, because I know he'll view this as me establishing a power position, so I say, "If anyone has any questions, Intern Jessica is all ears," then a couple of scattered laughs put an end to one of my least favorite parts of this job. I know that I should take the easy road on this, but that's not how I work. I've never liked the easy road- the times I've been detoured onto it have been unfamiliar and static.

When no one steps forward to give the next speech, I realize that I'm not allowed to end on a joke, so I add, "You're going to hate me more than you already hate me, but work through that hate, and you'll be rewarded with a collection you'll be proud of and enough money that your spring will be beautiful," I say, establishing that this collection is a good thing.

I can't help but think about Isabella, at home, missing this meeting. She needs to know this information, and I'll have to repeat my plan over dinner. I feel lucky that Isabella will most likely have noodles ready for me when I get home. I feel sad that she won't be sitting next to me on the train ride back to Jersey.

"James, would you like to say something?" Michael asks, noticing that I didn't discuss the ad campaign.

"Thank you, Mr. Lorrie," James says.

"You're welcome," both Michael and I say.

More scattered laughter- this time, it's nervous.

James steps forward, turns his hat backward, then begins, "Coco Chanel once said-" but he's cut off by hissing and eye rolls so aggressive I can actually hear multiple sets of eyeballs make a slimy rotating noise.

"No?" James asks, "Fashion royalty not good enough for you people?"

A silence causes James to hurry up, "I have a lot of amazing things planned for M.Lorrie. I'm carefully working with Michael to make sure we combine our aesthetics and burst out of the gate with the most exciting campaign in M.Lorrie's storied history. Everyone has been so welcoming to me, and as a guy that was once a paparazzi, I appreciate a warm welcome more than anyone else in the world. Most of you don't even flee when I enter the room. Cindy in marketing has been a downright doll, and Donna in accounting has the *best* coffee cake I've ever tasted. Anyway... we're ready for an exciting year at Michael Lorrie, and I can assure you, by the time this collection hits the runway, history will be made and your lives will be changed forever."

James looks around, then starts clapping aggressively. The rest of the crowd reluctantly joins in, and this suddenly feels like a Wal-Mart employee pep rally.

Michael and I both seem ready to put an end to this meeting, but when I see that my brother is stepping up, I step back. I willingly relent, while Michael demands the floor. This is how it always ends.

THE COAST

"I miss home. I need California. I just want to go home," Isabella says, under a pile of blankets, hidden in my bed. Nothing brought this on. There was no catalyst for this behavior.

Isabella's current state could be extremely detrimental to my plans.

"Your hair looks good," I tell her.

She smiles, only for a moment, then returns to her homesickness just as fast.

This collection seems to be a virus for the girls who are inspiring it. Lux is becoming distant; Isabella wants to go back home to the West Coast. If either of these girls escape before the collection is done, I'll end up designing pedestrian sweaters stamped with block letters that read, "I DON'T WANT TO BE HERE." The fashion bloggers would eat it up, but the insanely rich women who I view as my customer base would find the pieces unsexy and "bleak." I have two options- chose this direction, or redirect everything.

And just like that, the weekend is redesigned.

I rent a car; Isabella packs us food.

We go down to the shore.

The summer crowd is back in school, back at work. The normally congested areas now feel intimate.

We smoke pot in the rental car, while watching the waves crash, as Björk's *Post* plays from Isabella's phone.

We don't touch the water, and we do buy junk food, and we don't mention model diets or the fact we didn't even pack toothbrushes.

We don't meet up with anyone and that's good because we don't need them.

Isabella buys no souvenirs because all of her money is being saved, so it can be converted into Yen and spent somewhere far away from me, she tells me, but not in those exact words. I nod at her plan and focus on the waves.

The sun falls and the beach becomes attractive to Isabella.

The burnt, charred remains of Seaside Heights cradle us as we lie in Cassie's Acne hoodies and we watch the waves roll in.

"Sure it's the other side of the country, but you have to admit, it's close to home," I say.

"Our weather is better," Isabella tells me, then hides her hands in her sleeves/ "Our waves are better," Isabella tells me, as the same crashing noise heard on every coast negates her statement/ "Our boardwalk doesn't look so Dante," Isabella tells me, as she looks back at the cinder remains of a place that had been under a Haiti-esque assault these past couple of years.

"Then go back," I say, not meaning it, but desperate for her response.

She puts her head on my shoulder and it's enough of an assurance for me.

"I'll stay if you get me to Japan," Isabella says.

I nod, agreeing to the demand.

"Is that a confirmation that you'll get me to Japan?" she asks, feeling my head move.

"Walk for me this spring, then I'll get you enough money to stay in Japan from June to August. That's the best time for modeling there. You can build your book," I tell her, inflating her rate because I would pay anything to keep her around.

"Okay," she responds, then neither of us say anything for a very long time, because this all has a predestined end- like the ballet of The Boy and The Girl in the loop inside the house on Scotland Road.

THE PUBLIC SCREENING

"I need those pieces from the archive. Come on, Jessica," I bitch unnecessarily- possibly to make it clear to Lux that I don't view these new people to be as essential as she is. I want Lux to feel important again.

"Why do you have white slaves?" Lux asks, genuinely curious, following behind me down the hallway of the workshop.

My work phone buzzes, and I look down at it to find a picture with a play button begging for a touch. I move away from Lux and press down on the video. The scene begins to unfold, and I watch with impatient curiosity. In the foreground, is an empty chair, and in the background, bad hotel room shades are drawn closed. I wait for the kitten to pop into frame, but that doesn't happen- instead, a young model sits down in the chair. The model- brunette, pointy chin, Vlada bags, too much blush- seems nervous. If this is a casting video, so having her sit makes absolutely no sense because there are no chairs involved at all in the job she's being interviewed for.

James, off-camera, asks, "How old are you?" and I turn the volume up on my phone.

"Look at this. James is creating these 'screeners' as part of our castings," I say to Lux.

Lux walks over, and we both watch as the model in the video, after a confused pause, attempts to answer James' question. "Are you looking for my model age or my human girl age?" the girl asks.

"Either," James says, fluent in both units of measurement.

"I'm 19," the model says, not qualifying the age.

"I know that girl," Lux notes casually.

"Worth watching the screener?" I ask.

"She's addicted to laxatives," Lux responds, inflection-less.

"Currently?"

Lux nods, "That's probably why she's sitting down. If she stands up for too long..."

I press down on the video, pausing it, then I slide the phone back into my pocket after this comment. "I need to be the one casting the show. James is going about this the wrong way. He doesn't know how castings work. He's treating these girls like they're auditioning for single-episode roles on a CBS sitcom. This is why LA doesn't do fashion. Fucking casting couch bullshit."

Lux doesn't respond.

In an attempt to sound less like a ranting psychopath, I ask, "Remember that girl, Kearley Carmichael? I've recently been thinking about her look for this collection."

Lux nods, admiring one of my new, naked, grayish mannequins, and she tells me, "Two weeks ago, Kearley broke her ankle and three toes and has to learn how to re-walk."

"Shit. That's horrible," I say.

"If you think so, you've never seen her do runway. Kearley's walk made her look retarded so everyone is actually saying this accident might save her career now that she has to learn how to walk like a physical cripple, instead of a mental one," Lux offers, her husky voice exhaling all of this information matter-of-factly.

"Right. My thoughts exactly. Of course everyone is saying that," I respond. "What do you think about Lily Hawke?" I ask, moving on.

"I saw Lily floss with her hair once," Lux says.

"Well, she does have big teeth," I respond, worried that my second casting ended up even worse than my first.

"With her *hair*, Andrew," Lux emphasizes. "She was flossing with her hair."

"At least she flosses. That's better hygiene than most people."

Lux nods, giving up on her crusade to defame Lily, then she moves on, "You know someone tried to make me feel bad recently by saying that the average woman is a size 10, but it just made me feel awesome and superhuman."

"You are pretty super awesome," I say.

"Maybe in your outfits, but when those come off, I'm nerdy Peter Parker. I'm doofy Clark Kent," Lux mopes. This dual-identity theme she's co-opting seems too on the nose for the way she's been acting recently.

I don't pursue the conversation further, because I can't that deny my pieces do have a transformational quality to them. Maybe that's why I'm rehabbing M.Lorrie; so much of ready-to-wear is formed with the intention of helping the average woman hide her imperfections. The cuts add an hourglass curve to a pillar-shaped woman/ The ruffled sleeves draw attention away from a flabby jiggle/ The high-waisted, wide-leg pants cover the varicose veins and cellulite.

My ready-to-wear pieces will be constructed so that they both define themselves and also fix problem areas that my customers may have. Hiding never appealed to me, because I crave transparency, but my bias cut naturally produces side effects that my customers love.

Lux takes a step toward me, then says, "Since we're casting all weird..." but she trails off into nothingness, and ends up looking at the gray tiled floor.

"Yeah?" I ask, waiting for the question.

"Never mind," Lux says.

"What?" I ask, curious.

"I said never mind," Lux responds, her big eyes finally meeting mine. "I have to go," she informs me.

"Can I come with you?" I ask.

"I'm just going back to my apartment."

"That sounds good," I say, inviting myself.

Lux looks me up and down, then asks, "Will you pay for a cab?"

I don't have to nod, I merely grab my Saint Laurent jacket, then we walk out into the chilly October afternoon. After the weekend at the shore with Isabella, summer fled, and it couldn't have ended better.

I immediately flag down a cab, and it works out so perfectly that I have to look around to make sure that James isn't standing next to Lux.

Inside the cab, Lux texts non-stop, but she also holds a conversation with me while doing it. I'm asked all the right questions, so I just look out the window at the city passing by, and it makes Lux's interest in the mystery person on the other side of her texts tolerable.

When we reach Lux's apartment, I pay the cabby in cash, then grab Lux's hand, as she slides across the seat. She feels cold, and I let go of her as soon as she's standing.

"Let's get food," I suggest, walking away from Lux's apartment, since I can't shake the fact that her body felt dead when I touched her.

"I'll make you food. Come on," she tells me, then she walks inside her building. I follow, only because I want to spend time with her.

Again, Lux's roommate is gone. I make it a point to look around for her, but abandon the search quickly, and I settle on a futon.

Lux goes into the half-kitchen to start the meal.

Directly across from the futon is a coat closet, and my heart starts beating faster when I focus on what's hanging in the closet. I'm instantly transported back to a forgotten season.

"Will you put it on?" I ask.

"What?" Lux responds, turning to me, as eggs crackle in the frying pan in front of her.

I gesture with a flick to the piece hanging in Lux's closet. It's from our last Andrew Lorrie collection. I didn't give it to her.

Lux drifts over to the closet, leaving the eggs. "Oh. Yeah. Uh. So... turns out the Chinese wanted to pay me in a bit of trade too. They liked that you were using a Chinese girl for the fittings."

"Did they offer you a job?" I ask, standing up.

"I got some trade. I wanted it," Lux tells me, not totally answering the question, as she moves toward the garment instead of me.

"Why that piece?" I ask. During the fittings, Lux never expressed excitement over this dress. The look is too safe for her. It's nearly ready-to-wear, and I know that she'd never select it if she had the option of so many other Andrew Lorrie pieces she verbally and physically confirmed she loved.

When Lux goes back to turn the burner off, I study my work- a silk chiffon, pea green, triple spaghetti strap dress. It's bias cut from the hip, left to right, with the fabric bunching at the edge of the cut. Three layers of fabric were sewn below the slice, to keep the dress from being vulgar. The final layer of chiffon- ultra thin, ultra sheer- reached halfway down Lux's shin during the fittings.

The look was inspired by a night I spent waiting in my then-girlfriend's car, outside her mother's house, as she made the announcement that she wasn't going back to USC, and she'd be moving to New York because it was her 'last chance' to model. After she left, we collapsed and I lost track of the girl. She got sucked up in the international travel ring/ the rotating apartment ring/ the depression ring; fashion. Even though the girl was gone, I never lost track of the moment, so this piece, singular in its message, is a rare flash of color for me. The green I used is not dark and it's not foreboding. At the time, I didn't feel like my girlfriend should worry about what she was doing, or about the decisions she was making. The piece was built with splashes of envy, and money, and sickness, and spring promise- that's how I chose green. That night looked nothing like the piece, but it absolutely felt like what is hanging in Lux's closet.

Frozen at the stove, Lux turns the burner back on, finishing her food prep before a rare post-runway fitting. She prolongs the moment, so she can tell me, "I chose that dress because- believe it or not- people kinda liked some of your collection, and that piece- among others- went into production overseas. I'm guessing you haven't seen the pictures, but a couple of Chinese actresses have been showing up in the more wearable pieces of the collection. That dress is my favorite of the productions pieces. Do you remember the day we had the final fitting for it? That was a really good day."

I squint my eyes, devoting all of my brain power to recall the moment Lux and I finished the dress. Lux senses my struggle, so she reminds me, "One of the seamstresses brought her dog to the loft, and the pup would lay with me during the downtime, when I was in my street clothes. It was just a really fun afternoon. It was toward the end of the August- our first cool day after the hottest summer ever- and it started to feel like everything was coming together."

"I remember that day," I say, feeling warm.

"The piece got softer as the day progressed because of how purely good things were. We leaned toward ready-to-wear because facing the world didn't seem so scary that day. You dulled your pain and brightened up the design. It still makes things feel promising," Lux says, as her personality displays an optimistic shine I thought I had inadvertently robbed her of.

"Will you put it on?" I ask, again.

Lux makes sure the eggs are done, then attends to my request.

Dressing and undressing and redressing Lux remains one of the purest pleasures I've ever known. I feel grateful, not for the overseas success of the collection, but instead for Lux's nostalgia regarding "just another day at the office."

I watch, feeling accomplished, as Lux undresses, then carefully takes the piece off the hanger. After she slides on the dress, she holds up a finger and goes back to the closet. She takes out the matching pumps I designed, then puts them on- first the right, then the left.

When I look at Lux in the piece, I appreciate not only our history, but also the situation that brought about the design. This moment, combined with my beach weekend, provides me with a feeling of contentment that I previously thought was unattainable.

THE AFTER-PARTY HANGOVER

When I walk into my bedroom, I notice the door to the porch is open.

As I make my way toward my favorite feature of the house, I catch a glimpse of Isabella sitting on the deck chair we hauled up from the basement a day prior. Based on the blue glow her face is bathed in, I know that she's looking for something on my tablet. I get closer, and I can see her swiping through my pictures of the Andrew Lorrie after-party, where we met.

As I drift directly behind the deck chair, Isabella stops swiping and studies the picture in her lap. In the upper left corner of the photograph is a girl looking like she's not enjoying herself. I let out a little laugh, amazed that a background girl has come to mean so much to me. I now want to study these pictures again, so I can see who else I might have missed.

The calm of the moment is suddenly fractured, as Isabella makes a frustrated noise, stands up, then places the tablet facedown on the chair. I try to piece together what just happened, as Isabella wordlessly pushes past me, then stomps into the house.

"What was that?" I ask, stepping back into the bedroom.

"You're doing exactly what I worry people are doing behind my back every time I'm in a social situation like that. You are literally behind my back, confirming my worst fears."

"Oh, come on. It was a cute picture. You couldn't see my smile. I love the dichotomy of that shot."

"Do you? Yeah, it's great- the contrast between socially well-adjusted people, and fucked up Isabella," she spits at me.

"I like how you look like a model, and the band looks like rock stars, and the rest of the strangers look like, well, normal people."

"Why are there no pictures of just me from that night?" Isabella asks, returning back to the porch, grabbing the tablet, then putting in my password.

"Don't. That's not intentional. I was getting smashed around in the pit there. I was being begged by the action. I just shot-"

"-whatever grabbed your eye."

"Don't simplify it like that."

"Your talent comes from instinct, Andrew. That's why you're so good at what you do. Your sixth sense saw me, then placed me as background."

"I can't believe you're indulging in your own misinterpretations," I say, leaning on the door frame.

"When you were indulging your passion, where was I?" Isabella asks, then walks away again, before I can explain that I handed my camera off as soon as I saw her in blue velvet.

Instead of arguing with delusion, I sit down in the chair on the porch, then review the pictures to see if Isabella is right. I refuse to believe that I overlooked her, until I spotted a piece from my collection. Is there a possibility- however remote- that Isabella is not the announcement of a brand new talent, but instead just a conduit for my own extreme narcissism? I continue scrolling through the pictures. I find that someone, most likely Lux, continued to take photographs of the party long after I left. I flick through the captured moments, and I find that some of the pictures are pretty good. I'm about to e-mail a couple of great photographs of the band to the intern at Matthew's label, like she's requested I do numerous times recently, but I stop on a photograph of another beautiful girl. Again, what should be the focus of the picture is merely part of the background. The high cheekbones demand my attention and pull my gaze toward those almond shaped eyes that I cannot look into. I don't want to see what those eyes will tell me. I'll remain ignorant. I feel an absolute disappointment in the fact my lens had somehow disregarded the two most important women in the entire party. I vow to never make this mistake again.

It begins to rain, so I take the tablet inside, then get ready for bed.

As soon as I lie down, I begin waiting for the footsteps.

I made sure the curtains were open because The Boy and The Girl will only perform in the sliver of golden light from the street.

I need something to materialize. I need a vision for my collection. Isabella remains my primary influence, but I can't depend on her to stay for the entire time it will take to design and complete all of the pieces. If my designs end up reflecting the pleasure Isabella has given me, when she leaves, the collection will mutate; I'll lose my perspective. My pain will be absolute, and the pieces will all be dipped in my inspired acid. I either need an assurance that Isabella cannot leave or I need to manipulate her into staying. I'm not Michael, so I choose to seek the help of the Japanese. I'll remind Isabella that she'll be in Japan by the end of this collection, if she just cooperates. Hopefully, this promise of absolute distance will keep Isabella close to me until she walks for M.Lorrie.

I hear the floorboards creak, and I'm thankful for the thud of footsteps. I look to the patch of light. The Boy enters the illuminated slice of the room, wearing an ill-fitting suit. He reaches into his pocket and pulls out a small rectangular box. The Girl steps into the light. She's wearing a sleeveless red scoop neck dress that seems to make everything else look black and white in comparison.

"Did you steal a camera?" The Girl asks in mock horror.

"I put it in my pocket, but I didn't take it out because nothing..." The Boy stops talking, and quickly lifts the camera. The room flashes bright, then returns to dark.

"Nothing what?" The Girl asks, moving from the beam of yellow light into the pitch black.

"Nothing inspired me, so I didn't take a single picture."

A hand reaches out from the void, and grabs the camera from The Boy.

The Boy smiles, and the flash illuminates the room again.

The Girl returns to the sliver of light, and I freeze when she points the camera at me. My heart stops. A manicured finger presses down the plastic button and a flash blinds me. When the spots in my vision fade, so do The Boy and The Girl. All that's left is the drumming of the rain on the balcony.

THE GEARS

In the damp morning, I pick up my tablet and flip through the pictures that intern Jessica uploaded of Michael's previous M.Lorrie seasons. What I find is collection after collection of bland, proficient, wearable clothing. The last collection, the collection that caused Michael to be desperate enough to call on me, is so completely devoid of excitement and creativity that it makes me wonder if there was even a designer assigned to create these looks, or if this was the output of a committee of fashion students armed with pattern books. No choices were made, no risks were taken. The last M.Lorrie collection arrived and departed with bored models, lukewarm reviews, and virtually no impact. If this collection never existed, nothing would change.

Feeling curious about the high fashion line Michael showed last season, I go to *style.com* and review thumbnails of Michael Lorrie S/S for the first time. What I find is so completely different from the RTW designs that even a layperson wouldn't believe that both collections came from the same man. This puts me at ease, because if Michael allows for this cavernous distance to remain, I'll be able to put whatever I want on the runway.

Hidden in the past M.Lorrie collections, I find pockets of excitement. I don't mind taking inspiration from Michael's work because cribbing has always been part of fashion design. *Harper's Bazaar* debuted in 1867- we have that much history to pull from. To neglect the past, while creating the future, would be moronic and handicapping.

I write an e-mail to Karen and send it. "Stylist Questions" is the subject, to make it clear Intern Jessica will be pulling all the pieces I reference in the body of the e-mail. Karen has always respected me as a designer, so I make the effort to respect her as M.Lorrie's stylist.

My work phone begins to vibrate, and I experience a jolt of dread when I see the caller ID displays "My Partner."

"Hello, James," I say, answering the call in a way that makes my displeasure obvious.

"Did you watch my screener?" James asks, excited.

"Why are we casting this show so early?" I grumble, mainly so I can know how to get Isabella locked in for runway.

"Michael says that casting is a year-round job. He always casts early," James says matter-of-factly.

"Does he, Mr. Paparazzi? Michael *always* casts early, huh? I assume you're basing this knowledge on your experiences working with him prev- oh, wait. That's right, your previous experience is in stalking reality TV stars," I snark, hoping that James will realize I view his "screeners" as a waste of time.

"Listen, I know you think you're the casting expert, but Michael put me in this role because, unlike you, I'm a guy who doesn't have hang-ups that prevent him from doing the job he's given," James says, spitting this into the phone because he wants to be powerful, like Michael.

"I do my job," I say, calmly.

"No. You do *a* job. I do the job I'm hired for," James says.

"You've never done this job before. You've never worked in fashion before. How are you so sure what you're doing is right?" I ask.

"Because I'm following Michael's instructions," James says, with conviction.

With a smile in my voice, I respond, "Then you're definitely going about it the wrong way."

"Are you coming to work today? That Chinese girl from the meeting is here," James says, changing the topic of our conversation when he senses he's fighting a losing battle.

I quickly ask, "The Chinese girl from the meeting? Which meeting? What Chinese girl? Where are you, James?"

"At Michael's office. Where are you, dude?"

"I'm getting clothes pulled from the archive," I say, half lying. "Who's the Chinese girl? Lux? The investor's daughter who walked for me?" I ask, trying to remain calm.

"Do you wanna stop by my hotel room tonight?" James asks, dodging the question, seemingly uninterested in the girl.

"No. What? No. Why would I do that? James, *why* would I do that?" I ask, caught off guard, desperate to know if Lux is at Michael's office. I gulp down a bubble of fear that James' question was actually posed to Lux and the phone's mic just picked up on it.

"Alright, fine," James says, audibly hurt for the second time during this conversation. "I just thought a little working dinner would be good for the team. I thought you could help me smooth things over regarding the Regis situation. I guess I'll handle him myself tonight."

"I'm there," I say, since James cannot be left to his own devices with Regis.

"You're... where?" he asks.

"I'm at your place tonight. Text me an address, a dress code, and the time I need to be there."

"Okay," James says, then he giggles, "Irina will be there."

"She better be," I respond, then I end the call.

THE PIXX

James takes his key card out of the inside pocket of his gray pea coat, then turns to me, then says, "Prepare to witness what you could have had if you didn't hate your brother."

The card is placed into the door mechanism, a green light blinks, then we enter a generic looking hotel room that contains neither Irina nor Regis. The door clicks shut behind me, and I find myself relieved that the setup of this room is different from the hotel room James shot his screener in. I decide that I'm going to make my way into the bedroom at some point tonight, just to confirm that the screeners are shot in a different New York City hotel.

"I'm regretting my decision," I admit to James, but I don't provide additional details regarding where my regret is placed. I find it harmless that James is happy with where he's living. I no longer feel the need to spread misery everywhere I go; I save it for the important places, like my sketches. When I moved out of the hotel into a real home, an edge was rounded. It's a comfort I haven't felt in a very long time, and it allows me to appreciate the places that make others feel the same way. This empathy will enhance my designs, I'm sure of it. Ready-to-wear needs to be grounded in practicality, and now that I don't have to wholeheartedly wrestle with the instinct to escape, I can focus on my surroundings.

James' cell rings, but before he answers it, he takes off his pea coat, then carefully hangs it on a hotel provided wooden hanger.

Answering the call with a faltering, "Jimmy- uh, James. James speaking," he reveals his true identity for a short flash, and I pretend not to notice, but this slip confirms something for me.

"Not many people call you, do they, James?" I ask, but he just puts a finger up to hush me.

"Of course I'm ready, Andrew and I just ordered room service," James says, then points at a black menu on the table in his small "living room."

I grab the menu, and quickly decide on a burger, but when James doesn't ask Irina or Regis if they want anything in particular, I realize that if anyone is going to place an order tonight, it's going to be me. Michael definitely made James put up his own credit card for the incidentals.

James ends the call, then says, "Supermodels," and points at the phone, while making an annoyed face.

"Why are we having this little get-together, James?" I ask.

"I want to go through my visual plans in greater detail," James reveals.

I nod at this, accepting it. I usually don't plan everything so early, but then again, I usually don't design ready-to-wear, and I usually don't let a photographer cast my shows. I guess I've started doing a lot of things I don't usually do, and so far, it's been pretty painless. I allow James to play host. He takes out a bottle of white wine from a paper bag that was sitting on the table. I realize that this bottle of wine is the "room service" he told Irina about.

Before the wine can be uncorked, a knock at the door sends James into action. He twirls around, fixes his Yankees hat so that the curl of the brim is aligned evenly with his glasses, then he walks to the door casually.

"Don't do that Andrew Lorrie thing you do," James requests, turning to me, spinning his fingers in the air.

"What thing?" I ask.

"Yes- this creepy stare you're currently giving me- that's the thing. Get it out of your system now," he responds.

After I blink, James opens the door, revealing an un-airbrushed Irina. For a moment, I don't believe this our guest of honor. I tell myself that I'm looking at an impostor hired by the real model to do *FashionCut* interviews or the other shit Irina would never do- like show up to this meeting.

"This isn't a sex thing, is it?" Irina asks, walking into the hotel room, dodging James' attempt at a hug.

"I promise I'm not here to strangle you," I joke to Irina, and she pauses, then looks at me. She looks *switched on*. That's what I think to myself. She's switched on, and it scares me.

Regis follows behind his girlfriend, and I step toward him for help. He smiles at my fear, then displays an identical unease when he turns and notices Irina's unbroken stare. Acting fast, he makes himself the center of attention by saying, "Irina likes to be strangled during sex, so the strangling thing still would be classified as a sex thing."

"That's insane," James responds, chuckling good-naturedly.

"Only for three seconds," Irina clarifies, her eyes moving off of me, "You can't die from three seconds of sex strangle. Eight seconds of unrelenting sex strangle is insane, *then* it's attempted murder."

"What if he crushes your windpipe in three seconds?" James asks, deathly serious.

"There isn't enough blood in his arms to do that," Irina says.

Regis, for some reason, feels the need to defend himself, and says, "When you get a boner, all the blood doesn't just rush to your dick. I mean, some does, but the rest of your body still has decent blood pressure. Enough to get a quality strangle going."

"It's counter-intuitive, because sex is about creating life and strangling is about taking it," James maintains.

"You can do both without the negative side effects," I add.

"I want to pick the song I walk to," Irina says, immediately changing the subject. She sits on the sofa at the far end of the room, her legs doing a young

Sharon Stone impression. The aggressive oversexed intro, followed by the blindsiding demand, is a tactic that beautiful women like Irina often employ.

Irina's request instantly bothers me, not because I feel like she's overstepping her role, but instead because I've been designing collections for pop musicians and socialites for so long that when I was finally able to choose Sky's songs for my collection, it made me feel like I was finally in control. To take the playlist away from me would be a demotion. Music wasn't chosen for my runway shows as much as it was forced upon my designs for maximum cross-selling. I've watched some of my best work walk down the runway to a fuck dreadful song about "the club."

"Well, are you going to let me pick it?" Irina asks, when I don't respond.

"I'm 50/50 at this point," I say.

"Aren't you going to ask me which song?" Irina questions me directly.

I look to Regis. He's flipping through the room service menu. The prospect that James' room service would be billed to Michael reminds me that we have a giant company backing us so we can afford pretty much any soundtrack. "What's the song?" I ask.

"It's a Vanessa Carlton song," Irina says, then smiles sweetly.

I sigh. "No. No way am I letting my models walk out to 'A Thousand-'"

"-'White Houses,'" Irina interrupts me.

"A thousand white horses?" James asks, initially skeptical of the title, but he slowly comes around, ultimately declaring the choice, "Majestic."

"No. Houses. And she doesn't specify how many there are," Irina says.

Given the fact that Irina is Brazilian, there's a nearly infinite number of awful songs she could have selected. "White Houses" seems like a lesser evil. I squint, trying to recall the lyrics to the song. All I can think of is that it's about losing your virginity. "Will you send it to me?" I ask, needing to hear the song one more time before I can make a decision.

"Expect a CD and a bottle of champagne at your doorstep by the time you get home," Irina says, and as soon as she makes this promise, Regis glides into James' bedroom, almost like he's been put in some sort of trance and was just given his next objective. If a woman was going to put someone in a trance, Irina would be the one to do it. I have to genuinely consider if I'm in a trance right now because I'm slowly warming up to her song selection. I feel a budding generosity that demands I grant Irina her choice. The song was the first serious topic of the evening- it means something to her.

"You know I'm not going to let you call all the shots. We're making choices based on my judgment," I say to Irina, curious as to how she'll react to this.

She shrugs, then says, "That's fine, but I think that there are some areas-"

"-I know you've heard a lot about me on the internet and-"

"-I'm in. No discussion necessary... I'm in," Irina interrupts me.

"Just like that?" James yelps, slapping the table to his right. It's clear he was hoping that I would become the enemy, and he would become the trusted point-person at Michael Lorrie.

"Just like that," Irina confirms to James, taking noticeable pleasure in his frustration.

"Why?" James asks.

"I think that you're working against the team, James," I point out.

"Because I'm a Michael Lorre exclusive right now," Irina says, then she asks, "Do you know what type of hell that is? Do you see the boring pieces I'm placed in? Do you know that sometimes the pieces are designed *too big* for me because Michael only cares about those fat ass size six actresses and their Oscar attire choices?"

Regis re-enters the room when he hears Irina getting worked up.

"Are you afraid Michael Lorrie is changing your image?" I ask, seeking permission to do the same. Irina, despite being a supermodel, becomes an Andrew Lorrie girl simply because she has the talent to be anything her client burns for.

I see something in Irina flicker, then she counters my question with, "When have you ever seen my image change?"

She looks different tonight, and there's a reason why. There's a secret that I don't know, that she's keeping from me; it scares me and turns me on.

"Actually. Perfect introduction, Irina," James says, flicking the brim of his hat up. "Come with me, I want to show you something," he beckons, moving into the bedroom.

The three of us all seem to be mentally questioning if tonight actually *was* planned as a sex thing, but when we recognize each other's worry, we head into the adjoining room, confident we can outnumber James.

We find our host reclining in an office chair opposite a queen sized bed. When he sees us, James opens his arms, and between his arm-span is a line of three computer monitors with snaking cords that hook up to a laptop. Connected to the laptop is a line of labeled hard drives that are blinking in different time signatures.

James hits a few keys, then a green and black window on the far left screen is quickly minimized. On the middle screen, I see a small rectangle of the screener that he sent me, and I fear that we'll have to watch more of these pointless exercises tonight. When James closes the video player, I feel instant relief.

James' desktop wallpaper is the iconic picture he took of social!heavy, the night before they had their first concert at the Staples Center. Dakota Dabney and Kristen Paxton, paired up with their boyfriends, look out of their town car, staring into the camera, smiling. This photograph, and the corresponding story run by *OxygenWaster*, propelled James' career beyond that of a lowly paparazzi. Refusing to assist Paul Dabney in the betrayal of his own daughter was a moment that painted James as a man unwilling to fall in line with the "standard operating procedure" of the predatory entertainment industry. According to what I've read, after the story went viral, James expanded his fingerprint, continuing what he was doing with his photography, but on a bigger scale, with a supportive audience this time. He was prying into lives, then reporting what he found on a five-nights-a-week segment that ran during a quirky, campy CTV show where news that belonged on the internet was placed on TV for those who favored antiquated distribution methods. When it became clear to the viewers that the "Jimmy Pixx" extolled in the *OxygenWaster* piece was an authorial construct, James went back to being viewed as just another skeevy pap.

After leaving the photo up on the screen long enough to remind all of us that he was part of this important moment in pop history, James clicks to open a folder on his desktop. He selects a single file, dramatically hits enter, then all three screens start to slowly fill with small one-inch by one-inch squares. Inside each square is a letter of the alphabet. "I present to you, the Pixxitorium," James says, opening his arms again.

"Is this a database of girls you date raped?" Regis asks.

"Better..." James says, "...it's my oeuvre."

"Finally," Irina breathes a sigh of relief.

"I know, I've wanted to compile everything for so long," James says. "Want to take it for a test drive?"

Irina hums a whine, "But you just said our meeting was over."

Regis immediately hops on James' statement, and says, "Show me the Pixxitorium."

"Well, you know how Michael has those lookbooks and that online archive of every piece Michael Lorrie and M.Lorrie has ever put out?"

We all nod, as James sets up the Pixxitorium to be his archive.

"Now I have one of those for my work. Took me forever to compile."

"Click on 'R,'" Regis requests.

James' smile falls for a moment, then he clicks "I" instead, because all of the photographs that James has taken of Regis only exist because of who he's standing next to.

When the "I" is pressed, the squares flip over, and the letters are replaced by thumbnails of celebrities- Ian Hope, Ingmar Lenz, then eventually, on the second screen, Irina.

"You have every picture you've ever taken on these drives?" Irina asks.

"Well, every picture I've taken of you, but not every picture I've taken."

"I thought this was your archive?" Regis asks.

James rolls back in the office chair, then makes a rectangle with his hands. When he begins to hover the rectangle over his lap, Regis reaches over and clicks on Irina's name.

The tiles flip again, and now hold another afternoon of peace in Irina's life shattered by Jimmy Pixx. The tiles stretch across all three screens, and when Regis moves the mouse to right, the tiles continue to scroll horizontally.

"Nice interface. User-friendly," Regis notes, like he's leaving a short review of the Pixxitorium.

James' expression shows that he genuinely appreciates this comment.

Irina makes a noise, pleased by the pictures as they continue to scroll. California moments that escaped her memory have been archived here without her knowledge. The pictures date back to her early days as a model. I imagine the older pictures are what Irina is so pleased about. As her name grew, so did the number of photographers following her. James isn't some 20-year-old with a cell phone camera- he's a guy who's honed his on-the-run photography skills for 20 years.

Regis and Irina silently look at a checkerboard of their experiences together, and they both look like they're on the verge of laughing hysterically, then crying hysterically.

"Take her for a beta test," James says, popping out of the chair, absolutely glowing. I don't think he anticipated that Regis and Irina would match his excitement regarding this passion project.

Regis takes the seat and selects one of the squares. All the tiles on the screen flip, revealing thumbnails of a night that Irina and Regis spent on the Santa Monica Pier.

Irina slides her long body onto Regis' lap, draping a bony arm around his neck so she can slowly run her fingers through Regis' curls as they review their past. It's an intimate moment that James and I excuse ourselves from.

"That was a nice thing to do for them," I tell James, as we make our way into the other room.

"It was nice for me too," he admits.

James clearly still feels guilty that, under one of those tiles, the photographs that almost ruined Irina's extremely important cover are waiting to be rediscovered.

If the pictures that Jimmy Pixx took could cause such long-lasting pain, James seems to hope that maybe they can also heal a scar just as effectively.

THE START

Stepping back inside the house on Scotland Road, I begin to feel a small amount of pity for James. I make the decision to try and be more patient with him, because he's spending his nights in a hotel room, all by himself- another lonely stakeout for the paparazzi.

I'm happy that I didn't take the room from Michael/ I'm happy that I listened to Karen and called Cassie.

I decide to listen more and argue less.

At the small table in the kitchen, Isabella asks me questions about Irina while we eat the noodles with chopsticks. I'm glad I didn't get room service; this is better. Isabella brings over her MacBook and we watch an anime about a girl with detachable limbs who can only communicate by meowing like a cat. Isabella seems to love it, which endears me to the anime, just as James' love for his archive caught Regis' attention.

I sneak off to bed, as Isabella remains frozen next to the computer, her eyes widening as a man is eviscerated on the screen.

I brush my teeth, then slide under the covers.

I wait for Isabella to finish up the episode, then come upstairs, but time passes, and everything stays the same.

The halls are silent, the room is dark, so I get up, and open the curtains, until that familiar slice of light creeps in the room, then I return to bed and wait for The Boy or The Girl or *the girl*.

My work phone seizures on the nightstand, and I check it, hoping I'll find a picture that Lux took of herself specifically to send to me.

When I see that it's another screener from James, I'm thankful that Lux wasn't involved in this message.

I tap the screen, then watch as a black girl- a model I don't recognize- sits in a room that I *do* recognize. It's the hotel room from the last screener. I listen, as the eager to please girl talks about balancing being a parent and a model. According to her answer to James' previous question, this girl is 18. I ask myself,

How is she a parent? then, more baffled, I wonder, *How did a kid manage to squeeze out from between those tiny hips?* I can't watch another moment, so I mute the phone, then put it under my pillow. The screen's content is too depressing. This is the youth of America. It makes me afraid for these girls. I start to wonder where the parents are, then I remember that the skinny little girl in the chair *is* a parent. What a dangerous world this screener presents. Is anyone paying attention or are we all just watching videos of kids on our phones?

The girls in James' screeners inspire nothing besides fear in me.

Fear doesn't make me want to create. Pain is my fuel.

I never use a mood board. All of the important patterns, and textures, and images reside inside of me, and I can access them with surgical precision. Faces, and mistakes, and sensations from the past all collide together without the chains of logic or practicality binding them.

The idea of destruction as a side effect of creation is nothing new.

The idea of a brother being unable to measure up his sibling is nothing new.

Fashion came into my life by betrayal.

For me, the avalanche into designing outfits started early.

In the years before junior high, I had a very strict "fashion sense" that was instilled with unwavering purpose and zero aesthetic value. My wardrobe consisted of a teal Miami Dolphins Starter jacket, sports team T-shirts, black sweatpants, and bright orange socks. It was a clothing combination that one might find on a homeless man in any major city. It was not a fashion choice, but instead my fashion obligation. The orange socks were necessary because they were thick and had intricate stitching to indicate which side of the sock was the top. I took every precaution to make sure the stitching on my socks did not find its way under my toes. I seemed to be convinced that if something as simple as putting on my socks went wrong, everything else throughout the day could only follow suit.

I didn't have many friends, but the friends I did have were very close and forgiving of me. Intricate friendships were very important, and I worked hard to keep the good people in my life close by. My best friend, Pat Scanlon, shared my "sense of style" so what I was wearing was never questioned when I was in grade school. Then, when girls were introduced into the equation and junior high became life, suddenly there were shows on TV about what goes on at school, and none of the characters on the shows wore orange socks. I found myself at Pat's house, looking into his older brother's room, and seeing the same video games and sports cards that Pat's room was filled with, but he also had

Jordans, and colognes, and clothes that didn't have an expanding waistband. Pat's brother, Rob, seemed to be living a life that I wanted, and it didn't appear to be that far out of my reach.

One day, while at the mall with the Scanlon brothers, I decided not to follow Pat into the comic book store, and instead, I stayed with Rob. This time, I didn't breeze by the mirrors in the department store- I stopped and looked at my reflection. Rob, standing next to me, looked cool- I did not. I was led to the fragrance counter where Rob showed me how to get samples of the various colognes. He taught me that little vials of the cologne "Tommy" by Tommy Hilfiger were available on request. These "sample vials" allowed a person to go home and try out the cologne before a date or a day at the office. Following Rob's lead, I was able to score a vial from the reluctant sales girl. The next day, before school, I used the Tommy cologne, and I instantly felt a change. From that point, Rob taught me how to shape myself in an image that I could take pride in. The sweatpants were replaced by designer jeans. The sports team T-shirts were replaced by expensive hoodies that matched the hundred dollar shoes I circled in the mall, waiting for them to go on sale. My hair was cut every three and a half weeks, with very specific instructions to the hairdresser. I left Pat and the life we had enjoyed for so many years in favor of this refined focus. I still wear the Tommy cologne to this day. As grateful as I am that the vial found its way to me, it was also the first step in leaving behind a friend that did nothing wrong, other than accept me as I was.

Fashion enticed me to grow up, and I handled the situation like a child.

THE TIRED MODEL

The pieces that Intern Jessica pulled from the archive look much better in person.

"Do you wanna be here for the previews that we're scheduling with Vogue and Elle?" Intern Jessica asks me.

I shake my head no, mimicking Karen, who's standing to my right, shaking her head no.

Everyone knows it's better to have Michael and Karen host the previews so I can direct my focus toward what I'm naturally good at.

Lux tries on various archive pieces. They aren't tailored to her specific proportions, but they're a good indication of where I can tap a vein on M.Lorrie. I want my RTW collection to look like an M.Lorrie collection, but better.

"What do you think?" I keep asking Lux, as she stands in the focal point of the trifold mirror.

Anytime Lux's opinion is requested, she shrugs her shoulders in whatever stale smelling garment she's wearing. Maybe she doesn't have an opinion on these pieces because we didn't create them together. Maybe she doesn't have an opinion on these pieces because she hates that we've been demoted to ready-to-wear. The fact that Lux pursued a production piece from my Andrew Lorrie line proves that she can accept RTW, it just has to be infused with meaning.

I photograph Lux with my s1000. I no longer use Polaroids- they're too hard to find now. The s1000 is a beautiful camera, but you have to work to get a good picture. Most importantly, this unforgiving beast will not lie to me about the nature of these garments. If it looks good on the s1000, it's going to be transcendent on a real camera.

"Have you been going to castings?" I ask Lux, making small talk, afraid of the distance being projected out at me.

"When would I be going, Andrew? When? We're in here almost every damn day," Lux snaps, then she begins taking off the piece before I tell her I'm done with my pictures.

I avert my gaze, scratch my crooked nose, then mumble, "I was just curious. I can talk with your agent and-"

"-my agent doesn't give a shit," Lux says, pointed, definitive.

"Well, she's getting a fee from my brother and-"

"-don't talk to my agent," I'm instructed.

"Are you getting sick of this... of me?" I ask, tacking on the second part as an afterthought, despite the fact it's the entire point of the question.

"Sometimes I can't remember how I got to this point," Lux says.

"If you have to stop and remind yourself why you're doing something, don't do it," I tell her, as a general rule. When I finally gain the confidence to look back at the girl in the mirror, Lux turns away from me- the next Michael Lorrie piece hanging off her, unzipped, her nude back exposed.

"I didn't mean it like that. Don't... stop. Please. I need you. Don't stop," I beg, desperate. I try to surround her so she can't turn away.

Those big eyes look at me, and she says, "It's good advice."

"It's stupid advice. It's awful advice," I say.

"It connected with me," Lux admits, then shrugs again, like I asked for her opinion on the piece she's putting on.

"Are you trying to say that you're going to stop modeling?" I ask, putting my hands in my pockets to hide the shaking.

"Did I ever start?" Lux asks the mirror.

"Every day. You're modeling *every* day," I tell her, my stare slicing through her reflection.

"Then I'll never quit," she tells me. She reaches back and zips herself up, her arms bending in a seemingly impossible way.

"I thought you said I connected with you just now?" I mention, desperate for clarity.

"You did. I wasn't talking about modeling. *You* were talking about modeling," she says, then takes six steps back so I can look at the piece.

"I don't like it," I say.

THE POLO

I walk into the house on Scotland Road, and I want nothing to do with another piece of clothing for the rest of the day- possibly the rest of the week. The downstairs is quiet, but Björk is squealing through the floorboards, so I climb the staircase and make my way to Cassie's room.

In the room, on the floor, Isabella is doing her eye makeup in a mirror.

"What are you wearing?" I ask, horrified.

Isabella looks up from the mirror, deciding something, then she says, "My work uniform."

I storm into the room, as Isabella begins fixing the collar on an ill-fitting maroon polo, like the flipped neckline was the only issue I had.

I put my hands in my pockets, again. I feel everything closing in, not in a constriction, but instead in a collapse. "This shoot is for- what- a hot dog saleswoman?" I ask, my jaw clenched.

"I got a job at the movie theater. For extra money. For... model clothes?" she says, trying to spin it into something I'll support.

"The theater behind the train station?" I ask, my voice approaching a yell. This question is necessary so I know that I'm burning down the right building later tonight.

"Yeah, it's... close," she says, both of us only discussing the distance.

She's pretending this is a positive change.

This doesn't make sense to me/ This doesn't work for me/ This was *not* part of the plan.

I try to take the information casually.

I try to just accept it.

When that doesn't work, I say, "If you need money..."

"Absolutely not," she says, looking at me with disdain.

"I can call your agent and see what's available. I mean. Whatever they book you for can't be as..." I trail off because I know that Isabella didn't choose her uniform. She's only adopted this skin for safety; a safety she won't allow me to provide. Isabella might even feel she deserves this outfit. I hope that she's not using the polo as a self-defeating statement. This could be her showing me that she's not a model. She looks bad in the uniform. I'm of the belief no one can look good in this polo, but if it was placed on Lux, there's a chance she'd make it special.

I take out my work phone, then attempt to navigate the overly complicated interface with a shaking hand. I despise the phone because it makes me feel ancient and out of touch. It makes me resent technology- another sign that I will be phased out and replaced.

"Why are you on the phone?" Isabella asks me, as a glance becomes full attention.

"I'm making a call," I say.

"No," she says, springing up, pulling on my arm before I can place the phone to my ear.

"Don't worry. I'm not replacing one failing career with another," she says.

"You sound afraid," I tell her, my eyes focused on her face because I can't focus on her clothes.

"You've sounded that way since we moved in here," Isabella responds.

She considers herself "moved in." This should make things feel permanent, but I'm again reminded that this is not my house. Not anymore. What am I going to do? Buy it from Cassie? If I buy the house from Cassie, she'll never see The Boy and The Girl again, and I'll be trapped here, like them. I want her to see The Boy and The Girl- as long as they're in the right part of their loop. I need Cassie to see them, so she'll stop feeling so sorry for me, and start feeling nostalgic for me.

"Relax," Isabella says, grabbing her purse, "It's just until spring."

"It's only fall," I say, as she walks into the hall.

"It's *already* fall," she responds.

"It's *barely* fall," I yell, following behind her, trying to increase the severity of it all.

At the bottom of the stairs, Isabella turns around- a finger pointing at me, accusing me- as she hisses, "Listen, you wanted me around the house. Now I'll be here because I have to make my shifts."

"You're a model. You aren't a person who does... shift-work," I plead with her to understand.

"The clothes I'm modeling say otherwise," Isabella responds, then walks out of the house.

THE SKETCHES

I close off for a week. I sit on the floor of my bedroom with my pencils, and my black pens, and my large sheets of paper, and my tablet. Isabella brings me food; she moves the coffee machine upstairs. We don't speak often, but the look she repeatedly offers me indicates that she knows why there's a silence between us, and she's aware that she did nothing wrong.

I put on the score to *The Hours* by Philip Glass as I break this collection of bleakness down. Everything is sliced into an individual piece that can be focused on without the distraction of the whole. I need to separate my building blocks, despite the common threads.

When I have time, I will- piece by piece- fix each imperfect design, until it all works. The flaws will present themselves, and sometimes they'll cause a design to be discarded entirely; other times, the mistakes will be easily mended, and I'll stitch them without hesitation. I won't feel pleasure from my completed task, but I will exorcise some of my pain, and that's what matters.

The days on the floor spent sketching are scattered and daunting. I have too much to work from. The archive pieces/ The confusion/ The pain/ The new people in my life/ The old people threatening to leave/ The colder days/ The earlier nights/ The chains of Lux's social imbalance/ The pointless job Isabella is working/ The ugly history James is fighting/ The race against time that Irina is running/ The ugly fashion show that happens every day in the isles of the NJ Transit train/ The fact that everyone seems to be preparing for the worst, and as I sketch I begin to feel that's what I'll be providing them; it feels as though we're hopelessly limited now.

We need to be promised an escape everywhere we go; We need to be assured that the bullies of the world will be brought to justice and the wrongs will be avenged. Every narrative has to be filled with likable victims who defeat their aggressors. I won't follow the new requirements of content. I won't be a victim, and I won't present victims to the world as heroes.

I begin to pull on the scraps of time that momentarily shook me recently. I dredge up the scary moments:

-The 15-year-old model telling me, "I went through an awkward stage when I was younger."

-The rumor about an unnamed model at Flurry being a transsexual. When I pressed James for details on the model's identity, I was told, "Look around, dude. It could be literally anyone."

-The old review, e-mailed to me by a stranger, about a monochrome collection I released for a pop star. First sentence- "What's black and white and dead all over?"

-The advice a model gave me about dealing with Lux's distance, "We have the ability to change our expression based on exactly what's needed. If she's showing you something, she wants you to see it."

-A quote from Michael that the ready-to-wear collection from last season was crafted as "Rosemary's Baby meets all of Angelina's babies."

-The reporter from i-D who called, but immediately abandoned our scheduled interview, after reminding me, "The last time we met up, after I asked you about your controversial and disgusting statements, you mocked me for being a New York journalist with 'central Ohio thighs.'"

-Michael's e-mail after my first five sketches were photographed and sent to him, "You'll have to restrain yourself a bit. I think that's best for you- personally, and otherwise. Scale it back."

-My texts to James after a disturbing screener where the model could barely sit in the chair, her eyes at half-mast, "What the fuck is happening to these girls that they all look like zombies? It's not good," and his response, "Actually, zombies are very in right now."

-My realization that my biggest fear is being alone in this house.

I take the feeling of these moments and render them faithfully into looks.

I finish my sketches two days early, showing no one what I've completed.

I give myself the extra time to reconsider the designs, but I don't change anything, and at 8 AM on the due date, Michael gets his 43 sketches. I spend the rest of the day in the city, without Isabella, because she had to work at the theater.

While I'm waiting for the Dover train, I get a text, "Hey. It's Regis. Michael showed Irina the rough sketches. U pleased the unpleasable. Let's celebrate."

This message causes me to take a different train back into Jersey.

I arrive at the Hoboken bar that Regis is trapped in, while Irina does a night shoot on a rooftop a couple of blocks away. Regis tells me he likes my work/ Regis tells me it surpasses Michael's sketches for his new collection/ Regis tells me to keep it together/ Regis tells me that I haven't sketched the piece Irina will wear, yet.

The last thing that Regis tells me is, "Be careful."

On the Path train home, I dwell on this sincere warning, and I fear the plans that Michael has shared with Regis.

In my empty room on Scotland Road, I climb into bed, then wait for The Boy and The Girl to arrive. When I'm at the edge of sleep, footsteps thump closer and closer. I open my eyes, as the ray of light is breached, then The Boy speaks, "Okay. Here they are." His manner tonight is sensitive and insecure.

"Already?" The Girl asks, stepping into the sliver of spotlight. "This is insane. How do you work this fast?"

"They're only sketches," The Boy says.

"They're amazing," The Girl says, then bends down, disappearing for a moment, the edge of the bed blocking my sight line. When the Girl reappears, she's holding a sketch she picked up off the bedroom floor. "This one," she says, studying it, "This one is mine."

"I haven't sketched your piece yet," The Boy says.

"Yes, you have. I'm holding it," The Girl declares.

"Put it back," The Boy demands.

"Tell me I get this look or you don't get it back," The Girl says.

The Boy looks at The Girl, and the fear he wore on his face when he entered the room changes into a muted appreciation.

"You're a pain in the ass," The Boy says, with a warmth that doesn't match his words.

"I know what I like," The Girl responds, cutely.

"And everyone agrees you have incredible taste, which leads us to the problem," The Boy says, dipping into the darkness.

When he returns to the light, The Boy is holding about seven or eight sketches. Carefully lining up their edges, one atop the other, he makes a swift motion, tearing the sketches, then letting the pieces flutter to the floor.

"Are you serious, right now?" The Girl shrieks. She seems to know that she cannot fix what's been done.

"New direction," The Boy says, picking up the rest of the sketches, "I felt like the piece you picked didn't fit, but it's the rest that doesn't work. The other looks don't match your piece. I need to start over."

The Girl hands The Boy the design that changed things before a stitch was ever sewn.

The Boy and The Girl move away from each other, into the darkness, separated like the halves of the discarded sketches.

THE PLUS ONE

"These pieces are... complex," Michael says, going through the sketches on his desk, as James nods in agreement. Of the 43 looks I've brought him, I know that as many as 13 of them will be discarded. Normally, at this juncture in the process, I'd invite the pop star or socialite I'm designing for into a meeting, and the pieces would be discussed, then a vote would be taken about which looks belong and which don't fit. Today, that is not happening. Today, my sketches are being sorted into two neat piles by the man who built this house. This is not a conversation, it's a declaration.

"After we're done here, I'll begin building muslin concept pieces, based on Lux's measurements. That's the Fibonacci sequence of the female body," I explain, my hands clasped in front of me as I stand at attention.

"Such a talented composer, his music sounds like Heaven," James says, then he fixes his glasses when he sees that Michael and I have both taken note of this statement, and we're studying him, trying to figure out how a person like James exists in the real world.

James mimics the way I'm standing, and unfortunately for him, he continues his thought, "The way Fibonacci composed his sonic masterpieces is how we're going to compose this show." When he doesn't get the reaction he's searching for, he simplifies it further, "Basically, we'll be working with the mantra, 'No Fatties.'"

My designs utilize a bias cut, stolen from the queen of the bias, Madeleine Vionnet. This cut allows my work to appeal to larger women, once the design is no longer in a sample size. A bias cut, featuring a slice on a diagonal inside of a clean vertical line, is a technique that I find to be very romantic. Although fat women find the bias cut more flattering, I don't design with them as a consideration, because part of fashion is fantasy, and dampening fantasy for the acceptance of a slovenly culture seems criminal. Plus-size models cannot fit into the garments I've designed, however, if Michael's team blows out the pattern a couple of inches, these ignored women will look fantastic in my work. Michael has encouraged the bias cut because it will make my high fashion leanings easier to sell, but for me, the sales are secondary to making Lux look ethereal.

With Lux's emotional remoteness, I've become obsessed with her figure- the measurements remaining reliably the same, but their importance ballooning by the day. The models who wear my final creations will be chosen by James, with Lux's measurements as a direct reference.

People create in different ways and this is how I create. No one complains when a proven director insists on shooting film when most everyone has gone digital. No one complains when the veteran screenwriter hands in a screenplay written on a typewriter.

Every shade of skin will be on my runway because I'm interested in a body type this time. I don't need the screeners, instead, I need James to take measurements of his screener girls. If the model mirrors Lux, I'll demand her presence on my runway.

"Okay," Michael says, stacking 30 sketches in an orderly fashion on his desk. "These will do," he says.

James and I look at each other.

"You like them?" James asks, encouraged by Michael's accepting initial reaction.

"I've thought of a new name for the brand. The designs fit the new name," Michael says, making this about *his* accomplishment.

"What's the new name?" I ask, half expecting it to be, "Everyone Look At My Retarded Brother's Failures."

"MLORE," Michael says.

"MLORE?" James repeats, making sure he gets it right.

"MLORE," Michael confirms.

I nod, accepting it. "I can work with that. It's like *More* Lorrie, because there are two of us," I say.

Michael laughs at my statement for a very long time, like I told a good joke, then says, "Oh, Andrew. Never lose your sense of humor."

THE HAPPY MODEL

Lux calls me and tells me that she wants to hide in the bathroom, while I buy her drinks. The fact that she called and didn't text means that she feels bad about the archive fitting we did. I feel bad about it too. After I nervously e-mailed Lux pictures of all my sketches, she became excited and rejuvenated again. The bones of the collection seemed to remind Lux of what we're capable of achieving together.

Returning to the bar that comforted us the night before the last collection showed feels like hitting the reset button on all of the turmoil Lux and I have gone through since I destroyed our second chance. I order a gin and tonic, and a PBR. The bartender lets me flirt with her again. The night offers me a break from the panic. I consider that this coming winter might not be as cold as I imagined it would be.

Our usual hiding spot in the back room is vacant, so I sit down, then place our drinks on the table.

I text Lux, "There's a line forming for the bathroom," then I put my phone down and lean over to grab my PBR.

A moment later, Lux is sitting next to me, smiling.

"How'd it go with Mr. Lorrie?" Lux asks, happy. She's wearing an outfit that I've never seen, and I begin to realize that this outfit is probably why tonight is happening. Lux seems comfortable in her skin again, and she clearly wants to be seen. I don't care *why* tonight happened, so I don't give any of this a second thought, even though I don't agree with Lux wearing flats with an above-the-knee skirt.

"Michael- uh- approved the sketches," I say, still in minor disbelief.

"Makes sense," Lux responds.

"Why does it make sense?" I ask, then I point out, "It makes no sense. Even James was confused."

"When is James *not* confused?" Lux asks.

I laugh at this, then I tell my friend, "Thank you for inviting me out to buy you drinks."

"Oh!" Lux brightens up, "Speaking of buying stuff... I bought you a book!" she says, opening her purse.

I don't look in her purse because I find myself fearing what else it may contain.

With a jubilant vibe, Lux hands me a book with an orange spine that displays white block letters reading "IBSEN."

"Okay, I know you're going to be like, 'No,' so let me explain," Lux says.

"I like it," I assure her, but this seems to do nothing to calm her suspicions, and she begins her explanation, "Hedda Gabler, one of the plays in the book, is a very good piece of literature. Don't worry, it's nothing like that Invisible Man book I tried to get you to read. And, yeah, the spine is creased, but listen, I originally bought you a new copy, but the translation is shit, so this is my copy, and I'm sorry it has writing in it. I didn't return the shitty new copy so technically I still spent money on this."

I smile at Lux; this is the part of her I supremely love.

"Thank you," I say sincerely, "This means a lot to me," I tell her. I want to raise my hand up and touch her face, but I don't.

"I feel bad about the archive fitting," Lux quietly admits.

"We're in a weird situation. I just need you to keep it together," I say softly, maybe only to myself.

"I've started writing again, and I've changed therapists recently," Lux offers.

"How's that working out?" I ask.

"As expected," Lux tells me, and I nod at this.

"What'd you tell the brownstone guy?"

"What?" Lux asks, putting her drink down. "What?" she repeats when I don't immediately respond.

"How do you dump a therapist?" I ask.

"Oh," Lux says, then picks her drink back up, "I just said, ya know, 'I'm still fucking insane, you didn't fix me,' and the only response to that, is, like, 'True,' because it's an impossible point to argue, so we parted ways after I settled my tab."

"You had a tab with your therapist?"

"Yeah, I'm not the only model going there so she understood the... inconsistencies of... wait, did you tell me which sketches Michael denied?"

"The halter dress, the cupcake dress, the ape arms dress."

"He's dumb to pass up the ape arm dress," Lux declares. "Who the fuck doesn't want ape arms?"

"Girls who want skinny arms?" I presume on behalf of my customer.

"Girls with skinny arms have skinny legs so who cares about their arms?" Lux points out.

This is the old Lux. She has been resuscitated by my sketches, and her new outfit. Fashion saves another friendship, another life.

So many people look at high fashion as something evil. The evil things about the industry- trade/ UA girls/ the predatory photographers/ the debited expenses/ the EDs- are avoided or ignored in favor of the ever-popular attack that the fashion industry preys on feelings of inadequacy. The, "You're setting an unrealistic expectation for women." The, "You've photoshopped everything so much these girls don't even look like real humans." And, of course, the ever popular, "Real women have curves."

I understand how the fashion industry could seem cruel when a blue collar suburban dad- just to keep his daughter's affection- has to spend an entire month's paycheck on a purse named after Chloe Warren, only to see it get shoved into the back of a closet seven months later. That part of fashion sucks.

I feel the fear of the naturally thin girl who has to answer for the behavioral pitfalls of models who achieve a rail-thin look with the help of drugs or bad habits. Answering to allegations of unnatural diets when genetics is at fault is not fun. That part of fashion sucks.

I feel for the girl whose dream of modeling in New York City is destroyed by the hard reality of high rent and premium pricing. That part of fashion sucks.

I realize there are lots of things going on in the fashion industry that can scare people, but a girl who has been genetically blessed, bringing a designer's vision to life and inspiring people around the globe... that, I don't fear. That, I cherish. That part of fashion is incredible.

THE CHECKS

The Hours score plays over the stereo as I take out *Ulysses*, then spray the logs in the fireplace with lighter fluid.

I ask Isabella for her lighter, and she reaches into the waistband of her shorts, takes out the white Bic, then tosses it across the room to me, all while never looking up from the paper she's reading at the roll top desk.

Unexpectedly, I catch the lighter, and I'm a little sad that Isabella didn't witness this rare moment.

I light a *Vogue* subscription card on fire, then toss it onto the soaked logs. The flames roar up with a pleasing immediacy, so I sit down on the sofa and reward myself with a beer for all my hard work.

When Isabella doesn't join me, I arch my neck to see what she's reading at the desk.

"Why does Cassie have checks from Michael?" Isabella asks.

"She's a model, Michael is a designer," I say, then sip my Heineken.

"She's a model who has been a CK exclusive for- oh- seven straight seasons now, but these checks from Michael are dated as recently as last week," Isabella points out.

I try to focus on the fire- on the beer- on the moment that could be relaxing, if I allow it to be.

The CD ends, then there's a mechanical clatter as the changer switches to the next disc, The National's *Boxer*.

The paranoia eating at Isabella begins to nibble at me, and I say, "Maybe it's residuals... for... wait... the checks showed up last week?" I ask. I take a bigger sip from my beer, hoping to numb it all, but Isabella is right- this doesn't make sense. With no choice, I exhale, "Show me."

Isabella finally gets up, then approaches me, while explaining, "I brought in the mail because it was starting to burst out of the box. When I saw something from Michael's company, I thought maybe it was for us, so I opened it and..."

Sitting down next to me, smelling like dirty hair and a perfume I can't ID, Isabella hands over the envelopes. I open one, then review what appears to be a direct deposit check stub for a significant amount of money.

"Why would Michael be paying Cassie?" I ask Isabella her own question.

One of my favorite sights- Isabella's gap- makes an appearance when she realizes I'm following her train of thought.

Instead of marveling at this smile, like I usually do, I stand up bolt straight, then walk toward the front of the house where my jacket is.

"Where are you going?" Isabella asks.

"To call Cassie," I say.

From the other room, Isabella feigns offense, "I can't listen?"

"I want to protect you," I yell back, "If you're in danger here, I'm going to find a safe place for you."

I hear Isabella giggle at this, clearly perceiving my reaction to be melodramatic.

I grab my phone out of my jacket pocket, then with no hesitation, I make the call.

The moment Cassie picks up, I ask, "Why is my brother writing checks to you?"

"Why is my decades-since ex going through my things?" Cassie responds back.

Since I can't mention that it was the teenage girl I've moved into the house on Scotland Road who went through her things, I continue the conversation with an accusatory tone, "Michael Lorrie check stubs that came in the mail."

"I get the mail from the house shipped to me once a month," Cassie says, "I haven't seen it in a while, though. In fact, please ship the mail to me at the end of the month. I'll have my accountant review the check stubs."

"These aren't small checks," I say.

"So? Do I owe you a cut?" she asks, maybe covering, maybe not understanding.

"All I'm asking for is an answer."

"Why is the silly dog biting the hand that feeds him?" Cassie questions.

"Because he's worried about who's massaging the hand that's feeding him," is my answer.

"Then he should take a step outside of the food chain."

"Cassie, please. I'm trying to do the right thing here."

"No. You're trying to get answers because you can't be left out of the loop," Cassie says to me.

"I'm trying to close the loop," I say.

"I'll save you the trouble," Cassie responds, then I hear the line go dead.

THE SECOND ROUND

"Get me in front of her," I demand, walking into the center room of the workshop.

"Pardon?" James asks, looking up from his laptop. He has his back to the wall so that no one can see what's on his screen, and this is ideal for all parties involved.

"The screener you sent last night worked. I'm sold," I say, walking over to James. "I wanted to wear what the girl in the video was wearing so much that I'm afraid I'll catch myself in Isabella's clothes later tonight."

"Well, you do wear girl jeans," James says, raising his shoulders.

"They fit better," I defend myself, realizing that the jeans I'm wearing today were designed custom for my measurements, but they still look like womenswear. This is probably the reason Michael has someone else designing the menswear portion of MLORE.

To move things forward, I say, "I want to meet the girl from the screener so I can verify my first impression, but I gotta tell ya James, I think she's the first discovery you've made."

"Why?" James asks, with the brim of his cap angled toward the ceiling and his eyes looking at me from the bottom of his glasses. This reminds me of the look my father gave me when I told him I was going to MAFTA, just like Michael.

"I want to see her in person," I say.

"Nah, she's not model material," James declares, closing his laptop.

"What do mean 'not model material?' That girl is *nothing but* model material. That girl has no greater purpose in this world other than to be a model," I say, passionate that we've unearthed someone special.

"She looks different in person," James says, standing up, walking toward the door. I follow, not letting this slide, "Then why are we making screeners if girls look different in person? Isn't the entire reason that you're filming these little videos is so we can find girls, bring them in, interview them in person, then get them locked for the show? For once, I think your plan actually worked and you're sabotaging yourself."

"Okay. I didn't want to sound like a bully, but... she smells," James says, like I forced him into this pointless admission.

"James. Your comebacks need work," I say, impressed at how shallow his pool of insults has become.

"I'm stating a fact, Andrew. She smells awful," James says, his pace quickening.

"She'll still look great in our line. You can't see smell," I say, following my fleeing partner.

"She's not an option," James says, walking out of the workshop room, stoking my interest in the screener girl more with every determined step.

I continue my pursuit, campaigning for the model merely because James doesn't want her. "So maybe she smells. We'll have to warn hair and makeup, but we'll be fine. My girls are always under so many layers of powder that all of them smell the same."

"How much did you watch?" James asks me, focused on an unknown destination.

"All of it," I say, to please him.

"I don't think you did," James responds, sounding pretty sure of this fact.

"I did," I lie.

James stops walking, then flicks the brim of his hat up so he can get a good look at me. He searches my face, then either finds something or confirms something, and he tells me, "She's not coming back, end of story."

I stare at James, waiting for the real reason why this girl has been excluded so definitively. I push my tongue against my bottom row of teeth. James doesn't crack. He stares back at me. He doesn't even fiddle with the brim of his hat.

"Okay," I relent.

"Okay, we aren't going to see her," James says, not asks.

"Okay," I echo.

James immediately returns back to his casual self. "Besides," he says with a hard reset, "Tonight I'm meeting a model that's, like, a thousand times better than the last girl."

"If she's a thousand times better than the last girl who was- let the record show- as good as she is allegedly smelly, then let's just book this new girl right now."

"Respect the screening process," James says.

The screening process is a babysitter for James, so I decide to let the trivial game continue.

To confirm that models aren't being excluded merely because they refuse to fuck James, I'm going to watch the next screener until the end.

THE REPLACEMENT

Alone in the workshop, I drink out of the 24 oz Budweiser can I bought at some point between the first and second hour of waiting for Lux.

I'm unable to look at my phone, out of fear regarding what it will show me. I'm tired of having to witness beautiful women sitting in a hotel room, with a need to please in their eyes that seems absolute.

The moment I finish my beer, I hear the clack of heels in the hallway, and this immediately brings me to my feet.

Burning for the comfort of Lux, I decide I'll accept her excuse, but when I walk out into the hall, I receive neither the comfort nor the excuse. I receive something else, and I become unhinged.

"Who the hell are you?" I ask, walking toward the girl who just entered my space without asking. I know this girl is a model. I recognize her face from somewhere. It's not the face I need. She's not the person I need.

"Today. I'm... uh... Lux," the model says, strutting toward me with the trained runway walk that all my girls use.

"Is this some sort of joke?" I ask.

"No. I'm covering Lux's shift," the model responds.

"Modeling is not shift-work," I have to inform another beautiful girl, then I demand, Call Lux."

"She's busy."

"Doing what, exactly?"

"Things that aren't your business," the model says, not backing down.

"You're not wearing my clothes," I declare, staring intensely at the girl so she understands that whatever game she's playing, I'm not participating.

"Yet..." she responds, with a misplaced confidence, "...I'm not wearing your clothes, *yet*."

"You can give up on-"

"-good enough to sit front row, but not good enough to do a fitting for you, huh?" she asks, then smirks.

I close my eyes, and I say her name, "Madeleine." I can't help but feel like an asshole. I literally pulled this girl into the shitstorm of my life, then yelled at her when she attempted to stay. People leaving me is my biggest fear, and apparently, the second thing I fear is when they aggressively choose not to leave.

When I open my eyes, Madeleine asks, "I'm that forgettable?" then she takes off her long gray pea coat and hands it to me. I accept the coat, confirming that she's not wearing my clothes- yet- but it's just a matter of getting her out of the non-Lorrie outfit she arrived in.

Lux is missing, and that's bad, but with my minimal beer buzz, tinged with a high school embarrassment, I feel relief that Madeleine just performed a B&E on my life. This meeting in my workshop would've happened much earlier if I had a way to locate Madeleine after my show. I had ceased pursuing this girl because all I had to go on was a murky screenshot of her in the front row. I wasn't sure if she had an agency, and there was no libel-filled piece published online under her name that I could read and start hating her over. Her entire existence was a mystery, until now. I had given up on her, yet here she is. She hasn't given up on me.

"How'd Lux know to get in contact with you?" I ask, because all of this feels so calculated- like Lux planned to miss work- and instead of merely telling me, she set up an alternate model that she knew I couldn't refuse.

"I was in the kitchen making dinner, and she asked me," Madeleine says.

"You're Lux's roommate," I say, drawing the obvious conclusion.

"Indeed."

"And you were at the show because..."

"Lux gave me the invitation that Karen passed on to her. I'm- ya know- kinda a big fan of yours. Still," Madeleine admits, and it's clear that people who are my fans now file me under the "guilty pleasure" category along with reruns of *Gossip Girl* and social!heavy playlists.

"You're... Lux's roommate?" I ask, again, mentally filling in the backstory on Madeleine that taints her.

Immediately feeling the weight, Madeleine looks away, then locks her hand around the back of her neck, "She's talked about me. Shit. I promise I'm not..."

"It's fine," I assure her, "I know... you're..."

"A psychotic bitch?"

"Yes. Precisely," I say, then smile, "Sorry to hear about your breakup."

"Pardon?"

"Lux sort of let it slip that you were going crazy because of a difficult breakup, so she's had to skip out on me, to take care of you. It's fine," I assure her.

Madeleine stares at me for a beat, then says, "Yes, my breakup. Uh. Yeah. He left me without warning, so who better than me to show up when you're being ditched by your girl?" Madeleine quips, a bit sharp, not appreciative that Lux gossiped about her like that.

"She's not my girl, and I'm not being ditched," I say.

"She's not here," Madeleine responds, looking around the hallway.

"Did she say where she was going?" I ask.

Madeleine shakes her head back and forth.

"You didn't ask her?"

Madeleine repeats the wordless motion.

"You aren't curious?"

"I have an idea," Madeleine says, finally responding with words.

"What's your idea?"

"None of your business," she tells me.

I look at Madeleine. I need to keep her here because she has information I need.

"How tall are you?" I ask.

"Same as Lux."

"Really?"

"Yeah. We stood back to back and everything."

"You look like you weigh more than her," I say, testing the model.

"And you look older than your older brother," Madeleine says.

I smile, and admit, "Sometimes I feel older."

"I liked your after-party," Madeleine tells me, to steer the conversation away from the topic of Michael.

"Did you?" I respond probingly.

"Yeah. I liked that you said those things about the fashion bitches, then went and had fun."

"I said those things so this industry could start treating you better," I assure her.

"And now you're kicking me out of your studio. Sticking to the plan I see."

"You're right," I say, "Please stay. I'm sticking to the plan."

THE LOST ONE

While leafing through one of Cassie's *Vogues* in Starbucks, I stop on an editorial featuring the screener model that James wouldn't let me meet. I take a picture of the page, then reverse google image search the editorial on my phone. I get a name- Georgia Ashlock. I look at the other model in the editorial- she has her arms wrapped around Georgia's legs, and the expression on her face shows no indication that Georgia is stinky.

I google Georgia Ashlock's *models.com* profile, find her New York agency, then I immediately leave Starbucks, and walk upstairs and get on the NYC bound express train that happens to whoosh into the station seconds after I step out onto the platform. I look behind me to make sure that James isn't following me today. My timing is never this good.

An hour later, I walk into the Flurry office.

A text from Michael's Jessica reminds me that the name of our contact at Flurry is Randal Gooch, so I ask around until I'm directed to Randal's desk.

A man in his early 40's, whose every feature is exaggerated like a caricature of Rocky Balboa, glances up at me when I arrive at the edge of his desk and introduce myself.

"They liked the trade," is the first thing Randal says to me.

"Pardon?" I ask.

"Cori is signed with us, you know that, right?" Randal asks.

Maybe my original instinct was wrong; Maybe Flurry girls *are* my girls.

"I thought she was with Zebra," I say.

"Zebra?" Randal repeats, looking at me for only the second time. Randal's chest inflates as though he just swallowed a laugh.

"I'm actually here because I'm looking for Georgia," I say.

"Did you try a map?" he asks.

"The model Georgia," I specify.

"Georgia?" he asks, "You mean Virginia?"

"I thought all these models are foreign, why the fuck are they all named after states?" I ask, frustrated.

"I think Virginia left us for IMG," Randal says. "They were already Virginia's Paris agent. Yeah, I believe that she went all in on IMG. They're everywhere. They're a worldwide conglomerate. The UN should, ya know..." Randal trails off, abandoning his crusade.

I pace in front of the desk, and ask, "Why is everyone so apathetic about beautiful women in this city? Where *are* these girls?"

"Maybe they're in... Virginia? Georgia?" Randal mumbles.

"I'm not doing this who's-on-first shit with you," I say.

Randal looks up at me, for only the third time, then reminds me, "Girls disappear all the time. It's fine. Take a look in the lobby."

"Yes. Girls do disappear all the time... in an industry where unsupervised minors, too poor to bring their parents to New York, go into strange buildings, and meet with photographers who are required to prove nothing about themselves beyond the fact that they own a camera. How is that right?"

Something about James' screeners has made me keenly aware that the girls arriving at castings in this city are desperate enough to put themselves in compromising positions. Ever since this has been brought to the forefront of my consciousness, I feel an overpowering need to protest the system that's in place.

"It is what it is," Randal says, picking up his cell phone.

"Can people stop saying that?" I heave, pulling at my hair.

"It's generally what someone says when they want you to go away," a model says, passing behind me, and I don't even bother to look at her.

"I think you should be the last one to talk about saving models," Randal adds, but his tone is too limp to provide the bite the statement needs.

"I'm modifying that about myself," I say, fixing my hair. "I know that I'm incapable of change, but I'm pretty skilled at modifying," I admit, knowing that Randal isn't listening. "At least I'm doing more than putting young girls in debt," I jab.

When I don't leave, Randal decides to calmly defend his practices, "We give them an advance of money, debited against their future earnings. That's always how it goes. Sometimes, it doesn't end up yielding much for the girl, but that's because she's a talent that doesn't connect. When it works- it's amazing. We're their benefactors. If that makes you sick, pay your models instead of giving them trade."

I turn away from Randal, locking and loading another Andrew Lorrie signature rant, but I spot a familiar face that changes my plans. It's the black girl from the apartment Isabella was trapped in. She's waiting for me to finish this conversation, so I end it immediately, sarcastically mumbling, "Thanks, Randal."

I walk over to the black girl. Her hair is in tight braids and her true beauty is apparent under the bright office lights.

"Didn't mean to interject," the model says, and I realize that she was the girl who passed by me.

I need to speak to this girl, only because beautiful women are a band-aid for me.

"Who are you trying to save now?" the model asks.

She was actually paying attention to my concerns- something that the careless Randal was incapable of.

"Georgia Ashlock," I respond, "I wouldn't say I'm trying to save her- I just wish that someone could tell me where she is."

"I don't know her," the model says.

"What's a Blend girl doing in the Flurry office? Should I be concerned about this?" I ask, proving my interest is in gossip and casting, not hunting.

"I think I'm ready for a change."

"When you make that change, will you let me know where you land?" I request, unwilling to lose another fresh face in the shuffle.

"You got it," she says.

"Call me," I demand.

"I will, promise," she assures me.

"Not then. Now. I want proof you programmed the information from my card into your phone."

"Why?" she asks, suddenly nervous.

"Cards go missing, but a girl's phone never goes missing. She wouldn't allow it."

The black model nods at this, takes out her phone, and after three flicks, my work phone is vibrating.

I nod at the model, and in warm way, she asks, "How's Isabella?"

There's a pause in my response, and this sends me elsewhere.

It sends me home, to find the true answer to that question.

On the train, all I can think about is how easily Isabella could disappear like Georgia. California/Michael fires her/ Japan- the ways she could exit my life are multiplying. She has infinite potential, and all I have is her.

Approaching the house on Scotland Road, I see Isabella on the porch, the light from my tablet illuminating her face. I take out my phone and snap a grainy picture.

I make my way through the house, *The Hours* CD playing downstairs with no one is listening, the faint smell of pot hanging in the air.

Upstairs, I move through our room, and out to the porch.

Isabella looks over at me, caught off guard.

"How was your day?" I ask.

Isabella gets out of the chair, speechless, concerned. She's still wearing her work polo.

"Sit down," I say, lowering a hand, easing the situation.

When Isabella returns to her seat, I say, "I saw your ex-roommate at Flurry today."

"Everyone in that apartment was signed to Blend," she says.

"I guess you weren't the only one who wanted out."

"Why were you at Flurry?" is Isabella's next question, not, "Which one of my roommates did you see?"

"I was looking for a model," I respond.

"Ah, gonna move her into the basement?" Isabella responds, looking out to the street.

"What? No. Listen, James is recording these screeners, and-" I stop. I don't want Isabella to know about this strange process because she'll try to sit for James. Isabella, like Lux, is careful to make sure that she doesn't receive any benefit from being close to me. She'll forever do things "the right way" so that no one thinks she's walking MLORE because of her "connections."

"Screeners?" Isabella asks.

"James filmed a screener with Georgia Ashlock. Do you know her?"

"She's who you were looking for?"

"Yeah, I saw her in a magazine, and it reminded me that I wanted to look her up," I admit.

"I've posted so many pictures of her on my blog," Isabella says.

"Are they recent?" I ask, my hand gripping the back of the chair that Isabella is sitting in.

"The last photo set I posted was from a semi-recent Vogue ed. Why?"

"Just curious. Are there any recent candids of her? Any model-off-duty snaps?" I ask, my mouth dry.

Isabella turns to me, her red lips in a frown, "Are you trying to-"

"-I want her to walk for us, and she's missing, but I'm the only person who finds this troubling."

"I find it troubling," Isabella says, leaving it at that.

"I'm just trying to find her," I say, because I can't explain it otherwise.

"She probably went home."

"What do you mean she probably went home? The MLORE job could have been her break. She did a screener with James. He doesn't want to cast her, but I can't figure out why, and it's bothering me."

"Maybe he doesn't think the collection will work so he doesn't want to get her wrapped up in it," Isabella says, turning to me. I flutter five quick blinks, and I can see Isabella regrets her statement, so she circles back, "Or maybe there's another reason."

"Yeah. Maybe," I say, not letting Isabella and her infinite possibilities fix things.

"You were going to help her, huh?" Isabella asks.

"Yeah. I was," I tell myself.

"Cute," she says, and she doesn't mean in the kitten way.

"Come on. Don't do that. I was going to help her in the same way I'm helping you."

"The same way," Isabella repeats.

"Not the exact same way," I say, huffing out softly, "I'm talking about the work."

"Ah, yes. You're the picture of professionalism... living with one of your models, while you-"

"-what do you want me to do? Sleep in the workshop? Go back to LA where there's no scene? Get a hotel room on my brother's credit card? *This* exists because we need this house. We need to be here," I say, losing my temper.

"Do *we*?" Isabella asks, relaxed.

"Yes, otherwise you'll go home- because you don't believe in this collection- because you don't believe in me."

"Turn it back on me. Nice," Isabella says.

"Listen, I'm not on trial here," I defend myself.

"Does that mean I am?" she asks.

THE EXTENDED EDITION

I plug my personal phone into the charger, then I retreat to bed. I make sure the lamp on the nightstand is on, so that the only disruption I could experience would be Isabella stepping into the room. I'm not tired; the adrenaline from the fight out on the porch still courses through me. The casualness in which everyone operates regarding a potentially missing girl further exacerbates my distrust of this industry.

With nothing else to do, I find my work phone, then I review the pictures I took of Madeleine in my workshop.

I'm unable to edit the pictures on the phone, and I can't locate a notepad app that will overlay on the pictures, so I have to open my Gmail, then cumbersomely swipe between screens.

At some point between writing quick notes and toggling back to photographs I took, a screener starts playing.

I can't determine if I touched the screen the instant the video arrived or if the file started streaming automatically.

The setup is the same as it always is- A model in her late teens, wearing a white tank top and black pants/ A hotel room/ The curtains are drawn/ James is off camera.

The familiar checklist of questions about the blonde model's age, who she's signed with, and where she's from are rambled out with an inflection-less regularity that belies James' normal demeanor, but the voice coming from the phone is unmistakably his.

"I was scouted at a community pool/"I would like to make more model friends, beyond just the Brazilians- they accept anyone/"My career? I'd like to see it go anywhere! Besides LA," are the girl's answers.

As the screener progresses, the model's voice gets scratchy, and she begins coughing quietly into a balled fist before every answer. She's just another victim of the looming winter.

More questions are asked, one of them being, "Would you like a drink?" When this question is asked, I say, "No," out loud, like the model can hear me. The drink offer doesn't seem to be in response to the model's nagging cough. The question was asked only after the coughing fit had subsided.

I watch the model nod her blonde hair, confirming she'd like the drink, then someone off camera- not James- reaches an arm into the frame, and hands the girl a glass of water. The glass is tall- it's an iced tea glass- not the short stubby glasses that are the signature of every hotel in the city. I choose to assume the glass is from room service because this assumption allows me to continue watching the screener.

The model takes a massive gulp of what I hope is only water, then she relaxes and unleashes a smile that could appear in one of those unimportant clothing catalogs that are still shipped out despite an entire generation migrating exclusively to online shopping.

As the video continues, the model begins to look sicker, yet happier, and James' questions gradually leave the realm of the fashion industry completely.

"What's your favorite thing to do when you have a week to yourself?" is answered by the model with a dreamlike coo of, "Fuck. I like to find a beautiful boy, and I like to live at his place for a couple days, and I like to fuck."

I realize this will be the first screener that I watch until the end. I'm so focused on the phone that, what I wanted most tonight- Isabella sleeping next to me- would now become an unwelcome distraction. I desperately hope that the end of the screener is near. I anxiously hope for a goodbye that sends everyone in a separate, safe direction.

"You like to fuck?" is James' next question, the "k" pronounced with an unromantic sharpness. This is the first time he's followed up for more information after receiving a response, and this is the last question I want the girl answering.

Gradually letting her posture dip, her left shoulder angling toward the camera, the model smiles into the lens, and slurs slowly, "I find the most beautiful boys. I love beautiful boys."

"What about beautiful men?" James asks, and my spit begins to taste like copper in my mouth. I become an unwilling voyeur.

"I like all beautiful things," the girl gasps, and I panic. She's been drugged. I need to stop this- yet, I don't. I continue watching, my body sweating, my mind reeling.

"Do you think Michael's clothes are beautiful?" James asks, and I immediately fear that my brother *isn't* asexual, it just takes something this specifically fucked for him to get off.

"The beautifulest," the model stumbles through the word, but eventually gets it out. Then, when she bobs forward again, as though she's going to say something additional about the collection, she freezes, like her mind is taking a small break. I tap the screen because there's no sound and the girl is motionless. When I lift my finger from the upper left corner of the screen, I notice the curtain behind the model move. I touch the screen again, somehow interpreting this movement to be a result of my gesture. The curtain doesn't move after I flick the screen. I watch as the model coos out additional rudimentary thoughts, then the curtain begins to pull away, revealing a man in all black, wearing a mask with a red X on it. A chill rockets up my spine, and the shiver bobbles the phone out of my hands and off the edge of the bed. My heart hammering, my knees land on the hardwood, as I reach for the cell. Once I have it in my grip, I take six giant breathes, then I look back at the screen.

The model is gone, the chair is gone, the man is gone, the curtains are still, and the phone is silent.

THE HEAT

I stay home. I don't go into the office.

A text to James- "Up for a Jersey diner dinner tonight? My treat," is fired out from my work phone, then I walk away. I don't wait for a response, because I know that James cannot turn this invitation down. I leave my phone on the nightstand, since I'm unsure what type of information it's capturing about me. Michael has placed a hacked device in my hands.

Last night, I desperately searched for the file I was sent, but it disappeared as fast as it arrived. Michael has my work phone rooted, and nothing I do on this phone is safe or confidential. If people are worried about the government spying on them, they should be more worried about Michael Lorrie taking a peek because he can and will use that history against you. Two words sear my brain. Big. Brother.

I rush down two flights of stairs, then search around the basement, until I find Cassie's sewing machine. Inspiration hits, and I now want to create curtain-like dresses. I want my models to be mistaken for just background, until they step forward and stop hearts.

The curtains in the house come down. I tell myself it's for the line, and not because I require The Boy and The Girl to bring me predictable joy.

I leave the curtains up in the bedroom because I fear the possibility that The Boy and The Girl will go macabre, like the screeners, and I'll be surrounded by dread. I need to be able to shut out the demons.

I take out my personal phone, then text Lux, "If you come to South Orange, I'll pay for everything," then I drag the curtains down into the basement.

I tell myself, "This fabric is perfect for the line."

Andrew Lorrie, The Designer, immediately hisses back at me, "*This fabric has no place on the runway. What's the real reason you took down those curtains?*"

"Because I'm inspired. These curtains are going to be our next masterpiece," I tell The Designer.

"*The man in the mask walked out from behind the curtains,*" I'm reminded.

"Unrelated," I say, flattening the fabric on a long table.

"*Do you really think you can protect Isabella from what's happening by merely taking down the curtains? Are you trying to turn something you fear into something you celebrate? Are you finally collaborating with your partner?*" The Designer asks me.

I refuse to answer any more of his questions.

Without The Designer's help, I sew two full sleeves that I cut from the curtain fabric, then I check my personal phone. Lux hasn't responded to my text.

I search the house, until I find Isabella in the library, on her MacBook, video chatting with Matthew from the after-party band. Isabella doesn't see me so I walk behind her, and when I pop into frame, Matthew laughs.

"I didn't know you two were friends," I say.

"He spoke to me during your after-party," Isabella informs me.

"When?" I ask.

"After you went running," I hear Matthew respond.

I don't look at the MacBook when I ask, "Can you two continue this conversation in the basement?"

"Isabella, are you okay in that house?" Matthew asks with genuine concern.

"I only asked her that because I'm designing down there. I need Isabella for a fitting," I say, giving Matthew a reassuring smile so he doesn't tell Blend that I am abusing one of their models. I'm the Lorrie brother *not* hurting models. I want that distinction to be clear.

Isabella says goodbye to Matthew, then follows me down into the basement. When she sees the sliced up curtains, she asks, "Are we having a Sound of Music moment?"

I hear The Designer laugh at this comment, and I beg, "Please help me. I promise it won't take more than a half hour."

Isabella does the fitting for me, but she goes behind one of the curtains that hang from a rafter whenever she puts on the slices of a garment I'm making. I realize she's not wearing a bra. I don't think I've ever seen one of her bras. All of these thoughts are new for me because Isabella does my laundry now. I'm not even sure if the dry cleaners on South Orange Ave are still in business anymore.

After I complete a piece that *will* go into the collection- Michael's approval pending- I return upstairs to get my $1000.

When I grab the camera, I notice my work phone is blinking, but before I check the message, I get a Heineken, crack it, then down half of it.

Still unsteady, I press the button on the right side of the phone.

"I'll see you at 6," reads James' response to my text from earlier.

I look at the time on the phone- 5:40 PM.

"Are you in South Orange?" I text.

"I thought you were gonna stand me up," James sends back.

"Are you in South Orange?" I text again.

"Relax, dude," he texts back.

I refuse to follow the text's directions.

Two minutes later, I receive another text, "I'm on the train to Lorrieland."

The 5:18 arrives in South Orange at 5:49 PM.

I go back into the basement, and I tell Isabella that I'm meeting James, and she can't come.

"Um, Okay," is her response.

"I'm sorry," is my response.

"For?" is her response.

I don't answer. I go back upstairs and throw on my Saint Laurent jacket, then tightly pull a black scarf around my neck.

The walk to the diner is peaceful, and both of my phones don't vibrate. I begin to wonder if the only way I can control James is to become his best friend, then I wonder if that's what I tried to do with Isabella. Was it always my goal to make sure she had too many ties to me to drift away before her allotted release?

Luckily, I arrive at the diner before I arrive at the true answer to that troubling question.

Inside, I see James standing off to the right, surveying the mix of Seton Hall kids, young parents, street kids, and elderly folks all grabbing a greasy dinner-separate, together.

"Nice place," James says to me, as I pass him, then I slide into a booth, features a scenic view of the underside of the train bridge.

"This place is alright," I say. "It's no Chevy's..." I condescend.

"No, I think it's perfect," James says, as he sits down across from me.

James opens the menu I've flopped in front of him, then after a beat of silence, he asks, "So, which bank are we robbing?"

"What?"

"I think I saw an Investors Bank down the road- that might be a good choice," he offers.

"No, James-"

"-too far from the highway? You might be right."

"We're not robbing a bank," I say, quietly, and it makes me sound guilty.

"Our choice of restaurants says otherwise. Everyone here is planning on robbing a bank," James informs me with confidence.

I put my right hand on my forehead, while James, undeterred, continues his performance, only entertaining himself, "Well, that elderly couple in the corner might not be here to rob a bank- they might just be here because there are lots of soft food options on the menu. Then again, let's not count them out. Maybe they're like, 'Fuck it, we only have a couple of years left, let's go out in a blaze of glory and guns.' They'd get the same jail sentence for stealing a pack of gum as they would for robbing the bank because they won't live a week past the end of their trial. That's how we should do it- let's put this robbery on hold until we get older. There's no shame in doing something crazy when you're on your way out. That's the best way you could leave your loved ones. 'How did our father die?' 'Well dear, your father's best friend used his body as a human shield after they knocked over the Investors Bank down the street from the crime planning diner.'"

"That would fuck a kid up, maybe," I theorize, just to interject so James will shut up.

"Fuck him up with inspiration," James triumphs.

"I need your help," escapes my mouth before I can swallow the sad truth.

"You need the help of an absolutely pathetic, sociopath, celeb stalker? Well, gee, Andrew. Scraping the bottom of the barrel, aren't we?"

"I'm sorry if you've felt like I've discounted you. You know my limitations."

"Your limitations?" James asks, and I see him smile at this, "What pray-tell would your limitations be?"

"James-" I warn.

"-when you say your limitations, do you mean your selfishness?" James asks facetiously. "No?" he questions, then runs through a complete listing of my various eccentricities, "Could it be your vaguely Macbethian issues/"Your need to make everything a competition/"Your cyclical ability to place yourself in doomed situations/"Your distancing safety mechanism that places you into a near-constant state of crippling loneliness/"Your morbid curiosity that allows some asshole to sit across from you and list all your limitations as you press your hand to your forehead?"

I quietly say, "My anger." I make sure to keep my cool. "And I treat people poorly," I add. "I don't appreciate them," I admit. I have no fear of revealing this because everyone that I want to shelter from this reality has already become a victim of my limitations.

"Well, you buying me dinner is a great step on the long path out of Dickhead-ville, but I think you're wasting your time with me."

"That's what I'm worried about. I can't be wasting time."

"You need to relax. You sound insane," James says, then he smiles at me.

"No. Everyone is too relaxed. Everyone involved in this industry is too relaxed. It's causing these things to happen," I rant insanely.

"What things, Andrew?" James asks, playing coy.

"The... disappearances. The girls who just go missing. The fact that the face of our collection is twice the age of some of these models. The fact that-"

"-Brazilian genetics, man. Don't worry about it."

"You're not going to be able to write off everything that's happening here by just saying, 'Brazilian genetics.' That's not how this works," I inform James. I take a deep breath, then I take a deep inventory. Quietly, I confirm that I know something is up, and I hiss, "You're part of this."

"What are you doing in that house, Andrew?" James asks, "Self-medicating?"

I dig out my wallet, then I stand up, and throw down a fifty on the table.

Walking away, I say, "Enjoy your dinner, James."

This curiosity about the house on Scotland Road causes me to break into a sweat. Isabella is there, alone, in a house with no curtains on the first floor.

The ex-paparazzi quickly transforms into back into Jimmy Pixx, and chases me out of the diner, yammering, "Watch the videos. Maybe you'll get inspired by what you see. It's a point of reference. I mean, since when is Andrew Lorrie so interested in the welfare of all models?"

I pause for a short second, not wanting to lead James back to Isabella.

Leaning too close to me, James says, "What I'm doing is a building block in our collaboration on this line. What you're doing is sitting around your ex-girlfriend's house, with some man-jawed teena-"

My arm quickly raises, and I pull off James' glasses. Without hesitation, I drop the glasses, then stomp them into the sidewalk

"What the fuck!" James screeches, "Those were Oliver Peoples."

"Next time it's your skull. Don't fuck with me, James," I say, pointing to my destruction.

"Those were really expensive," James says, in disbelief- the sudden violence of it all catching him off guard.

"Now they're trash," I say to him.

"From luxury to trash. Who better to pen that story?" James responds, staring at me.

I can't walk back to the house, until I put an end to the conversation. All I want now is for James to take the train home. I only hope that it's late enough that he can't squeeze in a screener tonight.

"Michael and I have been speaking and he... clarified the situation for me."

This grabs James' attention. His hero worship of Michael as some sort of in-shape fashion Buddha allows me to portray my plan as a "Michael Lorrie plan" which, in James' mind, makes it the only option.

"The collaboration is going to be 40/40/10. You and I..." I start to say, then I swallow, feeling my pride hemorrhage, "... are equals. Michael is the final 10 percent. The approval is his game. He admitted he's too busy for the other shit. We need to get things to the approval stage, then refine everything until he signs off on it."

"Where's the last 10 percent?" James asks.

"That's what I've been wondering lately," I say, looking down at my phone to see if Lux has texted me.

"Can we just bump our percentages up to 45 then?" James asks.

"Sure," I say, tired. The percentages don't matter, I just need to be lowered to the vicinity of where James operates. Once we're on the same level, I'll start knocking on doors until I find the room these brutal acts are being committed in.

THE VIRGIN LIVES

I stare at both of my phones, and I wait.

I know that James will get revenge for what I did to his glasses tonight.

I wait/ I wait/ I wait.

Eventually, my patience pays off. My work phone vibrates, then instantly begins playing a video. This time, I didn't need to touch the screen.

The scene is familiar, but what sends me to my feet is the fact that, in the chair, is the black model from Flurry.

"So you're working with Randal now?" James asks the model.

"Yeah, I guess. I mean, he was so mean to Andrew that I almost-"

"-he treated Andy right," James assures the girl.

"He didn't," the black model says.

I grab the phone, and I desperately try to get my missed calls to come up, but the video will not leave the screen.

"What's your name?" James predictably asks.

"Libby Boken," the black model says.

I realize that James did something that I was too self-absorbed to do. I now know the black model's name. I want to know more about this girl, but I don't want to learn about her life moments before it falls into peril.

My need to call Libby becomes all-consuming. I turn the phone off, then immediately power it back on. After the Verizon logo appears, in the blackness of the screen, I see my reflection in the glass, and I look absolutely deranged.

Thankfully, the video doesn't start playing again, and I'm able to select the missed call from that day in the Flurry office.

When the video reappears on the phone, my call with Libby is already ringing. Both the audio from the call and the audio from the video play, layered. I'm almost positive that my work phone doesn't have this feature normally.

"What are the odds? It's Andrew!" I hear Libby say, when I put the phone to my ear.

"Do not-" James begins to bark, but Libby interrupts him by taking my call with a, "Andrew, you'll never-" but I interrupt Libby and instruct her, "Get out of the room. Now. Run. Now. I'm serious. This is not a joke."

"Get off the phone," I hear James scream, the audio echoing- the video a second ahead of the cell call.

"Get out of the room," I yell, trying to counter what James is saying.

The audio clatters, and I pull the phone away from my face. On the screen, Libby is no longer in frame. A glasses-less James is now in frame, and he's yelling to someone behind the camera, "She's not here for me, get that bitch. You're the one-" then the video ends.

I call Libby/ I call Libby/ I call Libby.

I transfer the number to my personal phone.

I call Libby/ I call Libby.

My work phone buzzes with a text, "Help," from Libby.

"Meet me. I can keep you safe," I send.

"Where?" she texts back.

"NYP. 1 hour," I text, then I realize she can't call me because she's hiding. "Or give me the hotel address," I text.

"NYP. 1 hour," she sends back, confirming my suggestion.

I lock the door that leads out to the balcony. I turn off the light in my room. I turn off the light in the hallway. I look into Isabella's room, and she's gone. I sprint down the stairs, and I find Isabella cutting up *Vogue* magazines in front of the giant LCD TV that plays a subtitled anime. It appears that the determined model is deep into a project for her blog or maybe a scrapbook. The magazine tears are being cut in long, inch thick strips.

All of the curtains are in the basement, sliced up, and I have to wonder if I didn't subconsciously put Isabella in all of this danger because I want to be her protector. Did I create a scenario that would allow me to be the hero who saves the princess?

My princess is in this castle, and I still can't rescue her because I'm running out the door again, sprinting through South Orange again, catching the last train again.

Quietly fighting back tears on the train, my head in my jacket, I don't form any semblance of a plan.

I get off the train, then dash through the crowd upstairs.

I finally find Libby, but she doesn't rush to meet me. She stands frozen, looking around to see if I'm going to drag her back to the hotel room by her hair.

I'm suddenly hugging Libby, as she lets out sobs that match those I huffed out on the train.

Without a plan, I ask the traumatized model where we should go.

She whispers, "Somewhere safe."

We leave Penn Station, but I realize that if Michael already knows about what happened tonight, he *will* send people to find us.

I try to think of a place where Michael wouldn't think to search, then I see the answer.

I pull Libby into a McDonald's.

Hand in hand, we approach the register and I start calling out random numbers, ordering far too much food, because I want Libby to have options.

When our multiple bags are ready, I seat us at a table far from the front window.

Libby keeps wiping her nose, eating fries, thanking me.

I keep checking my phones, texting Lux, texting Isabella, asking questions.

"Program the hotel's address into my phone," I demand.

"Which one?" Libby asks, looking at both my phones on the table.

I slide my personal phone over, and she takes it. "I'm going to bookmark the Street View of the hotel," she says.

"Please," I respond, opening my hands, as she hammers away on the screen.

When the address is entered, Libby gives me back my phone, then asks, "How do I know you're not part of this?"

"Because I watched James interview Georgia Ashlock in the same room you were in. That's why I was looking for Georgia at Flurry. I couldn't save Georgia. She didn't run out of that room. She, uh..."

Libby wipes her eyes, the cry returning, and she asks, "What happened to her?"

"That's what I'm trying to figure out," I admit, "That's what I'm trying to prevent from ever happening again."

"I'll- uh- help. Since you bought me naughty food," Libby says, smiling at her milkshake.

"Who else was there besides James?" I ask.

"There was this younger, kinda Jewish looking guy. James asked the guy, out of the side of his mouth, 'Do you have the juice?' then the Jewish guy offered me a glass of 'water.' I didn't take it because it seemed weird. It felt *off*."

"Was his name Regis? If I show you his picture, can you identify him?" I ask, getting worked up, immediately feeling guilty about being so obnoxious that I'm even violating the McDonald's patron standards of behavior.

Libby nods, and I pick up my personal phone, then flick through pictures of Irina, until I find the one with Regis in the background.

I put the phone down in front of Libby, and she glances at the picture.

"Yeah! That's him," she says, then takes a sip of her shake as a comfort.

"Okay. Here's the plan. Don't answer your phone if anyone from Michael Lorrie calls. Forward any strange texts to me. Don't participate in anything related to this collection," I demand.

"Listen, Andrew. I got dropped from Blend. That's why I was at Flurry. I have to-"

"-they tried to hurt you," I say.

"They didn't though. I'm fine. I'm... fine," she says, shaking.

I grab a napkin, then reach into my Chanel purse and take out one of the black pens that I use to go over my pencil sketches. I scrawl out a contract, sign it, then slide it over to Libby. "You've booked MLORE. You're going to be walking for me in February."

"MLORE?" she asks.

"We've rebranded," I say.

"Can you make that call?" Libby asks.

"I can cast you. I'm designing the fucking line. Yes, I can't make that call. Yes, I-I-I... am acting scary again," I say, first frantic, then totally aware.

"A little. But I didn't run. You're less scary than your friends."

I reach over and grab Libby's shoulders. I look her in the eyes, "Those people in that room aren't my friends. They aren't your friends. You cannot speak with anyone besides me, or your agent, related to this campaign. As far as you're concerned, everything you need can be handled through your agency or me. You deserve, to be able, to relax."

"You really want a black woman for your show?" Libby asks, race only becoming an issue after everything else had been addressed.

"Yes. I want you on my runway this season, and a hundred seasons after this. We will work together for many, many years. Do everything you can to hold up your part of the bargain, and I'll do everything in my power to hold up mine."

THE LIMITS

With the last train back to South Orange so far gone, and the morning train only hours away, I take a nap in Penn Station. I imagine that a minimum of seven F.I.T. girls will recognize me, snap my photo, then caption it, "Enjoying homelessness, you racist fuck?"

My phone vibrates me awake at 7 AM, and I immediately fear that I'm receiving a reshoot of Libby's screener. When I see it's only the alarm I set, I pull myself together, then I get on the train, and head back to South Orange.

When I walk in the door of the house on Scotland Road, I hear *The Hours* soundtrack playing from the library. I hesitantly follow the sound, unsure of what I will find.

Stepping inside the library, I see Isabella on the floor, next to a dying fire and a salad bowl half filled with a milky mixture. Isabella's hands are caked with a white chalk, and the *Vogue* scraps she had been cutting are now molded into a hardened mask of a face.

"I'm not interrupting some sort of witchcraft here, am I?" I ask with faux fear.

"I made something while you were gone," Isabella says to me.

"What'd ya make?" I ask, with a croak from my shot voice.

"A mask," Isabella says, then she lifts her project carefully by its sides, placing it in front of her face. She keeps it there, waiting for my reaction. I stare at the mask, and her eyes behind the holes. Her humanity is still present, so it doesn't bother me, but it also feels like a challenge. Will I look at her the same way if her face is obscured?

I want to pull the mask away.

"Where were you?" Isabella asks me, lowering the mask.

"You can't see James ever again," I tell Isabella.

"I'm not *seeing him*," she says.

"No. I mean, you can't be in the same room as him. Ever," I sit down next to Isabella, in front of the glowing embers. I didn't make a fire before I left. I glance at the bookshelf. She hid the lighter fluid back in *Ulysses* when she was done with it. Maybe she didn't need the lighter fluid at all.

Isabella stares at me like I'm the one wearing the mask now.

"Promise me you will never communicate with James, unless I'm there," my hoarse voice pleads.

Isabella presses her blood red lips together in an effort to restrain her opinion, but this fails, and she tells me, "This is getting excessive. This is getting bizarre. This is getting creepy." She keeps defining our relationship, searching for the term that will articulate just how fucked up things have gotten.

"I agree, that's exactly why we're taking these steps."

"The steps are the problem," she tells me.

"Not if they lead to the right destination," I say. "Isabella, listen to me. James is doing something to these girls"

"Do you trust anyone in this company?" Isabella asks, her eyes rolling under their near-amphibious lids.

"I trust you," I say quietly.

"Then why won't you let me in the same room as your co-worker?"

"Because I don't trust the guy behind the curtain," I say.

"We aren't at Kansas fashion week anymore, Toto," Isabella says, her wit always present, even during a subdued argument.

"The next time I get a screener from James, I'm going to let you watch it. He's hurting these girls," I say, but I'm too distant to be believed. "These girls are being hurt, on video, for..."

"He's a shitty film student, there's no cure for that," Isabella assumes.

"No. No. None of his 'stars' ever appear again, in anything. They're all... you know- uh- remember... when we watched that awful low budget movie on Netflix, where the plot was that some weird charm bracelet wearing construction worker would get men into his apartment, and he'd film them in all these gay scenarios, then it would end with a cheesy death scene?"

"Really? Your theory is that James is shooting softcore gay porn for Netflix? Okay, Andrew. I'll stay away from anyone who promises me a straight to Netflix movie role. Does that calm you down?"

"Only for a moment," I gasp out, taking what I can get.

"*This* is why people don't do you favors," I'm told.

"Isabella, just trust me on this. Have I steered you wrong so far?"

"We met after you put me in your-"

"-have I steered you wrong after I birthed your modeling career at the precipice of my failure?"

"I love that dress," Isabella says, like she's trying to remind me that some people don't think I failed.

"You cannot shoot with James. You cannot meet with James. That's final," I say, pulling at my hair.

"Or what?" Isabella asks.

"Or this is over," I say.

"What is this?"

"Did you stay up for me?" I ask, looking over at the pale model.

Isabella holds the mask up to her face, as she always does.

THE PART-TIME SAVIOR

My expectation for the day is that Lux will bail on our meeting.

I speak with my seamstresses.

I take pictures of two muslin garments, then send them to Michael and James.

Intern Jessica borrows Karen's driver's license, then buys me a 12 pack.

I act like nothing is wrong, when everything is broken.

Mentally, I always return to the pieces I made in my basement. They remain at the house on Scotland Road, because I secretly hope that Isabella will steal one of the looks and wear it during a night out with her friends. I want her to feel like she did that first night in blue velvet, again.

Intern Jessica keeps getting me beers from the fridge.

I set out all of the muslin pieces for Lux. Everything feels done- I just need to see it on my prototype girl to make sure it *looks* done.

Karen leaves/ James never arrived/ Intern Jessica leaves.

The day is over. I stay.

My work phone and my personal phone still have a significant charge because I haven't had to use either, unless I was checking the time or convincing myself I missed a message.

I wish the gray bodies of my mannequins would come to life for my trial and error tweaks because they're fine with being trapped in this workshop. I find myself now unwilling to deal with the rapidly revised social calendars of beautiful women.

A drumbeat banging on the door that leads out to 42nd street sends me walking down the long hallway. I check the date on my phone to make sure these aren't trick-or-treaters. I have nothing to give them besides beer and I'll need what's left of the 12'er if Lux stays gone.

I open the heavy metal door, and I'm immediately greeted with, a preemptive reintroduction of, "I'm Madeleine. Nice to see you again." She knows that this is going to be a battle, but she's marched onto the battlefield, when all the other soldiers fled to safety.

Madeleine to the rescue, again.

"You have a bad habit of covering for irresponsible people," I tell her, blocking the door frame.

"And they have a bad habit of habitually putting me in this position," Madeleine says, not bitter.

I nod at this, accepting it. We're in the same position.

Keeping her focus on the positive, Madeleine says, "Luckily, it was always my dream to sit front row at a fashion show, and other people's bad habits helped my dream come true. Then, I had a dream to wear beautiful designer clothes, and, well, my bad habits are getting me in those clothes."

"What's the next dream?" I ask.

"Next... I don't know what I want," Madeleine tells me.

At her base, Madeleine is a reliable, good friend, but without Lux, I'm second guessing everything. Lux is an instant soundboard- a trusted companion- a knowledgeable resource.

Madeleine has already captured her dream, and for this reason, her opinion contains no worth. All of the pieces she tries on, she loves. If she didn't have that reaction, she'd have to confront the fact that she worked so hard for a dream that- in the end- wasn't worth it. This would require a new dream. This would require starting over. This would require deep introspection. It's just easier to like the fucking dress.

Feeling misery inside a designer garment is extremely difficult to recover from. You can't shop it off, you can't fuck it off, and you can't run it off. If you go shopping, what will you buy when you've already worn the best? If you want to get laid, how are you going to feel sexy in jeans, when you didn't feel sexy in a dress that has been specifically tailored to entice and seduce? If you try to sprint away from yourself, you're going to do it in a sports bra and stretch pants. Running in anything designer would ruin the garment with the toxic filth being pushed out of your pores. Literally, just by being you, you'll have ruined the garment.

Causing destruction by merely existing is everyone's worst fear.

Madeleine brushes by me, demands one of my beers, then patiently works with me. She becomes what I need so I don't mention any of my doom and gloom thoughts. In the way that Irina is bound by the invisible handcuffs of loyalty to Michael, I'm starting to have a similar relationship with Madeleine. I'll be sure not to abuse this gift. Madeleine's type of loyalty is rare and precious- it can easily be exploited, but I refuse to trade it for temporary pleasure.

I need to protect this girl, and the thousands of girls like her.

Unfortunately, this means I have to put Madeleine in the path of danger.

THE TAB

When the last of the bagged muslin garments are picked up, I smile at Intern Jessica from across the long hallway, then I quietly say, "Thank you."

In response, Intern Jessica yells down the hall, "I still have Karen's ID. Let's celebrate."

I call Libby, and I call Isabella.

I call Lux, and I call Cori.

I call Matthew, and I call James.

Tonight, I decide that I'll max out my credit card by buying drinks and shitty food for my friends in a Brooklyn dive bar.

Everyone accepts the invitation to come out and celebrate the fact that the rough designs are finished, and the line is the Italians' problem for the next couple of weeks. Now, my job becomes focusing completely on making sure everyone pays for their "it is what it is" indiscretions. I want to punish bad behavior- I want the apathetic to finally care.

At the bar, I buy Libby a Mojito. I buy Isabella some sort of vegetarian bean dip. I buy Cori a glass of champagne. I buy James a full cup of scotch. I buy Matthew a Heineken. Right before I'm about to buy Lux a vodka tonic, she tells me that she "isn't feeling well" adding, "I don't want to drink here unless the bar sells NyQuil."

I keep pushing cash onto the bar, in addition to my tab. I fund this night because I want to reward loyalty.

The amount of money I'm putting out leads to strangers joining our party, and the strangers begin a post-*Reservoir Dogs* discussion of tipping.

Broke wannabe models and broke wannabe musicians surround the established professionals I brought out tonight.

The trust fund kids and the below-the-poverty-line artists share their reprehensible tipping stories with a misplaced pride.

Someone tipped a pizza man a coupon.

Someone tipped a Chinese food menu coupon to a delivery guy from a rival Chinese food place.

Someone tipped a room key.

Someone asks if the room key tip was a sexual advance.

Someone responds that the tip was made after a dinner with their sister, and she wasn't into incest or multiple partners.

Someone asks why they would tip a room key.

Someone responds, "It's fun."

Someone asks why it's fun.

Someone says that the room key tip was dickish.

Someone says that it was sexy.

Someone says that they like James' new glasses.

James says, "That cocksucker broke my last pair," then points at me.

Someone asks if everyone wants pizza.

Everyone does.

Someone asks, "Who's still open?"

I order a pizza from the kitchen.

Someone says that they don't like Brooklyn style pizza.

Someone says that they think they have a bit of a Brooklyn accent.

Someone responds that the new Brooklyn accent is, "Ewww."

Someone counters that it's not an accent if you're just saying, "Ew," in your normal voice.

Someone defends their impression by saying, "That's how people from Brooklyn start or end a sentence. They just make that noise, then point at things."

I have to step away from the conversation circle, and as always, I seek the comfort of a beautiful woman to restore my faith in the world.

Libby's roommate from the Flurry flat- a Russian girl with a heavy accent- tells me that she's thankful I bought her drinks. She informs me that she recently shot a lookbook, and with the money she made, she bought her mother a dishwasher. She says that her mother called her crying, thanking her, and this is why she loves modeling so much. She tells me that this is the prettiest part of the industry. Her story makes me almost tear up, and I decide that after my MLORE collection shows, I will never pay in trade again.

THE FUEL

Hungover, I sit in Starbucks with Isabella, and we read the September issues that- prior to this- had sat untouched on the front step. The issues are slightly wavy and waterlogged from the sideways rain that seemed to be the primary feature of this past fall. We each have a magazine- I have a *Vogue*. Inside, I read the stories about:

A divorcee who found love in a community college creative writing course/ A divorcee who had a skin cancer scare that ultimately taught her to embrace her pale complexion/ A divorcee who had such bad anxiety that she pulled all the hair out of the right side of her head, up to her temple, but everyone just thought she got a trendy haircut, and she ended up with a 19-year-old boyfriend as a result.

All of these articles are blandly familiar- each author abusing the same concepts of self-discovery and refreshed self-worth gained through menial experiences. None of what I read is new. It inspires neither emotion nor excitement- it merely fits in with what's demanded- a block of text between the perfume ad and the department store ad. Don't ruffle any feathers. Don't prompt any letters to the editor. Don't stray from the "cool mom" game plan. Find another woman who has no job- she'll have a great story about the "emotional cheating" that she feared would "devastate her family." If we really got the full story, her husband's response to the piece would be, "Finally someone distracted her, and I got to play my Xbox without her fucking nagging." This reality isn't important. This is the fashion industry at its purest.

Isabella closes her magazine, the motion causing my hair to puff back. I know that this dramatic flourish is a sign that she would now like my magazine. This is how Isabella makes her requests- silently, blatantly, only once.

I hand Isabella my *Vogue*. She hands me her *ELLE*.

"Anything interesting?" I ask.

"No, unless you think you might have a potentially homewrecking addiction and can't admit it," Isabella tells me.

I nod at this.

She watches my hands to see if I open the magazine. I don't. I reach for my coffee. She nods at this a single time, then opens the *Vogue*.

"Same with that one, it's only interesting if you have an eating disorder," I say.

Isabella quickly closes the magazine, lets out a huff, smiles down at the cover, looks back up at me, then gives me the finger.

I open the *ELLE*.

I read an article about something called mental dieting/ I read an article by a menopausal woman who "discovered" black men after her husband committed suicide/ I read an article by a woman who tried to write a book, but stopped writing after she finished about a dozen unrelated stream of consciousness paragraphs because they confirmed to her that she's a born writer, and didn't need a completed work as proof of this.

When I see the two pictures accompanying the next article, my brain forces me to pretend that the piece is about a cult of organ harvesting women who will do *anything* to get the livers that they sell to fund their high fashion needs. It makes the magazine spring to life. This fantasy is still a safe piece for me because no one would want my liver. I have to amplify these articles because they don't reflect my experience in this industry. The carnage has been cleaned up, the cancer subplot is secondary, the story is abridged. My aversion to the world that these magazines offer makes me wonder if I'm actually enjoying everything that's happening behind the scenes during the creation of MLORE.

THE PERFECT BODY COUNT

I stare past the white shirt, the black vest, the stubble beard, the tuft of brown hair, and I look out at the dark November sky, then I ask, "Could I have a moment to discuss something privately with you, Michael?"

Intern Jessica mumbles, "No problem," then quickly leaves Michael's office.

"Your casting director is- uh- destroying girls," I say quietly, after the door to Michael's office clicks shut.

"Pardon?" Michael asks, through his teeth.

"James is a fucking psychopath," I say, determined to remain calm, and already failing.

"He's a visionary," Michael says.

"He's probably envisioning playing cat's cradle with your intestines," I respond.

"It's funny. You two fight like brothers," my brother tells me, smiling.

"Georgia is missing. Libby was in danger. Michael, I'm getting these videos showing girls..."

"Who the fuck is Libby?" Michael asks.

"A MLORE girl," I tell him, my napkin contract completely binding.

"Well, if she had a screener, then..." Michael trails off.

This response makes it clear that James didn't tell Michael about Libby escaping whatever the fuck has been happening in that hotel room.

"I can't show you the screener, because I don't have any copies of them. They disappear after I watch them. *Georgia* disappeared after I watched her screener," I gasp out.

"So what's your theory, Andrew? The dumb model was kidnapped? She was roofied, then put on a Queensbridge bound train? What exactly do you suspect is happening here? Should we notify immigration? Should we call whatever Eastern European country that she's from and inform them in a frustrating conversation that she's missing? Exciting, we might find out her real age!" Michael says, openly mocking me because he knows I have no evidence. All of this is going just as he planned.

The plot isn't thickening- it's elongating. I need to pare it down, so I ask, "What's this all leading to? What's the goal of this entire scheme you have? How many people have to disappear before it's enough to satisfy your vampiric needs?"

"Oh, this isn't about *my* needs," Michael says, admitting things, while deflecting them simultaneously, "And it's not about the number of people. It's about the faces. It's always about faces. You know this."

"Why include others if this is about our last name?" I ask. The scope is too sweeping for this to be a revenge plot.

"Because it's about more than names. Because I can. Because it's fun. Because it will have interesting repercussions," he lists off slowly.

"And you'll be far enough away from it all that you'll feel none of these repercussions," I fill in the blanks.

"I'll be admiring them," Michael states.

"Of course you will be. Of course. Are you really this bored now that you have money? Fuck. Buy a copy of Grand Theft Auto. Get out of people's lives if you're seeking this destruction."

"Video games distract me from my work. But this... *this* makes me more interested in my work."

"When does it stop?" I have to ask.

"When you give up..." Michael says, letting it hang there. I don't respond, so he continues with his thought, "...which should be soon, since you seem to be ready to crack. Not that you have much at stake. You've fucked up your entire life. You've already destroyed everything that I'd want to take from you. If you want this to end, give up. Tell your favorite people- those fashion journalists- that you don't have what it takes to design for my label. Tell everyone that my shoes are too big to fill."

"Your shoes are too boring to step into," I say.

"James is meeting with another girl tonight," Michael shares, and this means that I've changed nothing. This is an industry where girls are silent about injustice and abuse because speaking up would hurt their ability to achieve their dreams. They just pretend the awful moment was a dream and work toward a better reality.

"Who's next?" I ask.

"What, are you going to 'warn her' that she's going to be transformed into a pile of dust if she attends the go-see?" Michael mocks me.

"What's her name?' I ask.

"She's a Marc girl, for the time being," Michael says.

"No one would jump ship to wear what you design. No one would run to that," I say.

"At least women can walk comfortably in what I design," Michael says, referencing critiques that sometimes my clothes are downright unwearable if the customer has a subway commute.

This doesn't bother me, and I counter, "Women will be walking in what I design this spring."

"You seem to forget that I have my high fashion label," Michael says.

"You seem to forget that too. Get to work, and stay out of my life."

Michael calmly reminds me, "Your livelihood is provided by me. Either give back what I've generously provided you or keep your work phone on, and watch a master at work."

THE ROOM

I text Lux, "RU free?" because I want Madeleine to appear at the workshop. When I don't get a response, I give in and involve another model.

"Going to the hotel to save a Marc girl," I text Libby.

"Just call the cops," she texts back.

"I know where it's happening, not when. I hope I'm not too late," I send to Libby, hinting that the exact time this Marc girl will shoot her screener is a little hazy right now. Before Libby responds, I send another text, "She's in trouble. If I don't text u again by midnight, call the cops."

"I'm not letting u go alone," is Libby's response. I knew she would be unwilling to allow these monsters to hurt another girl.

"You gotta make up your mind," I send to her.

"Meet me @ the hotel in a half hr," is the text from Libby that arrives so fast it's clear she immediately sent it after she was finished typing it.

"How r we gonna get into the room?" I text.

"Desk guy tried to get into my pants. I'll trick him," Libby sends, then includes an emoticon that seems proud of itself.

I accept this plan, then I cab to the hotel.

As I walk inside the golden lobby, my eyes run along the black and white maze-like pattern on the floor until they find a pair of black heels. My eyes climb the shoes, up to a jewel neck, dropped shouldered, oversized black and white houndstooth coat. Libby looks beautiful. Her only fashion misstep is that instead of a purse, she's wearing a backpack. As I walk over to her, I physically feel my circle expanding, then it immediately contracts when I remember why I'm here. I begin to feel as though there's only a finite space for the people in my life. As I let one person in, I push one person out. Tonight isn't about letting someone in- it's about saving someone. Tonight is about breaking in, then getting out, safely.

I smile at Libby, and Libby smiles at me, then arches her neck to draw my attention to the Gucci canvas backpack again.

"Whatcha got there?" I ask in a playful way.

"Picnic lunch, room service here sucks," Libby says, then sticks out her tongue at me. Raising her pointer finger, she takes control, "Wait here. I need to get our key. We're going up separately. I'll go first, then I'll text you. You'll wait five minutes, then we'll meet upstairs."

I accept this plan, then drift over to a high backed curved sofa close enough to the front desk that I'll be able to hear Libby's conversation.

"Libby. Baby," I hear the front desk guy celebrate. Based on my glimpse, the guy is Hispanic, with close-cropped hair, maybe 21, probably on the take, but not getting paid enough to willingly bypass a chance to get laid.

"You remember me," Libby says, her voice gaining a 'stupid model' bubbliness.

"I would have a hard time forgetting you," the desk guy responds in a way he probably thinks is suave.

"Stop. I'm blushing. Or maybe it's the cold. I went out to smoke a cigarette and- shit- could you make me a key? I left mine in the room," Libby says, positioning things as though she's been here all night. The realization she forgot her key was so natural that I almost believe that she was texting me earlier tonight, while smoking a cigarette outside the hotel.

"They gave you a key?" the desk guy asks, confused.

"Yup, but, hello, I'm a model so remembering stuff isn't exactly my- um- what's the word... asset? No... not asset... whatever. The guys left me stranded," Libby says, playing a character. "They went to a party. I still need to get ready. And I need to find a date," Libby adds, deepening a reality she created.

"A party?" the intrigued hotel employee asks.

"Yeah, I guess James hooked something up, but I'm gonna be late, and it will be so embarrassing rolling in there without someone on my arm. If I show up with someone, people will notice, and they'll assume that I was too busy getting my brains screwed out to arrive on time. I need that buzz."

"Same here," the front desk guy says, then laughs uncontrollably because he can't believe his luck, "I get off at midnight if you want to come down..."

"You're going to go to a fashion party dressed like a hotel employee?" Libby asks, making sure it's not too easy for him to get this date.

"If I take this bow-tie and black blazer off, I'm just a well-dressed guy who gives off a vibe like he's been screwing a beautiful model's brains out all night," the front desk guy says.

"I'll think about it," Libby's put-on ditsy voice responds, and this near brush off tells me that Libby has the key.

"I'll think about it too," the front desk guy says, and it's actually not a bad line.

I hear Libby's heels clack away.

I stay in the lobby and stare at my phone, until I get the text, "8."

I wait a full five minutes before I glance toward the front desk. The flirtatious card-maker has removed his blazer and bow tie, and he's now looking at himself in the front facing camera on his cell phone.

I quickly make my way across the lobby, and no one stops me.

In the elevator, I consider texting Isabella, but, "I'm meeting up with your old roommate in a hotel room," is a dumb text to send.

The elevator doors open on the 8th floor, and I step out, carefully.

Libby is waiting for me- just like her text promised- and she asks, "So what's the plan?"

"I take the key card, and you go on that date," I say.

"No. I'm not dating a bellboy," Libby says.

"It'll be fun," I tell her, because I don't want her to walk into that room- not again.

"Andrew, the only time you can tell me where to go is if I'm walking for you," Libby says, raising her pointer finger to me again. I agree to these terms, because I can't wait to have that power over her. For a moment, I feel like the critics actually did teach me something. There's a chance that I didn't have any black women on my runway because- in a way- I feared them. At this moment I still feel fear around Libby, but now it's for her safety.

Libby leads me to the door of the screener room.

We wait and listen. It's silent inside the room.

I'm handed the key, then Libby starts videoing our B&E on her phone.

Gently, I place the key in the mechanism. A green light blinks. I remove the key, then throw the door open.

Libby films... an empty hotel room.

"Mr. Lorrie, are you seducing me?" Libby asks. I shhh her, and she adds, "Because it might be working. This is way hotter than flowers."

Directly to our left is a bathroom, so I flick the light on, then carefully step onto the tile. A bar of soap is sitting on the edge of the white sink, unwrapped, still wet. The sticker that the maid puts on the toilet paper is missing. I slide the shower door open, but it feels futile. If someone was hiding in the shower, they wouldn't give up on their need for violence merely because they lost at hide and seek. I'm relieved when nothing is revealed. It dawns on me that I slid this door open because I have to check for blood in the shower. I look closely at the drain, but that distinct red is thankfully absent.

Libby continues filming, just in case we find something that can finally exist as evidence on a phone not owned by Michael Lorrie.

We leave the bathroom, and it doesn't feel like I'm moving through a hotel room, it feels like I'm walking onto a set. The room has an electric charge, but also a flowery ease.

"It smells like Daisy in here," Libby whispers

"Who's Daisy?" I ask, shaking, getting on one knee, preparing myself to look under the bed.

"The perfume," Libby says.

"Big deal. Tons of people wear Daisy," I respond, lifting the bed skirt, finding nothing.

"Tons of people weren't shot by Juergen for Daisy."

"Someone got shot?" I mumble, trembling as I move toward the curtains. I don't want to meet the masked man.

I don't want to be a victim of this brutal executioner.

"I think it was in Nevada. The desert," Libby says.

"How far were they from a hospital?" I question, not paying attention, grasping the curtain.

I'm tempted to rip this curtain down so I can steal the material and turn it into a dress for Georgia. Maybe she won't wear it, but it will be a dress for Georgia.

"Are you thinking that Juergen physically shot her with a gun? He shot her with a camera. He took her picture for the ad. Aren't you a designer?" Libby asks.

I tear open the curtain, and I find nothing besides a pretty nice view of Lincoln Center.

"Oh right. I was just joking... because... if I was going to kill someone... I would do it in the Nevada desert," I say, trying to sound like a force to be reckoned with. I pull open the other curtain, and find only the city, again.

"What the fuck is the theme of your collection? European hostel meets Eli Roth's Hostel?" Libby asks, moving her phone, videoing the absence of anyone.

The perfume still hangs in the air, and it's enough to tell me that it's not over, and I'm too late.

The screener was being shot when I was in the meeting with Michael.

"You have to go on that date," I say to Libby.

She scrunches up her face in displeasure, but she knows that I'm right. This isn't the last time we'll need to gain access to this tomb.

Tonight, we were too late. Next time, we'll be early.

THE DISTRACTION

The screener appears on a time delay. At 2 AM, I'm awoken by piercing screams. They aren't Isabella's, and I'm relieved by this fact. The noise of the streaming screener doesn't wake Isabella up, because she doesn't sleep in my bed anymore.

After the Libby screener, I presumed that James will be sure to never livestream again. I guess I'll have to set up my own feed to catch him.

I put my phone under my pillow, then I go to sleep.

I don't watch the screener because I'm powerless. The girl in the chair is already gone. Marc is going to need to do some new casting of his own now.

In the morning, after I shower, then text James, "Michael wants us to meet at the workshop to discuss the Irina campaign."

"Looking forward to it," James sends back.

As I get ready, I consider my options.

I can arm myself with a weapon, then beat the shit out of James/ I can tell Irina what goes on in that hotel room, and have her demand that James is removed from the campaign/ I can call the cops and tell them that James assaulted a model, then I can have Madeleine fake being a victim.

When I think about that final option, I realize I don't want to put Madeleine in that position. I can't make her party to the lying and depravity that powers Michael Lorrie.

I take the train into New York, then I wait in the workshop room at the end of the hallway.

The moment James steps into the room, I slam the door, then yell, "What the fuck is wrong with you?"

James smiles at me- like I only have half the information he does- and he says, "You should be more worried about what's up with the rest of your team."

"My team is fine," I maintain.

"Where's your new girl?" James asks.

"My new girl? Madeleine? She's *another* girl, not my new girl," I say.

"She's become *the girl* ever since Lux started getting dressed and undressed by some other guy," James offers casually.

I grind my teeth and close my eyes. I'm able to gulp everything down long enough to say, "Lux deserves a personal life."

"Guess she deserves a better part-time job too," James remarks, opening the door, then walking out into the hallway.

"Stop it, James," I demand.

James turns, and says, "When Michael told Lux he didn't have the cash to match her old salary, she certainly didn't waste any time finding other employment."

"What do you mean? You're making that up," I say. My heart grabs my rib cage and shakes as hard as it can.

"Your brother took on Lux as an independent contractor. She isn't making enough to pay her rent... but... she's paying her rent."

THE WEB

We had a meeting scheduled for today.

I drink, and I wait for Lux.

To pass time, I read articles on my phone, but I have to avoid the celebrity blogs because they remind me of James. I try to busy myself by tweaking various details on the working designs that I didn't send to Italy, but when I run out of alterations, the pieces demand Lux's presence.

I close my eyes and turn on some music, but every song I have on my phone is one I've listened to while working with Lux.

I have to be *reminded* of Lux because she's missing.

When I finally hear footsteps in the hall, I finish my beer.

The music playing from my phone gives away my location, as Matt Berninger croons about a glowing young ruffian.

I don't need to look to the doorway to know who's here.

"Lux is busy," I hear Madeleine say, and it's silent for a moment, then I'm given more information, "She called me, and told me that something came up. She mentioned you didn't need her because it's in Italy's wrinkled hands now, which sounded like a secret code, but maybe it means something to you," Madeleine says.

I'm seeing red. I want to destroy this city. I yell, "Had something? What did Lux have? What could she be-"

"-she said she had a job," Madeleine spits out, then she wears a look of immediate regret.

"She has a job. *This* is her job!"

Madeleine's eyes go wide, then she says, "Whoa there, mister territorial wolf. Relax."

"Tell me where she is," I demand, stepping forward.

"Andrew, let's get to work. I'll do whatever you need."

"You're not welcome here, until you tell me where Lux is," I say, snatching the fitting job away.

"It's not your business," Madeleine says.

"Then this is not your meeting, and you have to leave," I threaten, "I'll tell Karen to-"

"-is there a need to involve Karen?" Madeleine asks.

"I guess not," I say, relenting, "She's already too opinionated on this."

"She's jealous of your teenage house guest. She's jealous of your talent. She's jealous of your vision," Madeleine says, trying to misdirect my anger.

"Some of those things I wouldn't wish on my worst enemy," I say, then there's a short pause, which I stamp out by saying, "Without me involving anyone else, I'm asking you to leave. I don't want you working on this collection anymore because you're always covering for Lux. How can I be sure you even care about what happens here? I can't have two girls only half the time."

"I'll get her here, tonight," Madeleine squeaks, clearly unwilling to lose this opportunity. I was the one who picked her out of the crowd, and she seems to sense that I'm ready to return her there if she isn't careful.

"Good. Okay. That works," I say, calming down, running my fingers through my hair, "Thank you."

"But it won't be until 8:30."

"Why 8:30?"

"That's when his plane back to LA takes off," I'm told.

"Who is *he*?"

"I can't give you any details," Madeleine whispers.

"Do I want the details?" I ask.

Madeleine shakes her head no, pouts, and looks pained.

"Will this hurt me?" I ask, and immediately after I pose this question, my body begins trembling. My core vibrates, and I sweat through my shirt. Like a cat's purr, my body jitters in an ineffectual attempt to calm my insides down.

Madeleine scrunches her face.

"Is it bad?" I ask, punishing myself in advance.

"She says it isn't," Madeleine responds. The fact that she had to defer to Lux tells me so much.

I nod once at this, then Madeleine sends a text, punctuating her middle woman burden with, "She'll be here."

"Okay," I mumble, then add, "Stay."

Madeleine walks into the room, then takes off her pea coat. She's wearing a tiny T-shirt with the name of Matthew's band on it, and black leggings as pants, despite the fact it's way too cold for this outfit. She walks over to one of the tables, then lies on it like it's a bed, while I go to the fridge and get us beers.

When I arrive back at the table, I crack open a Bud tallboy for Madeleine, and she smiles at me. Despite my swirling emotions, I can't stop myself from smiling back. She sits up, and accepts my peace offering. We press our beer cans together, then gulp down a truce.

We wait until 8:30. Then we wait until 9.

Finally, we hear heels in the hallway. I step out of the workshop, then stare at the girl in the brown rabbit fur coat as she walks toward me.

Madeleine, back in her coat, scoots by me, trying to reach Lux before the argument starts.

After Madeleine whispers something in Lux's ear, she leaves me with my part-time model. I'm always telling girls that modeling isn't shift work, but it certainly feels like it is tonight. One model enters, one model exits. The model that left will be invited back, the model who enters...

"You can't do this one thing for me? I ask nothing of you, and you can't do this one thing that's for your own good?" I yell, immediately showing Lux that this repeated betrayal is not okay.

"Chill," is her response, "Everything is in Italy or at your house. I don't need to be here."

"Where were you tonight?" I ask.

Lux puts her back to the wall, slides down, then gets ready to have this conversation. Here. Now. "I was with him," she says.

"You chose him over me?" I ask, still standing, looking down at her.

"I had no choice. He's on a plane for LA now. I'm yours again. It's not a big deal," Lux says, not looking up at me.

"This is a big deal to me," I tell her.

"I sent Madeleine."

"It's not the same."

"It'll have to be good enough. I have no choice," Lux says.

"Explain everything. Now," I demand.

"Can we not have this conversation?" Lux requests.

"We need to have this conversation now. The time has come," I respond.

All of this is playing out like a breakup.

Lux wipes away the first tear, then looks up at me, and says, "You have to listen. You can't interrupt me if I'm going to tell you this. If you stop me like every five seconds, I'll get mad at you. Are you ready to just listen?"

I nod.

"Okay, if you speak at any point, this conversation is over," Lux warns. I don't speak, so she's forced to, "Um, I guess, let's start... with the start. Michael brought me on, but at a reduced rate, so I've been making money to cover the difference. I'm sorry that it cut into my time with you."

Lux is careful with the details, and she's reciting words that seem practiced.

To focus on the portion related to who I'm related to, I ask, "Reduced rate as in..."

"Your brother and I discussed that- uh- I was going to be an 'independent contractor' who doesn't work on a full-time schedule-" Lux sees me take out my phone, and warns, "-Andrew, don't. If you say something or call your brother, this conversation is over. Just listen."

I have to put my phone away, because I'm shaking and the normally sweltering temperatures we keep pumping in the workshop (the models are always cold) are not present today. I exhale and my breath comes out in puffs.

"Where do you work?" I ask.

"Remember that brownstone you picked me up at?" Lux mumbles, her big eyes on the floor, her chin pressed to her chest.

"You're working for your old shrink?" I ask, okay with this, feeling relief.

"I lied. My shrink doesn't have an office there," Lux says, eyes still on the floor.

"Then who does?" I ask, slowly walking toward the guilty looking model.

"A movie exec," Lux says.

"I- uh- I- Lux," I stammer out, my hand running over my chin, my heart melting inside my chest, bubbling and popping. "I just want you to be careful. Michael can be manipulative. He has a lot of money and-" I'm fighting back tears, I want to howl. I tell her, "Whatever you're doing. Don't do it. Trust me. I'm bending over backward just so I can design some shit that will be forgotten and eBayed in five months. I didn't set out to get fucked over by Michael, but that's what's happening right now. He's controlling everything and there isn't a damn thing I can do about it."

"The only reason I make rent is because of who I work for, so I have to be available," Lux informs me.

"Available for what exactly?" I ask.

"Are you serious? Are you a child, Andrew?" Lux asks me with hate.

"Why... would you keep all of this from me?" I ask, having trouble posing my questions, and having trouble listening to the answers.

"Well, I've been pretty obvious about this. Plus, I mean it's clear you have issues with money or whatever."

"I have enough money. I don't care about money," I say.

"You do, and yeah, you do," Lux says, "Everyone around you... is, like, rich. You have your... whatever, you just have issues with it, so I didn't bring it up."

"That's not a factor for me. What do I need money for besides cab fare and bar tabs?" I ask.

"You don't have money issues like you wish you had more. You have money issues where if people are well off, you automatically assume they're awful. Maybe it's because you're in a luxury industry or because your brother is so rich, Cassie is rich, Si-"

"-relax with your theories, Lux. This is about you. It's not about me, it's not about money. I don't give a shit about this guy, or what he does to make buckets of cash. I care about you being safe, and not ruining your life. I care about you not fucking yourself up."

"I already am fucked up!" Lux yells at me.

"You aren't as fucked up as you could be," I say quietly.

"All of this is safe," she tells me- a statement so naïve that for a second I believe Lux's fake age. "The site has all his information, and I tell Madeleine when I meet up with him. Lots of girls are doing the sugar daddy thing. You don't get it. You're from a different generation."

"You met some stranger on the internet," I say, my voice a whisper.

"The profile wasn't even important. He's not a stranger," Lux maintains.

"How is he not a stranger?"

"Stop it, Andrew," Lux demands

There's more. I crouch down and look into Lux's eyes, "Tell me how he's not a stranger and I'll stop."

"He's not a stranger because he's friends with Michael," Lux spits, then covers her mouth.

"Don't let him do this. You're better than this. Way better," I assure her in a trembling whisper.

"I'm 27, with *zero* life skills. I can do nothing!" Lux yells at me, "I have no talents, besides looking exactly how I'm supposed to look. That's not going to get me a job at Prudential. That *might* get me a job at a food court near the office building. My skill is looking 22 when I'm 27, and I'm in an industry that spits out anyone who's 23."

"You don't know what Michael and his people are involved in. It's an ugly reality, and I don't want it to be yours," I say.

Lux's pout is momentarily replaced with a flash of Michael's smile. "*You're* one of Michael's people, and we share a reality," Lux says, finally making eye contact.

"That's why I have this constant battle between needing to hold you close, while also pushing you away to safety," I say.

"What if you stopped worrying about it?" she suggests.

"Everyone has stopped worrying about it," I yell, splaying out my arms.

"Because nothing can be done," Lux says, shaking when she voices this perceived fact.

"I don't believe that," I tell her.

"And I don't have to prove to you that I'm right."

"Do you even like the line?" I ask, at the precipice of my work being destroyed.

"I see you in pieces... but not as much as I'm used to. Not as much as I want to."

I gasp in the rush of a jagged feeling, as the one thing I wanted to say to Lux is said to me.

"I guess I put you on a pedestal. I expected more from you. Way more," I say, sitting down, putting my back to the wall opposite the one that's holding Lux upright.

"And I expected more from you, Andrew. You're doing fucking ready-to-wear," Lux says, exhausted.

"Tell me what to do differently with the line," I beg.

"It's fine," Lux tells me.

"Fine?"

"Yes, and that's why it's shit," Lux says, going through her purse.

Punched in the stomach, but already on my ass, I puff out, "I'm... not..."

"Exactly. You're not using your talents. You're wasting your potential. You're just getting by. Maybe the next time you want to tell someone how pathetic and disappointing they are, you should check your own fucking reflection first," Lux growls, then takes out a Pall Mall and lights it.

I'm trying to assemble a puzzle in the dark, but everything is sand, and nothing connects. I can't explain any of this to a person who didn't see what it was like putting the line together. The girl on the floor is a stranger.

Looking over at me, Lux tries to distill the situation, "I'm not quite myself lately, and you're always you, and I know if you stop trusting me, you'll never trust me again. But, I really can't be worried about that."

I review Lux's statement. Am I capable of forgiveness?

My default reaction to failure is insecurity, depression, anger.

My anger will force me to seek revenge. Always.

So many actions that cannot be taken back.

Trust is glass.

Forgiveness is foreign.

I don't forgive Lux, but I do agree with her. I just hope that's enough.

"Get out of here," I say quietly.

Lux looks at me, then asks, "Why are you being so crazy about this?"

"Because, now, after all of this, the times you make me feel awful are slowly outweighing the times you make me feel good."

"Maybe now you get it," Lux responds.

I can't help but wonder if she's saying that this is how she's always felt on the other side of our friendship. My instinct to apologize is met with a slowly building instinct to save my breath.

I take the middle road, and admit, "You've hurt me. This hurts me."

"So, what now? I don't show up tomorrow?"

"For a bit, yes. I can't have... *this* in the mix. I have to separate this. I love you in both worlds, but those worlds need to be separate now."

"It's not going to work if you separate these worlds," Lux warns.

"It doesn't work when they're together, so I'll have to take that risk."

I have to allow this relationship to end, but if I do, when I need an opinion on the passion filled collection I've assembled, I won't have it. It's only Lux that I trust. It will always only be Lux that I trust.

"I need this to be fixed," I say.

We both want the same thing, yet what we want seems impossible.

"That's why I'm here. Why else do you think I cabbed all the way down to your space?" Lux asks me.

"Because you feel guilty."

"The guilt will be there. It will always be there," she states.

"If you don't listen to me, then, yes, you're right."

"Ugh. I know you're trying to twist this into some fucked up daddy issues thing, and I'm sure my therapist would agree wholeheartedly, but you can't free me from anything."

I look at a girl that I once couldn't stop looking at, and I tell her, "I hope the money can help you more than I could. I can't do this."

THE CATALYST

Even before I step into Michael's office, I'm yelling at him, "You forced Lux into ruining her life."

"And I'm different than you, how?" Michael asks, remaining seated, tenting his fingers.

A scared Michael Lorrie employee runs over and shuts the door behind me after I enter the office.

"I'm giving these girls an opportunity, while you're exploiting them," I say, pointing accusatorially.

"I absolutely am providing an opportunity," Michael says.

"I'm not making them compromise their morals," I respond.

Michael smiles, prepared, "So those dead animals your vegan models are wearing..."

"Oh please, those models are vegan because champagne doesn't come from a cow. If it did..."

"You and I are a lot alike," Michael says, and it's such an absurd statement that I immediately have to laugh, then clarify, "We're nothing alike."

"We're alike, but I'm just more direct in what I'm doing. You? You have to lie to yourself."

"You promise them a future, then you snatch the carpet out from under them. You place them in this trap," I say.

"You're right, Andy," Michael says. He looks up and to the left, then adds, "Remember that time I found a teenage girl that believed in all my bullshit, and I moved her into a house that I was- oh, wait- you set up that trap, not me."

"You can't equate the two. Everything you do is for your own sick pleasure."

"Want to know how this all happened?" Michael asks. He can freely lie to me because he controls everything now.

I don't respond because I don't know what the right answer is.

Michael looks past me, up to the TV behind me, then, when the tension causes the floors to warp and the walls to rot, he says, "A friend of mine was looking for an arrangement, and when we couldn't properly accommodate Lux, I made sure they had each other's information."

"Michael, why did you..."

"I didn't. Finance did," Michael says.

"Why did you have to negotiate with her? She's a model, she's not some supplier. She's a human being."

"She was told the figure and the terms. She knew the risks involved in accepting the agreement," Michael says.

"She wouldn't do this to me."

"Turns out she did. *For you*," Michael responds, loving this conversation.

"What did I ever do to you?" I ask, puzzled.

"What do *you* have to do with Lux's arrangements?" Michael plays dumb.

"Lux is the reason I have any success at all."

"She wasn't there for the early collections. Those were successful, don't shortchange yourself. It actually seems like she was only a part of your team for the failure and obscurity portion of your career," Michael says, practically begging me to permanently ruin things with one of the most important people in my life.

"Stop treating her like she's worthless," I say, and it comes out as a contorted whine.

"I offered her a job. I think that indicates I saw some worth," Michael says.

"As an independent contractor," I snarl.

"Industry standard," Michael responds, innocently.

"You have enough money that you can be better than the industry standard," I say, wishing I could drain the blood in my body because I don't want to share anything with this man. I will, however, hang onto our mutual last name because that's the one thing that Michael cannot take from me.

"I do have a lot of money, don't I?" is Michael's response to my challenge.

"Why would you choose to do this? What does this get you?" I beg for answers.

"Well, I accommodated your friend, which is what you wanted, and I helped out a friend of my own, but these were two people acting on their own accord, setting things up without me. I merely gave Lux the information, mentioned my friend was in town. Did I ask her to rush right over there? No. Did she? From what I understand, yeah. Apparently, Lux had been looking for... what was the term she used? Ah, yes, a 'sugar daddy.' That sounds so much better than the alternative. She told me she's on a site. Apparently, it's going quite well for her. You're not the only one who sees something in Lux."

"Give me his number," I demand.

"Andy?" Michael asks, mocking me, "Are you having trouble making ends meet?"

"Give me the number," I yell.

"Ask Lux," Michael says. "I know you want to make this about me- make me out to be the bad guy- but maybe you need to accept that your friend is a very naughty girl."

"You could have paid her more. You purposely shortchanged her and reverted back to predatory industry excuses to legitimize it."

"Listen, hired gun. I run a company, and I design. You're responsible for nothing beyond some fabric cuts. I could do your job in two weeks, but the fact is, I don't have an extra two weeks in my schedule, so I chose to pay you to take care of it. I also chose to pay Karen. I also chose to pay Isabella's agency so we can keep her as an exclusive."

"You what?" I ask, facing another assault.

"I wanted to make sure you had Isabella. Like you said, she's the fresh face for the line."

"I wanted Isabella to work. I wanted her to become a model! She's working at a fucking movie theater right now!" I'm screaming, looking for something to destroy.

"Well, considering the alternatives," Michael says, then smiles wide.

"You paid her agency so she couldn't book any other gigs," I'm wailing.

"Again, standard procedure," Michael says.

"And you didn't tell me this?"

"You asked for this, so I told James to get right on it. It's James' responsibility to coordinate casting, don't forget. Oh, and by the way, he modified the 'agreement' you went ahead and made with Anne. I don't remember you asking for my approval before you made those promises. Checks and balances, Andy."

"You didn't think Isabella could tolerate me for the length of time it would take to complete this collection, did you?" I ask, shattered.

"What *I* think isn't important here," Michael says, totally calm.

"You're treating models like they are goods instead of people. You're blackballing Isabella and pimping Lux."

"Come on, Andy. Lux is 27. It's not like she's young enough to be your housemate, so don't make it out to be more fucked out than it is. A 27-year-old adult doesn't need to be scolded for her behavior."

"Do you really think I'm that naïve?"

"Do you really think Lux is that naïve?"

"Michael, you placed her in this situation."

"Andrew. *You* placed her in this situation."

THE BREAK

I can't accept Lux in my life only part-time. I need her to be perpetually available. She's the first person I want to call when it's all going wrong. She's the first person I think of texting when I see nuisances like Dan Carrington making their way toward me at an industry function and I need to look occupied. Lux is the last person I want to leave, but to know that my calls will be ignored makes me want to sever all ties with her, completely. This is precisely why I would never let her work with other designers. I couldn't deal with her rushing off after my show to do the things she did for me, for someone else. The way I could possibly keep Lux would be to get her as an exclusive every season, and it's not that I can't afford the expense, it's that Lux won't take my money. What else can I offer her, besides freedom? Now that I don't have her- fuck it- she can have all the freedom she wants.

I demand honesty. I demand allegiance. I keep the same people around me because I'm unable to trust anyone new. Yes, any of the people I've known for my entire career could betray me at any moment, but this only convinces me further that I shouldn't seek out new friends or collaborators. Either I'm perpetually loving the wrong people, or no people are worth loving. Both of these perspectives cause my heart to rot.

Angry/ closed off/ cold/ obsessed with the fact I'm being singled out and abused- this is how I will always feel now.

I can't use Isabella to replace, Lux because I'm afraid of turning Isabella into Lux.

I refuse to force more rules on a woman that deserves a life free of the constraints of an old bitter man.

I throw myself back into my work, so I can funnel this new pain into something I can manipulate.

At the workshop, I needlessly tinker.

When I show Karen a collar I'm working on, she asks, "Aren't you worried that it's too 'Michael?'" and I proceed to have a panic attack. I tell Karen I don't care and the line is fucked and Michael already knows this.

The truth is, I can't even blame this on my brother. *I* designed the line. Michael didn't interject his style into my collars, because he was busy with his plan to destroy Lux. The more I review it, the less it appears the plan hinged on Michael's careful orchestration. All he really did was set up a situation, then he provided two adults with some information. He didn't force Lux to call the movie exec- Lux chose to do that. Michael didn't demand that Lux enter into this arrangement, he merely made sure the option was there. Michael has money, but he also seems to have no interest in sex. He exploits young girls, but not like the man that Lux has found. The fact remains, Lux was registered on the arrangement site before any of this happened. The movie exec might be one of many men that I share my fitting model with.

I compose myself in the bathroom, then return to work, spilling my pain again.

New sketches are bathed in darkness and fatalist doom. Mouth scarves run across perfect faces. An eye veil stripes across the head of a girl with arresting baby blues. Red splatters on blinding white. Another pure possibility is debauched.

I drop the sketches in the trash, then decide I'll get drunk.

I give up on the line. I'll let everyone else handle it.

I've done my part- Italy has what they need- I'll wait until it all comes back, then Karen can make the difficult decisions.

When I return from the bodega with my beer, Intern Jessica stops me in the hallway. "I saw you lose it with Karen..." she says.

I wait for her next comment, and she starts doing an impression of my stare, as she asks, "Why don't you ever ask me what I think?"

"Well," I say, from the back of my throat, drawing out the word so I can think of a valid defense. "We discussed the shoes. I asked you... about... pilgrim buckles," I mumble, then make a frowning face when I realize the intern is right. "I'll give you a really good recommendation," I offer, struggling to seem like a good boss. "I'll sign Michael's name on it," I continue, trying to sweeten the pot.

I open my Bud tallboy, and after the first sip, I realize that there are still people at Michael Lorrie who care about me. Here's Intern Jessica, calling me out for my distance, while I'm worried about everyone hiding from me.

I asked her for coffees/ I asked her for reference materials/ I asked her to make sure that the model in the bathroom was doing a planned throw up and not a stomach flu throw up that might be contagious.

Never once did I ask Intern Jessica what she thought of my designs. Maybe I was afraid she'd echo Karen's observations. I didn't want to tip the scales. If Lux agrees with Karen, it's just the correct opinion. If Intern Jessica agrees with Karen, and I disagree with them, the debate regarding if they're right could continue on in my head forever. I guess, instead of wrangling with Intern Jessica's observations, it just seemed easier to avoid seeking her input altogether.

No matter what, I can't discount the fact that she's been here, every day, since the collection began, providing me with the consistency and availability that I wrestled so aggressively for with Isabella and Lux. Intern Jessica has been giving me exactly what I've been demanding from my other girls, and I've ignored her.

"I don't want Michael's name on my recommendation," Intern Jessica tells me, "I don't care about a recommendation. Well- I do- but it's not why I've been here every day. Honestly, I was focused on getting an internship elsewhere, but I chose Michael Lorrie when I heard that you were taking the job. I knew that people would think I got the internship here because of nepotism- because my dad is on the board- but when I found out you were designing ready-to-wear, I was just so damn curious about what that looks like. I wanted to be a part of your process."

"Why?" I ask.

"Because I thought I could help you."

"You have helped me," I say.

"I thought you needed a hand, but you never took mine," she responds, and the guilt I feel is absolute.

Intern Jessica sips her beer, while I try to explain myself further, "You were so good with the other stuff, that you allowed me to focus on the collection. You know that I'm not great with the details, unless they're on a garment," I say.

"I helped with the other stuff, but my dream isn't to be a girl that does the *other stuff*. I want to do this," Intern Jessica says, pointing aggressively at the naked mannequins.

"You're so young that-"

"-Isabella got to be a part of it. I see her in the clothes. I don't see me. I'm nowhere in this collection. Isabella is younger than me, and she got everything."

"Isabella is different. You can't compare yourself to Isabella. You don't want to," I warn.

"You saw something in her," Intern Jessica says, then her silence implies I didn't see anything in my intern.

I nod.

It's time to modify my perspective.

I need to look at Intern Jessica as someone that I can trust.

I can't think of her as "Intern Jessica" anymore.

I need to think of her as my assistant, because I desperately need assistance.

"Do you see something in me?" Jessica asks, desperate to clarify the nod.

"You're on your way," I tell her.

"With your pieces, it's either there or it's not," Jessica says, about to cry.

"Well, like you said, you're not in those pieces so the rules are different for you," I respond, but then quickly add, "And, I think you're forgetting something. Remember when you pulled those Michael Lorrie pieces from the archive for me?"

Jessica nods, unable to speak because a cry is building behind her lungs.

"The orange mini dress you pulled from the archive for me is in one of those pieces we sent to Italy. Same with the black princess dress, and the pink bandeau dress," I ramble out, admitting to each inspiration. "You need to see the final pieces, then you'll understand. When you pulled the archive M.Lorrie pieces for me, it was because I saw designs that were almost there. I worked every day on getting them closer and closer and closer. You became part of the process when you brought that stuff to me. So, don't rush it. You might be enough for other lines, but you have a lot more work to do before you're a part of this to the degree you want to be."

Jessica nods. I know that this probably isn't what she wanted to hear.

In a moment that makes Jessica instantly younger than Isabella, she hugs me, and her mascara bleeds onto my shirt.

I want to protect Jessica. I want to protect Lux. I hate when women are being taken advantage of. I want to save these girls, but I'm misguided.

I defend strong women, and I defend weak women.

Both of these types of women hate me.

Both of these types of women view me as a confused little boy.

This proves their intuition.

This proves their intelligence.

Instead of speaking with these women, or about these women, I decide I'll start speaking to the piece of shit men who are pulling the petals off my beautiful flowers.

THE ROTTING MAN

I want to chew my lip off. I want to look as grotesque as I feel on the inside. I want to be falling apart in full view of everyone. I want to project an immediate warning of the disease I carry. I want a physical defect that the finest clothes cannot mask. I want to wordlessly inform people to look away. Stay away. Push me out of your mind. I am not a person. I am a monster, and monsters hurt people. Monsters are chased away. Monsters are avoided and shunned. Men vow revenge on monsters. There are gentle giants and misunderstood oafs, but monsters have no redeeming qualities. Monsters are never invited to the dinner table because you never know what the monster views as a meal.

This feeling of exhaustion is absolute. My face is yellow and purple, yet when I touch my padded skin, I feel no physical pain. I become aware of the organs in my body; functions that were on autopilot now require manual manipulation. It's like someone clicked off my focus, and now there are skills that have to be utilized to create simple clarity. I can't find a rhythm for my breathing. I feel like I'm going to suffocate myself. I hope that I do. I haven't eaten in 15 hours and I become sure that I won't eat for another 20. My stomach burns for nothing. It chews on itself. My brain spirals in a tornado, then stops sending hunger signals at some point. Why would you gas up a car that's barreling brake-less toward a cliff? Don't feed the monster because he eats flesh. Don't drip fuel on this fire. Let the fire burn out. Someone will find me and help me if things get too dire for too long. My brain corrects itself. *No. No one will find us. We are alone.* My arms protest my brain's need for relief. They attempt to distract the brain. They shake when they reach for the glass. *Just forget all of this shit*, the arms demand. They provide the alcohol that's supposed to bring hours of escape. The system begins to break down and the cogs search for preservation. The unessential parts fear their removal and push for their continued existence. The body needs order in the chaos, but nothing is synchronized. Everything is confused. The commands are written in a language that cannot be deciphered and the panic is now in charge. Needs are pushed aside. Indulgences are granted. The rules are broken and there's no use in rehabbing the existing protocol. Scrap it all and start over. Let someone else step in and fix things. Pass the responsibility to bodies more responsible.

I became sure that it's all over, and at that very moment, the girl who doesn't touch reaches out her hand, then pulls me back down into the basement. She demands, "Make me something."

THE FASHUN

The arrangement that Lux has with this man scares me. Now that she's decided her sexuality has a price, anytime she needs money, she'll calculate who she has to meet with, then she'll go out and do it. Lux's destructive short term thinking must tell her that the "arrangement" is "easy money." Nothing pays that well per hour- except maybe fashion- and there's a reason why. Lux considers herself immune to the risks involved with this "sugar daddy" concept. I can't deny that she's an intelligent girl, but Lux has never been a man, nor has she intimately known enough older men to realize the risk she's running thinking she can meet them for coffee, provide 30 minutes of conversation, then head back to their bedrooms to quickly finish the job. Being dirty is not that clean.

I know how dangerous this situation is because I'm a man.

I know how dangerous this situation is because I work with girls in fragile positions all day long, and over the years, there have been days when a model arrives, and she's not okay, and she tells me why she's not okay, and so many times a man's vile actions are behind the breakdown.

It's the booking as a "model hostess" that carries extra expectations/ It's the photographer undoing his belt buckle while snapping photographs/ It's the vague job that comes with specific demands.

I know how dangerous it is for a young girl to go into a hotel room with an older man because I'm sitting here, on my bed, watching a Hungarian girl in James' latest screener. I accept that she'll be gone in minutes, if she isn't already. Those girls have paid a price that I don't want added to Lux's debt.

I hate Isabella's theater job, but it doesn't squeeze my heart like Lux's part-time job. There's an old adage that a girl is considered dirty because she has sex with men, and a girl is pure when a man hasn't touched her. It's a simplification, but it works for what I have with Isabella.

I want Isabella to respond to my texts/ I want Isabella to get excited when a new anime series shows up on Netflix/ I want Isabella to look forward to modeling my clothes.

I don't want Isabella to fuck anyone, including myself. I want Isabella to exist as an intangible being. She keeps part of herself private. No one even knows her last name. If she was to have sex with Matthew, or one of the other models she's around, I'd want her to sneak the boy in, then I'd want him to disappear as soon as it was over. I need to be lied to, but when those lies start to affect my life- when those lies pull the person I love away, I can't abide that. With Lux, I'm okay with her having sex. I don't know if she has a boyfriend, I don't care who she sleeps with, but I do care when she makes herself a commodity, a possession, a toy. When Lux turns herself into a screener girl, it makes me want to say goodbye now because she's not worth the pain. I know how this will end.

Even in the back of my mind, the thought of these beautiful women fucking does little for me. The electrical current of sexual need I felt in my 20's has dulled, mellowed. The excitement of the release has dwindled. It's become something that I do in the morning, like taking a pill or ironing a shirt, then it's done. The need to procreate resolves itself in tissues before my morning shower. Now, a laugh is more exciting. Now, a quiet gesture is better than a moan. I fear this will infiltrate my work. Before, it was never about the sex, but the sex was there. I wanted my women to feel sexy. Now, I'm not sure what to do about the sex. Do I add it? Is it still there? Is it essential? Am I playing into the hands and minds of men who will destroy my customers?

Initially, women's fashion was interesting to me only because of the sex. I began an obsession with fashion models thanks to my mother's Victoria Secret catalogs, and the runway shows that ran every Saturday morning on CTV. During the televised fashion shows, the network would show uncensored nipples. I would tune in every Saturday, and I'd start searching the collections for the type of fabric the designer used, hoping for something sheer, something loose that would become revealing in motion. I arrived horny and left interested. I could see breasts on cable and they wouldn't be blurred out because it was part of the art. This established fashion's importance beyond just covering shame. Sometimes fashion shows that shame- sometimes it helps a person conquer that shame.

Shameful people gravitate to fashion.

A boy snaps sneaky pictures of a girl taking off her expensive dress.

The girl drives to the studio of a designer who creates a template that dictates in the near future she must be smaller, slimmer, taller, with better posture.

The girl leaves the fitting and meets with a man who gifts her a dress, then requests that she fill her end of the "arrangement."

It's hard to cover shame with luxury fashion because the more garments you need, the more shame you have to hide. The shameful act for the money; the money for the clothes.

Part of this is why I'm avoiding Lux, and part of it is why Isabella has stepped closer to me.

Isabella has taken the week of unpaid vacation that she's allowed, and she's devoted her entire focus to helping me get out of a situation that feels beyond my control. When Isabella was falling apart, I took her home, and now that I'm falling apart, Isabella takes me to work.

In the middle room of the workshop, I stare at a wall of digitals that Jessica has printed out. This mural is comprised of the 60 girls that James has taken an interest in. The agency-snapped photos are lined up so that Michael can "approve" them. I notice that some of the girls on the wall have already starred in screeners, and suddenly this collage feels like James' comprehensive hit-list.

I'm unable to tell if any of the girls look right for what I'm trying to accomplish, mainly because I've lost the pulse of my ready-to-wear designs. I ask, "Isabella, as a fashion blogger, what's your opinion on these casting choices?"

"As a fashion blogger?" she asks, making sure I really want this answer. Her eyes scream, *Get out now. Abort this line of questioning.*

"Yeah. What would a fashion blogger say about this casting mural?" I ask.

"You're a racist asshole," Isabella says, not sugarcoating it.

"What?" I yelp, bouncing out of my skin, then reaching up and pointing at the blacks and the Asians, a Mexican and maybe an Eskimo.

"Doing that makes the fashion blogger in me feel like you're very racist," Isabella informs me.

"I have everyone here. We even included this girl. She could be Haitian," I say, pointing at a particular picture.

"Exactly, Andrew. It's too deliberate. It's not true diversity."

"It's a fucking rainbow of teenage pussy," I say, not understanding.

"Now the fashion blogger in me says you're a misogynist too."

I sigh.

Isabella patiently explains, "Putting every race in there is artificial. It's pandering. It's insulting. It's as though a girl was picked merely because you're afraid of what will happen without a black model. It's racist."

"Okay, I'll fix it. How about I get rid of the Haitian? I'm keen on getting rid of the Haitian," I say, bartering, lost.

"Fuck you!" Isabella screeches.

"That was a joke," I say, putting my hands up. "What jokes are safe to make around fashion bloggers now?" I ask.

"Hmm," Isabella thinks for a moment, then says, "Ones about using men for money."

With that can of worms springing open, I say, "My jokes, my models, my business."

"And yours alone?" Isabella asks, still in fashion blogger mode.

"No. You can have an opinion, it just needs to be delivered with a little tact. If someone makes you a dinner and it sucks, you spit it into the napkin, then throw the napkin away. You don't say, 'this sucks,' then try to ban them from cooking."

"If someone makes you a dinner with expired ingredients, and you can't stomach it, you might puke. You shouldn't hold in your puke- it could be fatal," Isabella says.

I nod, then say, "Luckily, I've carefully selected my ingredients."

"According to a dated recipe-"

"-that has worked for hundreds of years. Just because it's not your taste doesn't mean it isn't palatable."

Isabella smiles at me, "You engaged fashion blogger mode, so you brought this upon yourself."

"I'm going to go see what Jessica is up to," I say, fleeing Isabella until I can exercise the blogger from her being.

"Jessica is a fellow fashion blogger," Isabella warns me, and I give her a chuckle as an acknowledgment.

I find Jessica in the room to the left, cleaning up scraps, pretending to not notice me standing in the door frame.

"You do have a blog, don't you?" I ask, because she's not paying attention to me.

"Yeah, I told you this the day we met. I'm the girl who writes about the girl next door," Jessica says, pointing a handful of scraps toward the room I just came from.

"The girl next- oh," I say, realizing that she means Isabella.

I approach Jessica as though I can't tell if she's a dog or a wolf, and I ask, "Everything okay?"

"Yes. Just. Busy," she huffs.

"Don't make yourself crazy over this," I say.

"Over what? The scraps, or the fact that you bypassed your team and choose the expertise of your teenage model gi- know what, never mind. Do you... need... something?" Jessica asks, a hurricane of cadences and postures.

"Listen," I say, sensing her issues, mentally acknowledging that- like Lux- I've gone back on my word almost immediately after a promise was made. "I know that counting buttons isn't glamorous, but at the end of this, I promise you, I'll help you get an internship with someone that will better utilize your talents," I tell her.

"What's your defect?" Jessica asks me.

"I don't do anything the right way, the scheduling, the casting, the timetables-"

"-no. Not like that. I know how you're different. I want to know how you can ignore me, while becoming deeply involved in *everyone else's* shit."

"You don't want me in your life. You've read the reviews," I say, saving the girl from the monster.

"Why are you so obsessed with those reviews?" Jessica asks.

I shrug, then say, "I'm just taking responsibility for my mistakes. And your generation wants me to never work again." I pause, wondering why Jessica is still torn up about my failures, then I consider that she thought she would be granted more responsibility when Lux left, then I brought in yet another beautiful and talented girl, whose opinion I demand relentlessly. I brace myself for the bitter response- a response I deserve.

"Do you think I'm unaware of how people feel about you?" Jessica asks. "Do you think I Wikipedia'd you five minutes before my Michael Lorrie interview? I fucking hate what they did to you, Andrew. Only an industry based on fear could ban one of its premiere artists. The fashion industry is an institution that starves itself for imagined reasons. It's insanely frustrating that we work in a field where elevating and evolving the art form can be put on hold for trivial or imagined reasons."

"I can't agree with this," I say, then I crack a smile and mumble, "I might agree with it, but I *can't* agree with it."

"Ray Lewis probably stabbed a man, and not only did he return to football after the knife was cleaned off, but he was the Super Bowl MVP. That was only allowed to happen because he's good at his job. Chris Brown beat the fucking shit out of his girlfriend on the way to the Grammys, and not only did he get to perform there a couple of years after, but they also ended up giving him a Grammy. That was only allowed to happen because he's good at his job. You said words that made people angry, and they banned you from doing what you do. You had to go behind their backs- in secret- just to perform the job that you're very good at."

"But they let me show another collection," I say, not sure why I'm battling against someone trying to stick up for me.

"Make no mistake, *They* never forgave you. *They* didn't let you show another collection- some Chinese guys who had no idea what they were getting into let you show a collection. *They* joined together, to stop you. And now here you are, designing for someone else's line, again."

"I don't think that our industry will ever be like those other industries," I tell Jessica, and she nods her head in agreement.

Jessica doesn't cry this time. With clear eyes, she informs me, "This industry is too worried about what a bunch of strangers on the internet think. The rest of the world can hurt people and still keep their jobs because of their talent, while you had to go into witness protection for a couple of sentences. They gave you more of a punishment for your sound bites than they gave to the people who physically assaulted another person. So, that's why I'm fighting for you, Andrew. I'm thrilled to be interning at Michael Lorrie, but I'd feel better about this industry if I was interning at Andrew Lorrie. The truth is, I fucking hate that you're reminding me of Michael- bitter and angry at the world, yet too lazy to even try to get better."

THE REBOOT

I become envious that I'll never create a piece that causes the type of devastation I'm currently feeling. I'm drenched with an emotion that fashion can't touch, and this fills me with inspiration.

I have one muse more distant than she's ever been, and another engaged in such a way that if someone suggested this possibility in September, I would've openly laughed in their face. The frail and bewildered girl has become a solid source of comfort. Isabella is here for me, always, at any hour, when my stitches pop and my wounds need redressing.

I still have the Italy garments being constructed, but I start sketching, aggressively, and instead of a collection built by transference, I find my new designs to have qualities of reflection. In my previous work, I would get out all my emotions, then the critics would pick it apart. Now, I'm dissecting the feelings, and I'm confronting what's haunting me, all during the creation process.

A second MLORE collection begins to announce itself. There's the Andrew Lorrie collection I failed with, the MLORE collection in Italy, and now... there's a third, final collection, revealing itself in inspired sketches. Last fall, I had been given a second chance, but I didn't change, and now that second chance means nothing to anyone, besides me. The evolution that Karen spoke about was always a lie. I don't need to adapt- I just need to part with what's holding me back. I've become a snake dragging my dead skin behind me like the train on a dress.

I make a plan to shed the excess.

I know that I'll have to give up my corpse brides and that will change my style. As a young designer, I viewed anyone who abandoned their natural signature as being desperate for acceptance and recognition. I always felt that they were running from what they *wanted* to design, so they could broaden the number of people who wanted to wear their line.

Yes, giving up my corpse brides will be a failure, but in a landscape so densely populated with my endless missteps and pitfalls, this concession feels minor. After failing so frequently, the abandoning of a makeup signature would appear as more of the same for me.

It's clear to me that my winter will be spent in a very specific work-related turmoil that I'll control completely, leaving out Lux.

Lux, I cannot control/ Lux, I cannot speak to Lux, I feel I no longer know.

Despite the distance, and also because of the distance, I miss her every day.

Suddenly, almost as though Cassie walked into my life and picked up a sketch I wasn't sure about, I'm redirected, and I *see* what MLORE needs to be in order to become viable.

With the help of four very different girls who choose to believe in me when I'm at lowest- Isabella and Jessica, Madeleine and Libby- I begin to climb out of the rubble.

When the dust settles, I find myself in Michael's office.

I inform him that almost everything I sent to Italy will be scrapped. I make a promise, "I'll give you a better collection, in time for fashion week. If you like the first one more, you can keep the first one. No problem. Thing is, I'll also give you a second collection, that, according to the terms of my contract, you'll also own. You're getting a BOGO."

"A... BOGO," Michael repeats, as though I'm speaking Spanish.

"Buy one, get one," I explain, trying to sound positive, attempting to become a salesman.

The silence allows me to assume that Michael is okay with my new strategy.

"Things have changed, and my new collection will be better," I promise.

Michael smiles at this because it's a failure on my part. This is me arriving at Michael's office, confessing that everything I've done since my last failure has been a pile of shit. He tells me I have one week to sketch the new line.

That's precisely what I do, and, somehow, it gets approved.

Michael never actually tells me my new sketches match what he's looking for, he just never stops me from working on the designs, and he allows the team he's given me to devote their full energy to my new vision. Italy stops their work and waits for the shipment I promise to deliver by December 15th.

Isabella meets me in the basement for the muslin draping, and the designs change again.

Everything comes together at a speed that only becomes possible when the artist devotes himself completely to the escape.

I feel energy flowing through my veins. A body that was once unwilling to simply exist, now works at a relentless speed to create.

Everything makes sense, and the broken pieces within me align into an entirely different animal.

The collection I *must* create inhabits a territory that exclusively mimics glass. Reflections/ fragility/ transparency/ heat/ pressure/ permanent in its destruction/ dangerous, if not carefully handled. These are the qualities of my line for MLORE. The old M.Lorrie branding was too confusing. Too traditional. Too safe. Too obvious. MLORE is what this brand needs to be. It's a focus on the lore. It's the woman in white. It's Bloody Mary responding to her buzzed-about name. MLORE is about stories. They don't have to be true, but they have to be interesting. I believe in the supernatural and M.Lorrie was too natural.

I fill my suitcase with the muslin pieces, and I transport them on the train, like drugs.

Karen recognizes the trance I'm in, and once she notices that the mannequins in the workshop are wearing new designs, she freaks out. This is another attempt to stop me. She'll fail, as usual.

"What the fuck is going on here?" Karen badgers me.

"We're pivoting," I immediately say, spraying lighter fluid on the flames of her fear.

The old sketches fade. I wake up from a past-dream. I become obsessed with the present. Clean away the clutter. I have awoken completely.

"We can't throw away everything we've done. I'm not going to let you abandon this collection," Karen says, in her signature monotone.

"Go worry about the accessories," I say, referencing the fact that she's trying to work a job she no longer has. "Italy is getting sent my designs on the 15th. We're going to box all this up after some last-second fixes, if you want to help."

"You're literally burning money at this point," Karen warns me.

"MLORE will be printing money, in the spring," I say.

"What's happened to you?" Karen asks with disgust.

"I've just made a breakthrough," I announce proudly.

"This isn't in the budget," I'm reminded.

"I'll sell the LA place," I say, my focus remaining singular.

"You're going to sell your house to work on your brother's label?" Karen recounts my plan slowly, so I'll realize how dumb it sounds.

"Sure," I say, my eyes fixed on a point in my mind, somewhere else- the shore.

"What happens when Cassie asks for her house back?" Karen questions me.

"I'll start paying rent."

"Oh, you're going to start paying, very soon," Karen responds.

"You can't stop me. Your dulling techniques are void."

I hear Isabella laugh at this.

"Andrew, I'm asking you to be logical," Karen says, "You can add a couple of new side dishes, but you can't go back into the kitchen and start from scratch, because the ovens are already full."

"I think you might be using a cooking metaphor right now," I say.

"Yes, I am. I might be taking some ingredients off the table here, but you're still the chef. Get cooking with what you have," Karen says, trying to divert me.

I look at my ex-assistant and, in a parody of her monotone, I say, "Don't let Michael change you, Karen."

"Andrew, there are things about you that need to change, but what doesn't need to change is the line you've created. We need to be prepared in advance because you know what happens when you're allowed to fly by the seat of your pants?"

"I create a totally unique vision?" I ask.

"You fuck things up for other people- other people who do their job incredibly well, and end up receiving no credit, or recognition, or even a moment to exhale and appreciate their work, because some sort of crazy shit is always flying out of your mouth immediately after the runway music cuts off."

I'm calm. With a syrupy cool, I ask, "Okay, but can we cast like regular human beings and wait until we have a set collection so we know what faces we actually need?"

"No. We can't. Do you want to venture a guess why we can't do that Andrew?"

I mock her voice, saying, "Because I'm an awful grumpy-"

She stops me, and takes over, "-because this is a minor line. Because you have a toxic reputation."

"Okay, so what happens when we have 30 goth girls walking for a cupcake pink line?" I ask.

"You're designing a cupcake pink line?" Karen nearly gasps.

"I'm using extremes to make a point. Remember when we were doing the kitchen thing a couple of minutes ago?"

"Please go more extreme, because I don't understand your point," Karen requests.

I want to scream, "*James is abusing these models and no one gives a fuck,*" but I try to think of another way get Karen on my side regarding the screeners. I need to come from a practical angle- appeal to her business side. "The problem with these screeners is that we're reviewing suspects for crimes that haven't been committed yet. It's backward. The girls have to match the clothes or it looks silly, and I'm still making the clothes."

"That's your fault. The videos are groundwork. Whenever you decide what your vision is, we'll at least have the groundwork done," Karen says, reading out of the Michael Lorrie playbook.

"What happens when Glinda the good model gets addicted to pills between screeners and her head doubles in size with water weight? We could have a Romeo + Juliet-era Leonardo DiCaprio in a screener, but by fashion week, we could get The Departed-era Leonardo DiCaprio, without the goatee... or actually, who knows," I say, then I momentarily blanch when I flash back on the *Titanic* conversation at Irina's condo.

Karen continues to tow the party line regarding the screeners, "To make sure the models still look good, we'll bring them back in, and-"

"-why don't we just bring them in closer to fashion week if it's such a chore to get them to stand in a room with a pariah like me?"

"Because this is a slow time and the girls are available. We're pulling them away from nothing, and we can get their agents excited about this. It's advanced money."

"Are we giving them money in advance?" I ask.

"Well, no, but Michael Lorrie's name is-"

"-as good as money in the bank. Right, Kar?"

"Yeah, Andrew."

I turn around, not letting Karen harsh my crystal vision, and I remark, "If you blow up the bank, the charred money inside is worth nothing."

"And the man who carries out the act is worth the same."

THE ONE

The 15th arrives and the second-chance garments depart to Italy.

With the true MLORE collection flying somewhere over the Atlantic, I focus on paying back the girl who gave me everything.

My hands no longer shake, and with precise taps, I send Michael a text reading, "It's done. Now I want you to meet the girl you paid to stay available for the line. Either she walks this show, or I walk from the collection."

"You don't have that power," Michael responds.

"I feel like I do. I have a second wind," I type back.

Michael wants to knock this wind out of me, so he texts, "Bring her in."

"Thought u don't have time for a meeting?" I send.

"Won't take long," Michael texts dismissively.

Isabella quietly accepts the fact that we're meeting with Michael today. I know that she's shy- I know that the idea of a formal meeting is horrifying to her- but she doesn't express her hesitation in words, which allows me to keep my directed focus sharp and passionate. In turn, I don't express my displeasure when Isabella delays us so she can smoke a bowl and watch an episode of a TV show where an entire school is turned into mindless, well-behaved zombies who are fixated on drinking milk.

In the cab, Isabella- made up perfectly for the meeting- glances out the window at a city that both intrigues and scares her.

"Hey," I whisper, to get her attention.

She looks at me, nervous, and I tell her, "Thanks."

"I'm not splitting this cab fare with you," she says, then smiles at her joke, her gap peeking out.

"I only have enough money to get us halfway there," I tease.

"We're almost there, so we'll walk, but I'm wearing four-inch heels, which will make you look very Tom Cruisey when you're next to me," Isabella says.

"I think I just remembered I have some money in my suit coat," I say.

There's a silence, and Isabella doesn't ask why I thanked her. I feel the need to make sure she knows why I'm grateful, so I say, "No matter what happens in there, remember... Japan."

"Remember Japan," Isabella repeats, "I think that was one of the battle cries that got us into World War II."

The cab stops, and I say, "Get ready for World War III."

I pay the driver, then we step out of the cab, taking a moment for ourselves at the curb.

We've carried each other to this point, and I find myself wondering if this is a wrong turn.

"Come on," Isabella says, walking a bit in front of me so I don't feel Cruisey.

"Why aren't you questioning any of this?" I ask her, as we walk into Michael Lorrie HQ.

"You took me to the burnt beach when I was having a tough time and that got me through it. One of us always has to make the sacrifice to be happy and agreeable when the other is sad," Isabella explains.

"You don't *have* to be happy," I say, knowing this is not her default setting. I wasn't surprised when Isabella referred to happiness as a "sacrifice."

"Sure I do," she says, "If we're both sad at the same time, drinking problems will develop. A small indie band will have to be formed. You remember the Blend apartment- *that* is communal sadness."

I laugh at this. Suddenly, both of us are happy, and it feels like we'll be able to defeat Michael, together.

Isabella checks her gapped teeth for lipstick during the elevator ride up, and when she appears confident with her reflection, the doors open.

Michael's Jessica is waiting for us, and she warmly introduces herself to Isabella. Then, it's dead model walking, as we make our way to the corner office.

When we get to the door, Isabella freezes. A panic I haven't seen since that night at The Imperial Hall- or maybe that day on campus- returns to Isabella's face.

I take three steps forward, then turn back and hold up a pausing hand to the girls, indicating that a short private exchange will be required before the meeting can begin. Jessica nods with an immediate understanding, then commences the same tour she took Karen on. Isabella blankly follows along.

As soon as I shut Michael's door, he asks, "Did you abduct one of Blend's models?"

"*Now* you're worried about abducted models?" I ask.

Michael nods at this. "You have to give her back," he says to me, like I'm a child who stole the neighbor's cat.

"Since you've kept her out of work, I want her to open your MLORE show," I reveal. This is the reason for the meeting, and I wanted to have Isabella here before I showed my cards.

"She already walked for you," Michael says.

"Yes, in a collection that's been forgotten," I respond.

Michael grins widely at this, then says, "Hold that thought, let's not keep the young lady waiting."

I nod, knowing that we're pausing the conversation to enhance my humiliation. I allow this to happen because my failures seem to become easier to tolerate with Isabella next to me.

My coping mechanism during this pain soaked season can be distilled in two words, *find Isabella*, and that's exactly what I do, again.

I leave Michael's office, then search until I locate the girls in the break room, drinking tea.

"He'd like to meet you now," I tell Isabella, and she smiles, for me.

I walk the now-confident model into Michael's office. I have no idea what Michael's Jessica said to Isabella, but I'll be sending flowers to the front desk as a thank you.

"Isabella, this is Michael. Michael, this is Isabella."

"I loved your last 'Irina' collection," Isabella gushes.

In a pang of jealous competition, I attempt to move the conversation forward, "Very good, now maybe you could-"

"-and the body bags to the Vanessa Carlton song. Incredible. Fashion history," Isabella says, still standing, towering over me.

"I agree, I agree. We're using Vanessa again," Michael says.

I never listened to the CD Irina sent. I knew it wouldn't matter.

"The new collection is stunning. I'm obsessed with the draft pieces," Isabella continues, a confident stranger, "I'm thrilled with what you guys are doing. I'd walk for trade, no questions asked."

"She doesn't mean that," I say, sweat climbing out of my skin.

Isabella eyes me, then says, "This line looks incredible. He practically had to pull me out of the workshop every night that I had the privilege of being there."

"You genuinely like the pieces?" Michael asks, his interest piqued.

"I mean, I could be a plant by Andrew. I live with the bastard," she says, then pauses, and her nerves get the best of her. She backpedals, "Not to say that he's a bastard as a reflection on his parental situation... because... you both have the same parents. Or had. Or... Okay, nice meeting you Michael, I'm gonna go stare longingly at the M&M's Jessica has in that glass bowl on her desk," Isabella says, immediately leaving the office.

I sit down in the chair across from Michael, unsure if Isabella provided enough compliments to land her this gig.

Michael just stares at me- his face a neutral mask- so I mumble, "I'm curious, what do you think about her?"

"She seemed high," Michael remarks.

"Well- I mean- yeah," I confirm.

Michael studies me, then provides a recap of where I'm at right now, "You're hanging out rent-free in your ex's house, getting high with a teenager..."

"My life does sound pretty awesome when you summarize it like that," I say, smiling.

"I don't think we'll use her. Her look is too jarring," Michael remarks.

I squirm, but try to play it cool, "Don't you want people to be jarred? You brought me in to shake things up."

"No. Don't confuse yourself. I brought you in because I can't design for my lesser labels. You can't design couture, so you were assigned my ready-to-wear line. Please be very aware of the situation," Michael says.

"She's the future," I declare.

"She's not the future of MLORE."

"Then the future for this company just got a little less bright," I say, crossing my arms, "I need another set of eyes- her eyes. Did you see her eyes?"

"Your intern has eyes," Michael says, checking his bulky black watch.

"Yes, but I need an additional set of eyes."

"Your intern isn't going blind, is she? Did you get a defective intern?" Michael asks, as though there was an intern assembly-line, which- yeah- he probably does literally view it like that.

"My intern's eyes are fine," I say.

"Just admit it. You're fucking her, Andrew."

"I'm not," I maintain.

"So she sleeps in a different room than you?" Michael asks, clarifying.

"She has her own room," I say, the semantics giving me away.

"Do her parents know?" Michael asks, then adds, "Have you verified that you're not her parent?"

"Fuck you, Michael. I'm trying to revolutionize your staggering line."

"Well you do have experience with staggering lines, don't you? That seems to be your only experience now that I think about it."

THE PROOF

I have experience with staggering lines. And beautiful women. And hidden killers. And widespread apathy.

"Why do you put up with me?" I ask Isabella as the cab sloshes through the December snow, on the way to the workshop.

Isabella turns to me, then says, "I'm constantly becoming other people at those fittings, and you're always no one but yourself. I guess I envy you a little bit."

"You're much better off than I am," I assure her.

"You're wrong," she assures me, and I believe her. *Why do I believe her?*

"And I know you miss *her*," Isabella adds, and she's right.

To forget about Lux, I threw myself into my work, and now I find myself at the dangerous point in the creative process where my complete attention is no longer necessary. I'll have some free time after today, and I hate it.

My work phone has stayed quiet. I wonder if the screeners have stopped, or if they're just being streamed to a new audience.

"Just get through this meeting, then it's Christmas vacation," Isabella frames things, noticing my furrowed brow.

I don't want to get through this meeting because, after, we'll return home, then Isabella will pack her bags and leave for California to spend Christmas with her family.

As soon as Isabella and I walk into the workshop, we find Karen frowning at the designs that didn't have to be shipped to Italy because I made them in the basement, and they can be finished here.

"You can't use this much plastic in ready-to-wear," Karen tells me.

"Why?" I ask, casually.

"Because it's tacky."

"People are tacky," Isabella points out.

"People are tacky *and* boring," Madeleine says, walking by, wearing one of my nearly-finished pieces, as a seamstress scuttles behind her, carrying a porcupine of a pin cushion.

"And they don't like garments that they have to dry clean," Karen adds, pointing out- probably correctly- this plastic won't stand a chance in the dryer.

"A MLORE t-shirt starts at $139.99. If they are paying that price, I think they can pick up a dry cleaning bill," I say.

"The buyers are going to have a problem with you using plastic," Karen tells me.

"Okay. I'll make it removable, but that's more work on the shoulders and callused fingers of our team. We'll all be very busy working on this new requirement now so I don't want to take up your time."

"Andrew, the entire collection has to be wearable," Karen says, not giving up.

"Madeleine's wearing a new piece right now," I say, arching my neck, looking for her.

"This is ready-to-wear," Karen attempts to remind me.

"Not all of it," I say, "There's still so much work to be done."

"Don't play stupid. You need to show a ready-to-wear collection," Karen says, her annoyance peeking through her monotone.

"Madeleine!" I yell, "Show how ready you are."

Madeleine walks toward us in the piece.

"How are things?" I ask the stomping model.

"Things are cool," Madeleine says, her pace consistent.

"See. Things are cool," I purr.

"She doesn't care," Karen responds, trying to throw me, knowing my weakness.

"Madeleine. Do you care?" I ask.

"About, like, causes?" Madeleine asks back, confused.

"Sure," I respond.

"Causes are good. Cure things!" Madeleine says, brimming with faux enthusiasm.

"See? Things are cool," I say, being an asshole to Karen, "Things are being cured. I feel cured."

"I'm calling Lux. You're losing it," Karen responds.

"Let me know how that goes," I say.

"What did you do to her, Andrew?" Karen asks, the lure of gossip driving this question.

I ignore Karen, because her curiosity has nothing to do with her concern for Lux. This question was asked because Karen can't tell if she's already been phased out. Beyond her accessories task, I'm unsure what Karen's purpose is anymore, so I let the silence provide the answer.

THE GIFT

We're sitting in the back of a taxi on the way to Newark International, when Isabella reaches down to get an H&M bag she's kept by her side, while her luggage sits in the trunk. From the bag, she removes a Christmas present, wrapped in taped-together *Vogue* magazine pages.

"What's that?" I ask, my smile joker-wide.

"Are you gonna be okay? Home? Alone?" Isabella asks me carefully.

"Sure- nail on the basement stairs, heat up the doorknobs, Christmas ornaments on the floor under windows. Maybe I'll treat myself to a toothbrush approved by the American Dental Association," I say.

"Ew, you might deserve to be home alone for that one," Isabella declares through a smile, then she hands me the present, almost as an apology.

My Christmas gift to Isabella was the plane ticket home to see her parents, as well as the ticket to return back to New Jersey in mid-January.

"You really didn't have to," I say, holding a present I didn't expect.

"Open it!" Isabella demands, excited.

"You shouldn't have spent money on me," I mumble, tearing open the wrapping, bisecting one of the models in the Vogue editorial Isabella re-purposed.

"I didn't," Isabella says, "The designer gets trade for once."

In my hands is a red sweater that I instantly like.

"This is perfect," I tell Isabella, and I mean it completely.

"I knew you'd like it," she says.

"Excellent choice."

"It wasn't a choice. I mean, you literally designed that sweater for the Vanessa Thach collection you ghosted for," Isabella says, a perfect ID.

"How did you find out I was behind the Thach collection?" I ask, worried that she also got my resume from Karen.

"You have a fingerprint, Andrew. Once I knew where to dust for your prints, I googled for a bit and as soon as I saw Vanessa's collection, I was instantly like, *I know this. Ah, yes. Andrew. I see him.*"

Isabella is right, completely.

I've always been aware of this fingerprint. It's passion and pain. The collections I design are an exact reflection of Andrew Lorrie during that particular season of my life. This is why high fashion lines are named after people, not abstract ideas. A diary cannot go by any other name than the owner's.

I try to remember why the blood red sweater made it into Vanessa's collection. The sweater wasn't about my anger- like a therapist would assume- I'm pretty sure it was about the sliced forehead that I suffered while I was sketching out the collection. Anger was tangentially involved, but the model was the one who was angry- *she* threw the mug. The handle on the coffee cup, upon impact with the wall, spiraled into my forehead, leaving a small gash the length of a sewing needle, directly over the fat vein snaking down from my hairline. This cut proceeded to spit blood down my face. I took my gray sweater off to sop up the bleeding and it quickly became soaked during the frantic car ride to the hospital. Before I got out of the car, I looked down and found a *new* sweater, stretched larger, dripping all over me.

The cut/ the sweater/ the affection I received/ the stitches I received/ the promises I received- all of it went into the piece. I don't have a scar, I still have the vein, and I don't know what happened to the sweater that made its way down the runway. What's in my hands, is a reproduction. I'm filled with warmth now that the sweater has been remade, softer.

Isabella explains why the gift is trade, "I'm able to knit in the box office, since Oscar season sucks. It's like, 'Do you want to watch the slavery movie or the slavery movie?' and I gotta say, the youth of South Orange... not that interested in slavery. Which is good on a fundamental level, I suppose."

I laugh, and I feel warm in the winter.

The cab pulls up to the terminal, and I help Isabella with her bags.

The cab leaves, and I step into the airport with Isabella.

Once we hit the security line, we both hold our presents tightly, and I wish the Cali girl a safe trip.

I make sure to keep a golden last image of Isabella, because it will maximize my nostalgia and feed my creativity.

Isabella leaves, and I'll be alone for Christmas.

THE SEASON TO BE JOLLY

I pessimistically assume that I'll never see Lux or Isabella again.

I leave *Post* playing in Cassie's room because it helps me pretend that Isabella is still here.

On Christmas Eve, I don't go into the workshop, because the employees who didn't leave deserve their freedom, just like those who did leave. As I look at the pictures that line Cassie's room, I realize it's Isabella that I want to spend this day with. I leave the room that *was* Cassie's and *was* Isabella's. Both women have plans to return, but plans are easily broken.

All night long, I look to the sliver of light, expecting a three-months-younger version of Isabella to drift into the room at any moment.

On Christmas day, I find no stocking at my feet, no Isabella by my side.

Two texts- both wishing me an identical, "Merry Christmas," arrive from my two muses, and this makes me restless. When I look at the holiday greeting from Lux, our other texts still sit in the stream. The messages are angry, bitter, and they hurt to read, still. For some reason, I begin my Christmas day reading these messages over again, as though there was something else that I could uncover. I search for the gift of clarity on how to persuade Lux to spend her holiday with me.

Madeleine's "Merry Christmas" text vibrates my phone, and it makes me feel strong enough to start my day. I respond to the text, then I get dressed in my lone Christmas gift.

It's a white Christmas and, my leather jacket won't be enough for the aimless trek that seems inevitable. I find a beige double-breasted, button closure, belted-waist Burberry trench in the coat closet. I try to remember if it's mine. I don't think it is. I put it on, gifting it to myself.

I begin my walk up through the snow to the university. When I get to those black bars, I see that the path to the gate is covered in untouched snow. All of the students are home, like Isabella. I don't trudge a path through the crisp snowfall; I turn around and walk back down into town. I buy a ticket from the machine inside the overly warm train station, then I walk up to the platform and sit, alone. I look at the new ads that have been put up, all of them promising precisely what the previous ads promised. I wonder if anyone has found their happiness yet. I turn and find that the suicide hotline ad is still there. I wonder how many people have given up on being happy.

The train is practically empty, except for uniformed service workers in bad polos. Minimum wage employees need to get to their job so that they can attend to singular people such as myself. I immediately push this thought out of my head because it makes me feel guilty for decisions I had no part in making.

My plan to surprise Lux at her apartment fails when I reach her doorstep, and like the house in South Orange- like the university- it appears the apartment is empty. I don't text her because I don't want to know how she's spending Christmas.

I flag down a cab, then hop inside.

After a destination rumbles its way out of my mouth, I sit, tense, in the back seat of the cab, and I quietly list all the reasons why this trip is a bad idea.

I need beer, so I have the driver stop at a place that seems open, and I assure him that I'll be right back. I'm guessing that, because it's Christmas, he waits. I return with a 12 pack of Saranac in my arms, and when I get in the cab, I reach up and offer the man one of the beers. "Merry Christmas," I say, and the man takes the beer, then places it on the front seat like a little glass co-pilot.

At every stoplight, I have to fight the gripping instinct to toss every cent I have into the front seat, then run.

I look out the window, and it reminds me that I have nowhere to go.

I find that New York City on Christmas looks so different from the part of New York where I spent my holidays as a child. Maybe this is why I choose not to flee the taxi for the remainder of the ride.

After I pay my fare, then Christmas-tip my (most likely) Muslim driver, I walk up to a building that I've only been in once, but the doorman opens the door for me like I'm a resident. Here he is, out in the cold, opening a door instead of spending Christmas with his family. My repulsion regarding this decision allows me to speak confidently to the obviously Jewish, not sad looking, front desk girl. I'm quickly let inside and I don't wish the desk girl a Merry Christmas.

During the elevator ride up, I remove my scarf and unbutton my coat-gestures that I will most likely rewind in mere minutes.

I get out of the elevator, and I persist with my bad decision.

I approach the closed door, and when Karen doesn't show up to stop me from doing this stupid thing, I decide to go for it.

After two of my knocks go unanswered, the door swings open.

Michael stands before me, completely put together in his Michael Lorrie uniform, yet his mask of cool falls when he sees me, as though I'm an apparition.

"Merry Christmas," I say, holding up the box of bad beer.

"Merry Christmas," Michael says, dryly, looking at the beer, intimately familiar with it because it's what our father would buy every Christmas.

"I hope I'm not interrupting..." I say, waiting for Michael to move from the front door. Michael doesn't respond because he would have to admit that he's alone on Christmas, and that would be the only thing more pathetic than spending Christmas with me. He's dressed for company, but there's no indication that he has company over, and his shoes- a soft soled cranberry loafer-indicate that he won't be leaving anytime soon. When I try to think of who Michael might spend Christmas with, I come up with an empty list. I think that's why I'm here.

"You dress like that when no one's around?" I ask, impressed by his effort.

"You dress like that when people *are* around?" Michael responds, eyeing my sweater.

"It was a gift," I say, defensively.

"The existence of that sweater at no time involved a gift," Michael declares, like he too recognizes it from the Vanessa Thatch collection.

"Are you going to let me in?" I ask, then I stare at Michael until he reaches out and pops open the flap of the beer box. He takes out one of the Saranacs- a Belgian Pale Ale- then makes a disapproving face and tells me, "I hate this shit."

I have to convince myself that his comment is about the beer.

Michael walks into the apartment, leaving the door open, so I follow him.

Inside the apartment, I hear a distant whisper that hisses, *All of this could have been yours if you just shut the fuck up.* Michael's home is carefully kept and universally smooth. The edges of everything are rounded. There are no right angles anywhere. The ceilings are vaulted/ The carpets are circular/ The furniture is plush/ The electronics are hidden. There's no TV, but when I look toward the far wall, I spot the circular cut out for the projector lens. This is such a stark contrast to the aged rectangles in the house on Scotland Road. Michael's apartment has a sterile composition that's usually limited to the doctor's office or a museum. There are no trinkets. There are no clothes on the floor. There are no dishes in the sink. The walls of this apartment are a Michael Lorrie hall of fame- Blown up magazine covers/ Sketches carefully framed/ Awards across the mantelpiece instead of family photos. The apartment is huge- in comparison to most New York City dwellings- and Michael tells me that the entire space is soundproofed, which is required for him to find inner peace during his morning meditation session. He's actively chosen to sacrifice space for proximity to "everything," then he sacrificed even more space to make sure the walls were thick enough to keep any evidence of "everything" out of the apartment.

Fleetingly, I have the desire to invite Michael to my house. The space/ the privacy/ the history/ the creaks/ the cracks/ The ability to not only host a party, but also offer sleeping arrangements for the guests- this is what defines a home. I much prefer to commute into the city when I need to work, or see a girl, or save a friend. I can experience everything the city has to offer, then after my task has been completed- or at least attempted- I can go back to Jersey and relax, or nurse my wounds.

If I was to share these thoughts with my brother, he would tell me that it's essential that I live in a "fashion capital" because there's no way to find out what's next until you see what's now. The people who buy the next collection will be from a capital/ The people who critique the next collection will be from a capital/ The people who can afford the next collection will be from a capital. The pulse is too weak in the suburbs. Michael lives in a city built for the rich, who only keep the poor around to clean up the mess left after the party.

"Why are you here?" Michael finally asks, holding out an empty hand in an incredulous way.

"Because it's Christmas," I respond.

"Dry off by the fire," Michael says, pointing to the rounded fireplace.

"You're going to make a fire?" I ask, with a snigger.

"Yup," he says, then picks up a black remote and clicks a button. A fire instantly roars up, then Michael carries the box of beer over to the fridge.

Accepting my demand for a Christmas together, my brother returns with a fresh beer in each hand.

Usually, when two brothers get together over drinks on Christmas Day, they take refuge in watching whatever sport is being televised. Today, the projector remains off, the game goes unwatched. No matter the sport, every player on a specific team wears the exact same thing and that does not appeal to us. There's a reason it's called a "uniform."

I finish my first beer, then immediately take the second that Michael left for me. When no conversation begins, I check my phone, looking for a, "New year, new start?" text from Lux, or a simple, "Wish we got a tree," text from Isabella. Both models are busy having a Merry Christmas with their friends and family. They're going about their holiday, occupied, distant.

Michael leaves again- this time for so long that I have to wonder if he's left the apartment. Eventually, he returns with two more beers pressed tight to his white shirt, while also balancing a bowl in each hand. He sits down next to me, in front of the fire, then hands me one of the bowls. He keeps the other bowl and both beers.

In my bowl is half a grapefruit with a cherry in the middle.

"So here we are. Dad's beer and Mom's grapefruit," I say.

"Don't do that," Michael requests.

"Last year, I drove all over LA to find grapefruit in December," I tell him, laughing a short scuttle of a laugh.

"Waste of time," Michael responds, then sips his beer. With this statement, I have to take a bit of grapefruit to remind me of Mom. Michael's single sentence fragment is evidence that he hasn't changed. The conversation that I thought he might be starting with this late breakfast never arrives.

Waste of time.

When Mom was in the assisted living center, Michael only flew to LA to visit her once. He was in LA for a meeting, and decided to call me to see if I could take him to see Mom.

When I walked Michael into Mom's room, she didn't recognize him. In that moment, our mother committed the ultimate sin, and it was the last time Michael saw her alive. "She didn't remember me. It's a waste of time," was Michael's response when I would ask him to visit again after that one unfortunate afternoon. Michael's line is called Michael Lorrie. His name is his brand. If people don't know his name, then they don't know his brand, and if they don't know his brand, Michael's status is obliterated. When Mom couldn't remember Michael's name- couldn't recognize his face- it was the final goodbye. He checked out when she checked in. She didn't move to LA for treatment- she was sent there by Michael. I was given the responsibility to keep Mom company, as she slowly faded.

Following my regular pattern, I searched for a beautiful woman to help me cope with what was happening in my life. A young girl, who understood exactly what I was going through, had recognized me one day in the garden that Mom and I would walk in. From there, we coordinated our visits to the assisted living center. The visits were easier when we could share conversation, our silent mothers by our side. When we discovered that we had both been decimated by both public opinion and private pain, we became each other's support system.

This girl recognized me because she had become the namesake of one of Michael's handbags- "The Chloe Warren." While working with Michael, Chloe must have also read about me, which probably annoyed Michael. Things got worse with our mothers, as things got more personal in my friendship with Chloe. She forced me to remember that life is full of progression and possibility, at a time when degeneration and finite loss seemed overwhelming.

We would go to McDonald's after the visits because the salad bar at the assisted living center was not to be trusted- Ms. Donnelly would pull her wheelchair up and eat from the communal trays as though they were her plate.

I was with Chloe the first time I saw James. Through the windows of the McDonald's, he took a picture of Chloe holding a Big Mac. At that time, James was Jimmy Pixx, so during his segment on CTV that night, he did five minutes of jokes about how Chloe was "packing on the quarter-pounders" again. I should not have put this moment behind me in favor of collaboration, because James Pickens ended up even more toxic than Jimmy Pixx.

I take my phone out, and text Chloe, "Merry Christmas." She immediately texts back "Merry Christmas, Andrew," and before I put my phone down, it vibrates again. I look at the screen, and find a Getty Images watermarked picture of Chloe wearing look 16 from my last Andrew Lorrie collection. I realize that the Chinese investors must have been able to sell some of the line in America, but that isn't the victory that I'm smiling about. Chloe is no longer a size zero, and she looks so healthy that I have to blink away tears. She changed. She saved her own life, despite people like James trying to pull her back down. "Don't tell Michael," is the text that follows the picture. Michael named a bag after the *old* Chloe- the Chloe whose body was being ravaged by an eating disorder- and now the *new* Chloe can be seen wearing one of my designs, with a true smile. I win.

I bet Chloe didn't text Michael today.

I bet Michael didn't text Chloe today.

I bet Michael has forgotten about her.

For every girl that survives MLORE, I'll do my best to make sure they end up like Chloe- better, healthier, an inspiration.

I stand up, then wish Michael a Merry Christmas.

I leave, unable to recognize the man I chose to spend Christmas with.

THE BEST DAYS

I get the first shipment of garments from Italy on the same mid-January day that I pick up Isabella from the airport. I feel relief. For the first time in my career, I allow myself to slow down and stabilize, because I recognize that things are shaking, and I fear the impending explosion. For my own safety, I develop a routine that seems to allow the days to breathe.

Every morning, I brave the cold and walk to the train station. I go into the office on the 8th floor, because no one is at the workshop. They give me my own desk. I feel normal. I assign Jessica responsibilities, like she requested. I remember to include her in some of my calls. I teach her about the standard procedure in the industry, then I explain how I do things.

By 3 PM, I'm back at home, answering e-mails, clicking through previews of James' test shoots with Irina. After dinner, I'm usually on the sofa with Isabella, streaming bad movies about lesbian vampires. I drink Heinekens, while Isabella smokes pot or these new colored cigarettes she's started buying. After the movies, we'll go up to the bed, and Isabella will practice her Japanese on my tablet, while I read *Hedda Gabler*- the play that Lux gave me. I always stop reading first. I become used to falling asleep with the light on, or waking up when Isabella turns it on, returning home after the 10 PM showing gets out. I never ask Isabella about her job and we never go to the movies, even though she could get us in for free. When I'm being an evil asshole, Isabella will stream *Vapid Shallow Models Must Die!* the softcore low budget gay porn disguised as a movie that we once accidentally watched, and I misguidedly used as a parallel for James' screeners. When Isabella selected the movie the first time, we thought we were going to watch a b-movie that would lampoon our silly industry. We knew it would be gay, but we didn't know it was going to be *that* gay. The screeners have become a distant nightmare, no longer arriving, so I can watch the shitty movie without too much real life anxiety. We don't talk about movies, unless they're terrible or anime, and the only book Isabella reads, I can't read, unless Isabella teaches me Japanese, but she's still figuring it out herself. The book that she focuses on is a tiny baby step toward her leaving me. I would never follow her to Japan. I barely even followed her into New York City and there's an express train that goes there. Gradually, through our movie picks and internet searches, we "adopt" celebrities in an almost ironic way, obsessing over them, sending articles about them back and forth. When Isabella is high and I'm drunk, we'll go on a micro-blogging platform and write mean comments to a mentally unstable female model named Charlie O'Shea, and our pleasure surpasses our guilt. Charlie responds to the comments and we can't stop laughing. When Isabella has her panic attacks, I read her my favorite Stephen King short story about a virus that has wiped out most of the population. It's about a boy and a girl on the beach. The boy realizes that the girl has the virus and that she'll be gone soon. Given all of this, living this golden January, my favorite January- I still know how it ends.

I won't chase the one person I should chase.

I'm a man with a single point of reference.

I don't change, and for that, I'm punished.

This punishment could be avoided, as most can.

Instead, I just choose to go back to sleep.

THE DEMON

Somewhere along the way, I had started using my work phone again. The e-mails about silhouettes/ The questions regarding a model's whereabouts/ The missed train/ The GPS drain on my personal phone- more and more I embrace collaboration, and the second phone becomes necessary.

I'm in bed, exhausted after a marathon day of fittings for the pieces Italy sent over, when a vibration wakes me up to a reality I've been avoiding. I reach under my pillow, and take out my warm work phone, which shows me that it's not over.

On the screen, a model sits down in that familiar chair, with the familiar curtains steady in the background.

I've planned for this moment, and I immediately spring into action. I pull the charger cord out of my work phone, then I walk quickly out of the room, my personal cell phone also in my hand.

I'm going to watch this screener, and I'm going to record it.

I rush downstairs, then I make my way to the island in the kitchen because the lighting isn't harsh enough to produce a glare, but it's bright enough that the recording won't be washed out.

I hold my personal phone over my work phone, then I hit record.

The predictable calm is still on the screen. A familiar young model is sitting in a chair, and when she answers James' question about her agency, I recognize her voice. I know the girl in the screener.

Charlie O'Shea is James' next victim; she's already been my victim.

I realize that if I call the hotel, they won't stop this. James isn't dumb enough to live stream again. I try to remember if I touched the screen to start the video or if it was playing as soon as I picked up the phone. I was in too much of a fog when the message arrived, but now everything is clear and sharp.

With a shaky hand, I record what happens; the brutality of it all captured digitally for the second time.

After a series of questions, the curtains start to move.

Charlie tells James about how people have a really strong reaction to her.

I have to blink tears out of my eyes, and when I do, I see the hooded man step out from behind the curtain.

I desperately want to call Charlie, but the only way I know how to contact her is by her blog URL, and the messages that I've sent there in the past have had nothing to do with Charlie's well-being.

The hooded man slowly approaches the unaware model, as she explains her sense of style- "I like old T-shirts, and fake fur, and aliens, and shoes with chunky soles."

My breathing is rapid and sloppy.

The hooded man is gripping a crowbar, stalking forward.

My sobs are heavy and my hands have to hold my personal phone, so I can't cover my eyes.

I watch as the hooded man cocks back a weapon- oh fuck, it's a crowbar- then he swings, connecting with the side of Charlie's head.

I vomit onto my shoes, my head between my elevated arms. I hear the strikes (*multiple*) and Charlie makes no noise because she was sent into a seizing shock with the first blow.

I wipe my puke and tears on my sleeve, then I look back at the screens.

The screener cuts off before I'm shown what they do with the perfect body, and for that I am grateful.

It becomes clear that the only way I can stop these screeners is to enter the picture myself.

THE ANGEL

I text James, "I don't care about Charlie, but if you ever touch Madeleine, I'll fucking kill you," then I go to work.

I know that James will set Madeleine up for a screener tonight. I make sure that the MLORE files are updated with Madeleine's agency and contact information.

I convince myself that this is the right thing to do.

I hum to myself as I buzz through the workshop.

After a long day, when I'm finally alone, I take out my phone, desperate for assurance that I'm not becoming Michael. The muscle memory action of reaching for Lux- like a cigarette or a cheap can of beer- is finally gone. I scroll past Lux's name, but when I don't find what I need, I take out my work phone. I select the number I was looking for, and six rings later- a recording, "Hi, you've reached Jessica. I'm not-" I hang up the call. Jessica is a young girl in the best city in the world. Young girls work all day so they can have their nights open. They go on dates, or go to shows, or go to filthy Brooklyn apartments and do drugs. Young girls don't drop everything to meet old men late at night. Not for free at least.

With no one around to warn me about what I'm setting into motion, I make an inciting call, pushing things further.

A half hour later, I lean into a cab, pay the driver, then take Madeleine's hand to help her over the snowbank at the curb.

"Did you even ask Lux?" is Madeleine's first question.

"Huh? Have we met?" I respond, dry, tongue-in-cheek, referencing that first day in the studio.

Madeleine looks puzzled for a moment, but eventually smiles, and says, "Nice to meet you. I'm a model, slash best roomie of all time, slash design consultant."

"What a coincidence," I purr, "I was actually just waiting for a model, slash best roomie of all time, slash design consultant. Do you have a moment to help me out?"

Madeleine checks her non-existent watch, then bites her lip. "I only have four hours, so make it quick," she says, then I pop open the door, and she walks inside the workshop.

While we're making our way to the far workroom, Madeleine quietly admits, "When we started that little exchange, for a minute I wasn't sure if you really did forget me. I felt ugly."

Thanks to the position Lux has placed her in, Madeleine can't be sure if she's in the workshop because I want her here, or if Lux just flaked out again, and I'm desperate for a substitute. This is a common problem for people who are dependable and discrete- two attributes that rarely remain in tandem because they become crutches for the manipulative and sick.

"I was attempting to flirt. My advances are usually met with disappointment and discomfort, so I thought everything was going as expected," I say, hoping it will make her feel better. "You were correct in your reaction. Let me make it up to you with an equally creepy follow-up. I want to do you a favor."

"I don't need favors," Madeleine quickly says, "I'm here *as* a favor. I'm not here *for* a favor."

This statement is a testament to her power. Madeleine's ability to compose herself, while everyone around her melts, makes me think, *Yes, this will work.*

"So let's talk about walking MLORE. Which piece do you want?" I ask, leading the conversation.

"Peace of mind. That's what I want. James called me and said I had to meet with him tonight. I was like, 'Schedule it with my agent,' but- Andrew- I thought- ya know- I had a spot already," Madeleine says. I feel her hurt, and it fucking kills me. It's clear that walking MLORE isn't a favor for her roommate, it's a job, and Madeleine wants to prove to her agent that- yes- this face has pull. The face stares at me, and I assume she's disassembling me with a glance, like I've done to so many people before.

"Oh," I mumble, "Yeah, that meeting has to happen. Michael's rules."

"Okay. Fine. I'll do it," she says, a little disappointed in me.

"Madeleine?" I almost growl, moving closer to her.

"Yeah?"

"You've been with me this entire time, so I'll be with you in the same way," I say.

Her big eyes get a little wet, then she looks away, whispering, "Holding you to that."

"No matter what, you *will* walk MLORE..." I say, then add, "...but I need a favor."

Madeleine looks at me, disappointed, again.

I take a deep breath, then begin to explain what I need her to do. I couldn't discuss this in a cab, or on the subway, or on the phone. Getting her inside the workshop was the only sure way that this conversation could remain completely private. This had to happen tonight, and it had to happen here. I know that James has a renewed confidence in his brutal process, because I was unable to save the Marc girl or Charlie, and my text this morning assured that Madeleine would be the next girl required to star in a screener.

I give Madeleine enough guidance that I'm confident she'll survive, but I leave out key pieces of information, knowing that if this ends badly, it will be on my shoulders. I accept this reality, because I don't know how else to stop James, and the executioner in the mask.

I have the footage of Charlie's death, but I need video of the man behind the camera. That is what I will get tonight.

Madeleine, calmly, with a perceptible distance, agrees to my plan. She doesn't say, "You owe me for this," nor does she ask me for money. I try to think of a way to pay her back, and that's when I remember I have a collection worth of designs that I abandoned in Italy. I hope Madeleine likes one-of-a-kind garments.

The timeline shrinks and everything is urgent. We cab to the hotel, and I send Madeleine in first. I wait five minutes, just as I did with Libby, then I head through the lobby. I still have the key card from the first time I tried to catch James in the act. It's possible they've changed the lock programming, but we didn't leave a trace of our presence in the room so maybe they didn't.

Madeleine, like a good model, follows my directions precisely.

When I meet her on the 8th floor, she calls the number James texted to her. I hide behind a jutting wall so I'm not visible if someone comes out into the hall to get her.

"Okay, I'll meet you there, leave the door propped open," I hear Madeleine say into the phone.

I don't peek past the wall, I merely look at the screen of my phone, then I put in my earbuds.

Madeleine makes her way down the hall, then enters the hotel room, phone in her hand. After she's introduced to Regis, and reintroduced to James, she sits down in the familiar chair, then she lays her phone in her lap exactly as I coached her.

I know all of this, because Madeline is recording everything, and streaming it to me. I had this camera app I had used when I was the creative director for a pop star who had nine other businesses revolving around their 360 deal, and I often had to use my phone to show them designs, while they sat in their hotel room in Australia and attempted to look somewhat coherent, occasionally vomiting off-screen. I had to have a recording of the conversation, because, often, the pop star would forget it occurred.

Now that everything is set, I walk to the door of the hotel room, so I'm close enough that I can help the damsel in distress, as she flees.

The way Madeleine has placed her phone in her lap, I have a clear view of the front door of the hotel room. Her back is to the curtains, and I'll get the view from the camera filming her when the screener starts- assuming they go live.

Even if James streams this on a delay, I can listen to the audio from Madeleine's feed right now.

I watch as James offers the "juice" to Madeleine, which she refuses.

With my phone in one hand, I try to fish Isabella's lighter out of my coat pocket because I need to set off the fire alarm in the next minute for all of this to end safely.

When I look up from my phone, I see Irina standing at the end of the hallway. The breath jumps out of my lungs, and not for the usual reason this happens around a supermodel. The single most troubling part of this surprise is that Irina looks her age.

"Andrew?" Irina coos, looking at me like I'm a high school friend she hadn't seen in two decades.

I pull out one of my earbuds, then ask, "Irina, what are you doing here?"

"I don't feel so good, Andrew," she exhales.

"You look good to me," I assure her, because if I tell her the truth, no one will feel good. She'll make sure of it.

As Irina begins to walk toward me, I look at the door to my right.

"Don't go in there," she says, as a warning.

"Are you part of this?" I ask in a distressed whisper. Despite starting this unexpected conversation, I'm still listening to the feed in my earbud. James is sticking to the script.

"This isn't your responsibility, Andrew," Irina says.

"It's not yours either. Walk away," I tell her.

Irina looks at me, and shakes her head, almost in disbelief. "You don't know," she observes, breathlessly.

"I know everything. I know what's about to happen and-" I hear a whimper in my earbud, so I reach for the handle to my right.

In a split second, Irina slams me against the door with such force that the frame buckles, and the door flies open.

Suddenly, I'm on the carpet, the wind knocked out of my lungs. I'm coughing, gasping, desperately kicking my legs.

I look over, and I see Regis and James scrambling, then I see the executioner moving toward a shrieking Madeleine.

I try to yell "Run!" at Madeleine, but nothing comes out.

Even without hearing my command, Madeline figures out what must be done, and runs toward me.

Regis grabs the executioner, Irina grabs Regis, James reaches down for me, and we all move in slow motion.

I'm thrown into the hallway, and with my back to the wall, I see Madeleine running to my side, but something stops her, and I look toward the room, to see James rushing at me again.

When he reaches me, James grabs my shirt, and stares into my eyes, searching for something. I stare back, until James spins away from me, then kicks the wall in anger.

The door to the hotel room is now almost closed, but the broken frame prevents it from sealing shut.

I can hear things being broken, hidden, and destroyed.

I hear a man scream.

Why did a man scream?

"You were gonna let him kill me," Madeleine yells down the hall.

"No. Now. Okay," James says, raising his pointer finger then putting it to his lips, "I can explain what's been going on, but you need to-"

My veins are swollen with adrenaline. I immediately get up and push past James, then I throw the door open to the screener room.

"Andrew!" James yells, grabbing onto my arm, but I go back inside the room, pulling him with me.

The bathroom door is shut and everything in the hotel room looks the same, except the laptop is gone and the window that's usually concealed by the floor-to-ceiling curtains has been opened. I pick my phone up off the carpet, then I hesitantly approach the open window. When I'm close enough to feel the light breeze, I stop. I realize why the previously closed window is now open. They want me to stick my head out of the open window to look down, then they'll push me to my death. "Failed Designer Commits Suicide," the headline would read. *The New York Post* would merely print "That's A'Lorrie."

I don't fall for the plan. Instead, I restart the chaos. I make my way to the closed bathroom door. There's no noise coming from the bathroom. All three people inside must have agreed to be quiet. I have to enter this bathroom because the computer and the camera must be in there. I need to get as much evidence as possible, so this will stop, for good.

I glance back at James, who looks like he's trying to figure out if he needs to restrain me, and my icy glare informs him that if he tries anything, he'll be the one leaving out the window.

James raises his hands- an attempt at innocence.

I throw open the bathroom door, then immediately gag from the carnage everywhere. The air is humid. The floor is streaked in blood. Regis is trying to break a severed arm over his knee so that it will fit in a trash bag. He's somehow eviscerated Irina *and* the executioner in under a minute, like he was a human blender.

"I need your help," Regis begs, and I look back at James, whose eyes are closed tight, and he's possibly mumbling a prayer.

"Why-how-why did you do this?" I ask Regis.

"I really need some help... then I'll give you answers," Regis says.

"You killed the face of my collection," I say, trying to rush toward him, but the blood on the bathroom tile makes my boots slip, and I quickly become Bambi on ice. I grasp the edge of the counter, before I end up weak and defenseless on the floor.

"I didn't kill Irina," Regis says, "Why would I kill the one person I spend my entire waking life protecting?"

This is the question that I'm unable to resolve in my mind.

"Look at the pieces around me. They're from a man," Regis says, holding up the arm. On the arm is a black glove.

James says, over my shoulder, "We caught the bad guy. Congrats team. We did it," then he starts clapping lightly.

"Irina is dead," I hear Madeleine say, and I turn to see her standing next to James, like the fearless super-girl she is.

"Irina is fine," Regis maintains.

"Oh, yeah? Where is she? I rushed into the hotel room and searched the entire place. She's not here."

"She slipped out when you weren't looking," Regis says.

"No. She didn't," I say, sure of this fact.

"She's very skinny," James comments, like this matters. In his defense, this fact usually *does* matter.

"She would have to be invisible to sneak out of here, and she's the opposite of invisible," I point out.

"Call her," Regis says fearlessly, the arm in Regis' hand gesturing at me with a flopped limpness.

"Don't point a severed arm at him," Madeleine warns.

I take out my personal phone, to call Regis on his bluff.

I select Irina from my contacts.

The phone rings once, twice, then someone picks up.

"Hey, Andrew. Is everything okay?" a voice with Irina's exact accent asks. A slight breeze brushes over the mic on her phone. It sounds like she's outside. I peek my head out of the bathroom, then look toward the open window.

"Where are you?" I ask.

"In the hotel. Please help Regis. We had to fight that man. We stopped him," Irina says, but her voice doesn't tremble.

"How did you get out of the room?"

"Are you seriously playing this game right now? Help my boyfriend clean, then meet me in the lobby," Irina demands.

"No. This isn't my mess. I'll be down in a minute. You better be there," I say, then I end the call.

I grab Madeleine's slender hand, then begin to pull her out of the room, until Regis' loud demand of, "Hold on," stops us. Regis is covered in blood, and when someone is covered in blood, I usually don't ignore them, for fear I'll end up covered in blood too.

"You aren't going to tell anyone what you've seen here," Regis informs us- it's not a question.

"It's over," I say.

"What does that mean?" James asks.

"Can you clean this all up before the cops get here?" I ask, then I raise my phone.

"You wouldn't," James says.

Regis goes back to cleaning, and casually explains, "You call the cops and they *will* ask what you were doing here- how did you come upon all this as an innocent bystander? They'll be very curious why *all* the missing girls told their roommates they were going on a go-see for a line you're designing and casting."

"Well, I think the massive amount of evidence I have will send their investigation in a different direction," I theorize.

James reaches down and touches the pool of blood on the tile. He stands up slowly, steps forward, then with Irina-like speed, his arm jets out and hammers me in the chest. A bloody smear wets my shirt.

"Explain why you're covered in the victim's blood," James says.

"I have this," Madeleine declares, holding out her phone, showing that she's recorded everything.

James, in a flash, grabs the phone, then throws it against the mirror on the bathroom wall.

Mirror shards, glass, and electronic innards rain down into the blood puddles.

Eyes wide, Regis barks, "Can you not smash mirrors while I'm cleaning up a murder?"

"Can you not yell 'murder' when you're cleaning up a murder?" James yells.

"A guy's body parts are everywhere, and my phone is now broken. Can things can't get any worse tonight?" Madeleine whines, puffing out her lower lip, looking at the slices of bloody mirror everywhere.

"Come on," I say to Madeleine, "We have to meet Irina downstairs."

"Then we have to buy me a new phone," she adds.

"Yes, then we'll buy you a new phone."

Madeleine and I leave James and Regis to clean up the phone glass, and the mirror shards, and the blood of the executioner.

It's time to have a meeting with the most visible invisible girl in the world.

We leave with questions, but we leave unharmed.

The mirror is broken in the bathroom.

The lock is broken on the hotel room.

The executioner is dead.

The girl is safe.

The cycle might be broken.

THE ROOFTOP

Madeleine and I stand in the center of the elevator, staring straight ahead, as we leave the scene of a murder.

"So- uh- weird casting," Madeleine says.

I glance at her and smirk.

She turns to me and grabs me by my blazer, angling me toward her. She slowly buttons my buttons, covering the bloody handprint, then she brushes some lint off my shoulder.

Even after the chaos, Madeleine is here to take care of the wounded and dysfunctional man by her side.

"The vibe of this new line is... not very Michael Lorrie," she says.

"Thank you," I tell her.

"I'm not sure I was giving you a compliment."

"I wasn't responding to what you said," I tell her quietly.

"Oh," Madeleine squeaks, then the elevator door opens, "You're welcome," she tells me. Her reaction makes me wonder how infrequent a simple "thank you" is in Madeleine's life of favors.

We walk out into the lobby, and Irina is nowhere to be found.

I take my work phone out, but Madeleine snatches it from me.

"Insurance," she says.

"I'll get you a new phone," I assure her.

"After we speak with Irina," she says. "After you buy me dinner at the rooftop restaurant."

I think about this, then exhale, "That sounds good." Madeleine is entirely unique. She's never frantic. She's never fragile. She doesn't need me to save her, and tonight I didn't save her; she got out on her own. Suddenly, Madeleine doesn't feel right for my line, and it kills me that this casting resulted in two casualties. No longer do I imagine her in my clothes, because nothing about Madeleine is glass. She's the stronger synthetic replacement that's introduced when the glass keeps breaking.

"Okay, while we're waiting for Irina, let's go over what we know," Madeleine suggests.

"About what happened up there?"

"Don't you think it deserves a bit of a post-game review?"

"We know for sure that the girls who showed up for the screeners are dead," I say, keeping my voice low.

"We know that the dude who was killing the girls is dead," Madeleine says, almost proud.

"Who killed him, though?" I ask.

"Regis or Irina. Both. A wolverine too, maybe. Did you see? He was eviscerated."

That's the term the model uses- *eviscerated*.

"Where was the rest of him?" I ask. "If he was murdered in that bathroom, why were there only *some* pieces of him in there?"

"The window was open," Madeleine mentions, then both of us start running through the lobby toward the entrance of the hotel.

We burst outside, and the city roars back at us. The chaos returns. There's snow and people everywhere, but no body parts- no pieces of the executioner. There isn't even a scrap of black fabric. If a body part fell out of the window, there would be at least three girls photographing it, then uploading the picture to their social network of choice.

I glance at the ballet theater to my left, and I start to feel tired of this dance.

A hand locks onto my shoulder, then pushes me. I swing around to face... Irina. I stare straight into her beautiful eyes, and I'm immediately struck by the fact that she looks stunning, refreshed, airbrushed, younger- fixed.

"You're pretty light on your feet when you're in the middle of a grisly murder scene," Madeleine says to Irina.

"Who's this?" Irina asks me.

"Don't play stupid. We know you were headed into that room for her," I say.

"I was out in the hallway with you, remember?"

"You threw me through a fucking door."

"I know!" Irina responds brightly, "It finally seems like I'm seeing results from my twice-a-week Pilates class."

"How did you get out of that room? How did you get out of the hotel?" I ask.

"I left," she says simply, then begins her return back inside just as casually.

"She's headed back to the scene of the crime?" Madeleine asks me, the pieces not fitting together, like if we tried to reassemble the executioner.

"Are we idiots to go back in there? Is this a trap?" I ask.

"Guess there's only one way to find out," she says, then follows in Irina's footsteps.

Unable to argue with this logic, I walk with Madeleine back inside, then through the lobby.

When the elevator doors open, I dash forward, claiming the center of the box, making sure that Irina is distanced from the "bait."

Irina enters the elevator and stands to my left, then Madeleine takes her place at my right. My hand juts out, and I press the 12, but not before considering choosing 8 to force her to confront what happened in that room. The 8 still feels like an infinity sign- a repetition.

"Why 12?" Irina asks.

"Let's have a drink," I say.

"Who am I to say no to that?" Irina responds.

"Who are you- that will be one of the questions we discuss over the drink," I mention.

When we arrive at the rooftop restaurant, we're immediately seated by a server, not in the open air portion, but instead inside, next to a sprawling non-indigenous plant. I'm sitting between Madeleine and Irina, in front of a small, red, cubed table with a candle flickering in the center.

The server converts himself into a waiter when he recognizes Irina, and our order is dutifully taken.

Either the staff is aware that Irina is involved in murders being carried out in this hotel, or she just tips really well.

"So," Madeleine says, looking down the line. She takes a deep breath, then asks a series of questions that are smiled at, but not answered, "What the hell was going on in that room/"How was I going to be saved if the lock wasn't broken/"Are all those girls really dead/"Why would you kill all those girls/"Why would you film it all/"Where did the rest of the curtain goon go/"Are you buying this dinner for us/"Is this all-inclusive or will I have to pay for the alcohol/"You are aware that I'm too broke to pay for this alcohol, aren't you/"I'm underage and I think you've already done enough illegal shit tonight, don't compound your issues by providing alcohol to a minor/"I mean, yeah, get me alcohol, but don't charge me for it. Leave it on the table, then it will somehow disappear."

"Crazy day," Irina responds casually, like she missed her train and had to race across the city to make an appointment.

"We need answers," I demand. "Where were you hiding in that hotel room?"

"I stepped out for some fresh air. It smelled like someone... well..." Irina trails off.

"When I saw you in the hall, you looked like fucked up Galina, and now you're ready to shoot a cover, over 20 minutes later? A little fresh air? That fixed you? Bullshit," I say, not buying the cause of the transformation.

"The outdoors does wonders. Maybe you should consider a little fresh air yourself, you look... stressed," Irina says to me.

"I'll go out there and call the cops," I threaten.

"And then they'll haul both of us away," Irina says, "After that- well- it's fairly obvious that your brother will bail us out. Michael to the rescue, again. His lawyers are so good that we'd probably end up back here tomorrow morning, with the best table in the house. Correct me if I'm wrong, but I don't think you'd like that." She's right. She knows she's right, so she continues, "There's no way you'll let Michael get involved in this. I mean, I get you, Andrew. I know you. You have no daddy issues, yet you burn for an oppressive force that you can rally against, so you constantly make your brother out to be this angry villain. You devote yourself to separating your image from his, but he's so buttoned down that you just fuck up your life- over and over- because it's the opposite of what he's doing- which is succeeding."

"I can't help but feel as though you're redirecting the topic at hand," I say. Even though she's very right, the timing for this confrontation is off.

Without considering my interruption, Irina continues, "You're unable to grow emotionally so you cling to young women because you believe that they'll need you, but they-"

"-this... is... pretty personal," Madeleine says, her eyes looking down at my work phone in her hands.

"I'm not having this discussion. We need to talk about what happened up there," I state.

Irina sighs, then says, "No wonder therapists get paid so much, you wackos really are demanding."

"You wanna talk wacko?" I respond with a hard whisper, "There are pieces of a man all over the bathroom on the 8th floor. Someone tore him apart. Care to tell me what happened?"

"Stress. It was stress. Be careful, Andrew. You seem like you're under pressure. You could be the next to explode," Irina warns.

"You expect me to believe the executioner exploded?"

"I mean, it's not that far of a leap. He was exploded into pieces in there," Madeleine says.

"He exploded from stress. We're in a financial crisis. Times are tough. You've heard the president," Irina says.

"If he exploded, how come there were pieces missing? Where is the rest of the executioner?" I ask.

"In hell," Irina responds.

THE SHRED OF EVIDENCE

I decide to wash my own clothes for once, mainly because my shirt is covered in dried blood.

In the privacy of the laundry room that's lit only by the light angling in from the kitchen, I set my blazer aside, then carefully unbutton my shirt, avoiding pressing my fingers against the brownish-red crust. I throw the blood-stained shirt into the washer, then I feel a shadow pass over me. I don't look back because I'm not sure if it's Isabella or The Boy and The Girl.

Feeling self-conscious, I pick up a T-shirt from the laundry pile, then put it on. It's a white shirt from Madonna's controversial (at the time) "Blonde Ambition" world tour.

"You don't have to do that, you know. The laundry is one of the few things I handle around here. Leave it for me," I hear Isabella say.

"I felt like I needed to do it, just this once. I promise the rest of the pile is all yours" I say.

Isabella enters the laundry room, and hoists her long body onto the dryer. She quietly watches me, as I stuff my clothes into the washer. I immediately want my camera when I notice the light slicing across Isabella's face- her left side in the dark of the laundry room- her right side in the glow of the bright kitchen. The slash isn't symmetrical. It cuts from the edge of her left eyebrow to the right corner of her mouth. Beauty is found in symmetry, but no matter which way Isabella's face is sectioned, it continues to be just as interesting as it was the first time I was mesmerized by it. I watch her, and I wonder if she views me as being careless about fashion now. I used to be extremely regimented in my dry cleaning schedule, and because of this, my designs always looked perfect. My reverence for the careful preservation of garments dulled once I started caring about the people wearing the clothes.

I take out everything I've stuffed in my blazer, then I drop the garment- currently crusted with blood- into the washer.

Isabella takes the wrappers and loose bills from me so I can finish shoveling a mix of our clothes into the washing machine.

Before I can grab my pile of underwear, Isabella asks me, "You bought another phone?"

"Huh?" I respond, leaving the pile on the ground.

"This receipt. It's for a new phone," she says, studying the long slip of paper.

"Oh. Yeah," I say, reaching over, taking the receipt.

"Can I see it?" Isabella asks.

"I want to keep the receipt. The place we bought the phone was a less than reputable establishment," I say.

"No. The phone. Can I see the phone?" she asks.

"I... don't have it," I respond, and Isabella folds into herself.

"It was a gift," I add.

"For me?" she asks in a tiny voice, giving me the option of just providing her with the phone so we can drop this.

"You have a phone," I say, because she does. Because I have no phone to give her.

"Yeah, an old model," Isabella says, and she lets this loaded statement hang. *An old model.*

She thinks I bought a phone for Lux.

"I broke a model's phone today," I say.

"Why did you throw it?" Isabella asks, immediately assuming the worst because she knows me well.

"I didn't throw it," I respond. Sure, it was thrown, but *I* wasn't the one who threw it.

"Then how did you break it?" Isabella asks.

"I was looking at her book," I lie.

"She keeps her book on her phone?"

"Yeah," I respond, feeling caught.

"Makes sense. Anyone can look good on that small of a screen," Isabella responds, and I begin to sense not only curiosity, but also pangs of rare jealousy from her.

"She just wanted to show me a shoot," I remark casually.

"And it was so good you dropped the phone?" Isabella asks, then makes a snort of a noise.

"No. I just... had a lot of coffee."

"Is that why you're sweating right now? A lot of coffee?" I'm asked.

I stare at Isabella, and she leans in toward me, her face moving away from the light.

THE UNAPOLOGY

I'm sitting at one of the sewing machines in the workshop, trying to fix a hem, when Jessica walks up to me, and asks, "Can we talk about what happened last night?"

"What happened last night?" I respond, playing dumb because I'm not sure if Madeleine can keep a secret.

Jessica lifts up her phone, then shakes it.

If she's confronting me about the cell phone I bought Madeleine, I'm going to buy my entire team upgraded phones so I have to stop answering for this simple purchase.

"I had a missed call," Jessica says.

I laugh to myself, then say, "Jessica, relax. I had a quick question. No big deal. Madeleine helped me out with it."

"What?" Jessica asks.

"I was going to ask you a question. We figured it out. I got the answer."

"What was the question?" Jessica continues to press, staring at me with sad eyes. I didn't expect her to pursue this further after I said it was resolved. My easy grin drops, and I'm lost for a moment. My mind races to a finish line I can't locate.

Madeleine, alive, appears in the door frame, and showing off one of her most inspiring abilities, she redirects this fraught conversation, by saying, "Hey! Jessica! What's up? I got a question for ya."

"Yeah?" Jessica responds, looking annoyed.

"Have you ever thought about how if Michael married his secretary and you married your intern, they'd both be Jessica Lorrie?" Madeleine asks.

Jessica pauses for a moment, then lets out a spit of a laugh, and I do too. Madeleine laughs along with us- a model trained to match the mood.

This quick comment keeps Jessica from having another intense conversation with me.

"If you're free, could you show me which piece you need me in next?" Madeleine, and Jessica nods to confirm she will.

After the girls leave the room, I take out my phone to text a thank you to Madeleine, but before I can, my phone vibrates with a new message. When I look at the sender's name, I feel electric relief.

Lux.

Finally, an apology will be issued, forgiveness will be granted, order will be restored.

"Do you have that copy of *Hedda*? It's the good translation. I'm writing an article for a magazine and I need that copy. Can you send it to me? I'll pay for postage," the paragraph long text reads.

The text is not an apology, it's an attack.

"It's awesome to know how little you care about me," I text back. I sit in front of the sewing machine, blank.

"Never mind. I'll get it online," Lux texts me.

I stand up, ready to end it here, but I know that if I say what I want to say, it absolutely will end what we have, and I don't think I want it to. "So that's the reason why you needed to speak with me? To get the one thing you've ever given me back?" I text.

"Well I'm sorry but if you just drop me for my roommate, what am I supposed to say to you?" she sends.

"Sorry would have been nice. That you care about me would have been nice. Now it's clear you don't so at least I have closure," I type out.

I try to figure out if this is closure, but before I can, another text appears, reading, "Well you know that's not true. I don't understand why you were holding me to some arbitrary standard. I know you said it was for my own good but I can be in charge of my own decisions."

This becomes about Lux, and I'm simply too tired for my first conversation with her in over a month to be only about her. I just need an apology, so I set out to guilt her into it. My fingers dance across the screen of my phone, and too frantic to punctuate, I type, "You honestly don't care I mean nothing to you."

When she doesn't respond, I send, "Hello?"

"I'm here," she texts.

I wait for her to send something else, but the text never arrives, so I continue the conversation, "What's your excuse?"

"That I can make my own decisions! I'm so tired of people telling me what to do for 'my own good' and it's like u were holding me to this fucking ultimatum that isn't fair," reads the excuse.

I need to hear her voice. I can't continue this over text. In an effort to either end it, or get her on the phone, I type out, "It's a good thing you needed that book or you never would have spoken to me again. Thank God for Hedda, at least I got some contact from you."

"Okay clearly you are not ready to discuss this. You are not going to listen to me no matter what I say so that's fine," is her response.

"So, what, silence again? You pretend like we never speak?" I send.

"That's exactly what you have been doing," she texts.

Our conversation hangs in limbo.

Nothing has been resolved.

Lux seems to agree and my phone buzzes with an incoming call.

When I answer the call, immediately, Lux asks me, "What's your problem?"

"All I want is for you to give a shit," I say.

"For a person who's constantly telling people to stop overreacting about things that hurt them, you're pretty sensitive," Lux spits back at me.

"I care. I'm not doing this for entertainment."

The line sizzles for nine cold seconds, then Lux says, "It's good that you've teamed up with Michael, I'm really starting to see the family resemblance."

Michael has to control everyone.

Michael has to know everything.

Michael has to be the one pulling the strings.

I try to think of how I'm different from Michael, but when I can't form a comeback, I have to accept Lux's observation. I nod, and I wish it was to silently confirm something, but it doesn't work. "Don't become like *them*," I beg.

"Not everyone is lining up to offend Andrew Lorrie," Lux reminds me.

"And you aren't lining up to make me feel any better," I say.

"That's my responsibility?" she asks.

"That's what friends do for each other," I say, teaching Lux a fact she should already know.

"I obviously do give a shit. Do you know how fucking upset I was all winter? I called my therapist and had to tell her the whole fucking thing which was *awesome*."

"I needed to know you gave a shit, and you continue to prove you don't. You gave up on me, then didn't speak to me again till you needed something from me."

"I do give a shit and that's why I called you instead of texting, and that's why I had to call my doctor."

"I feel like you ended it, and all I wanted to hear was that you missed me and you'd try to be a better friend, then the only contact from you is, 'Where's the one thing you might remember me by?'"

This causes Lux to explode, "You realize that I fucking poured all my pills out of their jars and was going to take them? You can't say that I don't give a shit. I don't think you're going to listen to anything I say, so I guess we'll discuss this at some other point if you still want to. I'm sorry you think I don't care."

"You can't even say it to me now. When you want to try to fix this, stop by the workshop and I'll listen."

"Well, it's embarrassing that I even considered doing that stuff. Obviously, I need some time. I'll stop by sometime soon."

"Goodbye Lux," I say, then I end the call.

THE DEAD MAN

I wake up at two in the afternoon.

I look at my work phone and the only notification I have is a text from Jessica that says, "Hope you're okay. Covered for you today :)"

I check and there are no notifications on my personal phone.

With the total destruction of the executioner, the screeners seem to be done.

I open my Gmail, and I find that Jessica has forwarded me a list of 30 girls that they want for the show.

Isabella is on the list. Lux is not.

This casting list for the show seems to answer a question. Libby and Madeleine helped me stop the slaughter of innocent girls, and it wasn't by asking nicely or arguing on the phone. It happened when a door was slammed open with violent force.

Lux's absence, and our shuttering of James' sadistic model-mill, has taught me that extreme action is highly effective and rarely punished.

Nearly hangover-less, I decide it's time to save another girl.

I throw on my Saint Laurent jacket and a black knit cap, then I walk out of the house on Scotland Road.

I take a taxi to the train, then I take another taxi to the brownstone whose ownership keeps changing. I had kept the link that Lux sent to my phone that day when I thought I was meeting her at her therapist's office.

The last time Madeleine mentioned Lux's sugar daddy, he had flown back to LA. I have to hope that he's returned to New York recently.

I walk up the stairs to the brownstone, then repeatedly hit the buzzer.

Eventually, a wisp of a voice asks, "Yeah?" over the intercom.

"Michael sent me," I say.

"Michael who?" the voice asks.

"Michael Lorrie. He gave you as a reference," I respond, bass in my voice.

"Alright, hold tight," the voice from the intercom tells me.

I don't know what I'm going to do when the man answers the door, but I know I have to confront him. I need to try to end this, for good. No one else in Lux's life will stop her from continuing with this mistake.

With Isabella, I'm careful to never fall into paternal behavior. With Lux, she requires me to take this role, so I step into it completely.

The door opens, and a guy- mid 30's, black hair, easily could kick my ass- asks, "How do you know Michael?"

I push by the guy, walking straight into his home. I can tell he lives on the bottom floor because I didn't hear him clatter down the stairs before the door was opened.

"Whoa, hey. I asked you how you know Michael," the man calls out to me, and my pace is quick enough that he doesn't catch up with me, until we're both in his living room.

The man grabs my arm, and once he whips me around, I say, "He's my brother. Michael is my brother."

The man stares at me, and now that my identity has been confirmed, he allows this to happen. The knowledge of just how powerless I am negates any initial threat I appeared to pose. The man walks over to his giant TV in the mahogany living room and turns it off. Everything in this room is the product of an interior designer. The brown leather, the autumnal colored books, the antique chaise, the vintage movie posters- none of it projects any sign of the man's personality, and this informs me about him. He's a man who pays premiums to keep up appearances, and at the same time, he doesn't care how obvious and desperate it all looks.

"Lux talks about you," the man says, relaxing in a brown leather armchair.

I grit my teeth and point at him, as I warn, "Just leave her-"

"-I bought Lux a piece from your collection," he says, realizing why he let me inside. "Andrew Lorrie," he repeats my name, putting it all together.

"Not the green piece," I beg, "That was from Karen," I add, unwilling to let him pollute my work. People can destroy me in the industry, but I won't let them destroy my clothes.

"Who the fuck is Karen?" he asks, "Who did you hear that from?"

"Lux," I exhale.

"And did this Karen tell you that Lux asked for trade, or did Lux tell you that?" the man inquires, shaking his head, "This is why the Asians are going to take over the world. They're always one step ahead."

"She told me she got trade from the Chinese. A dress and the heels."

"If you want to check out my bank statement, let me know. Your designs are actually pretty reasonably priced," the man says, his whispery voice becoming unnerving.

Lux's sugar daddy is using fashion terms and this is all beginning to feel very scripted.

"Michael put you up to this," I say. "Is he paying for... this?"

The man stares at me, marveling, shaking his head, pitying me, and he says, "You really are obsessed. Lux mentioned-"

"-fuck you."

"Yeah, bud. She mentioned you. Frequently. You should really think about providing health insurance for her. I'm not thrilled that I'm fronting that bill," the man says, smiling.

"I need you to stop taking advantage of her, immediately," I respond.

"I didn't force her into this. Even before Michael introduced us, she was signed up for the site. She was looking for guys. It's not just me. If I was to step aside, which I'm not going to do, someone else will scoop her right up. I only ended up with her because Michael recommended her, and she immediately agreed to meet up to see where it would go. We fast-tracked it because I was only in New York for a couple of days. We didn't want to waste any time."

"Where did it go?" I ask.

The man smiles at me, then says, "You don't want me to answer that question, dude."

"If you keep seeing her, I will fucking destroy you," I promise.

"Why is my arrangement your concern?" he asks, innocently.

"Because you're finding these girls on the internet and you're using them. They're only agreeing to your fucked up terms because they have no other option to make money."

Almost as though Michael had prepared him for the conversation, the man asks, "So, every girl that's walked for one of your little fashion shows, they all showed up through their agents, right?" It's almost as though he's amused by what he perceives to be my hypocrisy.

"Yes. How else would I find them?"

"The internet is a big place, dude. Lots of potential. Perfect for scouting. You certainly don't use it for finding girls, judging from what you're telling me. No- that would be too close to what I'm doing."

"That's nothing like what you're doing," I say, defending an industry I've become infamous for attacking.

"It's my understanding that models are discovered on the internet... or in malls, right?"

"By scouts. By agents," I say, trying to put up roadblocks against his logic.

"So, there's a situation where, instead of the girl applying on the internet, willingly providing her consent to become part of this circus, someone comes up to her in a food court and pulls her into that world? It seems like-"

"-you could draw that parallel with any job," I say, trying to wipe away this defense.

"Yeah, so what Lux is doing is like any other job."

"Are you seriously trying to have this debate?" I ask.

"As much as you aren't trying to have it," he says.

THE COVER

I throw open the front door to the house on Scotland Road.

I toss my hat, but I keep my coat on, as I make a drunk stumble toward the kitchen.

A crashing thud comes from the front of the house, so I backtrack, to see what else I've destroyed today.

When I reach the front door, I find The Girl framed by the light of the street, the rain hammering behind her. To my left, The Boy pops out of a mission style cube chair in the living room, leaving his book and a beer on the armrest.

The Boy searches behind The Girl, trying to identify the threat, and when he's unable to determine the cause of the dramatic entrance, he appears to realize that it's him- *he's* the threat. When The Boy locks eyes with The Girl, his concerned glare becomes admiration.

"Cover girl," The Girl squeaks.

"You booked it?" The Boy asks, with an excited pride.

The Girl walks over to The Boy's slice of light and presents him with a gift. A magazine. The Girl watches The Boy, searching to find his genuine feelings. I sense a dash of fear peppering the excitement in The Girl's eyes.

"They gave you the cover," The Boy says, overjoyed. His enthusiasm is pure. No fear is present in his reaction. The Boy runs his hand across the slightly warped cover.

"And you're right, I *did* book it," The Girl says. She takes the magazine, turns it over, then places it back in The Boy's hands.

"You're on the front and the back..." The Boy marvels, then the fear that was absent finally arrives, uninvited, inevitable. The pictures of The Girl conceal a combustible industry like the hollow copy of *Ulysses* in the library. People only pay attention to the surface, the rest stays hidden.

I turn away from The Boy and The Girl, because they do not exist. Not anymore.

THE SHOTS

Lux's text, "I can make my own decisions," becomes the closure I need.

I have a week of prep before my first presser, which will come in the form of a profile for i-D. Michael and I will be photographed, then a hastily written recap of our Wikipedia pages will accompany the shots.

As I look at the e-mail regarding the i-D shoot for next week, I notice that James isn't even CC:d. After the botched screener and the death of the executioner, James has had his role reduced. He's become a liability for Michael.

To be prepared for my foray back into the fashion journalism world, I research the Asian photographer who will be shooting the spread. According to his IMDB page, he directed a semi-noteworthy movie about a family of vampires who are "just like us" except they're "more patient with their educational system because the children remain children for eternity."

Outlined in the e-mail, the photographer's concept for the shoot is that, up close, portraits will be taken of Michael and myself. They'll slice those portraits down the center, then splice them together in Photoshop. I instantly agree to this concept because, as a photographer, I know what's trying to be accomplished, and I will undermine the intended outcome.

During the week leading up to the shoot:

I make sure I do a fantastic job for MLORE/ I place the finishing touches on my pieces, and I don't overthink it/ I'm kind to everyone, and I don't get visually or verbally frustrated/ I don't ask Michael for more money, and I don't e-mail him, because he's a very busy man/ I don't yell at the seamstresses for stealing from the snack cupboard/ I ask Jessica for her opinion/ I have dinner with Anne from Blend, and I forgive her for the "miscommunication"/ I find myself pretending the models at the workshop are Lux. I don't look any of the girls in their eyes. My trademark stare is traded in for a below-the-neck focus.

"Why haven't you shaved?" Isabella asks me three days in.

"I'm working on something," I tell her.

"What, the 'divorcee on a fishing trip' look?" Isabella snarks.

"It'll be gone Thursday," I assure her, still worried about how she views me.

"What's Thursday?" she asks, her curiosity piqued by a set date for the end of my scruff.

"You can come along if you'd like," I say.

This tease is the only way I can get Isabella to join me on set.

Isabella knows me, in the way that Karen knew me, but she doesn't panic unless the focus is on her, so she'll let me go through with my plan at the i-D shoot.

"Thursday?" Isabella asks again, buying time, considering what could be happening. Being presented with the key to open a locked door, Isabella accepts the opportunity, and tells me, "Sure. I'll go with you. New York?"

"Hoboken, actually," I say.

Thursday comes fast, which is good because my growing beard is itchy and makes me look like an alcoholic, which is too matchy-matchy with my actual vice so my image becomes unfashionable.

Isabella and I take the Path to Hoboken.

As we walk to the shoot, she fixes my hair so it's pulled back, in a stubby ponytail, tight against my scalp. My beard is exactly as long as Michael keeps his. I unbutton the top two buttons on my white Michael Lorrie dress shirt that Michael's Jessica was able to secretly snag for me. I was unwilling to go to the Michael Lorrie store on 5th Ave and buy the shirt myself. I refuse to fund a store that would happily sell women to wealthy men if it was legal.

"How do I look?" I ask Isabella.

"You look very *Single White Female* with a beard," she assures me.

We arrive on set early for the shoot.

A young Chinese guy points me in the direction of where they're doing Michael's makeup.

As soon as I enter the room, I call out, "Big brother!" as though we're the closest of siblings.

Michael looks at me, looks away, looks back at me, then pops out of the makeup chair. "What the fuck do you think you're doing?" he asks, stalking toward me, a finger raised in the air.

"Taking control of this article," I say, moving past Michael, then I sit down in the makeup chair he vacated. "Do me like him," I say into the mirror, pointing over my left shoulder.

The photographer- Asian, fat, serious, dressed in a nearly line-less long sleeve black shirt and black pants- looks at the fire breathing Michael, then at me, then at a bug-eyed Isabella who wears the expression of a friend who was invited to the Thanksgiving dinner of a dysfunctional family and the first fight just broke out.

"This has changed," the photographer marvels in a gravelly voice. The glimmer of inspiration in his eye assures me this shoot will go exactly how I planned.

The photographer places his hand under my chin, then- in what I assume is Chinese- he speaks with the Asian makeup artist.

Michael immediately protests, "Oh, come, on. You're not going to shoot him like that."

"I am," the photographer confirms.

"You aren't, I'm shutting this down," Michael declares.

"You aren't," the photographer advises.

Michael storms away, already on his phone, but things are too far in motion to change what I've started. Michael knows what I've done. After the photographs are taken, they'll place Michael's face next to mine, and Michael's small eyes will be overshadowed by my driven stare. Michael's hairline will look further back when compared with mine. It will be clear that Michael is the older brother, and I am the younger brother. In fashion, it's *always* better to be the younger brother. Deviations aside, the uniformity of the pictures- our similar face shape and the genetic overlap- will force the writer of the piece to assemble an article underscoring how the two men blended in the photograph are different, instead of having a photo where our differences are clear at a glance. I want people to be told in explicit detail how I'm unlike Michael.

It was obvious that Michael wanted to look better than me in every way, and now he's going to have to prove that he is.

All week long, I heard the echo of Lux saying, "I'm really starting to see the family resemblance."

THE REFLECTION

As soon as I get home from the shoot, I shave.

After I wash my face, I look in the mirror for a very long time.

The longer I look, the older I get.

The simple solution to this issue would be to stop looking, but then how would I truly know if I'm aging at an exponential rate, as it appears.

The fear of not knowing if I look gross is grosser than the reality of looking gross.

"I need to go meet with Anne," Isabella says, walking by the bathroom.

"It's dark out," I yell to her.

"It's six at night," she yells back.

"I don't care. I'm worried about your safety. I think Michael has something to do with the missing girls," I say, wiping my face. I'm withholding information. I can't figure out if I'm protecting Isabella, or if I'm putting her at risk by doing this.

Isabella, unconcerned, yells back, "I wouldn't worry about missing girls. Models are flakes."

I walk out of the bathroom, and find an oddly determined model. She's wearing my Saint Laurent jacket, lacing on a new pair of black Dr. Martens. The lack of scuff marks on the toes confirms that the boots aren't mine. I realize that my feet are probably smaller than hers.

Isabella will be gone in a moment, so I have no choice but to lift the veil I've worked so aggressively to keep over her eyes. Calmly, but with my intense stare unwavering, I say, "I think Michael is paying people to spread rumors that certain models are unreliable... to cover up a crime."

"Then he must have taken out a pretty big loan because every person in the entire world says models are unreliable. Including my model friends."

"Exactly," I say, "Everyone will turn a blind eye if you go missing. I can't let you go. I think these girls are being-"

"-oh! Look at mister model savior springing into action," Isabella says, standing up, towering over me. "Are you passing out cookies backstage with magnums of Ensure? Are you adding non-slip grip to the bottom of the MLORE heels, then bandaging blisters like some self-appointed fashion Christ? Is that what you're up to, Andrew? Saving the world's models?" Isabella mocks me.

I fear I'm becoming an overprotective dad in Isabella's eyes, so I decide to let her in further. "Models like you are in danger," I say, very clearly.

"Oh. Danger? Well, they *are* casting your new collection. How are we going to throw a wrench in this one? Let me guess, bias cut pieces in dark ominous colors, worn by white models in black-face? So dangerous. The wall of hype is cresting," Isabella says, and thankfully, her tone isn't as slicing as her words, so it makes it harder to believe she actually feels this way.

"Why are you being so apathetic and jokey? Why are you making it out to be like my request is unreasonable?" I ask, bursting into an argument.

"After this collection walks, take a vacation, Andrew. You sound insane."

"Goodbye, Isabella," I say, as she opens the front door.

Isabella turns around, perceptibly softening, and he tells me, sweetly, "Goodbye, detective Lorrie. Listen... I have something that might help you. It's upstairs..."

I stop listening because I don't want to know what Isabella is taking to tolerate me.

THE CHASE

My personal phone buzzes, and a chill climbs my spine when a play button appears on the screen.

With a shaking finger, I press down on the sideways triangle, but the phone seems to glitch out.

In the darkness of the bedroom, I notice the black screen is still being lit by the backlight. I'm about to turn the screen off, when the darkness lifts in the center of the screen, revealing a silhouette. It's a tall figure with bouncing long hair, and the outline moves forever forward, away from the camera. I don't touch the screen. I should be checking to see who this video is from, when it's from, and what the file is named, but I'm afraid to lose the image, so I merely watch what I'm being shown. I turn up the volume on the phone, but there's only the sound of traffic. No footsteps.

I watch the figure on the screen. She turns back for a moment- like she senses someone is following her- and I'm chilled to find myself looking at Isabella's profile- that beautiful profile I've sketched a hundred times.

The camera doesn't stop when Isabella looks back. It doesn't speed up in a way that would indicate that the person carrying out this pursuit is nervous or worried about being spotted. The camera doesn't flinch, it merely continues to float forward. That's the feeling of this voyeuristic view- floating, not walking.

Isabella turns a corner and disappears from sight. The camera continues to float at the same liquid pace, never rushing to keep its target in full view. I strain my eyes and search the dark on the screen for a landmark. I need to know where Isabella is. I need to know how recent this footage is. Isabella has worn my jacket and all black too many times to count. This could be any night after the first snowfall.

Suddenly, the camera whips to the right, and trains itself on Isabella again, then starts to steadily gain speed.

I find myself biting my clenched fist so hard my pointer finger momentarily dislocates.

I scramble to find my work phone, but I realize it's in the pocket of the Saint Laurent jacket Isabella is wearing.

Without shoes, I flee my room. I keep checking the screen of the personal phone, pawing at it to bring up my contacts, but the image won't leave. I run out of the house and into the street, barefoot.

Scotland Road is empty, and I feel powerless, like I stepped back into the brownstone.

I look down at the phone. The camera veers so close to Isabella that I can see the detail on my jacket, then, suddenly, my phone vibrates, and the image of Isabella is interrupted by a message.

"You look lost," reads the text from "Private."

"Who is this?" I immediately type back. I try to swipe to the video, but the screen is locked on the conversation.

"I think you have more important questions that you need the answers to," Private texts.

"Why are you following her?" I send. I can't mention her name.

Private could be anyone because, other than the girl being followed, I only have enemies.

"I think you know why…" Private texts back almost instantly.

"Please. Don't hurt her," I hammer out on the screen, while moving back to the house to avoid being hit by the oncoming traffic.

"I have money," I text, when the phone stays silent too long.

"Do you?" Private responds, and I can't tell if it's with intrigue, or if I'm being mocked.

"Yes. We can make a deal. Just between us. If I get Isabella back, we'll forget about all of this. We all walk away," I frantically type, then send.

My stomach sinks as the response pops up on the phone. I stare at a screenshot of my bank balance.

"That's just a piece," I type.

"Not enough," is Private's instant response.

I've worked my entire life to build a cushion for when things would get bad, and now they're bad, but I can't afford to make things better, so it's almost like I didn't take any of those steps at all. I've always known that part of being a man would entail saving money so the people I love will be safe, no matter what happens. That's how things are supposed to work.

"I can get more," I text, because I have to.

"Paying for a girl?" Private asks, hinting at a knowledge beyond just the whereabouts of a model.

I'm not sure if Michael's people have her/ if James has her/ if the movie exec has her/ if the Chinese investors have her/ if Irina has her/ if Isabella really did just leave to meet with her agent and someone is just using this to their advantage.

"I've told NO ONE," I send, leaving the statement open-ended.

"Do you promise?" I'm asked.

"I promise you. I just want these girls to be safe," I send.

"Good," they send, and this is the final text from Private.

My relief and worry tumble over each other in a disorienting spin cycle.

I walk back into the house, and immediately notice that, on the armrest of the square mission chair in the living room, is an ancient cell phone. This device is both foreign and very familiar to me. Next to the old phone is an empty beer bottle- a small amount of foam is slowly sliding down the side of the bottle, then settling at the bottom.

"If you aren't careful, you're going to lose her too," whispers through the house.

THE SAME MISTAKES

I stay up until Isabella comes home. She returns a little after 11, and calls out my name. I have to remain in my room for four minutes so I don't cry in front of her.

When I "casually" run into her in the kitchen, I proceed to follow her around the house, asking her a constant stream of questions. Isabella answers me with a mildly annoyed *Whatever, I'm a model* cool that she exudes religiously, unless strangers are present. Her familiar manner assures me that it's just another normal night, and allows me to go to sleep.

In the morning, I make an appearance at the Blend office.

Anne confirms that she had a meeting with Isabella last night. A video chat with a Japanese agency was set up in a hurried scramble because New York Fashion Week is quickly approaching, and Isabella needs to solidify her post-MLORE plans. There was something about the time difference that required the meeting to happen at night. I keep saying, "Absolutely," and smiling wildly at Anne, as she tells me her plan for Isabella. I now have a comfortable trust with Blend as an agency, and I'll make sure that more young women are placed under Anne's care in the future.

In the shine of this mild winter day, everything feels better. My brow that was slick with a layer of sweat all last night is now relaxed.

When the sun sets, I return to the house on Scotland Road, unwilling to let Isabella stay there alone after dark.

I find her in her room, sitting Indian style on the floor in front of the mirror, getting ready to go out. She's wearing a blue and yellow pleated schoolgirl skirt and a sky blue angora sweater.

"Look at you," I purr, leaning on the door frame of Cassie and Isabella's bedroom.

"Stop it, Andrew," Isabella says, immediately seeing through me.

"You going out tonight?" I ask dryly, trying to keep things playful.

"I'm just meeting up with a friend," Isabella says. She's doing her eyeliner so she can't give me the bitch-face I know she so desperately wants to deliver.

I stay glued to the door frame, and I ask, "It's not James, right? Becau-"

"-no. It's not James. Why would I hang out with James?" Isabella asks, rolling her now made up eyes.

"I just want to be clear."

"You're clear."

"Good," I say, then I repeat it, like it's a second take, "Good."

Isabella angrily shakes an empty hairspray bottle, "This is bad, I'm almost out. My hair won't have any body."

"Are you sure more body is what you want?" I ask, trying to make her insecure- hating myself for it- convincing myself that I'm protecting her.

"See. That's exactly why. I need my hair to be as big as the rest of me."

"Maybe if you didn't use so much hairspray..."

"Maybe I wouldn't have any friends."

"I'd still be your friend, even if your hair looked bad," I offer, attempting to be *enough*.

"Judging you," she says.

When the nozzle of the hairspray becomes unclogged and finally exhales a perfumed mist, I say, "So, for tomorrow..." and I only ask this because I need a general location of where Isabella will be tonight. This way, if another one of those nightstalker videos appear on my phone, I'll at least know the direction I should start sprinting.

"Just ask me where I'm going, and who I'm going with," Isabella says, throwing down a lip liner pencil with such force that it snaps in two. "Socializing is stressful enough. I don't need this as a primer," Isabella tells me, then her rage condenses into a pout.

"What's the answer to those questions?" I ask. It's clear that she thought, by bringing up the questions herself, I wouldn't ask them again, because doing so would prove her right. Normally, she'd be correct in this assumption, but I simply cannot take any risks tonight.

"I'm meeting up with this- ugh- male model, and we're going to some Webster Hall gig."

"What gig?" I ask, trying to sound cool.

"Matthew's band," Isabella huffs out.

I feel myself sweating through my shirt. "Cool. Cool," I say.

Why the fuck is Matthew playing a local gig and not inviting me? I paid him to play my after-party. Well, I think he was paid. The Chinese were supposed to take care of that. I'm sure they did. They're a careful people. Regardless of if he was paid, the party was a good time, and I took pictures of the entire thing. Why didn't he invite me to take pictures again? I quickly remember that one of the items I had pushed down on my "to do" list was to send copies of my photographs to the intern at the label Matthew's band is signed to. She e-mailed me about it- a lot. At some point, I just filtered her e-mails to go right into my spam folder. All of this makes me feel like shit, and I hate myself.

"Which model?" jumps out of my mouth, and the brazenness of this question surprises me.

I tell myself that I'm doing this to protect her/ I tell myself that Lorrie girls are targets/ I tell myself that Isabella probably isn't into this guy/ I tell myself the male model is definitely gay/ I ask myself if Isabella is gay/ I tell myself that I'm sleeping alone tonight, and I'm struck with the unexpected fear that Isabella won't be doing the same.

"Trae Payton," she says, when I don't leave the room.

"The urban clothing guy?"

"He had a Ck One campaign, okay?" she says, defending him.

"What's an urban clothing guy doing at Matthew's show? Not really... his type of music."

"How would you know what his type of music is?" Isabella asks.

"Do you think that Matthew has a lot of black dudes at his concerts?" I ask back.

"Uh, Trae is going, so yeah."

"You're better than this," I say.

"Than Webster Hall? Of course. We all are." Isabella confirms her detour.

"You're better than going on a date with some urban model."

"Why are you so weird about race?" she asks, her face scrunching in disgust.

"I guess you really do have low self-esteem," I say, hating myself, while hoping that it's the only way to keep her from doing this.

"What does not eliminating entire races out of my dating pool have to do with self-esteem?" Isabella asks.

"Okay, this isn't a discussion. You're right and I'm wrong, so?"

"No, you can't just attack me like that," she says, her voice metering up.

I cross my arms and shrug; I need her to cry, so her makeup will be ruined and she won't go out tonight.

"This is disgusting," Isabella says, getting up, then pushing by me.

"You knew I was a piece of shit when we met. We met because of my speech," I remind her.

She turns around in the hall and tells me, "We met because you gave me a job."

"No. We ended up in the same place because of a job. We met because you supported me immediately after I sank my career, again," I say, spiraling into argument after argument.

"I was attracted to your gift, I guess I thought I could ignore the rest. Or. I don't know. Fix you. I'm such an idiot. I'm such a girl. Fix you? I can't fix you. You're too fucked up."

"Maybe you could-"

"-I can't Andrew, you're fucked up and you need to change."

THE HACKERS

I know that I'm right to worry about Isabella after getting those texts and that video, but I feel wrong. Anytime I convince myself that I'm making the correct choice, I remember who I am. I remember my history. I remember that I'm older, so I should be wiser. I should shoulder more responsibility for decorum.

I try to think of myself at Isabella's age. I drifted. I sought out the fire. I stuck my hand inside it. I burned, not because I wanted to, but because that's what happens. I accepted it, and I grew to need it. More and more, I've needed it. The burn of a shot, the burn of the sun, the burn of a slap.

Every second that Isabella is gone becomes an hour.

I walk around the house, and I smell things, searching for her scent, but sometimes I find Cassie's scent instead. I spiral deeper. I just need someone to walk through the door. Isabella. Cassie. Lux.

I have to force myself to go to sleep because living like this is exhausting. When The Boy and The Girl arrive, I put in the earbuds attached to my phone, then I bury my head under my pillow. The only information I need will come from my work phone. When the phone remains silent, I fall asleep.

My dreams are filled with gray, faceless beings. I recognize no one.

When I wake up, my bed is empty. Finding myself alone, I feel pain that can only be compared to a hangover. Everything hurts, I want to wake up from the present. I want to step outside of my body.

Of course, I have to know the worst. I've already expected it, now it can be confirmed. Another girl lost.

When I remove my earbuds, I hear muffled K-Pop coming from Isabella's room. I grip my phone tightly, and I wish I had a screener to watch to remind me that there are worse things in the world than being left behind.

I force myself to get up- to apologize- to remind Isabella that as long as the next two weeks go smoothly, I'll put her on a plane to Japan.

I connect my work phone to the charger, then lay it on the dresser. I pick up my personal phone, aware that- in a brutal twist- the screener I bootlegged might be what allows me to keep things together.

With careful footsteps, I return to the door frame of the picture-lined room.

I find Isabella on the floor, again, and this time, she's stuffing her few possessions into her backpack.

"Why are you packing?" I ask, stepping into the room.

"I'm cleaning up," she responds, without looking up from her task.

"You're cleaning up your stuff into a backpack?" I ask.

Isabella stops "cleaning up" and says, "Listen, the cost of the train is kicking my ass, so I'm going to stay at the Blend apartment for a bit. They have an extra-long sofa I can crash on. It'll just be for a couple of days, then I'll be back."

"Do you have any jobs lined up in the city?" I ask, as my heart kicks at my ribs.

Isabella puts her hair behind her ear, and presses her lips together, before answering, "Castings. You know. Things are sort of coming together. Finally."

"Things were together before," I try to remind her, convince her.

"Not really," Isabella says, still in her makeup and outfit from last night. "I'm not a model yet. I'm just a girl who has done some modeling. I'm just a person wearing clothes right now. I'm just trying to... what's that saying... strike while the model is barely legal?"

"It's sort of dangerous out there, don't you think?" I ask, even though I know for a fact that everywhere is dangerous.

"I suppose," Isabella says, then shrugs.

Her backpack is almost full, so I beg, "Stop! Please. Stop. Before you go, I need you to watch this," I say, holding out my phone.

"No, Andrew," Isabella says, zipping her backpack.

"I'm serious. Please," I beg. "You can leave after you watch this. I don't think you will, but if you still want to, you can go."

Isabella returns my intense stare, then I force my personal phone into her hands.

"Go to my videos," I say.

Merely to get me out of the room, Isabella chooses the video folder, then selects the only file available.

I move behind her to relive the horror, to remind myself that I'm doing the right thing.

"Charlie O'Shea looks like shit," Isabella says, "Is this her therapy session? Good for her, finally getting help. It's totally like Charlie to put up such a cringey over-sharing video. First, the bong .gif, now this." I watch Isabella soften as she thinks about our messages. "Our Charlie O'Shea era... such an important time."

I know that her perspective will change in moments, but I try to bask in the glow of her golden nostalgia while I can.

"Wait, who's... Wait. Andrew, what is..." Isabella asks, her eyes rapidly blinking, giving her short clips of what's happening.

"What the fuckkk," Isabella gasps in a sing-songy way, then casually she asks, "Can I have this video for my gore blog? The crying overdubbed on the video is a particularly pathetic touch. I like it."

"Isabella, Charlie is dead," I say.

"Right. It's perfect for my gore blog."

"That voice you heard was James," I say, getting annoyed she's not putting this together.

"What?"

"Charlie was at a casting that James set up," I say, shaken up again, reliving the horror of it all.

"That's fucked up," Isabella notes, then starts clicking the screen, "Can we watch it again? Minus the overdone puking noise, this is actually a pretty good campaign. Good on James."

I reach over her shoulder, and yank the phone away, "No. We can't. That's not a campaign. That's evidence. That really happened. My work phone gets sent these casting videos, then the girls go missing."

Isabella pauses, finally understanding what's happening, and she gasps, "Why didn't you tell me this?"

"I warned you. I warned you not to do anything with James."

"I thought you were just being jealous. I thought you were just being crazy. How was I supposed to tell the difference between a legitimate issue and an Andrew Lorrie panic spiral? Andrew, I could have been Charlie. Well, not in any other way, but in this crowbar victim way, yeah," Isabella says, temporarily confusing herself.

"I'm sorry. I tried to convince you that I'm not just sitting here wringing my hands and acting like a jealous boyfriend," I say.

"Have you taken this to cops?" Isabella asks.

"No, I need proof James is involved besides his voice. You can edit a voice in easily." I say.

"Let me see your work phone," Isabella demands, holding out her palm.

I return to my room and grab the work phone off my dresser. I check the screen to make sure that I'm not handing over a potentially violent message to her. I still have no new notifications.

When I walk back into Cassie's room, I find Isabella casually sitting on the bed, her backpack on the floor.

The work phone is handed over, and Isabella glances down at my background- a picture of Lux in a piece that I ultimately left out of the last Andrew Lorrie show. A lost design on a lost friend. The Chinese investors own the piece, and they also own the laptop which contains the video of Lux walking in the garment. It's possible that this piece was used by the Chinese to take the place of the "missing" blue velvet dress that's currently crammed into Isabella's backpack. The picture is all I have now, and the dress will end up in a CEO's closet- either because the CEO is a woman, or because the CEO has a very expensive secret. I supremely regret that I didn't back up the videos of Lux walking in every look of my last Andrew Lorrie collection. I'm afraid my memories will fade.

Isabella leans back on the bed, holding my work phone above her head, while swiping through screens. Those long legs, those knot-less branches, angle over the pink bedspread. It doesn't look like a comfortable way to relax, but Isabella is like a cat, and the way she reclines only makes sense to herself and the camera.

"It's Jimmy," she tells me.

"Right," I say, knowing that he's behind this. "But how do you know?" I add because I'm desperate for more information.

"Maybe because the videos are being streamed from a hard drive named, 'E colon slash slash PixxsPixx,'" Isabella says, holding out the phone to me.

I look at the path, and try to sound like I know what I'm talking about by saying, "It could be a decoy. A misdirect."

"A misdirect that perfectly captures the douchiness of Jimmy Pixx? If that's true, kudos to whoever Michael has running his spoofing shit."

"So how'd he send out the screeners, then remotely delete them?" I ask.

"It looks like James will cue up a video on his computer, then he'll share his screen out to your phone. Your phone would be like 'Hey, new data, I must show my master,' then it streams as long as James wants it to. Sometimes, it might download the file to your phone, then James will remotely delete the file when he sees activity on your phone. Get it? He watches your screen, as you watch your screen, and once he shows you what he needs to, he can remotely delete the file, then close the connection. This way, there's no local file for you, and he gets to screen his horror movies."

"So, if we find the hard drive, then we might have the videos?" I ask.

"I guarantee we'll have the videos," Isabella says.

"Don't be so sure, these snuff films could send James away for eight eternities. Why would he keep the evidence around, waiting to be stolen?"

"Without question, he still has everything," Isabella tells me, handing me back my phone.

"Why would he keep something that could incriminate him?" I ask, willing to rephrase the question again and again, until I find the source of her confidence.

"Well, let's look at our two options. One- the films are just that, films. Shitty horror shorts that Jimmy is recording as some backward ass, art school dropout, YouTube shit. Maybe he's hoping that- by some miraculous twist of fate- he actually has talent and becomes famous for something. At the same time, you were assembling pieces of a fashion collection, he might have been assembling pieces of a new career. Or, we have option two- we're witnessing murders. These are murders that no one wants to see, but James wants certain people to see them. Now, tell me, Andrew. How many pieces of your collection have you thrown away?"

"Well, there was that trash can fire I-"

"-how many of your pieces have you discarded *not* during a rage blackout?" Isabella amends her question.

"Oh," I respond, "None. Why would I throw away hours upon- oh."

"Yeah. And with guys, this killing stuff is almost always sexual. BTK jerking off in a basement, Gacy and his rope trick- I think Jimmy can spare a couple of gigs on his hard drive for his torture porn. I mean, he'd never delete this footage. He's probably jerking off to it right now."

"Why the fuck do you know this?" I ask, not sure where all this knowledge is pouring from. What sort of dark reservoir is bubbling inside this girl?

"Serial killer knowledge is sort of a side effect of being a fashion blogger," Isabella tells me casually.

"I've been in fashion for 20 years, and I've never been influenced by serial killers," I say.

"A collection you ghosted from six years ago had Manson-hair," Isabella reminds me.

"On girls."

"Still."

"How does a teenage girl draw this parallel between the shittiest humans to ever walk the earth and fashion indus- actually. Never mind. Let's proceed past all of that," I say.

"Well, since you asked," Isabella responds, not allowing my detour, "A teenage girl feels like she's invincible, yet also totally fragile. She feels she has the world figured out better than anyone, and she hates almost everyone walking- bigots, misogynists, racists, guys in fedoras- she's superior to all. I mean that type of narcissism and pure dark hate is pretty much in the serial killer cookbook. You might be able to relate. Here we are, sitting in the suburbs, in a house we don't pay rent for, in virtually idyllic surroundings, and there's something thrilling about an animal tearing into this peacefulness to shake up our lives. So, yeah, fuck shit up. Punk rock, and all that jazz," Isabella says, then makes devil horns with her fingers.

"I don't think you're supposed to end a 'punk rock' declaration with 'and all that jazz,'" I say.

"I stuck my tongue out and made that punk rock hand sign. It's fine," Isabella assures me.

"So. Miss Scream Queen, why is James doing this?"

Isabella doesn't have to think about it. She instantly shares her theory, "All day long, Jimmy used to take pictures of famous people, then there was that big story where he got personally invited to the social!heavy concert. That boosted his profile to get him the CTV gig, which boosted his profile enough to get Michael's attention. At that point, fame starts to feel achievable for him, and since the social!heavy girls somehow put out fucking awesome music, Jimmy probably saw that he could solidify his fame by surprising people and doing something in-your-face. In this case, he literally put it in front of your face. Think about it, those guys who stand on the sideline and take pictures of football players, you gotta assume, after a while, they start having these daydreams that the quarterback is hurt and the stand-in for the quarterback is hurt and the coach is like, 'Well, we have no choice but to put the camera guy in,' then in his fantasy he throws like a hundred touchdowns, and they raise him on their shoulders. I think this is Jimmy trying to get on some shoulders."

"Why are you so full of energy today?" is all I can think to ask.

"Death, destruction, mayhem," Isabella says, her red lips- a smile.

Finally, someone has answers.

"Now come on, we have to stop this whole model slaughter or I'll feel super guilty," Isabella says, then unzips her backpack and dumps its contents on the floor.

THE EQUALS

"He's in the room at the end of the hall. I made everyone else go home," is the text I get from Jess, my assistant.

Isabella and I face the blistering cold and hurry to the workshop.

"It's so hot in here I feel like we should be traveling by boat through a sea of tormented souls," Isabella says to me, my face tingling from the temperature change. I remove my Burberry coat, then drape it in the crook of my right arm. It's hotter than normal in the workshop today because I had Jessica crank the heat to 87 after Isabella and I solidified our plan.

Isabella breaks away from me and enters the first room, while I continue walking through the workshop, looking for James so I can start a fight.

I find him right where Jessica said he would be.

"What are you doing here?" I yell.

James flicks his Yankees cap up and says, "I was invited. Why are you not panicking about the fact your line walks in a little over a week?"

"I'm prepared," I say.

"You're still missing your Chinese girl, aren't you?" James asks.

"Hand in your campaign, then promptly go fuck yourself," I tell him.

"Not your call," James says, unwilling to back down. This is good.

"I'm sure I'm not the first person to tell you to fuck yourself," I say.

James places his hands on either side of the rim on his hat, gives it a more severe curl, then says, "You're right. My entire life people have been telling me to fuck off, but now I'm finally at a place where I don't have to listen to them anymore. So, Andrew, fuck off."

To continue the conversation- stretching it out intentionally- and I say, "That's something we have in common. Lots of people have told me to fuck off, too."

"Oh. Yeah. Well. Then you should know how much it sucks," James says, softening, realizing that we're both bad people. It's my bedrocked belief that James is a worse person than I am, and this allows me to say, with confidence, "You're done after this collection, James."

"Michael will help me," James says, clearly nervous. I've tapped his fear.

"He won't. He only brought you on because he knows you have no morals so you'll do all the shit that would be too expensive for him to have done otherwise. You're like a one-man sweatshop for carrying out fucked up ideas."

"You don't understand," James says, his jaw locking, "It doesn't matter why he brought me on. He's the one guy in my entire life that sought me out. I was a dedicated artist, who chased people. Every day of my life- up until Michael called- was a pursuit. Then, because of all my hard work, your brother gave me an opportunity. It was a relief to have someone believe in me, so I won't let him down."

"Okay, James," I say, easing up because this is becoming heavier than it should be. I was supposed to start a squabble, not provoke a man to pour out his heart.

We have what we need. I've made sure that our target, the pea coat, isn't in the room, and Isabella is already waiting in the hallway- I can see her thin, lurching shadow looming just outside the door.

"I'm not wasting another second with you, James. Enjoy what little time you have left in this industry," I say, then I slide my coat back on.

I allow James to stay in my workshop. I'm confident he won't sabotage my pieces.

As I start to make my way toward the hall, James calls out, "Wait," then adds, "Don't walk away from me."

I stop walking, because otherwise James will start chasing me, and that's when he's at his most comfortable.

"I'm not storming out on you, James," I say, turning around to face him again.

"But you're leaving. Why can't we just work together until this is over?" James asks.

"Because if I stay, I'm going to explain to you precisely why you and I are not alike."

"Lay it on me," James says, opening his arms.

I sigh, then tell him, "I work *at* Michael Lorrie. You work *for* Michael Lorrie. You say yes to shit that even Terry Richardson would find morally turbid. You were given your job merely because you have no morals, and once you've completed your task, you'll be eliminated."

"And you *do* have morals?" James asks me.

"Yeah, that's why you were sending me those videos, isn't it? Because I care... because I'm the *only one* who cares," I say.

Out of the corner of my eye, I see the shadow in the hall slowly disappear, and this proves me wrong. Isabella also cares. I know that she's not leaving because she's offended- she's just moving on to her next destination- and I'm right there with her, so I need to make sure I keep James here with me. I tell him, "You're a talented photographer who regularly shows just how little he cares about others. That's the only reason why you're here, and that's the reason why you'll never work again.

"Really?" James asks, "You think I'm talented?"

"Yeah. I do," I confirm.

James nods at this. The only thing he got from what I just told him was that I think he takes a good picture. *That* was the part that surprised him- he already knew everything else.

"So why did you end up with this gig, Andrew? If you're so much better than us, why are you here, with me?" James asks, playing into my hand.

"Because Michael was tired of being ashamed of his ready-to-wear collections," I offer.

"Seems like he was also tired of being ashamed of his brother," James adds.

"Exactly," I say, "Michael is a businessman, and businessmen focus on reducing their risks. He couldn't have me show him up again, and he couldn't have me fail again because then his last name could potentially be sold to one of those dreaded department stores."

"You have it all figured out, huh?" James scoffs, not impressed.

"More than you know," I tell him, as a warning.

As usual, James doesn't heed the warning, and he says, "We're alike because we both have secrets. You're just too much like Michael to admit you're a fuck up too."

"That is exactly what I hate," I say, gearing up to release the anger that's once again built up inside me. "People are dead because of your mistakes. No one died because of my mistakes. People got their feelings a little hurt by what I said, but people physically felt pain from what you did. People died because of what you did. Everyone walked away after I made my mistake. No one could walk away from your mistakes, James. The only way they found to escape your mistakes was to run fast enough that they didn't get their soul eaten."

"They shouldn't have lost their souls. I do feel bad about that," James says, a little quiet. He pulls the brim of his hat down so his lack of humanity is hidden.

"No. You don't feel bad about that. You lost your soul long before any of those girls did, yet by some catastrophic mismanagement of the universe, you ended up providing even more souls for the sacrifice. You're going to pay for that, for all of eternity, with only momentary breaks when they pull your soul out of hell, just to connect it back to that fucked up brain of yours so they can inflict the same torture you masterminded for far too many."

"Ca-alm down, Andy," James says, marveling at me.

I nod at this, knowing that damning James to hell was a bit much, even though he had damned souls himself. Once again, he and I are not alike.

"What do you say we go grab a drink, and talk this over?" James suggests, likely trying to rewind things back to that day where we shared some Coronas.

This happy hour will give Isabella time to get into James' hotel room, steal the drives, then meet with us at the bar, so I say, "Sure. Fine."

"Come on. I know a place," James says, gesturing to the door.

"I need to text Jessica and make sure we can get out of here," I respond, then I take out my phone, and read a text from Isabella, "Got the card. Keep him busy. I need 2 hrs."

"No prob," I text back, then I turn to James, and say, "Know what? I'm the boss. I don't have to check in with her."

"Damn right," James says.

Isabella is already gone so I feel no fear walking through the workshop, but I watch carefully when James grabs his pea coat. The night he showed me his Pixxitorium, I saw him grab the key card out of the inside breast pocket of this coat. Luckily, he doesn't check his pockets.

We make our way out onto the cold street, and James, as always, flags down a taxi almost immediately. We could've just walked to a nearby bar, but I don't mention this, because I need to keep James busy. I want to give Isabella as much time as she needs.

James leans up toward the cabby, then mumbles a destination.

As we drive through a series of never-ending potholes, I hammer out a misspelled text, "Ina cab wigh James. You hve 2 hrs."

Isabella instantly texts back, "Won't need that long. Penn@8."

I look to James, unsure of where we're going, or why this ride is taking so long, but as long as we're not headed back to his room, it's fine.

"I don't think you're like him," lights up on the screen of my phone. Isabella is the only person to confirm what I believe in my heart. I take a screenshot of the text.

"Here's good," James says to the cabby, then swipes his Michael Lorrie company card to pay for the expensive fare.

We get out directly in front of Heathers. This "casual meet-up spot" is so out of the way from the workshop that the drive becomes purposeful. In this city, there's no reason to cab over 10 minutes just to find a bar, unless you're looking for a specific place.

I stop James, yanking his arm, physically preventing him from going any further.

James looks at me, and something seems to click in his head.

"Oh no. Did you quit?" he asks, concerned.

"What?" I ask, temporarily confused.

"Are you in 'the program?' Am I enabling you? Are you off the sauce?"

"No. James. I want to know why you chose this place."

"Your blood pressure. Must be... high," James says, his eyes bugging out. He walks up to the door to Heathers and tries to open it. It doesn't open. He tries it again.

"James. Heathers closed in October," I tell him.

"You're kidding," James says. His demeanor changes. He pulls the brim of his hat down, then takes out his phone.

"What are you doing?" I ask, growing tired of being the guy who constantly asks questions.

"I'm sending a text," James says.

"To?" I ask, moving closer so I can see his screen. He cannot lie to me.

"Oh, we were going to meet up with a model. I need to give her new directions." James laughs once at himself, then says, "Instead of it being a go-see.

I was like, 'How about a go-drink.'" As the words tumble out of James' mouth, he reads my face, then he quickly realizes I'm going to tear him apart.

"You've got to be kidding me," I say, breaking away from James, stomping down East 13th. I decide I'm going to call the cops. They'll be able to at least get James on supplying alcohol to a minor, and at best get him for the awful things he's planned for tonight. This has to stop.

"Come on, man," James says, jogging to catch up with me, "I'm doing things the right way this time. This is a public place."

"It's a closed bar, James," I point out.

I turn onto Avenue B, then I search the street for a cab or a cop. James continues his pursuit, and I need him close by so he can be arrested. I rant, "I'm not stupid. I know your plan. You were going to break in there, make up some bullshit about having a key, then you'd keep feeding the model drinks until she reached that sweet spot- at which point you were going to suggest that you two take some test pictures. You knew that place was closed, and you can't use hotel rooms anymore, so you're moving on to the next set. I'm not as naïve as some girl who only knows eight words of English."

"Naylana has only been here for two months. I think you should give her some time," James says tenderly.

"You're back doing the same shit. Now I know why everyone is so frustrated when I keep making the same mistakes," I bark at him, moving with purpose to an unknown destination.

"I have a show to cast," James says, defending himself, chasing me like he's a paparazzi.

"Not anymore," I tell him.

"Michael has been e-mailing me directly," James says, aware that he's no longer CC'd on correspondence.

"The way you want to cast this show is putting girls on a runway to hell. If you have any desire to be part of the selection process for who walks for me, you'll hold the go-sees in my workshop, with full supervision."

"Fine," James says.

"Fine," I say, not sure where I'm walking to.

"Can we still get a drink?" James asks, almost in pain, "Can you break your sobriety for one night? I won't tell anyone, I promise. If anyone asks, I'll tell them we spent the night in a church basement sharing our feelings and indulging in Folgers."

James' plea is effective, but it's almost as though he's pushing to keep my plan on track, and this sends me spiraling once again. I begin to fear that he *wants* Isabella to sneak into his room.

"If you see ANYONE around that hotel room, leave immediately/"Stay safe/"I need you to stay safe," are the texts I send, one after another, to Isabella.

"Hey Sweet Valley High, they'll let you text at the bar. Come on," James says.

I nod, acknowledging that a drink is now essential, and James stops walking, then says, "Andrew. Here."

I look at where James is pointing, and I feel even worse, as my suspicions are all but confirmed- I am part of James' plan.

"Why did you pick this place?" I ask, rushing over to him.

"Because it sells alcohol and we were looking to buy alcohol so, uh? That was the thought process."

I can't return to the red womb of this bar, and the fact that James has brought me here causes me to hold my crooked nose and blink repeatedly.

Lux knows this place well. If she was going to meet someone- a stranger- she would choose a place like this- a familiar place. She knows that she can hang out in the back, out of sight, and this arrangement is both discreet and public at the same time. I refuse to walk inside the bar, because I'm convinced that Lux is in there, with the studio executive, or a stockbroker, or just a guy who can build a really convincing online profile. James has spent months showing me things I don't want to see, why would tonight be any different?

"I want sushi," I say, and James doesn't start walking. "I'll buy the drinks on my card," I offer, and James immediately starts walking.

I start practically jogging, as James lags behind me. I need to get away from the bar, because if I see Lux sharing drinks with an older man, there will be yet another video of grisly footage that Isabella will have to retrieve tonight.

THE 2 OCEANS

On the train ride back to South Orange, Isabella and I are separated by her backpack. Inside her backpack, is the Pixxitorium.

"I had no idea you were such a skilled thief- first my sweater designs, now James' snuff films," I joke.

"Whatever, I'm a model," Isabella says, finally.

"You're kind of amazing," I tell the sleek cat burglar next to me.

"You're kind of insane. I mean, those texts..." Isabella says, and she can tease me about my paranoia because she wasn't hurt. This fact makes me happier than having the video evidence does.

"I was just... worried. I guess I didn't think about what I was asking you to do, until the plan was already underway. Once again, there was a girl that I want to protect, and I immediately put her in a dangerous situation," I say, staring at the blue seat in front of us.

Isabella leans across her backpack and puts her head on my shoulder. This is a girl who's been my safety net throughout the chaos of my personal and professional life while creating MLORE. Today, I asked her to take an active part in a dangerous game, and she willingly chose to help me. It's my responsibility to ensure that any retaliation for our actions tonight will be carried out on me, and me alone.

"Have you seen Regis or Irina?" is the text from "My Partner" that buzzes on my phone.

James must already miss me- or at least he misses his hard drives.

"Why?" I text back.

"I'm freaking the fuck out," James sends to me.

Isabella looks down at the phone, then says, "Call him 'pal,' because it's funny."

"Why's that, pal?" is the collaborative text I send.

"Someone is fucking with me."

"Did you check behind the curtains?" I text back.

"I'M FUCKING SERIOUS," is the text I receive, and Isabella laughs at it. "Caps lock. He *is* serious," she notes.

"Should I keep messing with him?" I ask.

"No," Isabella says, still leaning on me, "Just tell him."

"I have what you're missing," I text to James.

My phone rings.

"Send it to voicemail," Isabella says.

I ignore the call.

A minute later, my phone beeps, telling me I have a new voicemail.

Then, the phone begins vibrating again.

"Let me answer it," Isabella says.

I hit the speaker button on the phone, then Isabella says, in a very professional voice, "Bow Tie South Orange Cinemas."

"Who is this?" James yells.

"*Who Is This* is not currently showing," Isabella says, holding in laughter.

"Who is this? You're next, you fucking bitch," James growls, as Jimmy Pixx is reborn.

"*You're Next* is no longer showing, but I believe you can find it on DVD, Blu-ray, and On-Demand, sir."

"Give Andrew the phone, you stupid cunt."

Isabella stops laughing, and I start talking. "James," I say.

"It's not what you think," he gasps, the power draining out of him. He doesn't question my possession of his drives, and he doesn't deny what the drives contain. His interest is in mitigating the damage, shortening the reach, controlling the blast radius.

"I've already looked at the files," I purr.

"You don't want to hold onto that footage," James says, as a warning.

"I think I do. I think that's exactly what I want to do," I respond, but I don't use a smooth delivery to say this, because it would be too reminiscent of Michael.

"You don't want to get wrapped up in this," James warns.

"Have you been working with Karen? All of this is sounding very familiar," I say.

"Andrew, I'm not covering my ass here. You saw what happened to those girls, there is very, very little to keep it from happening to you."

"Or you!" I say, cheerfully, "Losing this footage is a big mistake. Imagine if people found out about what went on in that hotel room. By the way, you're on speakerphone on a very full NJ Transit train."

"None of this will end well," James promises. "You need to give me the drive back. Make a copy of it- I don't give a shit- I just want to make sure that when she finds out you have the footage, I'm not gonna get drained. I want it to be your necks."

"*You're Next* is no longer playing in theaters, sir," Isabella says in her professional voice, then giggles.

"I meant necks- between your shoulders and your empty head. In fact, she'll probably slice both your necks open- yours *and* the girl's. If that is your China doll with you, she'll probably end up beat to shit by one of her 'sugar daddies' before we even get to her. If it's Isabella-"

"-what the fuck does Isabella have to do with this?" I ask, taking the call off speaker, then bringing the phone to my ear.

"Come on, she must have helped you. You're computer retarded. The only computer story I've heard mentioned about you was a monitor throwing freak-out."

"Maybe you underestimated me, James?" I suggest.

"You have no idea what you're doing."

"That's the first time you've been right all day," I say.

"Let's meet-up and discuss this, Andrew," James begs.

"Sure. How about me meet at the diner again? Maybe now you'll be a little more receptive about what I wanted to discuss at that table."

"Okay. I'll be there. Bring my drives... please."

"Or what?" I ask.

"I know where you live," James threatens me.

"And I have the key to your hotel room, your career, and your freedom," I remind him.

THE COUNTESS

After I make sure Isabella is safe in the basement of the house on Scotland Road, I make my way to the diner. When I arrive, James already seated in the booth to the right, near the window. He's wearing his Yankees cap, black glasses, a black turtleneck, and black pants. I assume this outfit is intended to scare me into believing that he's going to break into my house tonight. If that's really his plan, I'll be home, and I'll be ready for him. It turns out we had a crowbar in the basement, and I've watched enough footage to know how to use one in combat.

James is immediately is on edge because it's obvious I don't have the Pixxitorium with me.

I sit down, fully in control.

James, looking like a kid in detention, asks, "How many of them did you watch?"

"Enough," I say.

I look for a waitress because I need plates to arrive so I can make this meal more casual. Right now, it feels like a powder keg.

A girl with a half blonde/half brunette ponytail takes our order, then James carelessly provides the spark needed for me to explode, "I don't even understand why you care about these disposable cunts."

Quiet enough that I don't attract attention, but disdainful enough that James knows exactly how I feel, I ask, "Are you really that threatened by these girls?"

James rolls his eyes, and I want to slap the stupid hat off his head, but I don't reach across the table, I merely answer his question, "They only have a *tiny* window to live out their dream and you've shattered that window for dozens of girls. How spiteful can you be? Why do you need to control something that doesn't even involve you?" As I ask this, I start to think, *Oh, yes,*

I know why James has carried out this sinister plan. It's exactly what I tried to do with Lux. This doesn't mean that James and I are even though. I have the hard drives, and James has nothing.

My stare demands a response, so James says, "The video thing is fucked up. Totally fucked up. I'm with you on that. After my first screener was finished, I was sick. I wanted to stop it, but Michael told me-"

"-you listened to him when he asked you to document a life being taken," I hiss, not comprehending how James was willing to revisit the filth he climbed out of when he left Jimmy Pixx for that social!heavy concert.

"It's not a big deal," James says, and he's almost smiling, "We used to do these staged moments with Paul Dabney all the time. We'd collaborate with him, then we'd fuck up his daughter's life. I thought this would be similar, but with models, then it got out of control."

"Ya think? You fucking vampires," I say, shaking my head.

James' eyes go wide, and he says, "Exactly! Good! You figured it out. That was going to be a bitch to explain."

"You don't have to explain that you're a vampire, you act like one every day."

"Wait. *I'm* not the vampire. She is. Or she's a succubus. I can't figure it out, but I know she needs their blood," James mumbles.

"She? Who's 'she?'" I ask.

Suddenly, the waitress is back with our burgers. It's clear they had them pre-made, waiting under heat lamps for the college students and boy-men to arrive at the diner with their predictable desires.

As soon as the waitress walks away, I ask, again, "Who's she?"

"She's Krista, she'll be our waitress tonight," James says, admiring her ass.

"No. Who's the succubus?" I ask, and the question seems laughable.

James flicks the brim of his hat up, then says, "Irina." His eyebrows lift with glee. He wiggles in his seat, takes a bite of his burger, then with a full mouth, he explains, "She's the one we were collecting these girls for. Right after the camera cuts, I walk out of the room, Irina walks in, then I never ask any questions about what happens. I just leave."

"What are you telling me? Spell it out for me, James. Break the story," I say, hammering my pointer finger on the table.

"Irina is, uh, pretty fucked up."

"Fucked up how?" I ask.

James laughs. It's a laugh devoid of any pleasure. Suddenly, another middleman is named. James is a rung under Regis. I'm climbing down the ladder instead of scaling up it. As a paparazzi, James' job was to capture what's happening, from behind the camera. He's not the man with the plan, he's merely the man who films other people's plans. He seems incapable of independent thought. If James was doing all of this for power, it's a colossal bust.

"Remember that wacko Countess Báthory?" James asks me.

"Sure she bathed in virg..." I start to say, then pause, and Irina's ageless face smiles at me in my head.

"...yeah," James says, becoming a ticket collector on a runaway train. All this time, I thought he was the conductor, but he's so far removed from having control that he's just along for the ride, and he wants to get out of this alive. "Irina kinda... believes she can be semi-possessed by the dead," James informs me.

"Are you high on the shit she's doing?" I ask.

"Virgin blood? No," James responds, "I don't have the taste for it."

"And what do you mean she's possessed? Does she have some multiple personality fuck-up?" I ask, information pouring over me, none of it plausible.

James holds out one hand in a motion that requests me to pause and listen, "She was possessed by that model that committed suicide... the Romanian Rapunzel, or something like that. Then... well... she said she got bit by a lesbian vampire backstage at that Michael Lorrie show that had the body bag finish. Apparently, she killed a Mexican, then they dragged the body out of the venue. As you recall, everyone loved it- your brother especially."

I lean back, looking up at the ceiling, and I ask, "What the fuck are you telling me, James? She'd be arrested for that."

"Apparently not. Not at all," James responds, almost like he appreciates Irina's power, "They didn't even question her. Or she ate the cop that questioned her. Either way..."

"Either way, Irina is eating models to stay young," I say to myself.

"And for pleasure," James adds, "She really seems to enjoy it."

"This is unbelievable," I mumble, "The face of our campaign ate the face of Marc Jacobs?"

"Pieces of it, yeah," James confirms, "And don't be so dramatic, she was only the face of the fragrance campaign, dude."

"And now Irina is... where?"

"Now she's at dinner," James says, looking at the time on his phone.

"Dinner like..." I say.

"The restaurants are pretty shitty in her neighborhood," James says, as though this is a reason that Irina could eat people without judgment.

"She lives in the East Village," I remind him.

James shrugs.

"Take me to her," I say.

"Take you to... the murderous succubus... who you just found out was... a murderous succubus?" James recaps my request slowly. "If you really want to meet with her, tell her you have the tapes," he says, a distant fear flickering in his eyes. "Then she'll come to you."

THE VISIT

"Holy shit!" Isabella yells, and the house carries her shriek up to my room.

I immediately search for the crowbar.

My text to Irina was sent less than a half hour ago.

Either is Irina already here, James has broken into the house, or Isabella has finally seen The Boy and The Girl. Has The Boy shown her the ugly side he now permanently resides on?

"I am literally in love with you," I hear Isabella yell, and this makes me fix my hair, then walk down the hall, hoping to see her looking up at me when I reach the staircase.

Of course, Isabella isn't waiting for me, and as I carefully make my way down the stairs, I hear a lightning-fast flurry of jokey rambling, which confirms who my guests are. I speed my pace up to match the rapid-fire words.

At the bottom of the stairs, the best greeting I can come up with when face-to-face with my visitors is a frozen grimace.

"Andrew," Irina says, then shoots me a smile, "I met your live-in model. She looks good enough to-"

"-what a pleasant surprise," I interrupt Irina, avoiding the innuendo she was about to unload. I move next to Isabella, so close that our arms touch, then I mention, "I didn't expect to see you here tonight."

Isabella agrees with the statement, but not the sentiment, by adding, "I know right, like when did good things start happening in my life?"

"Introduce yourselves formally," Irina demands.

"I'm Regis," is the quick-tongued response, then he reaches his hand out.

"She's Isabella," I say, then I step forward and shake Regis' hand.

"Relax," Isabella says, reaching over my shoulder so she can shake hands with Irina.

"This is fashion's Sid and Nancy," I say, properly introducing the couple.

"She's Sid," Regis clarifies, pointing at his girlfriend.

"Let's go have some diner food, or- you know- do whatever people come to New Jersey to do," Irina says, sensing that I want them out of the house and away from Isabella.

"Mostly, people seem to come here because they can't afford to live in the city, or they need to dispose of a body," Isabella says.

Irina shoots me a glance.

I shake my head, begging Irina to have mercy.

"I don't want to impose, but are you much of a cook?" Regis asks Isabella.

"Can we stop talking about food?" I demand.

"I hope you like Cup Noodles," Isabella says, then begins a runway strut toward the kitchen.

When she realizes no one is following her, Isabella turns, then asks, "Is that not supermodel food?"

"Irina likes the atmosphere of a meal more than the Cup Noodles part," Regis explains.

"Oh, well, we have a table... many tables... in this house. Nearly all of them can be used to simulate a diner-dinner. We don't need to leave," Isabella says, her pep being replaced with predictable shyness.

We arrive at a point where I have to make an incredibly difficult decision. I can invite Isabella to the meeting with Irina, essentially catering a meal with Irina's favorite food- young model- or I can throw Irina and Regis out on their asses, then I'll have to face the wrath of Isabella as she informs me that I haven't changed and I'm still "Lux'ing" models.

The tipping point, the reason why I let Irina stay, despite her deadly potential, is the fact that Isabella is finally enthusiastic about befriending another model. A supermodel has elevated the young girl's spirits and straightened her posture. Isabella is happy and this calms me down. It almost makes me appreciative that Irina is here.

I don't let myself forget that I too am a monster. What I did to Madeleine has haunted me ever since we left that hotel room. The only reason Madeleine is still alive is because Irina broke down the door and provided her with an escape route. This complicates placing blame for the event.

The bizarre pause that fills the house convinces Irina of something, then she walks by me, toward the library, even though there's no way she could know where the library is... unless Cassie had invited her to the house before. I always forget how old Irina is. She's not as old as Cassie, but she started so young that she doesn't have to be as old as Cassie to be in Cassie's circle of friends. Irina's instant fame put her in a different class.

Inside the library, Irina and Regis sit on the sofa to the right of the fireplace, while Isabella and I end up on the sofa to the left.

I wait for Irina to snap her fingers, instantly conjuring a fire in the fireplace, but when this doesn't happen, I begin to regret that I didn't take some time earlier to google what a succubus is capable of.

Regis, the voice of this operation, begins his rapid-fire delivery again, "Alright. We know you have the screeners. I want you to tell me what you think is happening, then I'll tell you what's really happening. Unless... now is not the right time." Regis looks at Isabella for a very long time, trying to figure something out. I hope he's not trying to warn her.

"It's the right time," I say, nodding slowly.

Isabella is the reason why we have the hard drives. I don't try to "save" her from this situation, because so often when I try to do that, I just make things worse. Isabella is part of this- she's been given information, she processed it, stole it, hid it, and after I forced her to do all of that, she did what Lux was unable to do, and she forgave me.

"So what do you think is happening?" Irina asks, relaxing on the sofa.

"If we're going to have this conversation, you have to promise not to hurt the people I love," I say.

"Like Isabella?" Irina asks, attempting to throw me.

I don't miss a beat because I want to be clear, "Like Isabella," I say.

"We won't hurt Isabella, and you know I'd never hurt Michael," Irina says. "So tell us what you've figured out, and we'll tell you if you're right."

"Okay," I say, leaning forward, my elbows digging into my thighs, "I think, you're some sort of ageless cannibal-"

"-whoa. Ga-ross. Cannibal sounds so fucking damaged," Irina says. Mimicking my pose, like we're shooting a MLORE ad, Irina leans forward further, then explains, "Here's the deal. I'm sort of the really attractive gray area between a lespire and a succubus. They don't have a good name for it, besides- you know- 'supermodel with an attitude.'"

"A lespire?" Isabella asks, and I pray that she doesn't start referencing the movies we Netflixed.

"We were calling it lespire for a while there," Regis confirms.

Isabella and I simply accept what we're being told. This normally exciting information now just seems like a handicap because we live in an age where vampire stories are no longer fun because if a vampire bit you now, you'd live forever. At this point, getting through today alone seems like an impossible burden, to add to it is a punishment.

"Lespire- lesbian vampire," Irina adds, then qualifies it, "I'm a lespire with a boyfriend. I met Regis before I became a lespire, and luckily he's very liberal. He's okay with me eating women, but if he eats another girl's pussy, I will bite off his dick, then eat his heart. It's a good understanding we have. We make it work."

"You can't eat girls anymore. It's wrong," I tell her straightway.

"How Republican," Irina sighs.

"How human. This is the human reaction," I say, standing up.

"Sit down," Irina demands, and I comply. "I'm not totally human, I told you that," she reminds me.

"How did this happen?" I ask.

"That's a story for another time," Regis says.

"Now is another time," I assert.

"It's complicated, and every time I go into detail, no one gives a shit," Irina responds. "A Latino dies," she adds.

"Lots of people have died," I remind her.

"And I never will. Bizarre to think about," she muses dully.

"So this will never end?" I ask, with fear.

"I mean, you could burn my body and it would end, but I don't think you'd be able to explain that to your brother. 'Hi, Michael. Sorry, I set the face of your collection on fire, but I don't believe in her lifestyle,' yeah, that would go over well. Imagine what the fashion bloggers would say."

"How'd you meet Michael?" I ask, then immediately shift my question, "More importantly, is Michael whatever you are?"

"Did you just ask if your brother is a lesbian vampire?" Regis questions, like I was the ridiculous sounding one in this conversation.

"I know you're all, 'I don't watch Michael's shows,' but you must remember the body bag show," Irina says.

"Don't describe what was inside the sheet," I request.

"Okay, since you brought it up... there was a real person wrapped in the sheet! Well, it was just a body at that point. That's what happens when you have a Mexican standoff between a Mexican with a gun, a Lespire with a crush, and a baby sister who I couldn't see get hurt again."

"I'm sorry that happened to you," Isabella says.

Irina's eyes flash with the cumulative souls of all her victims, as she tells us, "Now, because of the situation I've been placed in, I'm going to eat people, forever. Ya know how, in the movies, they're always like, 'Edward is a bloodthirsty immortal motherfucker, but he only eats cows,' well, that's not my deal. Maybe Edward is a River White style vampire, but with lespires and succubi, we eat people, straight up."

"She can turn into a giant bat-like creature too," Regis says, "That's how she escaped that day at the hotel."

"So what's your weakness?" I ask, unwilling to dignify Regis' ridiculous revelation.

"Well, I have to commit awful acts every day of my life, and eventually I'll watch everyone I love die, plus I have to be associated with all those shitty vampire books and movies forever," Irina says, then puffs out her bottom lip in a parody of a sad child.

Sensing that I'm confused as fuck, Isabella is starstruck, and Irina might be on the verge of a meltdown, Regis asks, "Do you want to take a break, and listen to a song?"

The entire room nods in agreement.

"This song is perfect for us," Irina says, staring at me, as Regis reaches into the waistband of his pants, then pulls out a CD.

"Perfect for what?" I ask.

"What we're putting together," Irina says.

There's the phrase. There's the chill. I can't use 'we' for this collection. Too many people would be implicated with that phrasing. *We* would mean Karen and me/ *We* would mean Michael and me/ *We* would mean that angry Italian guy halfway around the world and me/ *We* would mean Lux and me. Maybe that last 'we' is what I want, and I never use 'we' because I've accepted I can't have it. Maybe I want all the credit, but more realistically, I don't want to take anyone down in my vortex. If it's just Andrew Lorrie, the only one who's trapped in the rubble is me.

Regis removes either *Post* or *Boxer* from the stereo, then places his CD in the tray.

We're all quiet, as Regis walks back to the sofa to sit next to the otherworldly being he'd do anything for.

The sound of piano keys being stabbed surrounds us, then Vanessa Carlton's little girl voice begins to sing.

"I walked to Vanessa during my first show after I became what I am," Irina admits, almost sullen. Something about the statement- maybe the humanity in Irina's delivery- wins me over.

No. Not the humanity. It's the nostalgia.

Nostalgia is essential in my work. It is my fuel. Those grains of sand in the giant hourglass get pressed with the pressure of creation, then the hourglass becomes thicker- another transparent layer to warp the image of its contents.

No designer can resist nostalgia, and this is why I'll have my girls walk to "White Houses," a song that means something to the people who worked in this collection. I want to use it in a way that will enhance its meaning. I want its significance to run deeper.

"I'm afraid for us," I say, exhaling as the song plays.

The collection will premiere, and I'll do something bad.

Irina, breaking out of the trance the song put her in, asks, incredulous, "You think we should be scared, Andrew? Scared of what? The critics? The heels? The internet? I want you to show the collection you've always wanted to force into this world. I want to walk down that runway selling the shit out of exactly what you want me in. I don't care what *they* think. I've been in safe, clean garments getting rave reviews for so many seasons, and I can tell you both, designer and model, please understand that *their* approval won't fix anything. It will make you numb. You'll be left thinking, 'Now what?' instead of having that adrenaline pumping through your veins. Adrenaline tastes terrible. That's why I had the screeners set up. When people are willing and eager, they're soft and their soul is weak. It's hard to steal the soul of someone hopped up on the amazing freedom of riding a new risk. So, yes, I want to get my hands dirty. I want to make people question everything in their generic looking room. I want to confront these suburbabies, instead of just pandering to them. I want to show people what they want, before they know they want it. They'll listen, and I'll listen to you, if you listen to me."

"I can do that," I say, quietly, fearing I'm forming a pact.

Irina copies my intense stare, as she tells me, without a hint of her fading Brazilian accent, "If you hand me a safe garment with clean lines, it will be what you're buried in."

"In that case, I still need to design your piece," I admit, and Regis nods at this, pleased with the truth this impromptu meeting has been bursting with.

Gravely serious, Irina begs, "So, Andrew... you can continue on your path of complete and total destruction, but make absolutely sure it's all worth watching."

THE INVITE

I work on Irina's piece, while finalizing the cast with a confidence I've never had before. When Isabella saw the digitals of the "We Are The World" version of our casting, she was in fashion blogger mode and told me- yes-without a doubt, I'm still racist. It was clear that I needed help putting the cast together, and it was also clear that James would eliminate far more girls than he would add to the lineup.

During the creation of my MLORE collection, I found myself surrounded by women of color- there was Libby, Madeleine- and for a while- I even had Lux. Hell, Isabella is half-Mexican. Now, I even have the undead Brazilian, Irina. Considering that Isabella and Irina look white, I won't even get credit for them.

Brazilians seem to defy easy classification.

Back in LA, during one of our McDonald's trips, Chloe Warren took out her phone and showed me an amateur web page of a Brazilian girl who was practicing her basic English on a school monitored blog. The Brazilian girl, Maribel, had trouble articulating her excitement for Chloe and her bandmates, but the passion in her fractured writing was crystal clear. It was reminiscent of the hundreds of times I watched a foreign girl, who had been prematurely plucked out of school in the middle of her English lesson, struggle through a video interview with one of the growing number of fashion websites. The girl's nervous trouble with the complicated, occasionally illogical language was always a mix of endearing effort and nerve-wracking failure. Most of the time, I felt required to do the talking so these young models didn't have to worry about getting cornered into what could be an embarrassing interview. It turns out, maybe these girls were better suited to be speaking about my collections than I was. In the blog posts that Chloe showed me, Maribel, when she got too flustered, would merely write, "Come to Brazil!" as though it was a verbal crutch.

Irina has always had a complete mastery of the English language. She seems in control of all facets of her life and speech is no different. The *models.com* profile, and the small hint of an accent are the only clues that Irina is Brazilian. It's nearly impossible to tell a Brazilian by their looks. As I mentally acknowledge this, I start to think about Maribel's demand, "Come to Brazil." If we were all Brazilian, the race of my runway models would be a non-issue. Our runways would be filled with various tints of women, but there would be a unity that matched the ambiguity.

Could it be that when the Brazilians repeat, "Come to Brazil," they aren't making a request for travel, but instead are sharing a mantra that should be infused into a complicated industry? Maybe, if we all came to the same understanding that Brazil has, a lot of our problems would be solved. I've never been to Brazil to know if things are peaceful there racially, and I guess there's only one way to find out what it's like there. Maybe, after this collection, I will "come to Brazil" after being told so frequently, with such enthusiasm, that "Brazil loves you!"

I march up and down the hall of my workshop, studying my mannequins. I briefly wish that these pore-less, emotionless, stiff "women" could display my collection instead of the models. I imagine a conveyor belt scenario. *They* couldn't complain about the color of my models if all my models were this weird gray color, like the people on the suicide hotline poster at the train station. Sure, the feminists would destroy me. I'd be taking jobs from women. I'd be crowned "woman-hating" Andrew Lorrie, despite the fact that I surround myself completely with women in an attempt to establish some sort of order in my life.

To try and recreate the mannequins would run the risk of being inundated with cries of "gray-face" which seems like a topic everyone can get mad about. I'd (unsuccessfully) argue that the graying of the models allowed for the fairest casting possible because looking bland and being a uniform height and weight would be the only requirements to walk for me. Lux's measurements remain my prototype for everything below the neck. Eliminating the models would place the focus on my creations, and I wouldn't have to compete with God's masterpieces. I could sit with my friends and watch the show from the front row.

I was assigned Irina as the "face" of the campaign. That was Michael's casting decision. The rest of the girls, he doesn't seem to care about. All of the castings were about Irina.

Irina is the epicenter of MLORE.

Irina is the face of MLORE.

An image flashes in my mind- Isabella raising a mask to cover her perfect face.

Knowing what must be done, I key into the locked middle room in the workshop, then I make my way to Jessica, who's sitting at the sewing machine.

"I need you for something kinda important," I say to her.

Jessica looks at me, her blue eyes lighting up in a way that makes me feel like I have the best assistant in all of fashion.

"How are your paper mâché skills?" I ask.

"Suck my dick," hops out of Jessica's mouth. She puts a hand to her lips, but the words are already out. She seems to mentally review my question, then shrugs and sticks with her initial answer.

"I'm being serious," I say.

"I'm not some little kid you can send to the arts and crafts tent so she doesn't get too close to the fireworks," Jessica says.

"Is that a summer camp metaphor? I wasn't well liked at summer camp," I say, lost.

"I thought I proved myself to you. I'm going to be pulling some all-nighters for this Irina dress," Jessica whines.

"You did prove yourself. That's why I'm asking you to make 29 paper mâché masks from that stack of fashion magazines in the other room," I say, the number revealing my intention.

"You're using them for the runway," Jessica says. She smiles. She knows what I'm plotting and she seems pleased to be central to the plot.

Getting close to Jessica, in a hushed tone, I tell her, "You have to make these masks, off-hours, in secret. I'm going to give you a pass that will get you into the venue before the models show up for their practice walk. You need to get the masks in there, without anyone noticing. I'm leaving it up to you to get this done. I have a prototype of what the mask will look like. It's in my Chanel purse. Take it out when no one is looking, then go home for the day, and get to work."

Jessica whispers, "I almost missed the call again, huh?"

"I'm a firm believer in second chances," I say, "And, I was beginning to worry that I was molding you in my image, but you handled that second chance pretty damn well, so you definitely haven't absorbed as much of my technique as I feared."

THE ELIMINATION

Everything possesses a crisp clarity. All of the obstructions have been sliced away; the path is clear. I become absolutely positive of certain facts. Irina will not stop grabbing for the blood of the beautiful. I cannot destroy her. No one can break a determined person's drive. However, detours are possible.

After my meeting with the printers regarding my design for Irina's dress, I realize that I'm close to my friend's condo. I decided to show up at the American Felt Building, unannounced, the day after Irina showed up at my home, unannounced.

I feel equal to Irina now, and this equality makes me powerful.

Regis answers the door, reviews me, then gives me a nod, getting it, understanding the reason for this visit.

"Babe?" he calls out.

Irina walks out from the bedroom, looking like a beautiful woman, not like an undead slice of perfection and this excites me. My plan becomes etched in stone.

"Irina, I need you to do me a big favor," I say.

Irina rolls her eyes, as she struts toward me, confirming, "I know what I'm doing is-"

"-I want you to use your... power, affliction, skill- whatever you want to call it- to help me solve a problem," I admit.

"Isn't that what the runway show is about?" she asks, suddenly innocent and doe-eyed.

Regis' eyes are now slits. His initial trust begins to show cracks.

"This isn't going to happen in on a runway. It's going to happen in a brownstone," I say.

Regis steps between Irina and me.

"Ew. Andrew. Can you not?" Irina sighs, inspecting her nails, bored. Another guy trying to fuck her. Yawn.

"Exactly," I say, my blood pumping with excitement that she reacted with disgust when she thought I was coming onto her. "I want you to take that disgust and unload it on a man who asks innocent women the question you thought I was asking."

"Can you grow a pair and tell me what you need me to do, Andrew?" Irina requests, as Regis continues to body-block me from the dangerous succubus so I don't hurt her.

"I want you to do what you did to those girls, to someone else," I say, uneasy, more cracks appearing in my confidence.

"You were horrified by my actions, remember?" Irina asks.

"Yeah. I remember, but I'm more horrified by someone else's actions. I'll be okay with what you do, as long as you do it to the right people."

"You're not going to manage my meals," Irina says. Regis nods at this.

"I'm not trying to do that," I respond, raising my hands to show there's nothing up the sleeve of my self-designed dress shirt.

Irina rolls her hand, almost mocking my gesture, and says, "That's the fucked up part of this industry. Everyone wants to tell you what to eat. Don't eat this, do eat that, why haven't you eaten today, that's not good for you, that's not a substitute for real food, don't eat a teenage girl- it's like back the fuck off."

"Irina, please. I'm going to set everything up, all you have to do is walk into the room and become... you," I say, oversimplifying everything. "It's the clear-cut right thing to do," I lie to myself. I search for an example that validates my blood-lust, and I find it. "Remember that show where the serial killer only killed other serial killers? Maybe that could be you?" I suggest.

Regis shakes his head, then says, "No. She'd be the type of person who eats the showrunner after he stretches the series past its prime for three unnecessary seasons of pointless garbage."

"Maybe you could eat- I don't know- cab drivers and internet perverts?" I suggest, taking ingredients off the table, like Karen would do with me.

"Think about what you're suggesting. How can I put this?" Irina says, then the example hits her, "Imagine if you got a disease that made you suck dicks."

"I don't think you can catch gay," I say. "Can you?" I ask, in a quieter voice, merely because I'm completely at risk by exposure.

Irina giggles, then corrects me, "Actually, this is not about gay, it's something different. It's like... you become a... dick wolf. Imagine you need to suck dicks because you're a dick wolf that is powered by your awful hunger."

"Is this really a necessary alternate reality we have to craft?" I ask.

"It's the only way I know how to explain this to you," Irina says. "Where was I? Oh yeah, so you need dicks. Like you *need dicks*. You'll die without dicks. All you think about is dick, dick, dick."

"Okay, can we fast forward?" I demand.

"Well, dick wolf, what if I suggested that you only suck cabby dicks? How's that sound to you?" Irina asks me.

What started out as the most disturbing parallel timeline imaginable, slowly begins to make sense. "I'd seek out hot, clean, young people because if I'm going to be a dick wolf, I might as well make it as pleasurable as possible," I say.

"That's a bingo," Irina responds, pleased that I picked up on the moral of the story.

"And that's why you don't eat people with the most meat. It's not about the biggest meal, it's about the tastiest meal," I realize, but there is an asymmetry in Irina's actions, so I ask, "In that case, why did you eat the executioner?"

"Because I had to. I mean, I can eat guys, I just prefer girls," Irina says, illuminating things further.

"So if there was a good reason for you to eat a guy, you'd do it?" I ask, the wheels turning, plans progressing, problems being solved.

"For brutal revenge, sure," Irina says.

"I need you to eat Lux's sugar daddy, then you'll be the only face of my collection," I say, laying it all out on the table.

"You're forgetting something, Andrew. I already *am* your face," Irina responds with a bit of a laugh.

"I meant runway. You'll be the only face on the runway," I clarify.

Items that seemed meaningless before now hold a crucial purpose.

"I'm not wearing 30 looks. That's creative, but for me to have that much energy, you're gonna have to throw me more than just a Marc girl," Irina says.

"You'll have two looks. You'll open. You'll close," I say.

"Right, but there will be other girls walking, and you can't just remove their faces. Trust me. I've tried it before," the succubus informs me.

"That's the part that I have to worry about. I'm making a promise. You take care of a problem for me, and I'll take care of my end of the deal. After this meeting, I'll be working around the clock on your piece," I say, throwing out everything I can offer.

"You're promising this?" Irina asks, and the fact that she's curious about my proposition shows that not only do I have the upper hand, but she also believes in my ability to pull this off.

"I'm promising that you'll be the only face on the runway," I say, with an intimate pleasure.

Everyone goes somewhere else in their head for a moment, as though we're all finally accepting how extreme everything has become.

"I wasn't always like this, you know," Irina says.

"Neither was I," I admit.

"But here we are," Irina says, wobbly, until it's like she realizes something, then it clicks for her, and her posture improves, "Monday. We'll do it on Monday. I'm just showing up there and doing my thing though, that's it. I'm leaving right after. I have places to be."

These words probably mirror Lux's agreement with the studio executive, and for the first time, I *want* to watch.

Adding an additional clause to the contract, Irina says, "If this is a setup, I'll escape your little trap, then eat Isabella and Lux immediately after."

"This isn't a setup. I just want him gone. I need her back," I sigh.

"You're killing just to keep her?" Irina marvels.

"I'm not killing him. He made a decision to meet a beautiful woman in a hotel room. It's a mutual arrangement. He gets an experience, and she gets what she needs to survive. You'll meet up, and we'll see where it goes."

THE OPTION

"If u want to walk MLORE, meet me @Veselka @11. If u don't, goodbye," is the text that required four nervous drafts before being sent to Lux.

I chose Veselka in the East Village because they never close, so Lux will have no excuse for skipping this meeting; I'll wait however long it takes for her to arrive. I also chose this location because it's cheap, so this won't be another well-dressed man picking up a big check in exchange for his needs being met. I made sure not to choose the type of place an LA asshole would select. I know the places that an LA asshole would love in New York because I was an LA asshole for many years of my life. I remind myself that this meeting is about two disconnected friends sharing some cheap pierogi and beer. We'll either make up, or one of us will walk out. I know which scenario I prefer, but I'm confident I'll be able to handle either.

At Veselka, I find an open table alongside a big window that faces the mural painted on the side of a 24-hour grocery store. With this position, I can catch a glimpse of Lux before she sees me, as long as she's taking East 9th. I don't know how I'll feel when I see the girl I used to regard as my best friend, but now regard as just another model in trouble.

Ten minutes before our scheduled meeting, I order Lux and myself pierogi and bottles of White Lion. If the food gets cold before Lux gets here, it's completely her fault. If I finish my White Lion before Lux gets here, I'll just drink hers.

I respond to a text from Jessica about the printer, then a couple of minutes later, I approve her first mask.

The food comes, but I don't touch it.

Falling into old habits, I gulp my beer, but I'm aware enough regarding the situation I'm in that I slow down. I lower the bottle, and when I do, I see that, headed straight for my table, is a model I once knew.

Lux.

She's wearing a black Opening Ceremony button down with chain detail on the shoulders and cuffs, paired with sleek black jeans that almost shine. I recognize her black pumps, but I try to convince myself they aren't from the Vanessa Thach collection we designed together. Lux looks like she's headed to a funeral. I hope she has more black outfits, just in case the movie exec's wake is in New York and someone tips her off about when it will be.

I swallow hard, because I'm about to change things for Lux, but I'm not going to force her to choose sides. I'm going to leave the decisions up to her, something that she's consistently demanded.

I don't get up to greet Lux, and she doesn't make eye contact with me. She sits down at the table, then declares, immediately, "We aren't discussing him."

"Of course we aren't. You're never going to see him again, so…" I trail off, getting right down to it.

For the first time since she arrived, Lux's big eyes meet my intense stare, and she says, with an edge, "I don't remember you having the right to make that call."

"There's nothing that can change what's been done. But I can change, and so can you."

"What are you saying?" Lux asks, and the way she poses the question is hopeful.

"Here," I respond, sliding an envelope across the table.

Lux opens the envelope. Inside is a check. The first check. The first of however many checks she needs- even if it bankrupts me.

"Fuck you, Andrew," she says, tossing the envelope onto my plate.

I pick up the discarded gift, then slide it back in front of her. I start to explain, "I don't want-"

"-I don't want you doing this. I do not want this," Lux's voice waivers, then she puts her hand to her mouth, and after a second of silence, she recovers flawlessly.

"You're going to need this money," I say, dropping another hint.

"It's not a big deal. I wanted money. Not this money," she tells me.

"The amount on that check is a payment for overtime wages for the Andrew Lorrie collection. It's a check for your work, which was so successful, it generated revenue- for someone, I assume, hopefully, somewhere."

I sense a second of a smile on Lux's pouty lips when I release this unexpected statement of self-deprecation. The memory of the night before the Andrew Lorrie collection walked creates a golden moment that transcends whatever anger or offense is being cataloged at this table.

"I'm not taking this, but I will walk for you," Lux says, a compromise.

Before that happens, there's a discussion that needs to take place, so I say, "He's not going to be there. Ever again."

"I'll decide that."

"No. You won't," I say, slowly shaking my head.

"It's not your decision."

I pick up my fork, then I say, "The decision has already been made. Call him."

Lux shakes her fringe back and forth.

"Call him. Right now," I demand.

After a massive sigh, an eye roll, and an adjustment in her chair that could have been a consideration to flee, Lux takes out her phone. She presses the screen three times, then listens.

I watch, everything going according to plan.

Lux's big eyes get bigger when she hears who picks up.

"Sorry, wrong number," Lux says, then immediately ends the call. She looks at the contact on her phone, checking to make sure she chose the right person.

Lux's phone vibrates, and she drops it onto the table.

"What's going on?" she asks.

"Watch the video I just sent you," I say.

I toss a pair of white earbuds onto her plate.

"You're going to want audio for this," I add.

Lux reluctantly picks up the earbuds and puts them in. She plugs them into her phone, then presses on the screen.

A video begins playing.

"You're casting Charlie O'Shea?" Lux asks.

THE DAUGHTER ISSUE

I drop the i-D magazine onto Michael's desk.

"Check out the cover," I say, presenting him with a physical reminder that I took control of the shoot, and because of this, the story went from an interior piece to a cover piece.

The photograph, true-to-concept, is comprised of my face and Michael's face chopped down in the middle, then the halves are matched up. I'm on the left side, Michael is on the right side. As is the tradition with i-D, the cover subject is winking. Since they sliced the cover down the middle, I'm winking, Michael is not. They chose me to be the one winking- possibly because my signature stare into the camera was too off-putting, or possibly because my look was a wink in itself.

"I'm going to get a larger version of that cover for the apartment," Michael tells me. He doesn't seem annoyed. This is the first picture of me that will be on display in Michael's home. I begin to feel guilty about waltzing in with the magazine and presenting it as though it would be something toxic to him. He seems to like the cover. My momentary consideration of mercy is snuffed out when Michael says, "We only have a couple of days until the show, and we still aren't at the level of buzz we need."

The cover- a cover that wouldn't exist if I didn't intervene- becomes not enough for Michael.

"Maybe if your couture collection turned out better, the hype would be bigger," I say, reminding him of the buzz-less whisper the collection arrived with in January.

"Couture did fine. It did what it needed to do," Michael assures me.

"Well, I'm staying away from the press, just like you and Karen demanded," I mumble, not sure what else I can do.

"For the next phase of the publicity for this line..." Michael says, then pauses, constructing the wording for what he's about to mandate, "We're going to need you to do the Vogue piece and leak that you're Sienna's Wolfe's father."

I have to shift my body to conceal the gasp that escapes my mouth. My embarrassment about my conduct continues, mutates, balloons. I clear my throat, then say, "I don't think that's a good idea."

"Your track record with intuiting what's a good idea isn't that great," Michael points out.

I hold onto the crooked bridge of my nose, then release it. I ask my brother, "Don't you think I've fucked up Sienna's life enough?"

"Sure. Absolutely," he says, agreeing wholeheartedly.

"So, we shouldn't do this," I respond, hoping the idea was a temporary moment of sadism.

"*We* won't be doing anything. This is something that *you* will do," Michael tells me. "Unless, of course, you and Sienna both want to make the announcement together. I'll allow that since she photographs so well. That Cassie Wolfe DNA mixes nicely with the features that you and I share, and it's-why are you laughing, Andrew?"

"Because I'm not doing it," I say. I'm almost amused that, somehow, I actually thought that Michael might have given me MLORE to help me. "I'm not doing it," I repeat, to make myself clear. When I don't get a response, I ask, "Do you know how long it's been since I've spoken with Sienna? Do you comprehend how poorly my last conversation with her went?"

"She showed up to your after-party," Michael mentions, "It seems like she was reaching out. Offer her a part in the show as an apology. I'll make the sacrifice and let her walk. I'm sure that James can remove one of the girls we cast so we can make room."

"I'm not pimping out Sienna for your show," I say, my laughter evaporating due to the heat of my anger.

"Yes. Good. At least you're referring to it correctly. It's *my* show, and I'm telling you that I want to Sienna walk for me. You need to promote this line because that's what I used to do, but I hired you to do it. This is part of your contract. Do I need Jessica to e-mail you a copy of your contract?"

"I'll promote MLORE, but I need to put the finishing touches on the line, then I can go in full publicity mode," I say, the casualties becoming mere inconveniences. What the fuck has happened to us this season?

"What you're going to tell Vogue is, and if you want to write this down, you can, 'My daughter, Sienna Wolfe, will be walking the debut of MLORE,' or you can make up something about the fact that you became a Michael Lorrie man while working on MLORE, and you've come to realize that you can't run from responsibility, so you've decided to confront your failures as a man, and you're embarking on a quest to right some wrongs. Whichever option works for you."

"I'm not willing to put my daughter out there," I tell my brother.

Michael leans back in his throne, then says, "When I find a face I like, I'll personally go out and get that girl. I've been to proms, and open mics, and sorority functions, and rehab clinics. I think you can go to California for a day and see your daughter. Quite simply, you've failed to generate the buzz this collection needs, so you've placed us all in this position. Vogue is going to have to rush out the statement. This is very inconvenient for them."

"If you want the truth to come out, have Cassie make the announcement. I mean- shit- you're paying her, you might as well get something for your money."

"I already am getting something for my money," Michael assures me.

"What?" I ask.

"You don't want to know."

"Fantastic, Michael. Make Cassie do it. If you want this to happen, that's how it's going to happen."

"I don't think you're in a position where you can tell me how things are going to go," Michael says, and his words play over Lux's mirrored response.

"I won't do it," I say.

"Listen. I'm not asking you to lie. You've been lying for, what, 20 years? I'm asking you to tell the truth. Don't make me out to be the bad guy."

"I haven't lied about it. I've just... avoided the question," I say, shifting in my chair again.

"Exactly. Consider this a little bit of therapy," Michael advises me, and the mind-fucking mad scientist fabricates his psych degree right before my eyes.

"This little scheme isn't about fixing me," I say, standing up.

"You're not going to do it... because it's inconvenient for you? That's the situation that caused you to leave your daughter in the first place, isn't it? Fatherhood wasn't for you?"

I walk out of Michael's office.

As I make my way through Michael Lorrie headquarters, I realize what has to be done. I take out my personal phone, then select a number that I'm surprised still rings through.

"Hello?" a confused voice says, taking the call.

"Hi. Sienna. It's Dad."

THE END

Isabella goes up to bed, while I stay downstairs, video chatting with Jessica on my phone. I watch carefully as she alters the length of a flared skirt that connects to a leather bodice which will probably be converted to pleather for production because Michael doesn't want to get shit from PETA.

The last time I used this video conferencing app, Madeleine was entering the screener room, and now she's become a backbone of this collection, as she models this piece for us. Draping, fittings, runway, consulting- Madeleine is crucial not just because of her natural gifts, but also due to her tireless dependability.

I could have taken the train into New York for this detail work, but I decided to stay home and let my team have this moment.

This is Jessica's reward for finishing the masks.

This is Jessica's reward for *everything* she's done this season.

I'm silent, watching my girls work.

After Jessica finishes the piece, and Madeleine declares it perfect, my intern-turned-assistant looks into the camera on her phone, and says, "Andrew, this collection has really come together nicely."

I nod at this fact, and request, "Release Madeleine back into the wild, then go get some rest. We'll focus fully on the final piece tomorrow."

As soon as I close the chat, I find myself in a dark room. Streetlight pours in the front window, and the spotlight it creates is suddenly breached by The Boy and The Girl. I consult the timeline and realize we're reaching the end. I'm curious if the loop will click back over- like a track on repeat- or if it will end with the slam of the door. I thirst for the beginning of the loop, but to get there, I know that I have to confront the end, again. This is the chronological nightmare I've signed up for in invisible ink. I turn my back because I cannot watch. I walk into the kitchen, but the voices echo in this old house- the fact that they're being yelled increases their clarity. The Boy is drunk. The Girl is not. The Girl *cannot* get drunk because if the Girl gets drunk, the innocent will suffer. When

The Boy gets drunk, sometimes there are innocent casualties, and this forms the topic of conversation for the night.

"Not never, just not now," The Boy says, as though this is an acceptable answer.

"Not now? Then when?" The Girl asks.

"Later."

"Later she'll still be here."

"And the opportunities won't," The Boy says, with a shortsightedness that betrays the idea he can somehow predict what people will want *tomorrow*. Even worse, he follows this up with the ugly question, "How could you do that to your body?"

"How could I do *that* to another person?"

"It's not-"

"-fuck you for saying that. Fuck you for saying that," The Girl screams. I remember how her face looked, and it makes my eyes fill with tears.

"We have plans that can't be canceled. They're time sensitive."

"But this can be canceled? This isn't time sensitive?" The Girl asks.

"Yes and no."

"In that order?"

"In that order," The Boy says coldly.

"You're disgusting."

"I'm not going to lose my life. Not yet."

"You're going to gain a life," The Girl says, unconvincing in The Boys eyes for the first time.

"No. I'm not. Either way, I lose a life," The Boy says.

I hear The Girl plead. I hear the glass shatter. I hear the door slam. I hear The Girl sob. The loop is complete. Now, the story is fresher in my mind. Now, each experience will gain a further layer of sadness.

The entire length of the time I watched The Boy and The Girl, things played out exactly the way I remembered them, and that's a shame. I needed there to be a deviation, but there was none. In this rare situation, I craved change, yet everything remained stayed the same. I lose two essential people, again, and even though I knew it was going to happen, it still hurts just as much as it did the first time. I despise The Boy because I know the type of man he grows up to be.

When the loop begins again, The Little Girl will no longer be invisible.

THE FAVOR, RETURNED

The text that pauses my morning reads, "I'm quitting modeling and I'm gonna try writing again."

I become immediately convinced that Isabella heard The Boy and The Girl, and she left last night.

Thankfully, I'm wrong. The text is from Lux. She seems to now believe that her body is damaged, but to me, she looks exactly as she did when she was the innocent Asian girl walking into my loft to put a hand on my shoulder when my shoulders were caving in from the pressure of it all. I don't understand how she can view modeling a job, instead of a calling.

"Meet me at the workshop tonight at 8 PM. If you want to quit after our conversation, I'll let you," I send.

I refuse to fight Lux's decisions anymore, but I will try to keep her close to me. This season has taught me that I can manipulate outcomes, without manipulating people. It's about transparency and creativity. It's about bold action.

The first step in my plan to show Lux why she shouldn't leave modeling is to get my old computer back from the Chinese. I go through my personal phone and find a number that I haven't called in a very long time.

"Hi, Eunmoo. It's... Andrew Lorrie," I say, then I give him a chance to hang up on me. He doesn't take it. "You don't have to say anything," I tell the silent investor. "I need some files from my old laptop, then I promise you'll never hear from me again after I get them."

"It's okay," Eunmoo says to me, "People hate you, but your clothes are doing nice sales. Maybe they cut off tag after they buy?"

A call that seemed hopeless suddenly has a redemptive silver lining.

"Can I stop by your office and pick up the old laptop today?" I ask.

"Sure. It is in the box. I will not search. That will be up to you," Eunmoo says.

"Thank you," I tell him.

"I send you good luck for Saturday," Eunmoo says.

"I'll bring you an invite," I promise.

True to his word, when I reach Eunmoo's office, I find a box filled with relics from my short-lived second chance. I remove the laptop and a few possessions that anyone besides me would view as trash.

"You bring back?" Eunmoo asks.

"How about you pick it up on Saturday?" I tell him, giving him a black invite to the MLORE show.

Eunmoo looks at the invite, smiles at it, then says, "Okay, Andrew. Okay."

I cab back to the workshop, then I sit down at my computer.

During the breaks I have while working on Irina's piece, I sew together moments.

At 8 PM, Lux doesn't show. At 8:15, I burst out onto the street, so I can walk to the bodega and buy beer. When I look to my right, there she is. Lux is here, smoking a cigarette, wearing her brown rabbit fur coat that would be beautiful if it didn't have call girl connotations that are too close to the reality of it all.

"You look cold," I say to say to her.

"And that's why I'm stopping," Lux responds, pointing her cigarette at me.

"What are you talking about?" I ask, approaching her glowing weapon.

"You saw me and the first thought you had was, 'That girl looks cold,' and that proves I don't have what it takes."

I walk closer and say, "I also thought you look beautiful, but-" Lux interrupts me with a snort, then flicks her cigarette on the sidewalk, "-but I knew that's how you'd react, so I didn't say it," I finish my statement.

I stare at Lux for a long moment, then I begin walking back to the workshop; I don't need alcohol tonight.

I hold the door open, and without being told to do so, Lux returns to where she belongs. I immediately want to dress her, but it's not my decision if Lux is still a model.

"Why are you quitting?" I ask, as we walk down the hall, past the completed pieces.

Lux becomes distracted by the new designs. She's smiling. I see that she's reconsidering retirement, like a rapper who has put out his "last album" only to realize there are so many words he hasn't even rhymed yet.

"I don't know," Lux says, touching the pieces, permitting them to catch her imagination. "Maybe I wasn't serious. Maybe I was being dramatic."

"Why were you being dramatic?" I ask. The exec is gone, the check is in Lux's bank account, and these truths should mean that there are no roadblocks for her. Modeling is her future, now more than ever.

"Because I'm a fucked up person, Andrew. Don't hold me to this ideal," she demands.

"That ideal is long gone," I assure her.

"Well, sorry," Lux says, her big eyes finally focusing on me, "Sorry models aren't emoticons. I know it would be easier for you, but there isn't just one setting on 'dumb model girl.' Every day I've cried recently, I've also laughed just as much. There's a complex balance at work here. Nothing is terrible all the time. The great moments, they're still there- muted sometimes, but they're there. The bad times, they're still there too- no matter what you fix for me. This morning, I felt terrible. Now, I feel..."

During the seasons when the tags inside my garments had someone else's named sewn in them, Lux would sit me down and give me a pep talk when she saw me slipping. It was 50 nights filled with the type of inspirational speeches they add to sports movies. I never asked her to do it, but it was essential that she did it.

My skills are visual. Words get me in trouble.

The ability to create something beautiful has been a skill I've exploited for decades. When it comes to explaining why something is beautiful, it borders on an impossible task for me, however, to explain why Lux must continue modeling is excessively simple. The reasons number in the thousands, and I will easily pluck and present them to her, one by one.

"Could I talk to you in the workroom?" I ask, motioning toward the end of the faux runway we're walking.

Lux doesn't say anything, she merely walks ahead of me, then enters the room.

"Sit down," I say, close behind her.

A lone chair is placed in the center of the fabric-filled room.

The chair faces a long stretch of pure white wall.

Lux obediently takes a seat, keeping her coat on.

That glassy, unfocused look, now all too familiar, appears yet again in Lux's eyes.

I walk in front of the confused model, then ask, "What's the main reason why you were thinking about making this your last season?"

"I honestly don't know the answer to that question, Andrew. I guess, maybe the fact I'm in debt. I'm the only person I know whose profession has put them in debt," Lux says, and a cry begins to surface, then gets swallowed back down again. Lux shows how completely in control of her body she is and not a single tear breaks the plane of her eye makeup.

I step to the side three feet, then I press a button on the small black remote to turn on the projector I bought for the runway show.

Lux faces the blank wall, then after a few seconds, Lux faces herself.

I hit a key on my laptop, then the projector sprays out our runway test for the last Andrew Lorrie collection, and my emotions swell.

"You didn't tell me you were filming this," Lux says.

The beautiful model on the wall keeps walking toward the even bricks of the building across from the loft.

"Guys do that. They film things and don't tell girls," I remind Lux.

Before, I was worried about a designer premiering Lux to the world. Now, I'm worried about an amateur pornographer doing it.

Lux looks away, ignoring her past self. I choose to stand behind her, and I ask, "Do you see that model?"

The Lux that's projected on the wall is a model I knew, or at least thought I knew.

"Do you see that strong walk?" I ask, "That's more than just purpose. That's someone tapping into a force beyond just copying what others have done. *That* is what makes me design."

Lux puts up a hand to her mouth, unable to watch a girl who was my most trusted collaborator- a girl that she seems to envy.

"Look at her!" I yell, and Lux jerks her head back to the amateur runway test that continues to play.

"What do you see?" I ask.

"Me practicing for a moment I never got to live," she responds.

Lux wants to derail me, but I don't let her. I narrate what's happening here, "I see a girl going somewhere. The walk she's on should be pointless, but there's an art to the moment. It's like looking across a long flat stretch of night, and from that darkness emerges a figure. There's tension and excitement. There's a heartbeat. Do you hear the heartbeat, Lux? Listen."

Click-click-click comes out of the laptop connected to the projector, as two sharp heels alternate hitting the floor of the loft.

"If that heartbeat stops, so does Andrew Lorrie," I tell Lux.

"Fuck off. You're fine without me," Lux says, moving through the standard options she provides herself to address moments that require self-reflection.

I see myself in Lux. I place my hand on her shoulder, as she did for me that night I was unsure of everything.

We watch as the clip hops to another look. I've edited a stream of 35 looks together- all of them worn and walked by Lux.

"You were always there for me," I remind her.

"And recently I haven't been. I get it," Lux says, turning my message vicious.

"This is what no one understands. I wanted a show with all one look. I wanted you to walk down that runway 30 times. That's why I filmed you walking without your knowledge. I knew you wouldn't allow it, because you seem incapable of understanding why I would want this. I had to keep it a secret, which means we both kept secrets from each other. So let's call it even. Can we do that?"

I look at the back of Lux's head as she nods in agreement.

"I couldn't send you down that runway 30 times because the show would be too long, so I put together this video. In the end, I got what I wanted, and I don't remember this collection based on Galina, or Cori, or any of those girls- I remember it just as it appears in this footage," I say, and it's the complete truth.

"What about Isabella?" Lux asks.

"Isabella is different," I say.

"Who wore the blue velvet dress better?" Lux asks, "Me during the runway test or Isabella at The Imperial Hall?"

Since she's always given me her unbiased opinion about my work in the past, I return the favor to Lux, even though it could be to my detriment.

"Isabella. That piece was created to be on Isabella's body," I say.

"See?" Lux says.

"No," I counter, "You watch this footage and tell me that we aren't unstoppable."

"We aren't unstoppable," Lux says.

"Okay. Then what are we?" I ask, my hand never leaving the brown fur of Lux's coat.

"We're just two fuck-ups who need each other," Lux says.

"Yes, we are," I confirm. "Never forget that."

"We've split apart, and we're living separate lives," she acknowledges.

"Why can't we just agree to care for each other?" I ask.

"We only care about each other to ensure that someone keeps loving us, despite it all," Lux points out.

"So let's love each other, not for the other person, but for ourselves," I beg.

"Love me so I'll love you?" Lux asks.

This is how we reach an agreement. It's always a problem when two people are unquestionably alike. It creates friction. It creates altercations. It creates a stalemate.

I want to be loved, so I will love, and I will become loved.

It feels too simple.

Lux turns back and looks at me for a moment. She smiles at the option I've provided her. It's a smile so girlish that I believe for a moment that Lux *is* 18.

We're silent, as we focus on the wall, and watch my designs parade before us/ We're silent, as we watch Lux match my designs, then elevate them/ We're silent, as the heartbeat of her walk click-click-clicks with reliable tempo, and we both become positive that what we have is still very much alive.

The runway test ends, and I feel proud of my past and excited for the future. Lux agrees to remain a model, until she decides that she isn't a model anymore. I agree to let her walk for me. The next time I see Lux will either be the day of the show, or any day she sends me a text reading, "Wanna meet up later?"

Lux will make the decision on which steps she takes, and the order in which she'll take them. It's completely her decision.

THE BOND VILLAIN

Thursday afternoon arrives, as does Lux, for Michael's final walk-through.

Jessica treats our new guest coldly, and I realize that she's protective of me in a way that's both similar and different from how Karen assisted me previously. Jessica has seen me hurt, and she's working to prevent that from happening again. She doesn't understand that the same pain she's trying to shield me from will form the inspiration for the next collection we collaborate on.

After the walk-through is complete, I agree to go to dinner with Michael.

The restaurant Michael chooses for our "celebratory meal" causes me to think about Lux's accusation that I have "issues with money." I realize that I hate every person in this poorly lit, fun-devoid, movie set of a restaurant. None of the women around me are women I want to dress, but they'll be the women buying the MLORE designs that make it into production. I can only hope that they have daughters who will steal my pieces away from the closets that will forever conceal the designs I poured myself into.

The server knows Michael's name, and I'm not sure if Michael is a regular diner here, or if Jessica just makes a note when she calls in the reservation that the staff should pretend like they care who Michael is.

While we wait for our food, the conversation Michael supplies is merely a recap of his recent successes, like he was introducing Michael Lorrie instead of *being* Michael Lorrie.

When the food arrives, I have to massage my jaw before I start eating, since it's sore from the clenching I've been utilizing to mute my opinions tonight.

Michael begins to aggressively devour his steak, and in between bites, he says, "I have to hand it to you..."

I don't respond- I merely wait for the completion of a compliment I didn't expect.

"...you certainly rented a lot of mannequins.".

I hold onto the crooked bridge of my nose, then say, "The collection. What do you think about the clothes the mannequins are wearing?"

"We're definitely going to have to spend more to get these pieces into production shape, but it's apt," Michael says.

"Apt, what the fuck does that mean? The collection is apt?"

"It means, given the circumstances, it works," Michael says, then he smiles as his wine glass is refreshed, and an arm temporarily blocks the hateful gaze I'm projecting.

When we're eye to eye again, I say, "Inform me of the *circumstances*, Michael. What *circumstances* did I design under?"

"Well," Michael says, then takes a sip of his Palmer. He wipes his mouth on a napkin, then explains, "As you know, with the last season's M.Lorrie collection, we had trouble getting established faces to walk for the line because the ready-to-wear pieces got a little... patterny. The girls didn't see the appeal in taking trade, so I knew- in order to reinvigorate that dormant interest- I needed to trick the models into thinking that my ready-to-wear collection *might* be good. Once they see the collection you've put together, they'll have to admit that trade is worth it, and their soulless agents won't shake my company down for cash. Next September, the models will work for trade, thinking they're getting your designs, but they'll get whatever cheap garbage a group of wannabe designers submits to me. Or maybe I'll use that first collection you designed, what did you call it? The POGO? Well, that's not important now. What *is* important is keeping these girls on their toes and out of my pocket."

"That's what you meant by apt?" I ask, taking the napkin off my lap, then tossing it on the table, nearly knocking over my half-empty glass of Palmer.

Michael takes another bite of his steak, savoring it. "Do you want to know... MLORE?" he asks, and this is the happiest I've ever seen my brother since we were children. When I don't respond, he continues, "No one will actually believe I designed the ready-to-wear line, but if people believe *you* designed the line, and they know they don't have to wear your albatross of a first name on their clothes, then they'll get everything they want. We went a little more high fashion on this one, and I'm okay with spending the money to have another guy come in and tame all your looks for the buyers. I'll explain it to everyone behind the scenes, and the people who aren't behind the scenes will just see a good collection and a rebirth of a brand."

"And all of us get used along the way?"

Michael shakes his head, "I think that's a little shortsighted. I've kept all of your friends employed. That's not cheap. I let you design exactly what you wanted, twice. That was expensive. I was so generous, and I didn't even make you take out a mortgage on your home in LA."

"What happens to your plan if everyone ends up hating the line on Saturday?" I ask, trying to bend Michael's carefully curated reality that he's so proud of.

"You want to talk worst case scenario? Okay. Let's see. You run my consumer label into the ground, then you never work again. I swoop in, have my team design yet another boring-but-safe collection, then I'll look like a genius who 'put things back on track' after your devastation. I'm the good guy cleaning up after the bad guy, and that's a damn good position to be in."

"Let me tell you, it's a shitty position to be in," I inform my brother.

"This *will* work," he, in turn, informs me.

"How ugly," I say, ready for dinner to be over.

"The collection looks great," Michael says, for the first time.

"I mean you," I say, staring at him.

Michael stands up, and remarks proudly, "I look great."

"For now..." I say.

After taking out his wallet, Michael pays for the meal in a small stack of hundred dollar bills, then warns me, "If you have anything planned for the show that's not on the itinerary, I'll ruin your life. Have a good night, Andrew."

THE JUICE

Irina stands in the far room of the workshop, modeling the final dress. Everything works. All of it.

Tomorrow, we'll show this collection, and I'll be truly happy.

Irina doesn't have a mask on, because she won't be wearing one on the runway. I promised her that she'd be the *only* face of the collection, and this concept remains a crucial part of my plan.

I know the plan/ Regis knows the plan/ Irina knows the plan- Michael, however, is unaware of what's about to happen. He'd never allow this high concept gamble to grace his runway. When he arrived to do his final walk-through, I made sure to present the "safe" version of the collection- a version that will only exist in the MLORE workspace. I'm not going to send another impotent Michael Lorrie RTW collection down the runway. I won't put my girls at risk. Tomorrow, there will be danger, but one of the biggest dangers to the success of the show is, "What do we do with Michael?"

"Nothing," Irina responds to my question, then Regis starts carefully helping her out of the dress. "You'll do nothing with Michael, or else it's your ass," Irina explicitly states.

This ends the conversation in my mind, but it's a conversation between three people, and one of those people does not take this statement as a completion of the dialog.

I give myself permission to leave, and while I'm on the train headed back to South Orange, my personal phone rings. I look down at the screen and see that it's a call from a 703 number. The phone seems to ring with a threatening tone despite the commonality in sound it shares with every other incoming call I receive.

I can't bring myself to send the call to voicemail, so I swipe the screen, then put the phone to my ear. "Hello," I sigh, staring down my reflection in the train window. The man who stares intensely back at me looks ready to receive news that will collapse what he was so close to completing.

"Hey. It's Regis."

"Yup," I say, clipped, waiting for the story about how the face of my collection slipped up and ate the girls who are supposed to wear looks 9 and 15.

"Earlier you asked what we should do with your brother so you can put on the show this line deserves, and- uh- I have a solution," Regis tells me. I can't tell if he's nervous because he's always operating on a sped up wavelength.

"Irina won't do it," I say, confident in Michael's safety when Irina is involved.

"Exactly. Which is why, when I tell you this plan, I never told you this plan," Regis says. There's a pause on the line as he waits for me to verbally agree to his rules.

"Tell me your plan," I say, quietly.

"You say anything to anyone about this call, and I feed you to my girlfriend," Regis warns again. Slowing down for the first time, he says, "We need Michael out of the way before we show the videos. The moment he spots a mask, he'll shut it all down, and that's a problem."

"No matter what, he'll be there. Maybe we could lock him in a closet or..." I say, searching for answers, then I'm provided one by Regis, "I know a harmless way to let Michael attend the show, but he'll be... relaxed."

"Wait," I say, pausing this plan before we get too far in, "You are aware, on either side of the runway, I'm going to show a video of your girlfriend's victims?" I ask.

"Yeah, no shit, but the film only shows two people- the model and Dan."

"Who the fuck is Dan?" I ask.

"Dan is who you walked in on. Twice. The second time, I was arm in arm with Dan, and his arm wasn't attached to his shoulder."

I hold my breath, then I exhale a request, "Describe Dan."

"Tan, tall, thick eyebrows, let's see, what else... uh, fucking psychotic," Regis says with no respect for the dead man.

"I know Dan," I say. "Dan Carrington. I saw him at almost every fashion function I've attended. He used to constantly leave me voicemails. I know him."

"You *knew* Dan," Regis corrects me. He adds, "The room was in Dan's name because he had to be hidden before anyone else arrived. Do you understand what I'm telling you? Dan is the one who will be blamed for what happened. After the videos come out, they'll trace the room back to Dan, then they'll trace the voice back to James. Irina was never on camera, and do you really think James is stupid enough to tell on Irina? Exposing Irina means the death penalty for James, and- as you know- Irina works a hell of a lot faster than the justice system."

After my last collection, I had a voicemail from Dan on my phone. Each missed call from him was either me dodging death, or bringing death upon an unsuspecting girl. I'll never be sure now. I'm still not clear on Dan's purpose in the industry, but I am clear on why he was at so many parties. He was scouting his victims.

Regis lays it out for me, "I'm clean, you're clean, Isabella's clean, Irina's clean, and Michael- by design- is clean. So unless one of seven people involved in this says something..."

"Seven?" I ask, then I fill in the blanks, "You touch Libby or Madeleine and I'll destroy you like you're a girl on film."

"It was digital. Film is too expensive," Regis says, not scared, hopefully because he views my two model friends as innocent bystanders.

"So what's the plan?" I ask, the South Orange stop only minutes away.

"Before the show tomorrow, we'll cheers to a successful line. There will be four champagne flutes- three filled with champagne, and one flute filled with a special little mixture Irina has access to."

"We're not poisoning Michael," I say.

"Correct."

"We're not drugging Michael," I fix my statement.

"Correct," Regis confirms again.

"So what'll be in his flute?" I ask, then Regis sighs.

I look at the phone, to make sure the call isn't lost, then in a rapid-fire explanation, Regis recaps, "When I met Irina she had a toned down version of this... mixture that originally turned people into total literally eat your heart out demons, but some dude dulled it to the point that it just turns you super agreeable and super lazy- all that idle hand shit. It's basically a really good way to get someone to sit outside themselves for six hours and do whatever you want them to."

"That sounds like a drug," I say.

"Do you know many drugs that turn you into a demon? A literal demon?" Regis asks, dead serious.

"I'm not turning my brother into a demon."

"Because he already is one?" Regis asks sarcastically, then seems to be listening for a laugh. When he doesn't receive his response, he continues on, "The demon part is dulled. Some hot blonde twins defeated all the demons a couple of decades ago and- you know what? Forget the back story, you have two options, come back to New York and try the zombie juice for yourself, or let me put it in your brother's drink and show the screeners."

"I don't trust you," I tell Regis.

"What do I have to gain by fucking you over?" Regis asks.

I go through the possible ways I could be double-crossed on this. Regis could want me to show the screeners so he can say, "Andrew Lorrie was the man behind the mask." Maybe this misdirection is the way he gets his girlfriend out of the mess she's created in New York. For some reason, this scenario feels unlikely to me. I begin to suspect that Regis may be using these tapes as an insurance policy so that- in the future- the love of his life will be more careful and less aggressive.

"What are the side effects of the juice?" I ask, almost on-board. Every person I know who's downed this juice has ended up murdered by a crowbar, then their souls were consumed, so it seems impossible to know the long-term side effects of the mystery liquid.

"He'll have a hangover," Regis says.

"Then?"

"Then?" Regis repeats, "I don't know, he'll drink a Vitamin Water and take a gross shit."

"Okay. Dose him," I say, with no other option. "Actually," I add, "Bring enough for me too. If things go awfully tomorrow, I'll want an escape, and what you described sounds kind of nice."

THE PREP

The closed fist hammering on the front door draws me out of the library.

As I make my way to the noise, I try to remember how The Boy and The Girl first arrived at the house. When the sounds don't match my memory, I grip the doorknob and the knocks on the other side are so forceful that I can both feel and see the tremors on the door.

No longer willing to give in to my protective paranoia, I open the door. Standing face-to-face with my visitor, my only response is, "Lux. Shit."

"Warm welcome," an extremely put together Lux says, stepping inside. Everything she's wearing is something I've seen before and this calms my nerves. The new Lux is dressed like the old Lux, and this makes it hard to differentiate between the two.

"Is everything okay?" I ask, gravely.

"Can you not? I'm just here so we can finish up before the collection walks tomorrow," Lux says, simply.

"Oh," I respond. "That sounds great," I add, and I mean it.

"You didn't do your final walk through with someone else, did you?" Lux asks. She does an impression of my stare that's surprisingly accurate. It's clear that she's practiced this impression to reach such an advanced level of mimicry.

"I don't think I'm going to do a nerve-racking late night walk through. Our walk through with Michael was good enough. I think I'm going to go listen to Björk and spend time with my two favorite models," I say.

I grab Lux's hand, and she lets me lead her into the library.

Isabella is sitting on the far sofa, reading her Japanese book, her long legs pinned under her butt. She looks up from the book, then immediately hops to her feet. "Lux!" she squeaks, "Hi. I'm Isabella. We- uh- are the same size."

I don't mention to Isabella that her arms are slightly longer because I'm happy to have both girls here, perfect the way they are.

"Hi, Isabella," Lux says, walking over, flashing a smile. It's a smile that says, "We've both survived the Lorrie brothers."

"I'm glad you're here," Isabella says.

"After no sun and lots of expensive makeup, I'm still here," Lux responds, acknowledging that not only Madeleine, but also Isabella had to cover for her this season.

I move to the sofa, then sit down- Isabella on my left side, Lux sitting to my right. "Wanna see the final cast?" I ask.

Both girls purr with excitement, bookending me, as I scroll through my phone.

Cori's name is on the list/ Galina's name is on the list/ Madeleine's name is on the list/ Lux's name is on the list/ Libby's name is on the list/ Isabella's name is on the list. Despite having the greatest cast I've ever assembled, so many girls who belong on that runway are missing.

"We're doing a straight runway, right? No zig-zag shit, hopefully," Lux says. Normally she would already know the answer to this question, but she's missed so much that she isn't sure of any of the details. I hate the distance between myself and the girl sitting next to me.

"Wait. Menswear already showed, why is Matthew on here?" Lux asks, looking at the list. The use of male models for womenswear became possible once the masks were introduced. The inclusion of Matthew was part of my attempt to explore the limitations of casting. When *They* see one body type walking down the runway, the subject of the model will become static. The small amounts of body hair on a stomach/ hands too big even for these giant girls/ an Adam's apple/ a misplaced bulge- unexpected elements that will keep things from getting stale. During a video chat session, I had Matthew practice the walk I require, and he nailed it.

"Here's the final piece," I say, bringing it up on my phone for Lux.

I watch the side of her face as her big eyes move across the dress, then close for a long three-count. "This collection is special," Lux assures me, knowing I need it. "I like the tribute to Charlie O'Shea," she adds, conscious of a personal touch that I'm particularly proud of. Maybe my words did hurt Charlie, but now she's become an important part of my work. James' extreme action took her off the runway, but I've made sure that she'll be helping close the show.

Isabella pauses at the complicated feelings that come along with the final piece that will walk the runway.

"To fix things," I explain.

Lux asks, "What was that quote she gave after you two cyberbullied her?"

Isabella and I look at each other. We're both able to quote the exact wording because we referenced it weekly, until it stopped being funny. Neither of us repeats the words, so Lux searches for the quote on her phone. I feel both great nostalgia and great shame regarding the things we said.

During the final fitting, Irina told me that James showed her the messages I sent to Charlie. She said, "I hope you never forget what you said to that girl," and I countered with, "I hope you never forget what you did to that girl."

"Here it is," Lux says, then she reads off her phone, "Don't become obsessed with people you meet on the internet. You will sit home alone, jerking off to your computer screen, until one day, you find someone just as fucked up as you are, and you two will spend all of your free time pathetically bothering others."

"Such an important time," Isabella says.

When the nostalgia fades, and reality overtakes everything, Isabella asks, "You don't think- like- ghosts are real, and the ghosts of the screener girls will sabotage the shoes I'm walking in, do you?"

"That won't happen," I say, "I'm sure of it."

"Why?" Isabella asks, this definitive statement intriguing her.

"Because the spirits won't be able to recognize you," I say.

"Can we not? This ghost-chat is creeping me out," Lux says.

"Remember that mask you made?" I ask Isabella. "All of the girls will be wearing them, besides Irina," I reveal.

Both of them say, "Oh," then, "Why?"

For once, this isn't about me hiding Lux. Tomorrow is about protecting the innocent and exposing the sinister. This becomes more intimidating because Irina will be the only model not wearing a mask. She's not ashamed of who she is, and she's not afraid of the repercussions of her soul reaping. Irina can destroy anyone who forces her to accept the blame for what she's done- and what she'll continue to do in the future.

"I'm using the mask Isabella created as a prototype, and I'm going to mask all of my models, besides Irina, so you won't be guilty by association," I say.

After a moment of silence, I add, "I know it sucks. This is your second show, and it's your first."

"You're forgetting something," Isabella says.

"What?" I ask.

"My art is blocking out every other girl on the runway. Now *that* is power."

THE GIRL

Isabella's call time and her important role put her on an early train into the city.

I wake up leisurely- Björk's "Pagan Poetry" playing on my phone as an alarm. This is how I wanted to wake up, like Isabella was still here.

As the song plays, I'm pulled out of the room and down the hall by an unseen force.

I step inside Cassie's room one last time, and I immediately notice a new row of photographs. All of these pictures were taken this fall and winter, yet their number matches the 19 years of piecemeal memories that Cassie had assembled. I don't touch the pictures, but I relive each one, and as I move down the thickened border of the room, I feel my pain dull.

When I reach the final photograph of the second row, I find myself staring at a picture of Isabella that I did not take. She's in the house on Scotland Road, seemingly unaware of the photographer's presence. She's looking down at the hem on one of my curtain pieces, as it sits on the table in the living room. In a house that I reclaimed as mine, a girl I wanted to be mine, looked at a piece of me, as someone I don't know captured her image. I fear that James took this photograph, until I notice a reflection in the mirror on the wall of the living room. Framed in this mirror, is The Boy, with his disposable camera raised, taking a picture, because he was inspired.

I'm pulled from this moment, by the noise of the creaky front door being thrown open.

"No. No. No," I chant, and instead of rushing downstairs, I return to my bedroom. I check the time. It's 9 AM. If Isabella is returning, it means she failed. If Isabella has failed, this collection is worthless; I'll burn it all. This is the worst possible ending for my season to have. If Isabella bails on the show, it will be impossible for me to pay her, and she won't have enough money to sustain herself in Japan. If Isabella doesn't go to Japan at the right time, she may never book jobs there. She might have to go back home to California, her dream defeated.

Accepting that I won't extend the luxury of choice to Isabella, I leave my room, then make my way downstairs, toward the front door, holding onto my own dream, willing it into reality. I try to guess what Isabella's excuse will be- "Everyone's wearing masks, you won't even notice I'm missing/ "I saw a suspicious unattended bag at the train station/ "Fashion week might be canceled/ "Whatever, I'm not a model."

All of these possibilities- besides one- are lies, and Isabella is the only person I have in my life who doesn't lie to me.

When I feel the breeze from the open front door, my phone vibrates in my hand. I look down, dreading and desiring what I'm about to see.

For the second time this morning, I tear up over a picture of Isabella. The photo on my phone is of Isabella, sitting in the makeup chair. She's smiling so wide, the gap between her front teeth is showing.

When I look up from my phone, I'm staring at The Girl in the bright living room.

I'm breathless and buzzing.

Slightly older, slightly more annoyed, The Girl says to me, "Nice place."

"Cassie," I whisper, slowly walking to her, looking her over, then hugging her tightly.

The Girl and I stand in a house we once shared for a short, beautiful, difficult stretch of time. Our experience here is so important that it continues to play out long after we've moved on.

When I release Cassie, I look her over again. She's wearing a sleeveless black lace dress that has a semi-sheer polka dot sweetheart yoke, and she's paired this outfit with Azzedine Alaïa leopard calf hair-paneled ankle boots.

"Thisss, is weird," Cassie hisses, in a jokey way.

I smile at the comfort I feel over another surprise visit. Ever since I walked back into this house, people I love have rejoined me unexpectedly, consistently surprising me with their forgiveness. And it's nice not to be so alone.

"Being here is a lot weirder than I thought it would be. I feel like I love you, and hate you, and love you again," Cassie tells me.

"I'm okay with that loop. It starts and ends nicely," I say. The fact that Cassie is back in the house, on the day my collection will be shown, reminds me of the checks Isabella found, and I don't waste any time addressing the envelopes. "Whatever he sent you here to do. Don't bother."

"What are you talking about, Andrew?" Cassie asks with sincerity, and she's not a good enough actress to nail a rehearsed line on the first take. I believe in her innocence. Her innocence should not be questioned in this house.

"Michael," I say, exhaling his name.

"Michael?" she repeats. "Michael didn't bring me here. You did."

"I'm sorry, but-"

"-come on," Cassie says, holding out a hand. This is a gesture she hasn't made toward me in 20 years. I place my hand in hers, because my entire being demands it. Cassie pulls me forward, then still locked hand-in-hand with me, she bends over and grabs an invitation off the top of her Chanel purse that's sitting on the floor.

The black invite is for my show today.

"You're going?" I ask, a smile breaching my confused expression.

This begins to feel less like an eviction and more like a welcome home party.

"Those checks were to keep me available for your show," Cassie admits, "It was going to be a surprise."

"Why would Michael do me such a favor?" I ask.

Cassie's hand squeezes mine, and she tells me, "Because he was going to make you do something that would infuriate me. He was relying on you to fuck things up between us."

"He asked me to issue a press release admitting that Sienna is my daughter," I say.

"And that's why I'm here. Sienna told me about the call you had with her. If what you told her is true, I want us to be in the front row today. I think it's beautiful," Cassie tells me.

"I need to get ready," I say, letting go, stepping back, "Will you stay?"

"I'm your ride," Cassie says.

"We're taking the train," I respond, trying to anticipate if there could be other reasons those checks existed.

"But it's so hard to divert a train into the middle of nowhere," Cassie jokes.

I stare at The Girl, then ask, "Were you afraid to come back here?"

Cassie smiles that smile that has earned her enough money to buy this house 20 times over again, then she tells me, "No. I want to be part of today. It'll be the first time that we're all in the same room, together, as a family."

THE TRUTH

I wait until Cassie is inside the venue, then I make my approach.

Someone yells out, "What's the plan?"

"Everyone gets to keep their seat," I say, and the editors walking near me laugh. I notice that they're all wearing very sensible shoes today.

"What can we expect from your first collaboration with your brother?" a woman with a microphone asks.

"A romantic exploration of nature and the turbulence involved," I say because it's hard to pin down in a sound bite what's about to happen. It's better if they just watch.

"I noticed you didn't include 'controversy' in that description," someone in the crowd says.

I stop and announce, to the group-at-large, "I don't owe you anything, and this afternoon I'll give you what's important, but it will be ignored. You'll write the story you want to write, and it will be wrong. That's how this ends."

I hang around, my gaze scanning the journalists and editors. They have nothing to say- at least nothing that warrants a response.

I head inside, the crowd buzzing behind me.

I search for my center in the quarantined backstage area.

Michael, knowing that I'm capable of great feats of self-destruction, agreed that camera crews and critics would not be allowed backstage for the first MLORE show.

"Cassie Wolfe is here," I say, approaching my beautiful roommate.

"I know," Isabella says.

"How? We just got here."

"I didn't see her," Isabella says.

"So you knew she was here because..." I trail off.

"I called her," Isabella admits.

"You called Cassie?" I ask.

"Yeah, you told me a secret, and the only other person who knew the secret was Sienna Wolfe. I remembered that you called Cassandra on your phone because of the check thing, so I... kinda went in your phone. I didn't look at anything else, promise. I just got the number, then made the call. I've kept that a secret from you. I'm sorry, but you seem happy right now so I don't feel guilty. I wanted to make sure you'd be smiling the exact way you are right now."

I want to show my gratitude for Isabella's gesture, but I'm temporarily choked up and I can't force out the words.

Isabella pulls her mask over her face, then says, "It's almost about that time."

Working against a ticking clock, I search for Irina. When I finally spot her, I'm pleased that she's wearing a bathrobe, just we discussed. She can't begin sliding into the final piece until the other models are already walking. Next to Irina is Michael, and next to Michael is Regis. Each of them is holding a champagne flute. If the plan is still on track, one of those flutes doesn't contain champagne.

With his head, Regis gestures for me to join them, so I can begin the toast.

I casually stride by the commotion, smiling at models and keeping my cool.

When I pick up a flute of what I hope is champagne, Michael growls at me, "What the fuck are those masks, are you fucking kidding me?"

"Relax, they're wearing them on the top of their heads when they walk, it's going to be MLORE unmasked," I tell Michael. This is a lie that Cassie suggested to me on the train. "Masquerade parties are fun and all, but when it comes time for the unmasking- that's the most exciting part of the night," I explain, then I raise my glass, and say, "May this afternoon be the most exciting part of the night!"

"That... doesn't make any sense," Regis points out.

Everyone cheers' their drink to Regis' accurate observation.

I watch Michael down the entire flute of what he presumes to be champagne.

"Fine, masks can stay on," he says, then begins a direct path toward the designated press area beyond the backstage, so he can do an interview and repeat the masquerade quote I took from Cassie. Everything today feels very *fashion*.

I step away for a moment, and I run through the possible repercussions of what I've planned. I remind myself that I'm the guy who worried about what was happening, when everyone else couldn't be bothered. Operating free from the apathy of a selectively concerned industry has given me power.

I peek out at the crowd- they're restless. I look back to the models- they're masked. I look around for Michael- I find him sitting in a folding chair, sporting a dumb smile.

Regis appears behind my brother, placing a hand on his shoulder, taking protective ownership of a man his girlfriend cares deeply for.

I look for Lux, but with all the identically built models in their masks, I can't find her. Jessica was in charge of helping Lux choose the piece she'll walk in. Lux was able to make her own decision today. Now that I don't know where she is, Lux becomes just another model.

I sneak out of the backstage area as soon as the lights go down.

Cassie is sitting front row, her invitation on the seat next to her, holding a place for me. On the other side of the invite is Sienna, my daughter. She's wearing the piece of I sent to her- not my design, from her mother's closet. Beyond a quick glance, I cannot dwell on her presence, because I need to remain collected, for now. I'm so excited for what we have planned.

I quickly make my way to the chair, then place the invitation on the ground.

Over the booming sound system, Brendon Urie starts crooning the opening lines of the Tommie Sunshine remix of "The Only Difference Between Martyrdom And Suicide Is Press Coverage," and on cue, the projectors start. On either side of the runway are massive white screens. On the screens are the screeners, so Brendon begins a duet with James. One by one, James will ask his questions, as Brendon swears to shake it up. Jimmy Pixx will finally get the attention he always wanted.

Memories will march down the runway- confident, cold, and masked.

The incoming avalanche of my last four months pins me to my chair.

Now, it's time for my masked models. There's been a change of plans; Irina isn't opening. She's the grand finale. Irina is the reveal. She and I both agreed on this. We had planned this collection as though Lux wouldn't be showing up. Since Lux changed her mind, Irina was removed as the opener and everything was adjusted accordingly by Jessica. No one was sent home. All of the girls who were cast for this show will be on the runway. Lux taught me how important a single show can be to a girl.

My opener- a model who could be Lux- stomps forward wearing the crashing waves, crackling fire, and singed edges of Seaside Heights. If this is my lost muse, it would be strange that she chose a piece inspired by a time she wasn't present for. Maybe she recognized the emotion in the piece. Maybe this piece wasn't just about the torched boardwalk. Maybe this garment expressed the possibilities available when rebuilding is assured.

The fact I can't be sure if Lux opened the show means two things;

One- Lux *is* a model, completely.

Two- I don't know the new Lux.

Before this causes me to panic, a model who could be Madeleine stomps forward wearing the sweaty, slamming crowd insulated by the solid walls of The Imperial Hall.

A model who could be Galina stomps forward wearing the chains of anonymous attacks. These chains accessorize her beauty, instead of holding her back. She's *wearing* the chains, not carrying them. This is a piece both see-through and impenetrable, clear and confusing. In the end, Galina comes out looking unscathed.

A model who could be Cori Poorman stomps forward wearing the slice of glow that The Boy and The Girl would reveal themselves in. Also present is the darkness that they would vanish into.

When the executioner brings down his crowbar on either side of the runway, the audience gasps, but they don't look away. The next screener begins playing.

A model who could be Libby Boken stomps forward wearing the concealing curtains from the hotel, sliced in a way that quickly reveals a hidden weapon when she's mid-stride. Sinister possibilities are shrugged off by a girl, untouchable.

A model who could be Isabella stomps forward wearing a red sweater, inspired by the red sweater she made, which was inspired by the red sweater that I made long ago. This is a piece that's both an injury and a band-aid.

The masked models continue marching forward, wrapped in my pain, and the Panic! ends, then Irina's song selection starts. Vanessa duets with the slurred speech of a fragile victim. On the screens, the eager to please models are savagely claimed, one by one, over and over, like a scene from a bad dream/ In the center of it all, one by one, powerful models step forward and achieve their dream.

A model who could be Maryna Mauden stomps forward wearing the nature scene torn from the label of the bad beers I shared with Michael on Christmas day.

A model that I sincerely hope is Lux stomps forward wearing a white flag- a peace offering- spattered in blood, with green stitching that seems to hold it all together, despite the fact that I know if each stitch was removed, everything would still hang perfectly, work perfectly, thrive. The stitching is purely cosmetic.

A model that has to be Matthew stomps forward, masked, almost totally waxed, in a variation of Michael's best RTW piece- a piece that I felt belonged in *my* first collection, not his. Now, this piece is in my first collection for Michael. This is me tipping my hat. This is me admitting that, sometimes, my brother and I *are* alike, and the fact that neither of us will ever admit this fact also verifies it. This piece unites two brothers through a single love- fashion. I take a picture with my phone, as Matthew passes, then I e-mail it to the intern at his record label.

More models- some black, some white, some Latina- show me more memories. I think back to that train station platform, and I realize that these faceless people have helped me find *happy*.

Now... it's time for the final look.

Vanessa is still singing, as Irina appears.

Irina isn't wearing a mask. She's wearing a smile- not a cover girl smile- it's a sick smile. Hanging off Irina's body is a one-of-a-kind dress that will never see production. The pattern on the dress is made up exclusively of Polaroids and digitals of the models that Irina destroyed during the casting of this show. The agencies willingly provided snaps of their clients when they learned the models would be receiving cash for appearing at MLORE. They didn't bother to contact their clients- or if they did- the calls went unanswered, but clearly no one was too worried about the reason why a girl they couldn't find was getting paid in real money. Jessica scanned the Polaroids, culled the digitals, then assembled them all in rows using Photoshop. After that, we had the images screen printed with a high-quality printer onto a piece of pure white silk. It cost me thousands of dollars of my own money, and we hadn't even started on the labor to assemble the garment. Once we were confident with our sketch, our prototype, and our source material, we hand sewed everything in the locked middle room of the workshop. Irina immediately agreed to the piece- not that she had a choice. She never showed any indication of having doubts regarding wearing her victims like she was a beautiful Jacob Marley. The photographs on the dress are grave markers for lost girls that will never be seen again, except when this show is replayed. Irina closed Michael's body bag show with her victim hidden from the audience. Now, she's closing my show by exposing the faces of everyone she destroyed. Everyone, besides the movie exec and the executioner. The question becomes- will this make any difference or will she get away with it again? I think about what Jessica told me- about all those people who did horrible things, and were able to continue on like nothing ever happened because their crimes were physical, not verbal.

I don't want forgiveness from the editors and critics, I want it from the models on the screens, and on the dress. I once read about a civilization or culture that believed taking someone's picture with a camera would rob them of their soul. My intentions with this final dress were to take pictures of these lost girls, and sew their souls back into my work. The tag, inside the dress, hand stitched by me, reads, "Since You Cannot Walk This Runway, You Will Float." The white silk flows gracefully with every precise movement of Irina's body. It's not enough, but my talent is the only gift I have, and I need to share it with these young girls who have given up everything so this show could happen.

When the final piano key of "White Houses" hits, Irina leaves the runway, and a cover of a song that Isabella would always play in the house on Scotland Road begins. The strumming of an acoustic guitar playing Björk's "Hyperballad" is joined by Whitley's whispery voice, which is joined by beautiful strings, as my masked girls return to the runway for one final march, in a long line. I view this collection with the same feelings I had when I saw it on my mannequins. This season, I trusted a substantial number of new people- and many of them met, or surpassed my expectations. If only I could have watched this collection alongside Lux and Isabella- Jessica and Libby. Regardless, I still have the best seat in the house, between the two Wolfe women who represent my past and future.

As Irina- the final girl in the parade- reaches the end of the runway again, I wait for her to double back, then I stand up and walk parallel with her, knowing the crowd views me- not her- as the monster. I overtake Irina's stomping pace, making sure that I get backstage in time so we can get Michael out for his bow.

"Hyperballad" soars, and I find that I'm too late, so I watch from the wings as Jessica pushes Michael toward the applause.

When Michael hears the roar of the approving crowd, he looks out at the celebrities, and buyers, and editors. He seems lost. The crowd- of course- interprets Michael's zombification as a display of out of body splendor. They make this about them- as they always do- and they continue clapping, letting out whoops, applauding themselves. They view this bizarre scene as Michael taking in the moment.

When I feel that my brother is stopped in his tracks for too long, sopping up the still chattering applause past the appropriate amount of time, I become embarrassed.

Breaking away from Karen, as she paws at me, I walk out onto the runway.

Michael looks over, and instead of casting anger at me for diluting his moment, he smiles a crooked smile.

I reach out to take hold of Michael's bicep, but he grabs my hand, then raises it. The applause roars back up, and I look at Michael, unsure if he was ever actually given the mixture Regis was going to slip him. Was this always in the plan? Are we creating a public testimonial that Michael Lorrie is such a strong lifestyle brand that it successfully rehabilitated the worst person in the entire fashion industry? Maybe Michael just wanted this moment with his little brother?

As I help Michael backstage, Karen and Jessica rush to us. Karen leads Michael away from me, while Jessica hugs me.

"Ready?" Jessica whispers in my ear.

"Ready," I whisper back.

If Michael thinks today's headline is going to be about how he calmed the savage designer, he better be prepared for more of my last second alterations.

THE FALL / THE SPRING

Nearly all of the models have removed their masks, and some of them are rushing off to walk their next collection. I feel no jealousy regarding their departure- only gratitude.

One model, still masked, approaches me. I immediately know who she is by the walk/ by the cascading hair/ by those eyes that stare with a mix of judgment and softness. When she reaches me, a smile creeps across my face. I lift my hand, then I carefully slide her mask onto her forehead.

"What now?" I ask, an eyebrow arched.

Isabella's long arm points to the exit that leads out to the crowd of critics and editors.

If Isabella was able to see the loop, then she knows that I'm capable of breaking the cycle of my past mistakes. When Isabella left the house on

Scotland Road, she made sure that an image of her stayed in that room. A home that haunted me has now become a landmark of redemption.

Since Isabella kept her promises, I know that I need to do the same. I reach into my suit jacket, and I pull out a one-way plane ticket.

"Konnichiwa," I say, handing the ticket over.

"Konnichiwa means 'good afternoon.' Sayonara is 'goodbye,'" Isabella tries to correct me.

"I know," I respond.

Isabella's red lips part and reveal her gap. She looks away, holding the ticket to her chest.

"Send me pictures. Thousands of pictures," I request.

Isabella is about to cry, but before a tear breaches her eyeliner, she pulls her mask down, and with my muse ready for her escape, I understand that it's time for me to take my bow.

I walk to the exit, into the flashes, toward the critics- some of them familiar, some not- all of them essentially the same. I feel a deep need to unleash complete harshness on all of them, still. I haven't changed, but I have refined what I want to tell them. I do not fear being destroyed, but I have others to worry about, and finally, I worry about them.

A statement has to be made. It's common knowledge that, if a collection requires being bailed out critically and artistically, it can *always* be saved by giving a quote that, "I make clothes for strong women. Being strong is beautiful. The type of woman I imagine wearing this collection has her own mind, and her own opinion, and she doesn't give a damn if you don't like her because she's absolutely the woman she wants to be. I want women to wear these clothes while they're taking over the world!" This quote is so vague and girl-powery, it's the equivalent of a politician explaining that he'll "fight hard for the middle class." It's a promise that requires virtually no follow, up because by the time anyone calls the speaker out on their bullshit, the quote is so far in the rearview it'll never be news.

The crowd I walk into is massive, merely because they know they'll be able to write a blog post about how they actively confronted a *piece of shit, racist, bigoted, misogynist*. It appears that tonight's question is... *Can Andrew Lorrie implode so incredibly that he takes down his squeaky clean brother as well?*

"I see that the only way you'll put women of color on your runway is behind a mask," a short ugly girl starts bitching, beginning the attack.

The extreme violence that has just played out on the massive white walls bookending the runway isn't addressed. It's difficult to say if my collection was the reason the critics were distracted from the gore, or if it's the police procedural Dick Wolf culture we live in that allowed the screeners to play out, then fade away.

I look at the journalist, editor, blogger- who the fuck cares- and I calmly state, "One of the girls that walked for me today- Lux- an Asian girl, will be the face of my next campaign. She'll lead the campaign. She'll close the show. So, there's your exclusive."

It's at this very moment that I become fully aware of the fact that I haven't seen Lux today. I don't know if she showed up to walk MLORE, or if another girl wore two looks, while Lux went to work at another very different job.

"Why would you spoil that surprise?" a woman with bad hair asks.

"Because Lux needs to know it will happen," I say, staring at the woman, not at her raised camera.

Even if Lux chose to skip this show, I've reached the point in my career where it's my personal priority to share Lux with the world, instead of letting the world take advantage of her, myself included. I choose to be understanding because it will keep Lux close, and she's essential to my happiness. The thought that the rest of my life would continue on without a friend who made me smile so wide, so often, has scared me into action. This is an apology. If I'm lucky, Lux will accept it, and she'll keep this apology close to her heart, like the fabric of the clothes I designed specifically to fit her.

A bald man, who doesn't seem gay enough to give a shit about any of this, asks, "Why are *you* making these announcements? Where's Michael?"

"Well, since you refuse to talk about the collection I just showed, I've decided to talk about my new line. This is my final collection for Michael Lorrie," I announce.

"This is your *first* collection for Michael Lorrie," someone I can't see attempts to fix my statement.

"Keeping score, how unexpected," I say sarcastically.

"How are you going to start a new line with all of this controversy around you? The backers from the last line can't be willing to take on that massive risk again," a smug Asian asks.

"I already have an investor," I say, sporting a smile, because my investor is the *best* investor, and I'm confident this investment will make me change. This is an investment in Andrew Lorrie- not the line, but instead, the person. This investment will repair my perspective on that complicated loop in the house on Scotland Road.

"Who on earth would be dumb enough to invest in Andrew Lorrie?" someone asks, releasing this question as a gasp, like they just watched a blind pedestrian walk directly into highway traffic. I didn't catch who asked the question, and since I don't know who to direct my gaze to, I unfocus my eyes, look at the group, then I announce, "I'll be designing my next collection with Sienna Wolfe."

"The socialite?" the smug Asian asks.

"The investor," I respond.

"But it's the same person, right?"

"Maybe, in a way," I say.

"Does Sienna Wolfe really have the money to fund a line? Why would Cassandra let her do that?" another ugly person asks.

"Because Sienna is a businesswoman," I respond, "And she's free to make her own decisions."

Sienna had the trust fund that I set up for her, and that Cassie also contributed to, but by the time Sienna turned 18, she had already earned more money on her own than what we had saved in her account. She's never touched that trust fund, and when I called her after my meeting with Michael, I asked if she was interested in working with me. Fashion has brought all these beautiful women into my life, and the loop in the house on Scotland Road reminded me there was another beautiful woman that I need in my circle. Chloe Warren once told me that one of her biggest regrets was tossing Sienna to the side in the same way I did. Chloe and I found strength, together, as we were caring for our mothers, and now that our mothers are gone, it's time that we started caring for the next woman who needs our support. Chloe will be working with us on this new line.

A woman in the crowd holding a laptop dismisses my announcement with a caustic remark, and I make my reaction just ask ugly, "Who are you? A journalist? Are you important because you can write something and people will read it? We have a new name for that position now, it's 'Every person with a MacBook,' and, yes, person-with-a-MacBook, there's enough money for my line because whatever I get, I'll put toward the designs and the models. I'll do this for free."

"How can you afford to do that?" the MacBook bitch asks.

"I have a sense of responsibility to do this, so I'm rich. Maybe not to you. But to me... I've learned a lot this past season. My new line will reflect that."

"How?" I'm dared.

"Each girl above the age of 18- which will be every girl that walks for Lorrie-Wolfe next season- will receive health insurance for a full year after the show. If they want to return for the next show, the option will always be there. It will be their decision. They can't age out. They can't gain too much weight and be shown the door. Lorrie-Wolfe will be a commitment to the same girls you view as disposable. May I remind you, these are women you write about, not commodities."

"So you're adding plus-size models?" I'm asked.

"I can dress anyone!" I bark, then immediately calm down, "I can dress anyone. And I will," I confirm softly.

"When will we get to see the list of girls who were behind those masks today?" one of the journalists asks, moving on from my health care reform because it won't earn as many clicks as the fact that I closed off the backstage to the non-essential industry trash.

"Never. You'll never know who walked," I tell them.

"Why cast all those models on the screens as exclusives if we can't even be sure they were on the runway?"

"Did you see what happened to those girls?" I heave.

"So you're going from exhibiting violence toward women, to giving them everything?" the MacBook bitch asks.

"No. Not everything. What they deserve. Those girls didn't deserve what they got."

"Why won't you tell us who's behind the masks? I loved this collection, but this is going to be such a pain in the ass to tag in a post. Were some of those models in your womenswear collection actually men?" a girl who can't be more than 16 asks.

I soften when I see this girl, aware that she's not like the rest of these entitled adults. She's working out of a place of curiosity, not bitterness. She just wants to learn who these models are. I think about what Isabella said, defending the collectors. I think about how Jessica and Isabella both have blogs. "Take this," I say, handing the girl my all-access pass, "Go back behind the curtain and ask to speak with my assistant, Jessica. She'll let you know everyone who walked. You'll have to keep it a secret, though. Don't post it on the internet. I'm not going public with this cast because I'm holding out hope that *They* will focus on the important stuff."

"Thank you," the little girl says, then smiles, clutching the pass.

"Ah, as always, keeping the focus on the clothes so you can avoid addressing your hateful ways," I'm dismissed by the Asian bitch.

"I didn't mention clothes," I point out.

There's a silence that I hope will be used for reflection, but I know will not be.

These editors, and bloggers, and journalists were shown unforgivable acts and instantly forgave them. No one has been arrested. No one is curious about what Irina has become. No one cares about the health of the girls on the screen.

Checks will be cut to Flurry, and Blend, and the other agencies who had girls in the videos. The agencies won't question a thing. The girls will remain missing, and no one will search for them. The numerous disappearances will be blamed on flakiness, on confusing schedules, on homesickness. This will be viewed as an agency lucking out when a failing girl finally took the hint she isn't ever going to be on those billboards in Times Square and- thankfully- they didn't lose any money on her failure. More faces will be scouted, and they'll replace the old girls, but they won't replace *my* girls. Anyone who wore a mask today will walk in my next show, if they decide they want to. Yes, the shoes will be dangerous, but if an ankle is broken, the girl will be rushed to the hospital, and she'll be treated under the health insurance that the company I run with my daughter will provide.

The same people who watched the brutal acts that transpired this season, now surround me with cameras, not to discuss the horrible things they saw, but so they can capture me saying a horrible thing that they can pretend to be outraged about.

These people don't care that young girls are being damaged and destroyed, because it's entertaining to them. It's easy to write about. It's a good blog post. It's edgy.

Everyone here feels victorious because they just watched a Andrew Lorrie collection walk down the runway, yet none of the clothes bear my name on the tag, which means they won, *They* destroyed my name.

However, what these people will never realize is that it's not about collections- it's about letting go. Letting go of the girl with the future/ Letting go of the shame of the flee/ Letting go of the anger that had been misdirected/ Letting go of the surface.

It's about letting the people become the important part, while everything else becomes incidental.

In the end, *They* got what *They* wanted, and I received clarity.

None of this would have been possible without the help of the people I grew to trust and depend on, but make no mistake, all of this was by my own design.

ACKNOWLEDGEMENTS

God – Thank you for providing me with the talent to write this book. Without you, none of this would have been possible.

Mom & Dad – Your continued support and guidance has been more than I could ever ask for.

Bret Easton Ellis – I rediscovered your *Imperial Bedrooms* when I needed it the most.

Andrew McCarthy – Thank you for providing me with Andrew Lorrie's voice.

My Editor – Thank you for helping me shape, clarify, detoxify, and solidify this novel.

I'd also like to thank: John Galliano, Hedi Slimane, Vanessa Carlton, Brendon Urie, Björk, Philip Glass, Brad Gooch, Amanda, Naj, Cailin Hill, The Gary Mitchell, IP, AP, RD, JJ, SL, GW, Kate, Caroline, and my brother, Sean, who isn't Michael Lorrie.

Purchase The National's *Boxer* using this link: http://shopusa.4ad.com/boxer-colored-vinyl

Purchase Björk's *Post* using this link: http://shop.Bjork.com/

Purchase Philip Glass' score to *The Hours* using this link: https://www.amazon.com/Hours-Music-Motion-Picture/dp/B00007BH3Y

Purchase Vanessa Carlton's *Harmonium* using this link: http://www.vanessacarlton.com/store/
Also, buy Vanessa's record *Heroes & Thieves*. It has nothing to do with this book, but it factors heavily into the prequel to this book, which I wrote in 2011, but the novel is so questionable that I'm pretty sure that no one has finished reading the manuscript besides me. If you're an agent who regularly displays extremely bad judgment, buy the Vanessa record, then e-mail me for a copy of the prequel to *Empire Waste*.

BORING LEGAL SHIT

Before you sue me about something in this book, e-mail me. I'll fix any legal issues related to this novel. Don't sue me. I live in Newark. I'm broke. What are you gonna win from me in court? My *Vogue* magazines?

If you have print, ad, or editorial work in any of the major fashion magazines, my novels will always be free for you. E-mail me a link to your modeling work and I'll e-mail you a free digital copy of my novel. If you write those boring ass articles in between the editorials, you get nothing from me besides a small amount of resentment and some residual jealousy.

Feel free to post excerpts of this book on your blog, Twitter, Facebook, or apartment walls. Please don't get any of this tattooed on your body. I once wanted a Thug Life tattoo. Imagine if I got my way.

If you downloaded this novel illegally... I honestly don't blame you. Paying zero dollars for a thing is way better than paying four dollars for a thing. I get it.

If you want to read more about me, visit: tjamesreagan.com

If you're an agent and you want to represent my unpublished novels, email me at: tjamesreagan@gmail.com

ABOUT THE AUTHOR.

T/James Reagan currently lives in Newark, New Jersey.

He is the author of lovetrust, *beach house burning*, *Famous For Nothing*, *Empire Waste*, *Leeds House*, and *Southland Tales: The Complete Saga*.

He has sixteen unpublished manuscripts available for query.